PENGUIN BOOKS

ANCIENT PROMISES

Jaishree Misra was born in 1961 and grew up in India, moving to England in 1993. She holds a Masters in English Literature from Kerala University, and two postgraduate diplomas – in Special Needs and in Broadcast Journalism. She has worked in the field of Special Needs in India and in the Department of Social Services in Buckinghamshire, England. More recently, she worked as a Broadcast Journalist with the BBC. She recently returned to live in India with her husband and daughter. This is her first novel.

D1390969

ANCIENT PROMISES

JAISHREE MISRA

PENGUIN BOOKS

PENGUIN BOOKS

Published by the Penguin Group
Penguin Books Ltd, 27 Wrights Lane, London w8 5TZ, England
Penguin Putnam Inc., 375 Hudson Street, New York, New York 10014, USA
Penguin Books Australia Ltd, Ringwood, Victoria, Australia
Penguin Books Canada Ltd, 10 Alcorn Avenue, Toronto, Ontario, Canada M4V 3B2
Penguin Books (NZ) Ltd, Private Bag 102902, NSMC, Auckland, New Zealand

Penguin Books Ltd, Registered Offices: Harmondsworth, Middlesex, England

First published 2000
1 3 5 7 9 10 8 6 4 2

Set in 10.25/13 pt Trump Mediaeval
Phototypeset by Intype London Ltd
Printed in England by Clays Ltd, St Ives plc

It was but yesterday we met in a dream.
You have sung to me in my aloneness, and I
Of your longings have built a tower in the sky
But now our sleep has fled and our dream is
Over, and it is no longer dawn.
The noontide is upon us and our half waking
Has turned to fuller day, and we must part.
If in the twilight of memory we should meet
Once more, we shall speak again together and you
Shall sing to me a deeper song.
And if our hands should meet in another dream
We shall build another tower in the sky.

(From 'The Prophet' by Khalil Gibran)

PART I

ONE

My marriage ended today. Without the lighting of oil lamps and beating of temple drums, but in a cramped little divorce court, in the manner of these things. Ma had said, as we left the court, her voice and eyes brimming with sadness, that it had been my fate. I had replied, attempting to comfort her, that I thought endings were really only beginnings in disguise. I'm sure she wanted to believe me, but she was still silent as she looked out of the bus window.

What would you have done if someone had offered you a temporary period of happiness? Pluck a figure out of the air . . . say, for instance, ninety-eight days. Ninety-eight days . . . of the kind of happiness that you thought existed only in dreams. With no promises of any more. *And* with the unspoken threat that you might lose everything else you had. Would you grab the chance with both hands and then use every trick available to you to get an extension of sorts? Would you shy away in alarm, convinced there was bound to be a catch in it somewhere, and let the chance slip away, fearful of losing what you already had? Or would you merely take what you were given, with gratitude that miracles could sometimes come your way too?

I'm not sure exactly which of those things it was that I did in the end. Nor, I'm sorry to say, what it was that I would do next. I took my ninety-eight days, oh yes, that I certainly did. With awe and with gratitude. I had come perilously close to losing everything else, of course, but of that possibility there had never been any doubt. No attempt had ever been made to hide the fact that that was very likely to happen. But now it was over. The dream was over, sleep had fled. And the status quo returned more or less to its original state . . .

I dropped a kiss on the top of my daughter's sleeping head. The old familiarity of my lap and the drone of the bus ploughing through the wet Kerala night had put her to sleep within fifteen minutes of our boarding it. She would wake up when we reached Alleppey, unplugging a sodden thumb from her sleepy mouth, looking around questioningly. She would certainly remember her great-grandmother's house, our ancestral home of forty-watt sadness. Rediscover her favourite nooks and boisterously revive every dark corner for a while. Ma, sitting up as close to me as she could get, seemed to be absorbing some much-needed warmth from our longed-for proximity. It was strange that I'd had to come back to her to be set free again. Almost as if it couldn't be done without that one final blessing. I looked out of the window at the wide brown arc of muddy water being thrown up by the wheels of the bus, soaking all the cars we were overtaking without regret or apology. Sending their windscreen wipers into irritated double-time.

England's roads, with their quaint little rituals of mirror-signal-manoeuvre-arm-raised-in-silent-thanks, felt miles away in the howling wet darkness of this night. It rains in England too, all the bloody time it seems sometimes. Not like this, though. Even the rain there was gripped by the polite desire to descend as unobtrusively as possible. With the apologetic air of a well-bred Englishman ('Would you mind frightfully if I . . . ahem . . . if I descended for a few minutes on your head, my dear . . .?') There was none of this unseemly drama and commotion. These lightning flashes and deafening claps of thunder. Could the driver see a *thing* through these relentlessly falling curtains of water? This was the monsoon all right, heavy rains were to be

4

expected. But tonight . . . tonight, in the seemingly unstoppable way in which it was raining, I couldn't help wondering if some God had finally given up His endless task. Had *finally* downed all his tools in sheer despair at the weight of errors and mistakes that He simply wasn't able to control any more. And had at last sat down to cry . . .

I'm sorry . . . I whispered into the wet night. I'm sorry for all the mistakes . . . such expensive mistakes . . . so many years and a marriage . . .

But I'm still not sure . . . was the mistake mine or was it Yours . . . was it a mistake at all or part of some grand plan? That's what I want to think it was. A grand plan, ancient and meaningful and free of blame.

There *has* to be a reason . . . nothing, as they all say, filled with faith and filled with awe . . . nothing happens without a reason . . .

But I really need to begin the story at the beginning. Everyone knows there are no proper beginnings and endings, of course. So I'll just start, for the moment, with my eighteenth birthday. The kind of day most of us do see as a kind of beginning, bidding final farewells to the desultory chaos of childhood.

TWO

It hadn't been like any other birthday. No cake from Wengers, no noisy schoolgirl outing to Bengali Market where coins would be poured in a heap on the formica table (and carefully counted) before the order could be given. It was, in fact, very late at night when I even remembered that it had been my birthday too. The day had been crowded with so many other unfamiliar events, culminating in a long car journey to my new home. I sneaked a quick look at my wristwatch. Eleven o'clock. I'd been married exactly twelve hours.

The house loomed out of the sticky Kerala night, a huge birthday cake in a gloomy, fly-infested bakery. With pink borders and roses iced on to white marzipan. Tall wrought-iron gates were opened to allow the small convoy of cars up the sweeping drive, past a central cement cup-cake with frilly edges and a grassy mound topped with the plaster-cast figure of a woman. Even the garage nestling up against the side of the house was a pink and white confection that some impatient party guest had bitten into. His teeth marks carving two large slots that the white Ambassador cars in front of ours slid neatly into now. Transforming it into a ghoulishly grinning garage with two Ambassador front teeth. The shivering had started again.

This was it, the house that was to be my new home. It would never in fact become my home. I was to flee from it soon, leaving wedding sari and wedding photographs and wedding pain behind. In a few years' time, which was soon

6

– or not so soon, depending on which way you looked at it. But, of course, no one knew anything about that yet and the knowledge then would probably have surprised me more than anyone else.

'Stay here,' instructions from a new mother-in-law, 'we have to get the oil lamp lit first.'

I stayed in exactly the same position I'd occupied for the past five hours, in the middle of the back seat, cream and gold bridal sari crushed ungracefully against my sweat-soaked body, necklaces awry. Someone must have reached inside me and flicked all the switches on for I was suddenly wide awake, watching people spill out from the other cars. Sleep-walking children, propelled along without their knowing. Drivers stretching after their marathon efforts, sharing some laughing driverly camaraderie. An Am-mumma bent over by the exertions of the day. Faces familiar only from the toe-touching, banana-milk ceremonies of the wedding. My new family. My family's new family, the Alliance they'd so wanted that now knitted us all together so indubitably. Would we really learn to love each other, as I knew usually happened?

'Ready,' an aunt with a kind face put her head around the door, 'come out and hold this vilakku with the flame behind you. Remember to put your right foot on to the step first.'

Not for the first time in the day all eyes were on me. My heart began its familiar drum-beat:

> Don't trip don't fall don't go and ruin it all,
> Don't cry don't say I should not be here at all.

I know better now, of course, that I was only fooling myself. I had been *meant* to come here all along. It had all been written so many centuries ago even the writer would have struggled to remember where the real beginning lay. And I was flattering myself if I believed this was just my story. A mere word in a paragraph on a page of the story, that's what it was. But, just as a woollen sweater would start to unravel if even one stitch were taken out, I don't suppose I could have asked for even a word in the story to be taken out or rewritten.

Right foot on the first stair, I began my lonely journey through the crowd, up three shiny, polished steps. Vijimami had warned me of this dangerously polished floor. She'd slid ignominiously on it, for about three feet, when my family had been here last week delivering the traditional good-token ten kilos of laddoos. Luckily she'd grabbed hold of my mother-in-law (to be) and saved the laddoos from descending to the floor in a sugary yellow heap. What a bad omen that would have been, she said. I could hear her shrieking laughter now as I gingerly picked my way down a verandah that reflected the flame of my vilakku in the half-darkness. Someone was taking pictures, someone else was shouting 'Right foot again at the door', there was a lot of giggling and joshing, all sleep forgotten. And then, shattering the still, humid night, an ululation in shrill female voices swelled eerily from the dark depths of the garden. The korava to keep evil spirits at bay. The servants of the house, gathered together under the jackfruit tree, ordered to ululate as fervently as possible so as to frighten off even the smallest, nimblest of spirits attempting to creep into this blessed night with evil intentions. I could barely discern the howling gaggle in the black night as they stood, with raised heads and swollen throats, their ebony skins invisible against the dark tree trunk covered with its bulky cargo of fruit.

As the plaintive howl rent the still night air, I stumbled into the house, goosebumps breaking out all over my body. I've taken it now, I thought in sudden panic, that last irrevocable step into my new life. I've gone past that point at which I might yet have been able to turn back. I'd said that to myself many times over the past few days. But, I wonder now if (and it's a bit of a silly if) . . . but just for argument's sake, *if* there really had been a Turning Back Point, what point precisely would it have been? The day before the wedding? The day I'd been seen at the bride-viewing ceremony? The morning before the saris had been bought and the cards printed? Now? Now that I'd just stepped into my new marital home? ('C-c-could I have some money for a taxi, please? I've just remembered, I have to get back to my family in Alleppey . . .' *That* would have brought that howling korava to a sudden halt. All those poor servants, ululating for all their worth, robbed suddenly of their voices, gaping mouths blowing out silent round 'O's of astonishment into the still night air . . .)

Instead I looked diffidently around the living room, handsome but cold, even on a muggy night like this. No squashed cushions, no scattered toys, just yards of gleaming printed velvet and smooth teak surfaces. Concentrate on your feet, I hissed inwardly, many eyes will now be observing you observe the house.

I was seated on one of the expanses of printed velvet. Another round of bananas mashed into milk was making its way towards me in a carved silver bowl. I hadn't eaten much all day. The wedding feast, served at midday, had shown every sign of revisiting the banana leaf on which it had been served, but I'd managed to quell the nausea and continue the pretence of eating. Just before lunch I'd had to consume endless spoonfuls of bananas mashed into milk, one spoonful per elderly relative. And now there was to be more, one spoonful per *new* elderly relative . . . was I allowed to say I didn't even like bananas very much? Probably not. And so I opened my mouth again dutifully while the cameras popped.

The night went on, old women sat around swapping their tales toothlessly, and wide-eyed children stared at me transfixed. Everyone else looked busy with something or the other. I stayed sitting, with my head bowed, trying not to look, trying not to think. Would it be better for me if this night ended or not – which would be worse? A pair of efficient feet under a sari edge had materialized before me and a voice belonging to them was saying something. I looked up. Mother-in-law. I stood up hastily. A tray was being put into my hands and I was being propelled towards a closed door. The heady aroma of the jasmines piled on the tray was a memory of all those weddings I'd attended as a guest. Now here I was attending my own. I quelled the inane urge to giggle. Among the jasmines lurked another glass of milk. Someone lit a bunch of incense sticks and, sticking it into a banana, placed that on the tray as well. The crowd, all thoughts of sleep completely banished now, started to hoot and bray. It was time for everyone else's best part of the day. Reminiscent of countless Hindi films where shy brides were symbolically deflowered, with a spilt glass of milk, or a crushed flower among the sheets. In the dark-ness of a cinema hall, these scenes were greeted with an uneasy hush among the rustling of popcorn and the crying of a baby quickly muffled by a warm breast. In real life, however, it seemed to be terribly good fun, as new uncles now thumped each other on the back and new aunties laughed behind their sari pallus, looking coy. A graceful sister-in-law with a long swaying plait was pushing me along, too quickly, towards a polished teak door. I couldn't walk that fast, I wanted to say to her, I'm not used to saris. I'll probably trip now . . . and fall and ruin it all . . .

It would be my turn first and then the bridegroom's. With the braying voices reaching a crescendo, I was pushed into a bedroom, nearly spilling the glass of milk. Someone slammed the door shut behind me and I could hear the latch slide in. I steadied the glass of milk and wiped a few splashed drops off the front of my sari. Milky deposits were making my tongue feel fuzzy and sour. I needed water before I could perform *any* other function. But there was no time now. I knew I was meant to arrange myself shyly on the bed before the braying routine was carried out on the bridegroom. My body felt sticky and my necklaces were starting to tighten around my neck, robbing me of breath. White walls were closing in around me, windows with grills looked darkly at me . . . was that a door? Without another thought, I dived into the adjoining toilet, still holding the laden tray. Kerala had never terrified me like this before.

My mother said I was a proper Kerala girl, even though I was born and grew up in distant Delhi. The first time I was taken there, I was three months old and screamed for 2,000 miles, turning the aircraft that was carrying us into a living hell for all the other passengers on board. After a brief respite at Cochin airport, still waiting to be overrun by Dubai-dreams, I took up the screaming again for the three-hour taxi journey to Appuppa's house. By the time we reached Thakazhy, I was a tiny, wet and trembling bundle, hoarse from having given my new lungs their first outing.

Appuppa had sent the big boat to accommodate our suitcases. We climbed aboard, my parents with their small, sweaty, talcum-powdered bundle, the boatman with the suitcases, and I am told that, for the first time that day, my screams were silenced. Ma said it was the watery rhythm of the punt against the side of the boat while Dad thought it was the hushed weeping of the wind in the palm fronds above. It's true, I was enthralled and converted in one magical instant into a gurgling blissful baby, but wasn't it clear that I'd simply been here before? Swum perhaps in these backwaters, so dark and deep. Or lain on their banks with a favourite friend and played childish games, a few centuries ago.

We went every year to Kerala, to visit my two sets of grandparents. Taking an Indian Airlines flight to Cochin and then a taxi to my grandparents' house at Thakazhy. The road from Cochin always ended abruptly in the empty summer-time playground of Thakazhy Primary School, which is where the cars had to be parked. For years I lived with the logical notion that this was where the world ended. In Thakazhy, at the primary school. From here started the 'other' world that lurked behind the chaotic, car-filled one that ended so suddenly in the empty playground. If you took the small path behind the school that led down a flight of mossy stairs, you came to what was called the backwaters. Here was, quite suddenly and inexplicably, a world of stillness and dark green depths. The world that my father's parents inhabited in Thoduporam, their large lazy house that sprawled on the banks of the canal, staring all day into the green mirror at her feet, like some beautiful water-maiden.

The boat ride from Thakazhy Primary School to my grandfather's house was one that changed little in my childhood. The same summer holidays, the same water hyacinths bobbing against the side of the boat, the same smiles flashing shyly from the banks of the canal, where women washed their clothes and scrubbed their pans. I was in my teens when The Road appeared, dusty orange, hugging the side of the canal as if a little unsure at first of its true business. Later it would find a new confidence, growing in status and width, even acquiring a coating of pot-holed tar. Eventually and unconcernedly it would squeeze all life out of the canal which would choke on its water hyacinths and concede to the competition without so much as a fight. But, long before the canal finally died, allowing lumbering, Dubai-fuelled Ambassadors to roar up and down its conqueror, there was Appuppa's boat. Long and shiny, oiled wood slicing dark water silently, except for the watery rhythm of the punt against its side.

It was almost always dusk when we arrived at Thoduporam. The house would be dimly lit and the lone oil lamp under the tulsi bush would be fluttering weakly in the gentle breeze.

Appuppa would cry out to Ammumma at first sight of the boat sliding up to the house and, without waiting for her, he'd run down the steps, crying and laughing and dispensing generously large, sandalwood-scented hugs. First his son, then his daughter-in-law and then the small, hoarse bundle who grew into his beloved granddaughter.

Appuppa, who always smelt of coconut oil and sandalwood, was only one of the reasons for which I loved Kerala. His hugs were among the most delicious smells in my childhood, right up there with warm unniappams at tea time and oiled, wet boat-wood. As I grew, I reached different parts of those hugs. For the first few years my nose buried itself squarely in the starched mundu that covered his legs, before I'd be whisked upwards to a safe shoulder or arm. Then, some years later, my face would squash right into his brown belly, a bouncy coconut-oily treat. But that was before I outshot him completely, and before he succumbed to the bullying progress of life, crouched in an armchair, giving up, like his canal, without bothering to fight. Capable now of only receiving hugs, sometimes without even recognizing the city-strangers who turned up every summer to dispense them. He had seemed well this morning . . . and had seen me off at Guruvayur with a wide, toothless, silent smile. But that was this morning . . . such a long time ago . . .

Even through two sets of closed doors, I could hear the crowd still braying. Was the bridegroom in the bedroom yet? I locked the toilet door very slowly, hoping desperately that the bolt would not squeak and give away my terror. First I had to get all the jewellery I was weighed down with off my sticky person. I struggled with the seven necklaces that Preethichechi had so expertly looped around my neck, using twine to shorten or lengthen them as required. Tricks she'd learnt at Preethi's Bride and Beauty Parlour in Bangalore. I had asked to be able to wear just my favourite two.

The traditional pachakallu thali around my throat and the mullamuttu in a long loop down to my navel. But Ma had worried that the Maraars and their wealthy friends and relations would think I had only two necklaces to my name ('You know, she *only* has a mullamuttu and a pachakallu thali, that too such a *small* one!'). She told me firmly that it was important to wear every single chain that I had. That way they might even think I had *more* tucked away in a few dozen red-velvet Bhima Jewellery boxes. Stubborn clasps and flesh-coloured twine were getting stuck in my trembling hands. I dropped an ear-ring, Ma's beautiful old seven-stone diamond! After ten minutes on hands and knees I finally found it, winking mischievously at me from behind the cistern, and put it carefully into its box.

What would he *think*, what would he *think*, that I was intending to spend the *night* in here? The man outside . . . my new *husband* . . . the word did not emerge from my numbed brain easily. It felt ridiculous, and again I could feel giggles rising up inside me. What would he do? Assert his conjugal rights, definitely! It always happened on the first night in films. Followed by delicate tamarind-chewing and vomiting. And then, exactly nine months later, out would pop the babies. Ma had tried to explain some of the facts of life last week, but it was a stilted little explanation and she was getting breathless in the course of it, her eyes sliding about everywhere. I startled her by telling her I knew, even though I didn't *exactly*. Leena and I had put our heads together at school often enough during lunch breaks to pool our meagre knowledge, and I had a fair idea of what to expect. I was determined, obviously, to postpone the thing as much as possible.

I had a long, slow bath, filling up water along the side of the bucket in another noise-saving exercise. It was the most silent and eerie bath I'd ever had, with none of the Asha Bhonsle trilling I often practised at home. A gecko family silently watched me, seeming as struck as I was by the seriousness of the situation. Through the open ventilator I could hear more noisy night-time creatures in the garden outside as I towelled myself dry. There were other frightened creatures like myself out there, but while they made cheeping and screeching noises to keep their adversaries at bay, I continued to skulk around the bathroom in grim silence. I wore the sari petticoat and sticky blouse again, as I hadn't had the presence of mind to grab a nightie on my panic-stricken way into the bathroom. Gingerly, and very silently, I slid the bolt and pushed the door open. The room was dark, the curtains had been drawn. I waited for my eyes to get accustomed to the unfamiliar darkness. I could hear a gentle snore. He was asleep! I couldn't believe it. The events of the day had worn him out too, fatigue had probably overtaken all other duties and desires. *Oh, thank you, sweet God!*

I slipped into the large bed next to him, without moving the covering sheet, half of which was draped over his sleeping body. I didn't really need it, the night was warm. Half an hour later, it wasn't feeling that warm and mosquitoes had started whining warnings of bites to come. But I decided it was prudent not to pull at the sheet, which was now wound tightly around him. You couldn't pull the covering sheets in bed from a complete stranger, could you? How had Ma and Dad done it? They'd barely known each other when they'd got married too. At what point did they decide they'd been married long enough to pull sheets away from each other in the night?

Despite my own deep fatigue, I lay awake for what seemed like most of the night, thinking mainly irrelevant thoughts. I suppose it takes being eighteen to have the ability to think of everything *except* the important things on momentous occasions. My fellow frightened-creatures-of-the-night were still occupying themselves noisily in the garden outside. It was now starting to rain. A tall garden light with a round glass dome shone wetly into the room. Branches and leaves were shadow dancing on the walls. I turned my head on the pillow to sneak a look at the man I'd married this morning. I could see only the silhouette of a largish nose, sort of hooked at the tip. He was snoring gently, taking in breaths through large nostrils and expelling them through a slightly open mouth. With a coo-wee, coo-wee sound. Like an unfamiliar nocturnal bird of prey. A hand curled itself around my heart again at the unfamiliarity of the sight. Just *pretend* that it's Arjun, I told myself hopefully.

I closed my eyes tightly, and saw . . . again . . . the flashing white of a crooked smile. Not-so-white cricket whites, soiled green at the knees. Green eyes (or were they grey, I could never tell) fringed with brown lashes, longer than mine. Brown, very dark brown, hair that riffled as he bowled or batted while I watched from the dusty edges of the maidan. Watched, taking mental snap-shots, worried I'd have difficulty remembering all the details later. Difficulty that I did have, funnily, after he'd left Delhi. (Lift your arm, sir, pretend to throw the ball, thaaat's it . . . click.) I had a whole album of those to keep me entertained all night if I wished. The only real one had been left behind in my room, hidden under a pile of glass bangles and old hairbands, with a few letters, two of them fast losing their special smell, in a Bata shoe box, on the bottom shelf of my cupboard. The cupboard that Dad and I had chosen in white to look dainty. And placed alongside my window which looked out at the jacaranda tree that would have started to weep lilac tears all over my marigolds at this time of year, just outside my room. At home in Delhi.

What was I *doing* here, lying on somebody's foam-mattress bed that smelt of shop-new latex, on such a frighteningly clean sheet? My back was getting stiff as I tried to keep from rolling on to the man next to me who wasn't

16

giving me my rightful share of sheet. The injustice of it was making my eyes smart. Tears that I'd managed to stave off all day, in some desperate bid to seem in control, were now rolling down the sides of my face, making the insides of my ears go squishy wet. I desperately needed to see my parents and tell them their dream wasn't panning out too well for me. To ask them to get me out, to take me back. To send me off (even if it *was* in annoyance) to my bed, in my room with its posters of Pink Floyd and Amitabh Bacchan held up much longer than expected by bits of crisping, yellow Sellotape. In my *home*, with its squashed cushions and familiar smells. As far from Kerala as I could get.

THREE

Home, for virtually all my life, had been Delhi. Big, busy, bustling New Delhi. Two thousand miles away from Kerala, which is about as far as you can go in India, without tumbling into the Indian Ocean. This, I suppose, had always been the chief paradox in my life. That these two places ran together in my blood, their different languages and different customs never quite mixing, never really coming together as one. And when, as a Malayali girl growing up in Delhi, with Malayali parents but Delhi friends, and Malayali thoughts but Delhi ways, I also decided to fall in *love* with a Delhi boy, who was never really going to be welcome in my Malayali home, I should have been able to look ahead and anticipate the brouhaha to come. But I didn't, and in the manner of the very young and the very foolish, I coasted into my troubles without fear or shame.

It was outside school, two years before my marriage, that I first met Arjun. I'd been enrolled in the Irish convent school, because my parents wanted me to speak English well and get a head-start in sophisticated Delhi society. Arjun was at the boys' school next door, whose population was carefully separated from us by high bramble hedges and gates that were kept permanently locked.

'Hey yaar, Janaki, have a look at that one there, he's the one I'm going for outside the gates today.'

I peered through the dusty leaves of the hedge, spotting a tall, lanky figure bowling a pretend googly. 'The one in the cricket kit?'

'Nah, not that chitta wimp, the one next to him. Tall and dark, raaaather nice.'

My friend, Leena, had a sexuality that seemed to be developing in leaps and bounds ahead of my own. In huddled little lunch-time sessions I'd been treated to the details of her various horny escapades and had discovered that she had a certain penchant for what she described as boys 'tall, dark and hands'. I'd certainly felt breathless titillation at some of her tales of said hands wandering around parts of the anatomy that for me were still reserved for careful examinations in bathroom mirrors. For the time being, though, I was content to twirl and pout for hours in a state of undress, filled with admiration for the burgeoning curves I could see in my mirror.

'Come *on*,' I said, tugging at Leena's reluctant sleeve, 'Sister Seraphia will be upon us in a minute, if we aren't careful.'

'Oh all right, spoilsport, but watch my speed outside the gates this afternoon.'

The Gates were where the school architects and the Keepers-of-our-Collective-Chastity seemed to have made hopeless miscalculations. At the end of the school day, girls and boys from both schools poured out into this common area to board the school buses. In the ensuing chaos, countless pairs of eyes met, countless dates were made and countless parents' hopes of ensuring good English, high morals and pure thoughts by sending their children to expensive convent schools, were thereby dashed.

As we joined the blue and white exodus that afternoon, Leena unbuttoned her starched collar and pulled her shirt out of her blue pleated skirt. She then flashed me her wicked smile and proceeded to roll the waist-band of her skirt around itself, once and then twice. This was one of the tricks of surviving convent-school life that had been handed down many generations of schoolgirls. Regulation ('no more than *one* inch above the knee') voluminous skirts could thus be transformed into the cutest swishing little things, designed to set hapless schoolboy pulses racing.

'Hang on, yaar,' said Leena, pulling me back in the mêlée outside the gates. We had got past Sister Seraphia who'd failed again in her policing duties to notice the length (or lack of it) on Leena's skirt. She'd nodded briefly at Leena's loud, 'Good afternoon, Sister' and carried on scanning the crowd, looking for tell-tale signs of blue uniforms mingling with grey. This the authorities *had* got right. The girls wore blue skirts and the boys wore grey trousers and it was relatively easy to spot any undesirable interaction that might take place between trouser and skirt.

Leena had sighted her quarry and was getting ready to move in for the kill. 'Behind that bus, Jans, hurry!' I was pulled at great speed around one of the buses lazily gorging itself on schoolboys. We were on forbidden territory now and I felt the down on my arms prickle and rise.

'Hello,' said Leena in what she imagined was a sultry, mysterious way, 'I'm Leena and this is my friend, Janaki.'

We were facing Leena's 'Tall, Dark and (hopefully) Hands' who was now smoking a surreptitious cigarette, and his cricketer companion, whose fair skin had been cruelly dismissed as 'chitta' by Leena. 'Hands' was clearly pleased at the unexpected encounter, but dragged slowly on his cigarette, threw it down, crushed it with his shoe, and then drawled, 'I'm Jai and this is Arjun.'

Arjun had greeny-grey eyes. I'd never seen eyes that colour before. The prickling sensation on my arms had now travelled up to the back of my neck. I was aware that my concentration on the conversation was poor and that my eyes were darting furiously about in sheer terror of a nun's habit materializing amidst the grey of the boys' side. How on earth did Leena manage such admirable insouciance in the face of possibly life-long incarceration? She was laughing loudly now at something Hands had just said, sticking out her unusually long left thigh in provocative fashion. People were looking at us, bigger boys with envy and smaller boys with 'oh yuk' expressions. Forcing my attention back to my companions, I noticed with a start that Grey Eyes had fixed them on me, admiringly. I could feel my tongue slink down my throat in the wrong direction. It didn't look as if Grey Eyes was having that much success with his tongue either. Our eyes met for a few confused seconds and I quickly decided to concentrate instead on reading Today's Thought for the Day on the board outside the school church. In the two years that I had been at the school, I'd never read the thing with such fierce concentration. Plastic removable letters inside a glass box were sternly telling me, Let your conversation be without Covetousness; be Content with such things as ye Have (Hebrews 13, 5). Try telling Leena that, I thought. She was still engaged in covetous chatter with Hands and I sneaked another quick look at my companion-by-default. He was hitting his cricket bat on the edge of his shoe and chose that moment to sneak another look at me, and we drowned again in waves of silent, mutual mortification.

I never worked out, even years afterwards, whether the world had seemed to stop for those few minutes because I was plain scared. Or, because of something much bigger. Something so big I was certainly not to know of its existence then. Arjun and I laughed often, later, at the memory of that first meeting, and I convinced him that my dumbfoundedness was purely because Leena and I were on The Boys' Side and liable to be caught by Sister Seraphia at any minute. I wouldn't know until very much later that a new story was beginning to unfold. A brand new – or very old – story, depending on which way you looked at it.

I also wasn't to know that, among the snorting and

juddering of diesel-spewing buses that afternoon, something old and timeless and unstoppable had been set slowly
into motion again. Something packed full of dangerously
unfulfilled promises, bursting to get out. I have wondered
sometimes, *if* we had known then of how much havoc it
would wreak, so many years down the line, whether we
would have met again the following day. And then started
lying to our parents to be able to see each other again and
again and again . . . Would we have wanted the story to be
written at all?

*   *   *

But we did. We met again the following day, having said an
awkward, 'See you tomorrow.' Just to find our tongues and
find that we were able to chat casually too. Then, the
following week, Arjun bought me a leaf-plate full of
kulcchey choley from the vendor who always had the good
sense to set up his stall just outside Sister Seraphia's territory. Digging into the sour brown mess with bits of oily
bread and having to run to wash our hands at a corporation
tap nearby, we missed our buses of course. And had to
clamber on to a crowded DTC bus to make our way home.
Squashed up against each other, surrounded by bored
commuters, we not only found our tongues but found it
hard to stop chatting when it was time for me to get off at
Hauz Khas. And in that careless, unthinking way, and in
the space of a few weeks, Arjun and I became friends. It
would have been difficult not to, even if we had not liked
each other, because I was Leena's cover for her clandestine
meetings with Jai, which by now had almost certainly progressed way beyond just 'hands'. So, over the weeks, whenever Leena and Jai vanished behind an assortment of
convenient trees and shrubs at Nehru Park, Arjun and
I were left to hide our mutual embarrassment in garrulous conversation. That we were still talking long after
Leena and Jai had had an acrimonious split-up six months

later, was an irony that was not lost on us. Some time after that, and I'm not sure exactly when, I began to fall in love.

Despite all that happened afterwards, it still feels vaguely embarrassing to use grand words like 'love' for the emotions a sixteen-year-old is capable of feeling. But I have no other words to describe it. Arjun was to become someone whose well-being I would begin to care deeply about, sometimes more than my own. He occupied a great deal of my thoughts and his was the company I desired more than anyone else's. I liked him for not trying to be all hands as soon as we'd met. He made me laugh. We liked the same sort of music, and the same kind of books. I didn't like his cricket very much, but not enough to mind hanging around the edges of the maidan, waiting for him to finish. I glowed in his company, I melted in the crookedness of his smile and I drowned willingly in the green depths of his eyes. I wanted to be able to get into his head and wander around in it, exploring his innermost thoughts. I even risked the sorrow and wrath of my parents to be with him. If that wasn't love, then what is?

Leena's theory was simpler. 'He's got a great butt, yaar, and free access to his brother's motorcycle. That's what it is.'

I'd never needed to have secrets from my parents before, not even too many secret *thoughts*, most of which Ma was treated to as she went around the house doing her chores with me bobbing about in her wake. But I hugged these new, unfamiliar thoughts to myself with a secrecy that both puzzled and thrilled me. I was fairly sure my parents would disapprove; I'd heard Dad harrumph loudly at love scenes in films, worried they would fill my head with silly notions. Love, for him, had been the stirring in his heart when his mother had shown him the picture of a fresh-faced girl she'd chosen for him to marry eighteen years ago. This running-around-trees business was for film stars and fools, he often said. At that stage I had pitifully little to be guilty about, according to Leena. I'd certainly never run around any trees. BUT, Arjun was definitely the wrong sex to be just a friend in my parents' eyes. Even I wasn't very sure I could truthfully describe him as 'just a friend'. Briefly conscience and caution wrestled with each other in my mind until I finally decided I was going to chance it and try the fine noble path of a half-truth.

Making sure Dad wasn't around, I broke the news. I was lounging on the sofa next to Ma, trying to look as though I hadn't planned to be there, opening up with a forced enthusiasm, 'Ma, I've made a new friend! We have *loads* in common, similar schools, service background, the same tastes in books and music . . .' I knew I sounded gushing and decided to tone it down.

Ma only smiled absently, carrying on with her knitting, eyes fixed on her favourite Wednesday night *Chitrahaar* on television. I took a deep breath and ploughed on, 'He's really nice, can I ask him over with Alka and Leena for dosas one Sunday? I'm the only South Indian among my friends and they're always pestering me for dosas.'

This time, with the subtle use of a pronoun, I'd pressed the alarm button. Her eyes shot away from Dilip Kumar's lovelorn face on the black and white screen and landed searchingly on mine. I had nothing to feel guilty about, well, not *much* anyway according to Leena, but I could feel myself redden.

'How long have you known him? Who is he? How do you know him?'

Oh dear, maybe it hadn't been worth it after all.

'He's a Colonel Mehta's son. Goes to St Paul's. We met at school. Maaa, he's just a friend, don't look so alarmed.'

'I don't know,' she said doubtfully, 'I never had friends like that when I was growing up. You have to be careful, you know, there's lots of boys out there who will be only too willing to take advantage of pretty girls.'

'Oh, Ma! He's a FRIEND just like Leena, Alka, Anju . . .' I brought out my carefully rehearsed trump card, 'If he wasn't just a friend, would I be asking him around to meet you?'

I could see her struggling with this one. She clearly wanted to meet him as he was evidently already a part of my life. But would having him over to the house amount to giving the liaison her stamp of approval? And feeding him dosas? The messy, time-consuming treat we reserved only for our very best North Indian friends! That would certainly be an overly warm welcome, almost like announcing he was now part of the family.

'I'll ask your father, no promises. Certainly no dosas!'

Arjun did eventually come to my house, surrounded by my gaggle of schoolgirl friends – noisy camouflage to my growing feelings for him. He seemed only barely to survive their screaming jokes and gales of giggles, looking red and sheepish through most of the afternoon. But proving heroically his worth to me. I could tell he was faintly hurt by my parents' evident suspicion of him, answering Dad's questions politely but nervously. I hoped he would not hold it against me and made a mental note not to subject him to such an inquisition again.

In a roundabout sort of way, I could understand my parents' fears. They had lived straightforward, honest lives and wanted the same for me, their only child. Neither of them would have dreamt of doing anything without seeking their own parents' blessings first. They had left all major decisions in their lives to the wisdom of their parents, who had always chosen wisely and chosen well. They had been told by their parents to love each other, which they had learnt to do, without artifice and without effort. When they left Kerala for busy, smart Delhi, where Dad was to take up his first posting, they had already dug for themselves strong, deep foundations in the age-old traditions of their ancestral soil and suffered no mixed-up priorities. Unlike me.

My world was a confusing one for them. They were so sure that I would be safest among my own people, marrying eventually into my own community. But I had all kinds of friends and all kinds of experiences that were alien and that couldn't be stopped. Arjun, unfortunately, would fall firmly into that category – he was the wrong age (too young), wrong community (not Malayali), and came at the wrong time (I was too young).

I could see Ma clearing away the dosa debris in the kitchen. My friends, and Arjun, had left after an enormous lunch, leaving me glowing with pride. Arjun had eaten two large dosas stuffed with spicy potatoes, struggling with North Indian fingers to scoop up runny sambar with the dosa pieces, attempting to imitate my easy ability to do so. And had pronounced them delicious, better than India Coffee House dosas, he'd said. I ran up behind Ma whose hands were balancing a pile of plates and gave her a huge hug, nearly lifting her off her feet, 'Thanks, Ma!'

'Okay, okay, enough said! Only I know how long it took to persuade your father it wasn't a bad idea. But never again, okay? We aren't the kind of family that can encourage its girls to have boyfriends.'

*   *   *

And so Arjun never came again to my house, but Delhi was a big place and I had been careful not to promise never to *see* him again. It was on such technicalities that I would later assuage my guilt. I did in fact meet Arjun again very soon. Leena was to have a seventeenth-birthday bash on the day the schools closed for the summer. To which boys were to be invited too! As the daughter of an Air India pilot and an ex-stewardess who wore her hair clipped short and smoked cigarettes, Leena was the only one among my friends who was allowed to have boy friends. The two words existed separately, of course. Even Leena was really only allowed friends who happened to be boys, rather than *boyfriends*, but we were all filled with envy that she had the sort of parents who would actually allow a party that included boys. My parents had also earned my undying love – for not only giving me permission to attend but also agreeing that it would be better for me to sleep over at Leena's house rather than attempting to return home at night. Unaware of the boy guests, of course. Seven school-girl heads converged excitedly in the basketball court every lunch time that week.

'I'll get my mum to do her chocolate brownies, shall I?'

'Yeah, and the baby idlis you brought to the church fete last year.'

'Not *idlis*! Idlis are uncool.'

'Yeah, they're okay for fetes and things, not *parties*.'

'Yeah, for parties, *dance* parties, you've got to have Englishy stuff . . . like . . . you know . . . fish fingers and cutlets and things.'

'How about pizzas? My mum's learnt to do pizzas at her coffee club.'

'Yeah super! Lemme write that on this list, little pizzas.'

'How many boys will your dad allow, Leena?'

'Oh, he's cool, about seven or eight?'

'God! What a sweetie-pie! I hope my dad doesn't get any whiff of boys being there, or it's curtains for me all right.'

'My mum would *die* if she knew she was making brownies for *boys*!'

On the evening of the party Leena's mother's elegant living room was cleared of furniture, to make space for a dance floor. The dining table in the next room was groaning under the weight of assorted foodstuffs from various homes and an enormous chocolate cake from Wengers sat pristinely in their midst. Leena's father was re-connecting the music system with a long-suffering expression on his face.

'You shouldn't have moved this,' he admonished us mildly, 'all the wires have come undone. What's that red cellophane paper for?'

'Oh nothing, Papa, just to wrap over the light-bulbs.'

'What! You'll set the house on fire, you know. What do you want to cover the light-bulbs for, anyway?'

'Oh Papa darling, you don't know a *thing*,' Leena was camouflaging this rather rude and completely untrue remark with her arms wrapped around his neck and a couple of loud kisses, 'it won't set anything on fire, I've seen it done before. Anyway, I've asked Mama.'

Leena's room was like a teenage bomb-site, with clothes and shoes and cherry-flavoured lip-gloss being flung everywhere. Girls in various states of undress were tottering around in unfamiliarly high heels, doing each other's hair and make-up. My own hair, normally scrunched back in a bouncy pony-tail, had been hair-sprayed and tamed into a submissive chignon that startled me every time I went past a mirror or the polished side-board. Even demure little Renu, chemistry whiz and teacher's pet, was completely unrecognizable in a strappy top borrowed from someone else for the night. By seven, we had exhausted ourselves with the exertions of getting ready and with our efforts to refrain from falling over in shiny new high-heeled sandals. We sat around, waiting for the guests, trying to appear nonchalant. There was a renewed flutter as the Boys arrived in a flurry of throbbing borrowed motorcycles, and reeking of after-shave. Leena had already given Jai the strictest of instructions not to behave like a boyfriend under her parents' nose – an instruction he seemed quite pleased to be given as it gave him *carte blanche* with a room full of adoring schoolgirls. But Arjun, who had already been nicknamed Georgie, short for gorgeous, by some of the girls outside the gates and to whom I'd already silently and secretly given my heart, signalled a greeting to me from across the room. I didn't have to worry about parents' watching eyes on this occasion, but could feel my heart begin to flutter as I saw his tall figure push its way through the room to me. He was in a dark grey shirt and his eyes were a completely new colour tonight. Just to throw me into further confusion, I thought. I managed a faint hello.

'You don't mind if I monopolize you all evening, do you?' he whispered. In the few months since we had become friends, he had lost his shyness and was now grinning crookedly and confidently at me. I could see, from the looks I was receiving, that being monopolized by Arjun would probably make me horribly unpopular among my friends, but it was hard to pretend I minded.

'No, I don't think so,' I said, trying not to sound too keen.

I made room for Arjun next to me on the sofa, and introduced him to the others perched on it like beautifully coiffed and waiting vultures, surveying the boys with distant and careful disinterest. Together we talked of various unimportant things, while I wondered why Arjun's eyes were so dark tonight and marvelled at how they seemed to turn gentle every time they rested on my face. They were confusing me and overcoming me with feelings I was not sure I could name. It felt safer not to talk too much and to keep my eyes from looking into his. I rubbed my hand absently on the blue jacquard of Leena's mother's sofa. Arjun picked up my hand and said something about the new pink nail polish. We laughed and I did not draw my hand away, wondering at my boldness in front of all my friends. We were not to know, of course, that it would be on the very same sofa, many months later, that we would hold hands again. Not, on that occasion, with the tender awakening of new feelings but with the desperate knowledge of that fledgling thing coming to an end. After a while, still holding my hand, Arjun asked if I'd like to dance. On the floor, we would get a semblance of privacy but the music was loud and I was conscious of many pairs of eyes watching us curiously. Arjun seemed less concerned than I was and when the track changed and a slower number came on, he drew me firmly to him. I entered the crook of his arms with the oddest and, as it would happen, quite inaccurate feeling that I was coming home and that everything was going to be just fine. My nose, thanks to the three-inch heels I had borrowed earlier from Leena, hovered just over his shoulder and I leaned my cheek on the side of his neck. What a lovely smell, I thought, analysed later as being a combination of after-shave, talc and boyish sweat. God, I love him, I thought . . .

After an hour we were accosted by an unamused Leena, 'Look here, Arjun, you've got to *mix*.' She was shouting to be heard over the amplified crooning of George McCrae.

Arjun looked around at the large group of girls stuck shyly to the wall. 'Why? We're not bothering anyone here.'

'Yes, but I don't have enough boys to go around, you can't stick to Janu like this!'

'I'm sorry, Leena, I will talk to your other guests too, I promise,' and to make sure she would go away he added, 'but Janu's my girlfriend now.'

I wasn't sure if Arjun had said this to be spared the travails of striking up conversation with a whole bunch of wallflowers. Even if it were true, there seemed to be a sneaky unilateralness about his statement that I knew I ought to disapprove of. But I'd never felt so light-headed and so reckless before. 'Am I?' I asked, genuinely curious, after Leena had departed in uncharacteristic confusion.

'I'd like that very much,' he said, looking at me with a new seriousness in his eyes. I hadn't noticed the precise moment at which he'd progressed from being a red-faced novice to a confident suitor, but from his sudden smile I could tell he had no doubt in his mind at all of what I was going to say. I knew enough about the rules to be aware that I was better off pretending disinterest, at least for a while. But at that moment, I could see no logical reason for such an argument.

I reached up on Leena's stiletto heels and gave him a chaste peck on the cheek to seal our agreement. My feet were starting to hurt horribly, but now the night had to be danced away. Wrapped in Arjun's arms, the falsetto wail of 'Rock your baby' had never sounded sweeter. I was vaguely aware of seven other couples also moving slowly around us, all glowing a strange cellophane-red. The large band of wallflowers were glowering redly at us. But love is a selfish thing and the feelings of girls who had been my friends for a lot longer than I'd known Arjun seemed suddenly unimportant. My excuse being that I just didn't feel I was *me* any more. Apart from that, my knees felt weak, my tongue dry and my poor feet as though they were on fire. If ever there was a falling in love feeling, surely it wasn't this! But the spell of whatever it was broke at about midnight when Leena's father came in, turning on all the lights, 'Okay, kids, start winding up now.' The redness of the room dissolved away, leaving everyone blinking in the harsh light of reality. Loud groans had him retreat hastily and the lights promptly switched off again. Ten minutes later, however, he was back, this time with Leena's mother, both of them sounding very loud and very firm. After two or three bouts of the lights being switched on and off, it was clear our party was over. It was also clear, as Leena announced with a beatific smile, 'Arjun and Janu are now an item!'

We parted tenderly at Leena's gate, amidst the more bois-terous farewells and shouts of 'happy hols' flying around us. Our new status as an item had been unambiguously announced, and so we were being given our own private pool of darkness in which to say goodbye. I looked up at Arjun's face, lit faintly by a spluttering NDMC street light swarming with insects. I could hear one of Ma's many warnings whisper from deep inside me somewhere; 'These boys are all after just one thing,' it said . . . but the face looking down at me was amiable and suddenly irresistible. Even if it was after just one thing, tonight it was going to get it from me. 'I love you, Arjun Mehta,' I whispered, reaching up for a proper kiss this time. It was a long kiss, the way I'd seen it done in the movies, and it left a warm wetness on my lips that the child in me wanted to wipe away with the back of her hand before she finally slipped out of me for ever. The biggest milestones of our lives have a strange way of drifting silently past us without trumpets and fanfare and without flashing the warning signals that really ought to accompany them. Ma was to ask me once, some months later, when it was that everything had happened – and why no one had told her that her little girl had suddenly become a woman. With an air of such regret that she hadn't known exactly when to say goodbye. But then, no one had thought of warning me either. Not only that growing up was something that could happen so quickly, but that it was all so irreversible and so very final. And really not as desirable a state as I had foolishly imagined it would be.

Later, in the darkness of Leena's bedroom, I needed some reassurance, 'Is this really what it's like, Leens?'

'What,' she asked sleepily.

'I don't know . . . *love* . . . is it like this?'

Leena was silent, more from her desire to sleep than any attempt to ponder over my new confusions. I continued, speaking more to myself than to her in the soothing darkness of the night, 'My insides feel like jelly, my mind's just mush . . . and all I want now, *from life*, is to be with Arjun again . . .'

'Take it from me, yaar,' she said, turning over with a yawn, 'love is a bloody pain in the arse.'

*   *   .   *

'Kerala, you can't go to Kerala!'

'But I have to go to Kerala, it's the summer holidays.'

'Precisely, it's the summer holidays, you can't go to Kerala.'

'Arjun, this is getting like a conversation between two deaf men. I *always* go to Kerala with my parents during the holidays. I have to see my grandparents. You don't think my parents would even dream of leaving me behind, do you?'

'But it's the holidays. What'll I do without you?'

'Cricket . . . cricket . . . more cricket, no doubt.'

I looked carefully at Arjun, suddenly he didn't look that unhappy.

'Yeah, I suppose I *could* get some practice in.'

We were sitting under dusty trees at the edge of the cricket maidan. I'd made a quick trip to my eerily empty school under the pretext of cleaning out the contents of my desk and had rushed down the road, aware that I could squeeze in half an hour with Arjun before my deadline to reach home. Jai had already wasted ten minutes of our precious time together arguing with Arjun for having stopped practice early to flop down next to me.

'Oh get lost, Jai,' Arjun said, 'go and find Leena or somebody.'

Jai loped off, muttering. Already the world seemed to be conspiring against our love and I felt a sudden rush of tenderness towards the figure sitting in front of me, now offering me the last of the nimbu pani in his flask. I shook my head and rubbed gently at a long green grass stain on the knee of his trousers.

'Your mum won't be pleased to see that, it'll never come off.'

'Doubt that she'll see it somehow.' He laughed at my puzzled expression. 'She lives in England.'

'In England? Not with your dad?' I thought with some

horror that they were probably divorced. That wouldn't go down well with my parents at all. We didn't know anyone who was divorced.

'Dad didn't want to upset our education – and he also needed to look after our farm. Everyone thinks they're divorced, of course.' He tore at a clump of grass angrily.

'I didn't think that at all, lots of people live separately,' I said hastily. 'Is there any nimbu pani left?'

Arjun passed me his flask and I peered into it. Two tiny ice-cubes were struggling to stay alive among the dregs of murky lime juice. 'Finish it,' he said tenderly, 'I'm not thirsty any more.' The month of June in Delhi was hot enough to melt the tar on the roads and everyone was always thirsty, but I was starting to see the side of Arjun that was unfailingly generous. Even then I had a faint sense of being terribly lucky to have found someone like him.

'Who made the nimbu pani for you then?'

'Ramvati,' he said, 'she's worked with us since I was five.'

'Is she the one who answers your telephone with a confident "Alloooisspikking pliss?"'

Arjun laughed, 'My brother and I taught her that within a month of her coming to us. But she's firmly resisted all further attempts at being taught the Queen's English. Why don't you come over to meet them before you leave for Kerala?'

'Your dad won't mind?'

'Nah, he's like a pal, I can tell him anything. Even that I didn't want to go to Kerala if I didn't want to.'

I sighed, 'Arjun, my parents aren't like that. They *dote* on me.'

'Well, mine dote on me too, but they let me do what *I* want to do.'

I thought about this. There was no doubt in my mind that anything my parents *wouldn't* allow me to do sprang firmly from their love for me. Even Arjun couldn't convince me otherwise. 'Different people just have different ways of showing their love,' I said.

'I suppose you're right. But I'll miss you when you're in Kerala.'

'I'll miss you too, Arjun, but I'll write to you so often it might actually be better than when I'm in Delhi.'

'What do you mean?'

'Well, no one will check my letters, I know, but actually being able to meet you here will always be a problem. Even phone calls will really have to be sneaked out to you when there's no one around.'

'Yes, I was a bit startled yesterday when you suddenly addressed me as Renu in the middle of our conversation, babbling inanely about some chemistry equation!'

We laughed, and I hoped that Arjun would understand that my machinations were born of necessity rather than deviousness. But Arjun, straightforward and uncomplicated, still sounded puzzled, 'But you were allowed to have me around to your house that day for lunch.'

'Yes, but now it's different. I think it'll be hard to hide my feelings.'

I wasn't sure Arjun could understand my dilemma and I looked at him, worried that the bother would have him lose interest in me. But he was smiling his cheerful smile as he said with mock exasperation, 'Well, we'd better get going then if you want to be home by lunch time. Can't have you getting into trouble.'

We scrambled up, dusting bits of dry grass off our clothes. Arjun hailed an auto rickshaw while I gathered up our belongings. A colourful rickshaw trundled up, coughing its diesel waste into the hot air. The driver looked at us enquiringly.

'Mehrauli,' Arjun asked, 'via Hauz Khas?'

Given a churlish but accepting nod, we climbed in, pressed deliciously close to each other in the tiny confines of the passenger seat. The rickshaw driver scowled suspiciously at us in his rear-view mirror. Randy schoolkids, I could hear him think. I sat primly with my hands on my lap, while Arjun confidently stretched his arm out on the backrest. Holding hands was completely out of the question, even in the anonymity of this teeming city. Girls like me grew up knowing that careless behaviour either sent out wrong signals of availability to the millions of 'Roadside Romeos' that peopled the streets; or incurred the risk of having someone report you. I was sure this rickshaw driver wasn't beyond marching without ado into my house to give my parents the terrible details if I held Arjun's hand or kissed him, so I perched on the edge of the seat, wearing as demure an expression as I could muster.

'You can't be too careful, moral guardians lurk everywhere,' I whispered to Arjun by way of explanation. He waved his hand dismissively but laughed with me as I pulled a face at the back of the driver's head while he was busy negotiating the manic traffic on Janpath.

I could see that Arjun had understood my need for discretion as he tapped the driver on his shoulder just before reaching the turning to my house, '*Idhar rokna bhai ek minute.* Disembarkation point, just out of sight of your home,' he said to me, 'fifteen minutes late. I hope you don't get into trouble.'

I gave him a soft look to make up for the enforced chilliness of our farewell. I probably wouldn't see him for nearly two months now and couldn't find the words to tell him how much I would miss him. 'Enjoy Kerala,' he said ruefully, 'write to me about it. I'll miss you terribly.'

'Get my address from Leena,' I said, getting out of the rickshaw. 'Two months will fly by . . . I promise.'

He nodded silently and for a moment I forgot the hawk-like auto-rickshaw driver as I reached out with my hand to gently cup Arjun's cheek. He gave me a quick kiss on the palm of my hand and the diesel engine revved up an instant warning. I snatched my hand away and watched with my heart in my mouth as the auto rickshaw careered madly down the road. Oh please be safe and well, I thought, and please wait patiently for me to get back. I turned to walk slowly down the leafy road leading to my house, putting my palm to my face. Surely the world was turning upside down. I normally loved my summer holidays. I couldn't remember ever *not* wanting to go to Kerala before . . .

We went every year to Kerala, because my grandparents depended so much on those annual visits and prepared months in advance for them. Airing out the mattresses, frying neyyappams, ordering stacks of melting-soft bolis that took fifteen minutes to make and a mere minute to eat. Ma's parents lived in teeming little Alleppey, full of cinema houses that showed bawdy Malayalam films, so noisy you could sometimes hear the dialogues and soaring songs from outside the hall while queuing up for tickets. Dad's parents lived fifteen miles away in other-wordly, sleeping, dreaming Thoduporam on the banks of the back-waters at Thakazhy. Through almost all of my childhood, both houses had one set of grandparents each, and of course I didn't think then that, in a few short years, that would reduce to just an Ammumma in each house. And finally end with the complete eradication of Thoduporam and the transformation of the house in Alleppey from a happy holiday venue (where cousins gathered and food was served in batches) to a house of forty-watt sadness. Sadness that I, a favoured grandchild, would contribute to in no small measure.

The earliest holiday in Kerala that I'm able to remember was when I was four. That had also been the holiday that, I realize now, had left me with two myths that would follow me for a long time through my adult life. The first few days of my holiday had been spent in Thoduporam, where Appuppa had shown me a sleeping white water-turtle in a corner of the kolam. Perched next to Appuppa as he read his newspaper on the cement steps of the kolam, I spent long hours trying to wake the turtle up, using long bamboo stems to pierce the surface of the water, hoping to tickle the turtle awake. Our silent camaraderie in those still afternoons that zinged with insects was broken only by the occasional chugging of a motor boat on the canal outside and by particularly insistent calls for lunch. Indoors, Ammumma and my mother were usually busy either cooking or exchanging gossip about relatives. Appuppa and my father were far more exciting company, especially if they were going down to inspect the rice fields, which was lovely, squelchy business. But tickling an unresponsive turtle was starting to wear me down when it was time to move to Alleppey for The Wedding.

Raman mama, my mother's brother and my favouritest uncle was getting married. I was included in the female contingent that went to visit my new aunt's family with jewellery, clothes and sweets two days before the wedding. My new aunt, Vijimami, turned out to be small and round and sweet with a startlingly loud shrieking laugh. I adored her and was insanely jealous of her all at once. It was clear that Ramama and I were to be cruelly separated because of this small, round invader he couldn't seem to get his eyes off. Everybody seemed to be laughing a lot and Vijimami was receiving an inordinate amount of attention and gifts, all through which she laughed shriekily. I concentrated fiercely on the delicious rava laddoos that smelt of festivals and left little gritty pieces between my teeth that I could wrestle with for hours afterwards.

At the wedding, I was a thorough nuisance, Ma said, placing myself in between the bridal couple during the feast and the banana-milk ceremony. From this vantage point, I could observe my new mami's dimples and dental fillings and ensure she didn't get too close to Ramama. Afterwards, when we left the hall that now looked like a hurricane had passed through it, Vijimami was brought home, to Ammumma's house. She was brought to the door and had to carry a lamp with the flame spluttering behind her as she walked in. Her pretty face was lit golden from the flickering flames that filled the room and, through the pall of incense smoke, I could see that she had tears shining in her eyes. Certainly those shrieks had been temporarily silenced.

'Why is she crying, Ma?'

'Because she's left her mother's house to come and live with Raman mama and Appuppa and Ammumma.'

'But it's nice to live with Ramama and Appuppa and Ammumma.'

'I know, darling, but she doesn't know that yet. We have to make sure that she finds out soon, which means that you need to be a good girl too and be as nice to her as you can.'

I took in this information and held my resolve until nightfall when I saw Ma escorting Vijimami gently into Ramama's room and then beckoning with a big smile for Ramama to join her there.

'I want to sleep with Ramama, let Vijimami sleep with Appuppaaaa!'

Despite my howls, Vijimami slept in Ramama's room that night. Hopefully she soon found out that living with Ramama and Appuppa and Ammumma was really quite nice and her tears had been a bit of a waste that night. She certainly soon became a valued member of my family. An ever-present and welcome appendage to Ramama, Ammumma's faithful lieutenant, and Appuppa's favourite person, partly because she laughed her shrieky loud laugh at all his jokes . . .

That was what I thought happened after all weddings, a gradual wiping away of tears and more people to love and be loved by. I certainly didn't know then, and would have found it very odd indeed, that weddings were decreed in some other-wordly place where accounts were being totted up and re-

evaluated all the time to decide who should marry whom. My own horoscope had been written up at the time of my birth and lay in Ammumma's bank locker, carefully guarding the secrets of my future. Somewhere, a young lad had already been born who would have to be mine because it had been decided such a long time ago, it was silly to ask when. He wouldn't necessarily be the one I loved, of course, because that was another story altogether, possibly separated from this one by thousands of years. He had been born as well, obviously, and already our destinies and our many pasts were combining in a grand dance so meticulously choreographed, we could easily delude ourselves into believing we were making it all happen.

Even arriving in Kerala hadn't helped to raise my spirits. This one, holiday number seventeen, was a completely new experience. No longer was I interested in accompanying Dad on the boat as he went around Thakazhy on trumped-up chores to amuse me. To his hurt 'Moley not coming?' I would mutter lame excuses and hang around next to Appuppa on the verandah, taking up careful position at the front gate when it was time for the postman's visit. I longed for Arjun's company and wrote never-ending letters to him, perched on the steps of Appuppa's kolam, throwing bits of puffed rice down to my turtle. I couldn't wait to get to Ammumma's house in Alleppey, because no letters had arrived at Thakazhy and it was possible that Arjun might have used the other address. Yes! Two letters were waiting for me! One carefully disguised with Leena's name and address at the back and the other, in a completely different handwriting, with Anju's. When the third letter arrived the following week bearing Ayatollah Khomeini's name and an address in Iran, I was given a quizzical look by my father, but still asked no questions.

Arjun didn't seem to have particularly good epistolary

skills, his letters being about a tenth in size compared to mine. They were all about when he was playing cricket and with whom. But I could feel myself go hot and cold at the last line in Letter Number One that said, 'I miss you so much, it feels as if I love you more than anyone or anything else in the world.' And the second paragraph in Letter Number Three that said, 'I sleep on the terrace these days because it's too hot indoors and the damned electricity keeps getting cut. I'm also helping Dad to make sure no one steals our cabbages again. He's told me to sleep with the airgun next to me, just in case I need to scare intruders off. Sometimes I look at my airgun and wonder what it would be like if it was you next to me instead!' Any doubts that I'd nurtured were now dispelled. The tingling that schoolboy declaration left me with just *had* to be love, I thought.

There were three things that would later signpost that particular holiday in Alleppey as being different from all the others. It was the only time I was there but longing to be somewhere else. It was the first time I would be bought a sari instead of dress material. And it was, without any of us knowing it then, my last holiday in Kerala. Each of those three events was inextricably linked to the others of course, but the connection was to become apparent only much later. Afterwards, with the benefit of hindsight, I could see quite clearly that it was my girlish longing for Arjun that would make Kerala a place not just for holidays but for ever. And it was the rite of passage surrounding a girl's first sari that should have warned me of it.

But I trooped merrily down to Seemati Sari Emporium with Ma, Vijimami and Ammumma when the time came – pleased as punch at the prospect of owning my own sari, which Ma would have to *beg* to borrow from me. Ramama was paying for it, but neither he nor Dad could be persuaded to join us on our girlie mission. We left them discussing politics on Ammumma's verandah and walked down the main street, stopping to buy strings of jasmine flowers – an elbow length each for Ma and Vijimami, a palm length for my shorter tresses. We made slow progress down Mullakkal main road as half the population of Alleppey had heard from either Ammumma or Vijimami of our arrival, but still wanted to enquire personally of us, 'When did you come?'

At the sari shop, we were escorted like VIPs into the inner sanctum, reserved for silk-sari buyers, the privileged few who got to sit on red rexine seats and receive bottles of fizzy Limca on the house. A salesman was assigned specially to our party and we watched as he stood on the platform above us and wrapped, one by one, gorgeous silk saris around his weedy person. Although I had been treated to this sight on many occasions, I never failed to derive great pleasure from it and wondered if the pleasure was mutual. Untiringly, the hapless sari salesman, Alleppey's secret drag queen, would stick his hip out, flaring out the silken pleats, lifting his arm to move the pallu slowly around, making it float and drift gracefully down. The coquettish pouts that accompanied all this were setting Vijimami off in shoulder-shaking sniggers, despite Ma's imploring looks, and so we quickly chose a beautiful orange crepe silk with a gold border. ('Very ideal for mol's complexion,' the sari salesman said, wrapping it in tissue paper, pleased that his poses and pouts had not been in vain.)

That evening I wore my new sari for our evening visit to the temple. Mullakkal Devi's temple was always completely lit up with oil lamps, all along its sides. There were obviously enough people in Alleppey who had dreams they wanted fulfilled and our Goddess never lacked oil in her lamps.

This time I had a special prayer too and had asked Vijimami for a small bottle of oil. As I poured its contents into the large nilavilakku, I asked my family's favourite deity to somehow stop my lying and cheating over Arjun. Mullakkal

Devi would know how to reconcile my wish to be a good daughter with my love for Arjun. She was resplendent today in a deep maroon silk skirt, someone's offering for the day . . . Please sort this out for me, Devi, I whispered, looking at her face, glowing golden through the oil lamps. She looked as though she was smiling. As though *nothing* would give her greater pleasure. Could she see what was to come?

After the deeparadhana, we gathered under the banyan tree to give Ammumma the chance to show us off to her friends and to exchange the day's gossip.

'*Aiyyo*, here comes that Maheswari,' whispered Vijimami with a giggle.

'Mahee!' Ammumma called out. 'See my Mani and Janu are here. From Delhi.'

A large figure rolled up and peered at us through the falling dusk. Fixing its eyes on me but speaking to my mother it said, 'Enda, Mani! When did you come?' and, without waiting for a reply, 'So this is your Janu, yes, she's as pretty as you said, chechi. How old are you now, moley?'

Replies didn't seem important to her and so I only mumbled something. I knew I was being assessed carefully – face, figure, jasmine flowers, orange silk sari. And, yes, here it was . . .

'I'll call Padmaja Maraar straightaway and see what she says. They can come with their son next week, can't they?'

Ammumma's cat was out of the bag and she had the grace to look shame-faced when Ma turned on her after her friend had departed.

'What are you doing match-making for Janu, Ma? Have you forgotten, she's only just seventeen? She has to join college next year. In this day and age girls don't get married in their teens like they did in our time, do they, Viji?'

Vijimami who was always gloriously happy and giggly despite a marriage in her teenage years, fortunately for me, concurred.

43

I saluted Ma with three loud cheers in my head. The ancient branches of the banyan tree were whispering their wisdoms above my head and I looked up to twinkle a happy message through the evening star that would now be emerging over Delhi as well. Arjun . . . you and I are safe for now . . . it looks like we have Ma on our side, without her even knowing it. Dear, *darling* Ma.

I spent the rest of my holiday trying not to miss Arjun too much by accompanying Vijimami to several Malayalam films, their numerous songs and love scenes all reminding me terribly that I was in love too. I ate myself sick with plump, yellow mangoes and spun out in impatience what I didn't know was my last holiday in Kerala. Fortunately, Padmaja Maraar and her son never turned up, Ammumma obviously having had a quiet word in her friend's ear. They had been reserved for my next visit to Kerala. The final one.

*   *   *

Back in Delhi, the leisurely rhythms of Kerala faded very quickly in the busy routine of city life. It was our final year at school and the dreaded board exams were looming. Even Leena had taken to wearing a hang-dog expression and opening up conversations with queries about the dire Organic Chemistry syllabus. But for Arjun and me love flourished like those startlingly beautiful desert blooms that seem to need neither water nor nourishment. Growing into something as strong and steadfast as seventeen-year-olds will ever be capable of, despite the pressures of secrecy and impending exams.

Fortuitously for us, I had been picked to play the part of the son in the end of year production of *Monkey's Paw*. It was this unfortunate youngster's fate to die a gory death halfway through the play, which meant that I could slip away to meet Arjun, well before the end of drama practice. While Mr and Mrs White continued to tread the boards, lamenting the death of their only son, I would mount the pillion of Arjun's waiting bike and be taken to nearby Connaught Place for a shared cold coffee and sandwich. Sometimes, if we were hungry, we went instead to Bengali Market where our scraped-together pocket money went a little further because aloo tikkis and tea were cheaper. Arjun was always careful to keep one eye cocked on his wristwatch, worried that he would get me into trouble if we got too bold. It surprised me that he felt so responsible as I was getting increasingly tempted to throw caution to the winds, but I loved him all the more for it. It had started to feel as if all that really mattered were these snatched tête-à-têtes. And I thought about them far too often while staring blankly at my textbooks later.

We had by now managed to find one rendezvous point that was completely private – Chor Minar, near my house, appropriately meaning Thieves Tower. Here, in this crumbling abode of a gang of thieves that nobody had bothered to write a history about, we savoured our few stolen moments. All over Delhi there are similar monuments, left perhaps by the Archaeological Survey of India to be discovered by young lovers like us with nowhere else to go. The first time we climbed the gravelly steps up to the top of Chor Minar, unhooking cobwebs from our ears and spitting them out of our months, wc discovered that Delhi lay basking prettily below in the winter sunshine. And we watched in fascination while her Gulmohar tree cover turned gradually from heavy green to the most shocking shades of orange and red as summer approached. We made this vantage look-out point, once belonging to a gang of no-gooders, our own. Safe in the knowledge, like those thieves long ago, that no one would think of looking for us here.

This was our home away from home. Our little tower in the sky, a time-capsule of crumbling yellow stone that transported us effortlessly into a dreamt-up future. Here, I would push open the bougainvillaea branch that functioned as our front door as Arjun came in, say helloji-would-you-like-some-chai-ji, take his jacket and briefcase off him, ask him about his day at the office and tell him how much trouble I'd had with the kids. Here it was so easy to pretend we were together, never having to return to our separate homes again. To forget that we would have to sneak off before the street lights started coming on and the bats started to wake up, flapping irritatedly around our heads. It was among those ancient yellow bricks that our love played out its childish game of Let's Be Grown Up. Without being terribly sure of what being grown-up really entailed. It seemed to be enough if we were given an hour or so to sit with arms wrapped around each other, talking about this and that. Perfecting our kissing technique and memorizing each other's faces for the long periods that we could not be together. Here I forgot so easily that my parents loved me dearly too – and were waiting at home with hot food and trusting hearts and their own set of dreams for me. So different from mine.

Chor Minar was our solution to the problem of not being able to traipse freely through each other's homes. And, because our conversation never seemed to run out, there was also the telephone to compensate. Our Malayali servant boy would furtively whisper, '*Arjun bhaiyya*' to me, having answered the telephone with his customary, 'Menon speaking' (for 'May I know who is speaking?'). If either of my parents asked him to whom I was chattering on the phone, he would gravely reply, 'Leena didi' or 'Renu didi', jingling the odd bribe I was able to slip into his pocket. I had been to Arjun's house on two occasions. Once, with Leena, to play a raucous game of cards with Jai and Arjun's brother and once to meet Arjun's father who had given me a cautious but friendly welcome. Later Ma said that was because these things were always less worrying for boys' families. The reputations of families were carried on the shoulders of their daughters, she said. And parents of boys didn't have to worry about things like ... (this was her worst fear) ... *pregnancies*!

It was hard to explain to her, and by then too late, that a pregnancy was terribly unlikely because Arjun and I had never made love. Not in the proper sense, of which I still only had the fuzziest notion. ('Only on top, *not* below!?' Leena had enquired incredulously once, following that up with a worried, 'Under shirt or over?') Despite having Chor Minar to shield us from the world, its gravel-strewn floor covered in bat droppings was not conducive to real romance. And there was always the worry that another pair of lovers would come stumbling into our hiding place one day. Logistics, lack of privacy and plain old-fashioned fear all played their part in keeping our love unconsummated. Given time, they were all laughably fragile barriers that would probably have come down one by one. But time was what we were *not* to be given, although we didn't know that then. And if we had known that then, what course would that childish love have taken? Would it have died its natural death, like so many others do? Bequeathing tender or cringing memories, depending on the circumstance. Would its consummation have sufficed to pay off the debt that we didn't know of then? That we couldn't have seen waiting in the wings, like some angry, unfulfilled promise? To haunt me and follow me until it did exact its price?

And so, innocently and unthinkingly, we carried on playing the game. Drama practice and maths tuition providing thin cover. With guilt occasionally raising its ugly head, only to be promptly stamped down by the fecklessness of youth. If I had ever bothered to sit down and apply the law of probabilities to all my ducking and weaving, I would have known that it was only a matter of time before some little deception made its way out. I would have also recognized that there would be no getting off lightly. When it did finally happen, however, the punishment was the ending not, surprisingly, of our love. But of my life with my parents. Not such an unusual thing, you might say, happens to everyone sooner or later. Except that in my case it felt as if I had effectively taken a loving, safe childhood into my own hands and ended it for ever.

I had said I was at a special maths tutorial class when a friend of my father's spotted me on the pillion of Arjun's motorcycle. Returning from a shared bowl of soup noodles at Akasaka, a birthday treat for Arjun. Weaving carelessly through the evening traffic on Outer Ring Road. Really not caring at all by this stage that I might be seen and reported. A well-meaning telephone call had preceded my arrival home, because when I walked in later that evening my father's face was like thunder and I could see that my mother had been crying.

'Where have you been?'

I should have taken my cue from the cold anger of his words and spoken the truth, but instead I blurted, 'Maths tuition . . .'

I hadn't noticed the cane my father had in his right hand. Ma said later, tearfully rubbing Burnol on my legs, that he'd gone into the garden and hacked it off the hedge himself. In a blind, raging grief she hadn't been able to stop. In blind, raging confusion that his little girl had become a woman without anyone bothering to tell him. I heard a swishing sound, and seconds later realized he was slashing at my legs. Once, twice . . . I could hear my mother screaming at him to stop. All the anger . . . at having ever left Kerala, at having carefully attempted to bring up a daughter in a thankless place like Delhi, at having been deceived by the thing he most loved in the world . . . all seemed to be coming out at me, with that horribly swishing cane. Cut from the hedge in our own back garden, just behind my marigold patch. Dad, who had always overflowed with tenderness

. . . I was too shocked to get out of the way, and would not have believed what was happening if it wasn't for my stinging legs.

Great red welts appeared on my legs, and on my heart, the next morning, testament to my shame and deception. I was told that from now until my final exams I would be taken to and picked up from school. I would not be allowed to use the telephone and would be accompanied everywhere. There was to be no more drama practice and no more maths tuition. And no more roaming around town with boys. I spent hours in my room, staring at my textbooks through unseeing eyes and wondering if the world outside was still a normal place. Were people really laughing and loving in their homes? Had another pair of lovers annexed Chor Minar?

It felt as if my father almost couldn't bear to look at me after that, but I couldn't tell if it was his guilt or mine that was causing that awful rift. Stubbornly and, I suppose, a bit spitefully, Arjun and I continued to stay in touch, smuggling letters and messages through our friends, but fear was now the overwhelming emotion. The joy had been taken out of loving, and what was left was a strange silent thing.

After the exams were over, the scramble for college places began. It was plain that my parents had lost interest in their desire to send me to college. College was for those girls who were serious about their studies and who didn't waste their parents' hopes and money. I was offered a place at Miranda House for a BA in English, but it was decided that we'd make our annual trip to Kerala as usual in a couple of months' time and discuss the matter further while we were there.

Arjun, in the meantime, had decided to join his mother in England. Despite the churning in my stomach, I tried to sound happy when he first told me of it in a sneaked telephone call. He had been offered a place at Hull University,

which was quite near where his mother worked at Scun-
thorpe General Hospital. We had, neither of us, heard of
Kingston-upon-Hull before and I raced to my atlas to look
it up. There it was, a small black dot on the north-east coast
of England. It looked like it might be a port town. 'Is that
why it's called Hull?' I asked Arjun. He didn't seem to know
but thought it might be something to do with ships. I could
sense his growing excitement at the changes that were
about to take place in his life. He had been with his father
to the British High Commission and had been granted a
visa. 'I have to work on my accent,' he said, 'they kept
asking me to repeat myself. Aspiration of consonants, that's
the key.'

We aspirated in chorus, 'Puh . . . kuh . . . tuh . . . p(h)ot of
t(h)ea . . . p(h)iece of c(h)ake . . .' dissolving into hysterical
laughter. But, after putting the phone down, I buried my
face in my pillow, ashamed to find myself crying at Arjun's
happiness.

Although he was now very busy organizing his departure,
we managed to meet on a few wistful occasions, when,
despite everything, we still talked in terms of being able to
be together, *properly*, someday. When and how we would
achieve this was too exhausting and too distant to seriously
contemplate. But it was still preferable to think in those
terms.

The day Arjun was to leave for England finally came, not
even my most fervent prayers could stop it. I woke up
feeling sadder than I had ever felt before. Even the jacaranda
tree outside my window was bent over and weeping purple
tears for me in the early morning sunshine. Sadness is
something that usually shrinks when measured in hindsight but the sadness of this bright, beautiful morning was
one that would stay with me for a long time afterwards. I
often used it, later, to measure other sadnesses. In a game
I sometimes played to check the immensity of one sadness

against new and unfamiliar ones. Months afterwards, I could still remember the feel of it, in the hotness behind my eyes and the dryness in my mouth. Worse, I thought in retrospect, than the day I got married two months later, because that event at least had some compensatory joys, such as my parents' happiness.

Arjun's flight was to leave late at night. By afternoon I was desperate to see him once before he left, a telephone call just wouldn't do. I needed to see him, to look into his eyes and tell him that, whatever happened, I would always love him. I went into Ma's room to ask if I could go to Leena's to say goodbye to her before she left on a family holiday to Goa. Ma looked at my face, something must have told her of my unhappiness and, unexpectedly, she nodded a yes. I hastily washed my face and brushed back my hair and ran down the road to get myself an auto rickshaw. Leena's mother was out playing cards at her club and wouldn't be back for a while. How odd, I thought, that circumstances should all be falling so nicely into place when it was time to say goodbye. Leena made a quick phone call to Arjun. My heart was thudding, he's bound to have gone *out* for something, he's probably at *Jai's* on the other side of town . . . but he was at home, packing. 'I'm leaving right now,' he said, 'the packing can wait.' Twenty minutes later, he'd arrived at Leena's house, laughing that he was probably in trouble for having borrowed his brother's motorcycle without the usual wheedling. We were to get one precious hour together.

All the terribly important things I had planned to say somehow got stuck in my throat and remained unsaid. Coming to mind much later and much too late. Bitterly, I would later blame myself for not having told Arjun how much I really loved him and, despite everything, how glad I was to have found him. I couldn't remember either if he had said anything of consequence that I could have cherished for ever. We talked of inconsequential things, and of unimportant things. Did we talk of the future at all? Of how we would be together again, *somehow*, in some distant place? If we did, it would by then have sounded very hollow even to the two of us. There had been too many barriers and gates between us, even when we had lived in the same city. Too many Sister Seraphias (nursing their own broken dreams perhaps) watching out to see that young people did not make the mistake of even beginning to dream. Especially outside school gates, where parents paid good money to ensure that blue *never* mingled with grey.

Leena took a photograph of us. When it was developed a few days later, Arjun's face looked bright and optimistic. I, on the other hand, turned out looking pale and drawn. As if in anticipation of everything that lay ahead. I was sure we would never meet again, although I could not bring myself to say it out loud. Leena made us some toasted sandwiches and fresh-lime soda, and then left us to sit forlornly on her mother's blue sofa to talk some more of all those unimportant things that might somehow hold off the importance of this goodbye. Even Leena's kid sister, normally a pesky seven-year-old, stayed quietly in her room either under pain of death from her bossy sibling or because even she could sense that two young lovers were failing miserably to say goodbye properly in her living room.

When my deadline approached, Arjun hailed me an auto rickshaw on the road outside. He kissed me tenderly before I boarded it. 'I promise I'll be back,' he said to which I couldn't say that I didn't think he would. The feel of his lips on mine was still warm and wet when I saw him mount his motorcycle as the rickshaw-wallah turned his vehicle around. Almost physically unable to let Arjun out of sight, I lifted the back flap of the rickshaw and watched him ride away. In the opposite direction. It was all over.

FOUR

A few days before we left for Kerala I was told that a Maraar family were interested in me for their younger son. He had a degree in Business Administration and was tipped to take over the successful family-run motel business soon, with plans to develop it further. Letters and telephone calls from Kerala were bringing wonderful news. The older son was a college professor who was showing no interest in the business, so everything would almost *definitely* pass on to the prospective groom, I was told. Their string of Maraar Motels, acquired at the rough rate of one every two years, now stretched from Kovalam to Calicut. They were a highly respected family, had two sons and two daughters, a beautiful house and a fleet of Ambassador cars. And all those motels, of course, with plans of *more* to come . . . that too in *Bombay*, my dear, as Ammumma had been informed by the eager match-maker. So far they had turned down virtually every other Malayali family with a marriageable daughter in their quest for a pretty girl, preferably one from a family without *too* much money. Puzzled, Ammumma had to have it explained to her that Mrs Maraar worried that a girl from a frightfully wealthy home might turn out to be arrogant and 'unable to adjust'. So far their search, spanning two whole years, had proved unsuccessful – leading them to look at Malayali families outside Kerala. Not that they *really* wanted to take the risk of some Bombay-Delhi city type, but they had heard that my family were conservative and traditional and the match-making

Maraar relative in Alleppey had undertaken to stand as *special* guarantor of my suitability. For her pains she was receiving a Kanjeevaram sari, the general kudos of people and the undying gratitude of two families. And I? I was an incredibly lucky girl even to *get* a proposal of marriage from a family as wonderful as that.

'What about my studies?' I knew there was no point even mentioning Arjun, but my studies were surely good enough reason to put marriage off for a while.

'We've already discussed that with them. They said you could continue your studies in Kerala if you were very keen. English Literature is something you could even do from home.'

'I don't feel ready for marriage . . . I'm looking forward to going to college here.'

'Why? So that you can waste more of your father's hard-earned money pretending to go to college while roaming all around town with boys?'

'I've never roamed all around town with boys, as you put it, Ma. That's not fair! Arjun was my friend, just like Leena and . . .'

'Don't mention his name to me. You know how much you've disappointed us with your behaviour. Now think about this wonderful offer, proposals like this don't come every day. They're so keen to see you they are willing to drive down to Cochin the day we arrive there. Just imagine!'

I made a mental note not to get into any more arguments. All I needed to do was meet this family and then say I didn't think the boy was suitable for me. Too short, too tall, there were hundreds of excuses I could make. Surely no one was going to marry me off at gun-point.

When we left Delhi two days later, I had no sense at all of it being some kind of final departure. A final departure not only from the home and the city I'd grown up in but also from a general state of happiness for a long, long time.

I had packed my usual small blue suitcase with the clothes and books needed for a two-month stay. Looking out of the window, I said a casual goodbye to the city sprawling lazily under our climbing aircraft, and remembered how awful it had felt doing the same thing last year because then I was leaving Arjun behind. There *were* advantages to his being in England after all. In the two months since he'd left, a couple of letters had arrived for me at Leena's house and I carefully cherished them in the bottom of a shoe box hidden under a pile of glass bangles and hairbands. They were in thick envelopes perfectly made, unlike the skewed ones I was more used to, and smelt wonderful. As if from a far-away world where everything was fragrant and orderly.

The first letter said,

Janu my sweet,
I'm writing this on board the flight, with some paper very kindly given to me by the air hostess (very pretty, I might add!). I think she likes me, she even offered me a can of beer. Heineken too! I tried that brand once with Dad at Mr Mittkopf's and didn't like it very much, so I'm sticking to orange juice at the moment. I might succumb the next time she asks me, though, if she smiles very sweetly. Don't be annoyed, I miss you very much already. Even more than I miss Jai and cricket practice with him at the maidans!

Do call my father and brother whenever you can. I'm sure Dad in particular will be missing me and will consequently be thrilled to hear from you. I'm looking forward to seeing Mum of course, it can't have been easy for her, these past two years alone in England. So it's going to be wonderful for her to have me (her ray of sunshine, no less) with her now. In all honesty, though, at the moment I keep seeing your tearful face as we said goodbye at Leena's. Don't worry, Janu, it won't be long, just three years for me to complete my course. Keep yourself busy, as I intend to, and the time will just fly. I

promise you we'll be together someday. I'll post this letter at Frankfurt airport so you get it soon.
Many, many kisses,
Yours,
Arjun

Just three years, he had said. That seemed like an awfully long time from my point of view, three years would mean the rough equivalent of about thirty marriage proposals to stave off. Keep yourself busy. Busy with what? With turning down marriage proposals, with facing the grief and anger of my parents? Would that make the time fly, really? His next letter was shorter. I thought he sounded happier, more settled . . .

My darling girl Jans,
I've been here two weeks now and the weather's great. Lots and lots of cricket, on television, on village greens and virtually everywhere that you look. It feels like I'm in heaven! Here they play it properly though, all kitted out in white, with proper score boards. It was great seeing Mum at the airport, and I spent the first few days with her in her tiny hospital flat. On Monday, she took me to Hull where I met some of the Profs. I have my own room now, C 3 Nicholson Block. It's got everything I need, even a washbasin but the loos are down the corridor. Food's ghastly. Here they say 'tea' for 'dinner' and there's a fierce-looking woman with a moustache who serves it up. If you're ever offered something called Shepherd's Pie, remember to decline politely. I've made my first friend, a chap from Liverpool called Kevin. He seems pleasant enough, although I can't always understand everything he says.
I'll write to you again in a couple of weeks. Your letter took two weeks to get to me, is it the same from here?
Love you loads!
Keep smiling!
Arjun

Oh *Arjun*, I thought to myself, why don't you know what it's like? I'm leaving for Kerala *tomorrow*, where I'll be seen by some family for their son. I have to think up some very convincing excuse to get out of it. Then there'll be another and another and another. And each time I'll have to think up some better and better excuse. And all you have to worry about is whether it'll be Shepherd's Pie for tea!

* * *

The hot wet Kerala air hit us as we disembarked from the aircraft. The salty, fishy smell of the sea was drifting over the tarmac as usual, making my stomach turn in the heat. Raman mama was among the crowds to receive us. I gave him a big hug, my *favouritest* uncle. He took my suitcase off me, 'So, all ready to see your prince in shining armour? Or, more likely, prince in shining Ambassador, eh?'

Everybody laughed. So, Ramama was in it too. Surely he would disapprove? He and Vijimami were going to be my allies, they'd never agree to anything that would make me unhappy, would they?

We were taken to the house of a friend of Ramama's. His family were acquainted with the Maraars and it was felt that this would be the most neutral place to meet. I was helped into my one and only sari and told to stay in the children's bedroom until the Maraars arrived and I was summoned. I sat on a child's bed, which was covered in comic books, shivering in anticipation. It was going to be *easy*, all I had to do was say *no*. The two little girls whose room I had invaded looked at me sympathetically.

'You want to read my comics?'

'Thanks, yes maybe, which is your favourite?'

'Richie Rich.'

'I used to like that too.'

'Yeah, he's rich, with lots of money, but he's got no friends. That's why he's called a poor little rich boy.'

But no amount of scintillating conversation was going to

get my mind off the impending meeting. The *pennukaanal* that millions of girls had gone through over the ages, some with tremulous dreams for the future and some with the knowledge that this was in essence the end of dreaming. I heard the sound of car doors closing and realized, with a start, that They'd arrived. Through a chink in the door I watched with my two, small, new-found friends, the Arrival of the Maraars. There seemed to be about six people and the drawing room was filled with the sounds of shuffling and sitting down and embarrassed laughter and small talk. Did you find the house easily? When did the flight arrive? Did you hear, there are plans to expand the airport because of the Dubai rush? Did you know there's a girl in this room for whom it's the end of dreaming? After an eternity, I was called.

'This is our Janu, who has waited all her life for this beautiful moment, is it not so, Janu-mole?' I was being presented with a flourish by the garrulous man of the house, idiot father of those two lovely children indoors . . . more embarrassed laughter . . . 'Come on, moley, meet Suresh's parents, his elder sister Sathi, her husband Dr Sasi, *fay*mous nephrologist, and this here is . . . The Boy!'

I scanned the room, seeing only blurry figures with no faces. Ramama patted the chair next to him and I sank into it gratefully. The lady of the house brought in the tea things, she seemed pleased to have got the unexpected chance to show off her new Arcopal set (newly arrived with cousin from Kuwait). Ma followed close behind carrying a tray laden with goodies bought hastily from Cochin Bakery on the way down from the airport. Rocket mutais, luridly coloured cakes, special mixture with bright green bits in it, and rava laddoos that smelt of festivals.

More small talk in which, fortunately, I wasn't expected to participate. I could see that my father was being listened to admiringly. It was considered very good when one of Kerala's sons did so well in a big place like Delhi, becoming 'Such a Highly Placed Official'. I knew how hard he'd worked to climb the ranks of the Air Force and felt a sudden rush of pride in him. It seemed a long time ago that I'd last seen him look so happy. How much unhappiness I must have caused him with my deceit . . .

The Maraars looked like the Good Family I'd been told they were. All starched shirts and elegant silk saris. The Elder Sister asked me whether I could speak Malayalam. In my not-so-good Malayalam I replied that I could. Her husband, Dr Sasi-the-famous-nephrologist, asked me if I had any hobbies. I said reading and music but forgot to say amateur dramatics. Ma said later this was fortunate as they might have thought this drama-shama stuff unbecoming to a future daughter-in-law.

I noticed some whispering between Ramama and Dr Sasi-the-famous-nephrologist and heard Ramama say, 'Why not, these are modern times, are they not? Moley Janu, Suresh wants a private word with you, so why don't you both go into that room there.'

I could hear coy laughter ripple around the room in anticipation of this hopelessly romantic encounter as we got up and were ushered into an adjoining study. I sat behind the table and Suresh took the chair opposite. He looked like he had done this before. He spoke to me in not-very-good English, and I replied in not-very-good Malayalam. It could have been an interview for a job, which I suppose, in a sense, it was. He asked me what subjects I had taken in high school and what I intended doing at college. He asked if I knew how to cook and what sort of food I liked. He asked me if I'd like to ask him any questions, to which I said no thank you. Ma said later this was also good because it would have seemed quite forward of me to have asked him a lot of questions. Without intending to, I was passing my pennu-kaanal with flying colours.

Before leaving, the Maraars got into a hasty confabulation on the verandah and then came back into the living room to say 'Yes', throwing my parents into a confused delirium. Yes, they liked the girl and what did we think about the boy? Disconcerted looks flew around my camp. Such a quick and unequivocal response had not been anticipated. I could feel my heart pounding in my chest and my mouth went dry as I wondered if I would be consulted at all.

I heaved a sigh of relief as I heard Ramama say, 'They've only just arrived after a long flight and now we have to get to Alleppey before it gets dark. Could you give us till tomorrow morning to discuss things like Janu's education? We'll call you first thing in the morning, definitely.'

The Maraars seemed a little taken aback at not getting the instant and gleeful response they'd expected but left none the less, with a flurry of smiles and silk saris, in two white Ambassador cars. Disjointed voices were taking up a chorus somewhere.

'Didn't they seem *nice*?'

'*Verrry* decent people.'

'That sister and her husband looked so good, such a dignified couple.'

'I saw her *covered* in jewellery for her own wedding, very wealthy they are, these Maraars. Moley Janu, you are indeed a very lucky girl that they liked you so much.' This from the lady of the house who was clearing away her now gloriously defiled Arcopal tea set.

I thought to myself uncharitably that she was a silly cow who didn't have a clue what I wanted and that I didn't feel especially lucky that the Maraars liked me. They had, in fact, made my problem worse by doing so.

Probably guessing my thoughts, and wanting to avoid an

60

argument in front of the couple who'd so kindly loaned us their living room, Ma hustled us all into Ramama's car and we left for Alleppey. No one bothered me in the car. The talk was still predominantly about how nice the Maraars seemed and how lucky we were. I could sense the comments were all floating subtly in my direction. But I was exhausted now. The car tooted noisily through crowded towns and villages, angrily avoiding cyclists and children. I knew I had to close my eyes and blank everything out, even the darkening paddy fields and glimpses of sunset over the ocean that I always looked forward to seeing.

Ammumma was waiting eagerly at the door, 'How did it go? What did they say? They *did*? You *what*! You said you would tell them *tomorrow*? Are you all mad? What are they going to think? They could even retract their offer by tomorrow!'

Ramama sat me down gently, 'What's wrong? Suresh looked very nice, didn't he? I believe he's a very decent chap.'

'I'm sure he is, Ramama. I have nothing against them. I just think it's too early.'

'Why?'

'Well, because of my studies.'

'But they are willing to allow you to do your BA. The only difference will be that you will be staying in their home and not in Delhi.'

'Don't *you* think eighteen's too early?'

'Well, Vijimami was only seventeen when we got married, remember? In some ways, I think it's easier to adjust to new situations when you're younger.'

Suddenly everyone was talking again. Be grateful for what you're getting . . . We're just an ordinary service family . . . They could get their pick of any family in Kerala . . . They don't even want a *dowry* . . . It's nothing less than arrogance to say no to people like them . . . I want to see a grandchild of mine married before I die, your poor Appuppa went without knowing that joy, don't do the same to me . . . On what *basis* can we turn them down, especially as *they've* said yes! . . .

I looked around me, here were all the faces that I had loved virtually from the moment I was born. It would be *so* easy to make everyone happy, really. Oh, what am I to *do*, I thought forlornly. Ramama, seeming to take pity on my tired state, said, 'Go and have a wash, think about it before going to sleep. You can give me your answer first thing in the morning.'

If I said that I lay awake all night thinking, it would not be true. I was still at an age when little thought went into large decisions. I was exhausted, both from my journey the previous day and from the guilt I had wrestled with for so long over my relationship with Arjun. The fact of Arjun's departure was just starting to sink in as something real and permanent. He'd gone, not for a month or a year but probably for ever. Ma was right, it was crazy to expect we'd ever share a future together. We'd always occupied different worlds, now it could have been separate universes. Where everything, even envelopes, looked and smelled different. *He'd* sounded happy in his letters . . . I was tired and did not want to think any more. Were there eighteen-year-olds who dealt with grief in sensible, thoughtful ways? As far as I was concerned, it was easier just to pull the shutters down and hope for the best. I had no excuses to give Arjun, later.

The next morning I lay awake for a while looking at the parrots swing on the branches of the mango tree outside. Where are you, Arjun? It would be nine-minus-four-and-a-half . . . daybreak in England now. Are you sleeping in . . . it's Sunday . . . no classes today . . . What'll it be for tea today? In England, they say 'tea' for 'dinner'! I hope it isn't Shepherd's Pie. Do you think you'll make it to the cricket team next summer?

Vijimami put her head around the door, 'Coffee, molu?' I nodded and smiled at her. She came in and sat next to me, 'Have you thought about things? This is *marriage* we're talking about, not something to *worry* about. You'll just have more people caring for you and making sure you're happy. Mullakkal Devi will always look after you, like she's looked after me in this house, you'll be . . .'

'It's okay, Vijimami, I have thought it through. You can tell them I said yes.'

Her eyes widened and I could see disbelieving dimples appear in her fat, happy cheeks. She rushed joyfully out of the room to pass on the good news to everyone else. I leaned back on my pillow and felt strange waves of relief flood through me. The parrots were still engaged in their noisy dance, their green and yellow now blurring suddenly into the surrounding mangoes and leaves.

*   *   *

Cheyyat House
Mullakkal
Alleppey

Dear Arjun,

I'm sure we both knew this was coming, so here it finally is. I'm getting married in two weeks' time. To a businessman who lives in Kerala. I've met him once, he seems pleasant enough. I don't suppose you want to know much more about him, and there's little more I can add to that description anyway.

But to answer the question that must be uppermost in your mind . . . because, because, because I'm tired of fighting off my family, they've proven their love for me in the eighteen years it's taken to bring me up. And I just can't believe they'd push me into something that would be wrong for me. I know you think of it as a stupidly blind kind of trust, but there it is.

In any case, you seem so far away, I don't feel a part of your world any more. I could feel myself starting to lose you the

63

day your visa came through, and since then your excitement over UCCAs and halls of residence and new possibilities have felt pretty alien to me.

Your world and mine have grown so far apart, I reckon I've lost you anyway. And maybe I'll find some comfort in making my folks happy, for once! For a while they've seen my ways as being increasingly dissolute and uncaring, so here's compensation for all that in one fell swoop. And how! I've never seen them happier. It's hard not to let that infect me. But I'd be lying if I said I didn't miss you and think about you every day.

Don't be angry with me. Given a choice this isn't how I'd want it to be. Trite as it may sound, I want what's best for you as well. Five thousand miles away, I don't suppose that thing is me. Work hard at your new course and do well. Something tells me that somewhere along the way I'm going to see your name in lights. And that'll give me another reason to believe that what I'm doing today has been the right thing.

Please remember me well . . .

XXX
Janu

PS Please don't write to me again, it'll get me in trouble.
PPS I hope you make it to that cricket team next summer.

* * *

'Moley, Janu, come and try this on.'
I hastily pushed the letter into an airmail envelope and hid it between the pages of my book.
'Coming, Ma . . .'
Smiles were wreathed across her face. She was sitting on the floor surrounded by silk saris and had a pile of blouses on her lap. She looked like a plump, cheerful island floating on a multicoloured sea.
'The tailor's just had these delivered. I did tell him to do

one for a trial before cutting the rest. But it looks like he's done a good job, so hopefully we won't have to send them back. Look, Ammini, double-stitching around the waist and arms, so they can be taken up or down according to the fashion. Try this one on, moley . . .'

I made off to the bathroom with one of the blouses, leaving my mother and her sister cooing over the rest. No more jeans, unfortunately. We'd already assessed, from the few stilted meetings that had taken place, that my prospective in-laws had orthodox taste in clothes. And what was most important for the time being was to make sure I fitted in as seamlessly as possible. Without sticking out like a sore thumb, without sticking out like some Delhi-raised vagabond amidst their lovely Kerala-bred, sari-clad daughters. The blouse was a terrible fit, now what sort of an omen was that?

'Maaa! Come and have a look, it's awfully tight around the waist and arms . . . ugh!'

Ma came rushing in, smiles now replaced by a dark frown.

'I had told that fool Venu to stitch just one first, now we'll have to send the whole lot back for re-stitching. And only two weeks to go! What's wrong, it looks all right?'

'Well, it's tight and uncomfortable for one . . .'

'That's only because you're not used to wearing blouses. Wandering all around Delhi in those filthy jeans and tee-shirts. I should have made sure you wore saris more often, to give you more practice. Never mind, you'll get used to it.'

'Yes, like I'll get used to giving up my studies, my friends and my freedom?' I said, *sotto voce*.

Ma shot a quick look at my face, half-worried and half-angry, 'Now don't start that again. We've been through that a hundred times. It's been fixed now, even the cards have all been sent. Our family have all gathered here, from everywhere. Now be happy and look ahead to a new life, moley.

All girls have to get married someday. You're a lucky girl. The Maraars are an old and gracious family, half the families in Kerala would have died for an alliance like this . . .'

Marriages in Kerala were never just marriages, they were 'alliances'. Alliances between just whom was the bit that wasn't always easy to work out. The parents? Families? Whole clans, reaching back many ghostly generations? I was twirled around for the back of the blouse to be examined. 'Just think how lucky you are that they haven't objected to your having been brought up in Delhi. It's a good thing you're pretty. I think that's what did it in the end. Now lift your arms.'

There was the sound of running footsteps and the bathroom door was pushed open without ceremony. Even the *toilets* held no privacy these days with the house so full! It was little Mini, red-faced and breathless. She pulled her pants down, perched herself hastily on the toilet and fixed her eyes unseeingly two inches in front of her face. Once the urgent sound of hissing had reduced to a trickle, she surveyed the scene in front of her.

'That blouse makes you look like a cow,' she announced, 'look, it's got four pointies instead of two.'

'She's right, Ma,' I wailed, 'it's got darts in all the wrong places!'

I thrust my chest out for Ma and Mini to get a better look. I could see Ma's face darken, definitely four pointies. That Venu was going to die a painful death. 'Well, take it off, we'll just have to send it back to Venu-tailor. For the amount of business he's getting from us, it's the least he can do to make sure at least the *bride*'s blouses fit properly. *Kazhutha!*' She bustled off, leaving a cloud of annoyance in her wake.

I looked at myself in the mirror, feeling very unamused. Venu-tailor obviously had an impossibly idealistic notion of the direction in which women's breasts pointed, I thought,

adjusting my bra straps. My eyes travelled down the reflection I could see . . . the face and figure that had made the
Maraars like me and cast me into this new tangle. Ma didn't
usually tell me I was pretty, for fear it would go to my head.
I looked enquiringly at the girl standing before me in bra
and panties . . . what lies ahead for you now, I asked her.
Ammumma's old Belgian glass mirror always made everything look nicer than it really was. The hazy reflection
showed me an oval face, framed in black shoulder-length
curls. Limpid brown eyes looked sadly back at me. I smiled
at them, attempting to make them smile back, but they
wouldn't and started filling up alarmingly with tears. Those
damned tears . . . whenever I was alone . . . which, thankfully, wasn't often these days. A soft humming was issuing
forth from somewhere behind me. I'd forgotten! Mini was
still in the bathroom. She seemed to have settled herself
comfortably on the toilet, balancing her pink panties on
swinging upturned toes. From this vantage point she was
examining my figure with as much interest as I was.

'Why are you still here? Off with you now.'

'Can't I stay, please, Janu chechi? I can give you more
advice on the rest of your clothes too.'

'*No*, shoo, I think I've had enough advice to last a long,
long time, without six-year-olds being added to my list of
advisers.'

Mini obviously liked the tone of my voice and re-arranged
her features to receive with sympathy any more confidences
that I might be ready to unload. When I pulled on my kaftan
without paying her any more attention she tried another
tack.

'Chechi, your mother was telling my mother that you
had a *boyfriend* in Delhi?' She said the word as if it were
on a par with the 'bloodydamn' for which she'd received a
maternal smack the other day. Dropping her voice to
a whisper and widening her eyes into saucers.

'Mini, there's nothing that our two mothers will not tell each other. When you're a little older, you might want to beware of that. Remember, no hasty confidences to seemingly kindly aunts.'

'Yeah, chechi, but that's because they're *sisters*,' said Mini and, still hopeful of some stray confidences added, 'that means that, because we are cousin-sisters, we can tell each other everything too.'

I handed the little girl a mug full of water, 'Yes, Minimole, we can. But, sadly for me, not until you're just a few years older and can fathom the meanings of love and honour and tradition and duplicity and sham. For now, unfortunately, I'm alone in this and it hurts like mad, but you'd better be off because your friends will be wondering how long it takes for Simla-people to have a pee.'

Not comfortable with the turn in our conversation, she wriggled off her perch on the toilet, pulled up her panties and made off at great speed. I watched through the window as she rejoined the little gaggle of girls that appeared miraculously in grandmother's garden whenever we arrived on holiday. Through the mosquito mesh stretched across the bathroom window, the scene had a gauzy, dreamlike quality. Ten years ago, that was me and not Mini scampering around Ammumma's gravel compound, whooping with delight along with my new-found friends. The scene was the same, the same compound, the same little girls, the same flying pigtails. Only I'd been removed from it. To be grown up. To meet Arjun. To leave Arjun. And to ensure that I began to pay off some of the debts that had accrued against my name somewhere. My story was beginning to be written again.

FIVE

The wedding was to take place at Guruvayur temple, one of Kerala's holiest Hindu shrines. On my eighteenth birthday. It would be a double blessing, everyone said, a birthday *and* a wedding at Guruvayur. I'd been there many times before, of course, on happy if not especially worshipful occasions. Geeta chechi's wedding when I was seven; two years later her mewling baby's rice-giving ceremony when even I was allowed to smear some mashed-up rice into his unwilling mouth; Alleppey Appuppa's thulabharam, the following year, when he was weighed against a seemingly ever-growing mound of sugar. Guruvayurappan was greedy for his share of sugar, they said, because it was going to take one of His miracles to cure Appuppa of his cancer. Appuppa had succumbed soon after to the monster growth that took over his stomach, but now Guruvayurappan had been promised another thulabharam for bringing about the miracle of my marriage. I was to have my weight in sugar offered to Him on the morning of the wedding by my grateful grandmother.

It was four in the morning, but the dark wet streets of the temple town were busy with worshippers and pilgrims disembarking from Tamil Nadu buses in droves. Ammumma had given me some flowers and a coconut wrapped in a banana leaf to offer the Gods in gratitude at all my good fortune. I could feel the edges of my sari grow sodden and muddy with only one hand to hold it up and now my feet were getting caught in its wet folds. I couldn't walk very fast even though it had started to drizzle.

The enormous temple gates were open, little old ladies were scurrying in, their white mundus wet from the rain and their newly washed hair. Guruvayurappan had been given His early morning bath and was all shining black, stone-coloured in the dark interior of the inner sanctum. Later in the day, like me, he would be dressed in silks and jewels. Sometimes the priests who performed this task made his plain stone figure look so beautiful it could take your breath away. It was Guruvayurappan's magic playing out through their fingertips, they said. The priests at the door, however, were always angry young men, filled with the importance of collecting as much money as possible in as short a time as possible. And so they played their powerful game of Let's-push-poor-praying-pilgrims-along. But, among the pilgrim-shoving and the insistent clamour of the temple bells, the people who had had icy baths in the kolam and then queued up for hours got their longed-for glimpse of Guruvayurappan and were satisfied. Sometimes they even cried. Tears rolling down their faces in myriad unknown joys and sorrows.

'This way, here, climb up on this step-ladder.' There was no time for awkward fumblings in this efficient place. I clambered on to an enormous pair of weighing scales and watched while, amidst a lot of shouting and giving of orders, large tin drums full of sugar were carried out. One by one they were placed on to the scale on the other side. One, two, three, my equivalent weight in sugar, its sweetness carefully calculated by Guruvayurappan to cancel out the last remnants of bitterness in my heart.

'What do they do with the sugar?' I asked Ammumma as we hurried back to the hotel, past the kolam whose waters were gradually warming with pilgrims' bodies and the gently rising sun.

'Must be using it for the payasams that are then given as prasadam to the pilgrims.' That was a strange thought. Hundreds of pilgrims from far away places would at lunch time today be opening up their banana-leaf parcels to partake of my bitterness-turned-to-sweetness. 'Roll up, roll up, here have a pack of this special No-pain-any-more-payasam!'

The chosen muhurtham was eleven o'clock. The most auspicious hour of the day and most practical to serve lunch afterwards. It was also least likely to rain and upset the careful arrangements at that time of day, they said. But they were wrong. At about nine, the heavens opened up and it started to rain as though some broken-hearted Goddess just could not stem her tears any more.

Worried-looking menfolk gathered around, discussing quick changes of plan so that the guests did not get soaking wet. Women issued dark threats to children who might run out into the rain, spoiling their brand-new silk clothes. I sat in my room, now so dark it needed all the lights turned on. Outside, thunder rumbled forbiddingly. But inside, a life was being re-fashioned while a bride took shape and children ran up and down the corridors, screaming their heedless joys. Preethi chechi had been assigned to do my hair and make-up. She ran a successful beauty parlour in Bangalore ('waxing - bleaching - eyebrows - upperlip - and - full - bridal make-up') and took to her task with masterful aplomb, a monument to confidence in an ocean of confusion.

'Preethi, moley, look at that rain! What do we do, it will all be a mess now!' Ammumma said, scurrying in with my small, sandalwood jewellery box.

'Don't worry, Peramma, it will be okay. My make-up is all waterproof, imported from US. Rain, swimming, tears, *no* problem.'

I hoped she was right. Her confidence was comforting. Rain, swimming and, best of all, tears-*no*-problem.

The rain continued to drum its relentless mocking rooftop-rock while my powders and creams were put on. First base foundation, then a dusting of powder. Then liquid eye-liner and mascara, lip-liner, lipstick, blusher, bronzer . . .

. . . blouse (now down to two pointies instead of four thanks to the near-decapitation of Venu-tailor), underskirt, sari, jewellery . . . a bride was definitely taking shape. I looked in the mirror. She was glowing in deep-magenta silk that was shot with tiny gold threads. She looked luminous and beautiful. The picture of a school-not-quite-college-going figure, clad in jeans, was receding even in my head. I screwed up my eyes, blurring my reflection as much as I could to see if I could remember what she'd looked like, but she'd gone. Preethi chechi smacked my shoulder gently, 'What are you doing, Janu, you'll ruin your eye make-up!'

The rain did not let up all through the ceremonies. The Maraars arrived in their fleet of Ambassadors, starched shirts and silk saris gradually ruining in the rain. They were given the best seats in the hall while everyone else occupied whatever was left. People were fidgeting about, shaking out the water from their best clothes, laughing and pretending not to have minded a little rain. The bridegroom took his place, cross-legged on the flower-bedecked mandapam, while old women and children craned their necks to get a good look and then whispered and giggled secretively to each other.

I was ready by now, another proud product of Preethi's Beauty Parlour. All my cousins were lining up, eager and laughing, waiting to be handed the flowers and oil lamps they would carry on brass platters as they escorted me into the hall. Vijimami, Kunyamma and Ma started handing out the platters. They were all three in identical blue Kanjee-varam saris, looking like a small team of anxious and determined teachers out on a school trip. Mini turned around to look admiringly at me, her bright face flickering even brighter from the oil lamp on her brass platter. She whispered loudly, 'Walk slowly, chechi, there's no need to rush, you might fall.' I smiled at her and a sonorous drum-beat took up in my head:

> Don't trip don't fall don't go and ruin it all,
> Don't cry don't say I should not be here at all.

Ramama was beckoning from the top of the stairs. It was time for the procession to begin. First the aunts carrying lamps, then the unmarried girl cousins, big girls in front, little ones bringing up the rear. Then the bride and her parents, the father holding her hand, the mother following closely behind. The jeans-clad birthday girl was back, this time with Arjun. They were standing against the wall, laughing at the spectacle now, a special birthday treat laid on for her. Go away, the bride whispered to them, there's no room for you here, can't you see I'm busy getting married? They vanished obediently as she was led into the hall. Flashbulbs popped, necks craned, the nadaswaram shrieked shrilly and the sonorous drum-beat started up again:

> Don't trip don't fall don't go and ruin it all . . .

The rain beat down relentlessly outside. The streets emptied and became little rivers as pilgrims huddled for cover in shop doorways. The priests inside the temple picked up their enormous vessels, bubbling with payasams, and carried them indoors. The kolam became a small sea, washing its waves against stone steps. People said Guruvayurappan often sent a little rain down to signify his blessings. But this was not just a little rain. One priest, looking up at the tall golden kodimaram silhouetted against a churning black sky, remarked idly that it looked like even Guruvayur-appan was inconsolable about something today.

SIX

The rain continued unabated through the rest of the afternoon, adding chaos upon chaos. It even seemed to doggedly follow the convoy of cars that later took me to my new home on that long road to Valapadu. They were waiting, the whole convoy of them, at about six o'clock when all the ceremonies were done and it was time to leave Guruvayur. I hurriedly gave a quick round of hugs to my family who had crowded into the lobby of Elite Hotel to say goodbye. Dad was looking suddenly bereft . . . Ma, always practical, whispered a cheerful, 'We'll see you soon at the reception, moley . . .' Both my Ammummas were either crying or laughing, I couldn't tell . . . Appuppa smiled toothlessly from his wicker chair . . . But I couldn't be long. The Maraars were waiting, smiling, pretending not to mind waiting. 'We have a long journey now, you know . . . Five hours from here, it'll be midnight when we get there . . . Let's hope it stops raining soon . . . Is she ready to leave now?' Someone had already put my suitcase into a Maraar car. Ma patted me firmly on the back, a pat that firmly told me (and her) that it was now *really* time to go. I turned and, without daring to look anyone in the eye, made a quick dash for the car, careful not to spoil the cream and gold mundu-sari I had been changed into. The car smelt brand new . . . ('They change them every year, my dear . . .' Maheswari Aunty had whispered unnecessarily to a by-then terribly impressed Ammumma.) From the deep depths of the middle of the back seat, I watched my family crane their necks to see me better and to smile reassuringly. I smiled reassuringly back at them. They and the Maraars were exchanging nods and looks that indicated that the matter at hand now was one too serious for small talk. I found myself suddenly squashed as new husband and new mother-in-law got into the back seat on either side of me . . .

Nobody talked much during the journey, weddings are exhausting affairs and these were a few precious hours to be able to catch up on sleep. Every so often one head or the other would nod off, jerking awake a little later with a start. The car screamed noisily towards Valapadu, overtaking obdurate lorries and cars less new. The neck of the driver poured sweat in copious quantities that were wiped away at fifteen-minute intervals with a towel draped across his shoulder. I tried very hard not to drop off myself, terrified of putting an unaware head on an unfamiliar shoulder. But, in the drifting memories I now have of that long journey, I know that at some point I must have slept too. Closing my eyes and closing away knowledge of things too frightening to contemplate for any length of time . . .

When my eyes flew open again, it was to find that the convoy had stopped. Tall iron gates were being pushed open, revealing a garden and a house. We must have overtaken the rain somewhere on the national highway. It was now dark and hot. The car started up again, moving slowly up a concrete drive, carefully making room for the other cars. The house loomed out of the still night. Large and white, with all the parapets painted in pink emulsion. Some enthusiastic architect had created a large plaster rose-shaped design on the front of the house, just under the roof, making me think of a huge birthday cake. Birthday! It had been my birthday too today. Even my parents had barely been able to remember that in the day's excitements. This new family didn't know it at all. Happy Birthday, Janu, I said to myself, trying to be cheerful. Just imagine, a *wedding* for a birthday present, a big expensive wedding for a growing-up and going-away present. Eighteen now, everyone has to grow up at some time or the other . . .

*   *   *

The morning after the wedding was as full of watchful eyes as the night before. I'd found myself suddenly wide awake at break of day and slipped out of bed as silently as I could. The windows had heavy wrought-iron grills, painted black and red. The garden outside was sodden from the rains that pelted down late at night, every little leaf looked like it carried a burden too sorrowful to bear.

I remembered Ma's careful instructions from the day before. *Don't* go wandering out in your nightie! Have your *bath* as soon as you get up! Remember to *wash your hair* (in Kerala you haven't had a bath even if you'd scrubbed yourself mercilessly but omitted to pour at least a mug of water over your head). I opened my suitcase, holding the clasps down with my thumbs so that they wouldn't snap open making a noise. Gathering the set of clothes that Mini's mother had carefully chosen and placed in a bag right on top, I crept into the adjoining bathroom. I'd been told to take everything I'd need for the first few days, and there they all were in dear Ammini Kunyamma's neatly arranged pack . . . soap, soap powder, talcum powder, toothbrush . . . oh dear, no toothpaste! I rummaged frantically around the plastic sari-shop bag that had been carrying everything. No, certainly no toothpaste. I crept back to my suitcase in the bedroom, gingerly opening it up again. I knew I had to be quiet because I was terrified of awakening my new . . . the word refused to form itself in my mind . . . *husband* . . . In my head I was using the same tone of voice that Mini reserved for 'bloodydamn' and 'boyfriend'.

Still no toothpaste. I sat back on my heels and contemplated my first foray out into the gracious, well-dressed world of the Maraars, in my crushed clothes from the night before, unwashed body and, worse, unwashed hair, strange vagabond from Delhi, begging for toothpaste. ('Don't they brush their teeth where you come from?') I could picture the look of horror on my mother's face and knew I just couldn't let the family honour down. Creeping back into the bathroom, I slid the bolt silently shut again. I picked up the pasteless toothbrush and rubbed its bristles vigorously against my small pink bar of Luxury Lux soap. Taking a deep breath, I brushed the resultant pink gloop against my teeth. I'd never tasted anything so awful, but, twenty minutes later, I was scrubbed and clean, the ends of my hair bearing tiny drops of water like so many tremulous, glittering trophies. I got into the carefully chosen brand-new sari (yellow nylon 'Garden Hakoba' very-nice-madam-very-well-draping) that had been hotly debated back at home, Ma favouring a more formal silk and Kunyamma going for the more casual, about-the-house look for 'The first day at the Maraars'. Remembering the kohl in my eyes and a little red bindi on my forehead, I was ready for them.

The house was dark and no one seemed to be up yet. I could see, even in the half darkness, that everything was in its place and the cushions on the divan were eerily upright, like soldiers on parade. I wandered through a seemingly endless dining room with a polished table big enough to waltz on and then found myself in a small verandah. From there I could see some movements in the kitchen ... a Maraar! Gingerly I pushed the door open, startling a bent little Ammumma who was pouring oil from a large urn into two little bottles.

'Oh, it's you, Janu, you frightened me. Why are you up so early?'

I spoke my first words to a member of the In-Laws, 'I usually wake up early'... oh dear, my first words and they'd turned out to be a lie. Getting up early was something I only *ever* did to get to school on time and when I couldn't block out my father's shouts any more with warm blankets.

'Would you like some coffee? There's some in that percolator over there. I'd make it for you but my hands are oily.'

I went over to the percolator and contemplated the small steel contraption. Yes, I would like some coffee, please, but I was familiar only with the stuff that came out of bottles in a spoon. My second lie was on its way.

'No, I don't drink coffee, thanks.'

There was a busy sound at the door and my new mother-in-law entered the kitchen. She'd been the subject of most of our speculation in all conversations that had taken place about the Maraars back at home. The two families had met on a few occasions to discuss the planned 'alliance' and my uncle, amongst others, had developed a strong 'Janu's-mother-in-law phobia'. Mini's father, normally an easy-going sort of individual with a wicked sense of humour, had found his laughs drying up uncharacteristically in the presence of that forbidding figure. On one of his early attempts at breaking the ice, he'd informed the Maraars that my father's official designation of Director of Signals in the Indian Air Force really only meant that he was the man who stood on the airport tarmac waving cardboard lollipops at taxiing aircraft. This brought the usual round of affectionate sniggers that gradually bubbled away as my family realized, one by one, that they were the only ones laughing. The Maraars appeared to be taking their cue from the matriarch leading their delegation. She had fixed a cold gaze on Kunyachen, clearly signalling that no jokes demeaning The Alliance in any way would be harboured. Her son was marrying the daughter of a Highly Placed Official, and *nothing*, especially not the buffoonery of lowly uncles, was going to detract from that.

I unfroze myself and tried to sidle along the wall as she approached the percolator.

'Have you had coffee?' she asked, without seeming to

address anyone in particular. I shot a look at the Ammumma still pouring out her oils and decided the question must be aimed at me. Before I could reply, however, the Ammumma said, 'Janu doesn't drink coffee.'

My chances of getting some sustenance seemed to be slipping away. The taste of bath soap still lurked horribly in my mouth.

'Tea, then?' Still no eye contact.

I decided to take the plunge. Boldly, I replied, 'Yes, please.'

'Look, you're not in Delhi any more. Like it or not, you now live in Kerala, so I suggest you drop all these fashionable Pleases and Thank Yous. Here we don't believe in unnecessary style.' She accompanied this with a short laugh, perhaps attempting to take the edge off it. But the edge was clearly there. It tore a tiny little scratch inside me somewhere, and suddenly the many times that I'd been told off for forgetting a little kindness or gratitude seemed so falsely, so pretentiously *Delhi*.

Deeply ashamed, I pushed my back as far as it would go into the wall behind me and watched her briskly make the tea. Was her displeasure because I'd spoken in *English*? I cast about frantically for the Malayalam to use when she gave me the tea she was making, remembering vaguely that there were no equivalent words for a casual Please and Thank You. I couldn't very well have used the only option I knew, unless I wished to express the deepest, most flowery gratitude more suited to a court than a kitchen. Non-Kerala families like mine tended to mix up English and Malayalam into an easy, casual city-speech that had worked reasonably well on my holidays here. Now that I was here for ever, it looked like that brand of Malayalam was going to be woefully inadequate. Even worse, seen as *stylish*. Thankfully it didn't look like I was expected to join the rest of the conversation between the two women. It was about the food that would be cooked for the large extended family staying till the reception, and the old Ammumma appeared to be taking orders from her daughter. 'You can cut two kilos of beans for the thoran, and six carrots. Make sure you do it yourself, that Thanga will make a complete mess if you leave it to her. Last week the pieces were so big, I could not even chew them. You don't watch her closely enough, sleeping instead of supervising.' Nary a please nor a thank you, I noticed, and delivered in a tone of voice that was deeply frowned upon in my family, but we'd evidently got a lot of things wrong. 'Here's your tea.'

I walked to the kitchen counter to pick it up, 'Thank . . .' I remembered just in time to swallow my unbidden English gratitude with a hot gulp of tea.

As I was sipping my sugary tea, different members of the clan started to drift in. First Sathi (the older sister-in-law I had already met when I was first seen by the Maraars) followed by her brood of cheeping chicks (Vinnu, Annu and Joji), then Latha (the Kerala-brought-up-daughter-in-law . . . *washed, bathed* and not in a *nightie*), followed by various other aunts and cousins. The men were probably congregating elsewhere, in some distant and privileged verandah or living room, to which large trays of tea were being regularly despatched.

Perhaps out of kindness, I was not spoken to very much, which was a relief. It didn't sound as if anyone in this family had grown up outside Kerala, the Malayalam flying around me was fast, fluent and elegant. My years of growing up in Delhi and having to struggle with Hindi in school, had relegated Malayalam to a very low priority. It was getting clearer by the minute that my holiday-Malayalam, so comical it sometimes even made my grandparents giggle, was unlikely to endear me to this family. I hoped I could get away with looking sufficiently interested in everything going on around me *without* having to make verbal contributions. Don't appear *overly* agog though, I warned myself, that might be misconstrued as well . . . as being idiocy or something.

As the morning outside brightened, I noticed that the younger set had started to drift around and were getting ready to play some board games in the dining room next door. Most of them looked about my age, and I hoped I would be asked to join them when I saw Gauri, my new younger sister-in-law, carry out a large carrom board. She had not been a part of the Maraar group that had first come to see me, but had not shown any interest so far in getting to know me. She was Mother-in-Law's pet we'd been told, still a schoolgirl and the one that I had marked out to befriend in this household. She had looked busy all morning, chatting and giggling with the cousins who were visiting, now organizing them efficiently into teams to play carroms. That looked like much more fun than the kitchen activities and conversation that was all about people and relatives I did not know yet. I continued to play with my teacup, listening enviously to the gales of laughter emanating from the room next door. I don't suppose it would have done for me to be included in that happy set. They were the *daughters* of the family, and *unmarried*. It was okay for them to be unwashed at ten o'clock and wearing nighties, unlike me. I missed home dreadfully and hoped that the expression on my face did not give it away. A small frock-clad battalion of new nieces had assembled itself in front of me and was now observing my every movement with eyes that moved in perfect military unison.

'Hello,' I ventured softly. Annu, about four, slid hastily behind her mother. Two-year-old Joji showed me a furry bear and then hid it behind her back. Vinnu, who was probably about the same age as Mini, maintained an unbroken gaze. Occasionally her eyes would wander up and down my person, carefully examining an ear-ring or a toe. I wondered what to make of this careful inspection. She was looking at the chain around my neck when she suddenly piped up, 'Is it gold?'

No one else appeared to have noticed I was attempting my first full-fledged (Malayalam) conversation with a Maraar. 'It is,' I replied.

'Is *that* gold?' She was now looking at my ear-rings. I nodded.

Her gaze wandered to my hands, she wasn't going to give up easily. 'Diamond?' She looked like a suspicious jeweller.

I shook my head. It was only an ordinary Rangoon white stone that Ammumma had set in gold for me on my last holiday in Kerala. The little girl nodded in satisfaction, she'd finally caught me out. I thought our conversation had petered out, but a few minutes later she startled me by reaching out a small finger to stroke the yellow nylon of my sari. 'Imported?' she asked.

I didn't see my new husband until it was time for breakfast. The wizened old Ammumma, who had not stopped to rest once, had warmed two dosa griddles and was now turning out crisp, golden dosas at great speed. The Maraar clan seemed enormous and the meal-time routine seemed to be men first in the dining room, children alongside at the kitchen table, then the women, the drivers and servants and finally, after she'd fed everybody else, the old Ammumma. I thought of the fuss my grandmother would have made if anyone had ever attempted to relegate her to that position in our house.

Suresh came in with his father. Both of them smiled briefly at me as they sat down and were served their dosas with sambar and chutney.

'Do you eat dosas for breakfast in Delhi?' Hopefully a kindly, and not sarcastic, enquiry from Father-in-Law.

'Not often,' I replied, 'my mother doesn't get the time on working days, but we do have them at the weekends sometimes.'

83

'Well, you can't expect any better when women go out to work, can you?' This was another barbed shaft from Mother-in-Law. It wasn't taking me long to work out that my choice as bride had not been a universally popular one in this household. Had Suresh defied his parents' wishes to choose me? Perhaps from among the thousand hopefuls who, we'd been told, had been vying madly to become his wife?

I looked at the back of his head. He seemed to have had a bath as well. I was glad I had remembered to remove my washed underwear from the bathroom after finishing my bath, carefully spreading them out to dry on top of my suitcase. They would be nearly dry now, discreet and un-tempting on their perch under the bed. I was grateful that he had not forced himself on me last night and now strangely touched at the possibility that he'd perhaps defied his mother's wishes to marry me. I also knew by now that I was going to need an ally to fend off the many shafts that were undoubtedly going to be heading my way. He was the obvious choice to be that ally.

I couldn't remember the details of his face from that first awkward meeting, and hadn't needed to look at it during the marriage ceremonies yesterday. While walking around the flickering vilakku at the temple with my head bowed, I'd had plenty of time to observe his feet as he walked ahead of me. I'd felt a sudden lurching realization that I was getting more time to familiarize myself with the feet of the man I was marrying than his face! They looked about size eight, with slightly blotchy skin, the big toe was shorter than the one next to it, the nails were pale with jagged edges. That was when the shivering had started. I had quickly struck up an inner dialogue with myself to stop the shaking, which seemed to work briefly. 'Surely you must be able to remember *some* other details about him from that first meeting?' 'Nope, it's all a complete blur.' 'You're not *trying*.

Remember a largish nose?' 'Hmm . . . maybe . . .' 'Now try again, he's not very tall?' 'Yes, I sort of remember that . . .' 'Good And there's lots of other things you know. That he runs a verrry successful motel business, my dear. Developed (from scratch!) by his father. Verrry good family he belongs to also.' 'Yes! And now I also know the shape of his feet!' At that point my thoughts had been completely drowned out by the thumping of the temple drums and lowing of conch shells. The smoke from the oil lamps and the heavy perfume of the joss sticks had been threatening to throw me over in a dead faint. Maybe it was safer, I told myself hastily, not to think too much.

Here in the kitchen, I couldn't stare for too long, of course, but I could see in brief darting glances that he had a small bald patch developing at the back of his head. His back looked narrow, he was quite slim and wiry. Dark skinned. I knew he was twenty-six and a half years old. A fair bit older than me, but Ma had said that would probably make him protective and kind. Leaning on the kitchen wall, watching him talk to aunts and cousins, I felt weary at the thought of how much I still had to find out.

I was also beginning to get a sense of having a lot of reassuring to do. That hadn't occurred to me before, that this new family of mine might have developed a pre-conceived notion of me! Somehow I had to let these strangers know that I was kind-hearted and affectionate. That children and animals usually liked me. And that, despite Delhi, I was really not *too* stylish and had come into their lives very eager to love them. *Despite* having lost my heart once as a sixteen-year-old, which of course had to be carefully hidden from them. How on earth was I going to convey so much and soon? And in broken Malayalam! It felt like there was an awful lot of catching up to do, as there were obviously certain things about me that had already failed to make the grade. Beginning with an account in debit was *not* the best

way to set out on a new life. Suddenly I was terribly home-
sick again and very close to tears.

*   *   *

Over the first few days with the Maraars, I progressed into
little more than monosyllabic replies. This, I was sure
would be considered a good thing, as brides were expected
to be bashful. And a bashful bride from *Delhi* (who could
have turned out to be God-only-knows-what) would, I
thought, endear me to them greatly. It certainly wasn't
coming very naturally to me as there were times when I
longed to break out into animated chatter, joining in the
general conversation. But speaking in English would be
misconstrued as attempting to be stylish and speaking in
Malayalam had on occasion been greeted with sarcastic
laughter. I was better off pretending to be a bashful bride.

I now knew where the rice was kept, at what time lunch
was served, what everyone's names and relationships were.
I had even been taken by my mother-in-law to Dr Gomathy's
clinic to have a 'Copper-T' fitted. The thing that was going
to prevent inconvenient babies from arriving and interfering
with the BA my parents had been promised I'd complete.
It nestled snugly now deep inside me somewhere, having
been pushed in by Dr Gomathy's efficient rubber-gloved
hand, after which she patted my bare bottom announcing
sagely that I was now 'ready' . . . Ready for Lurve, I thought
anxiously.

The reprieve I had been granted on my wedding night
hadn't lasted, of course. It seemed to be quite late at
night that people began to retire to their separate rooms in
the Maraar household and I'd hung around the following
night until I was actually told to go to bed. Suresh was
already in the room, stretched out on the bed, reading a
magazine. Hoping that minimal eye-contact would
somehow have him fail to notice that I was in the room
too, I tip-toed about getting ready for bed. When I could put

86

it off no longer, I finally perched myself delicately on the edge of the bed, swinging my legs demurely over, quickly tucking them under the sheet. I could hear sounds of a magazine being put away and of an arm reaching out for me and knew I couldn't put it off any more. When it finally came, with an ungraceful conjoining of arms and legs, and clothes and sheets, with buttons and hooks adding to the chaos, I greeted it with the stoic sense of one of those things that had to be done. Like a visit to the dentist, where things went on in intimate parts of you that you could neither see nor control. Love didn't seem to play much of a part. And laughter, that might have been more comforting under the circumstances, didn't come into it at all. It felt awkward to be kissed by a mouth that had not had very much to *say* to me up to that point. I tried to quell the feeling of revulsion that rose in my chest. And decided I was no nearer either to feeling loved or to wanting to love. Even my few tentative explorations with Arjun had not prepared me for this sudden invasion. Later, looking up at the ceiling fan, feeling sore, mentally and physically, I wondered why Leena had advocated chasing after this thing with such fervent enthusiasm? Perhaps it was one of those things that would *grow* on me, I hoped, watching my figure whirling slowly around in the steel cap of the fan above. Next to me, the eerie night-call had started up . . . coo-wee . . . coo-wee . . .

But there was at least a kind of rationale to the nights that my days in the Maraar household still seemed completely devoid of. It was getting clearer that it was the *Maraars* I had married, not Suresh. He had not been unkind, but had not seemed to want to spend much time alone with me. The couple of hours before breakfast he spent discussing business with his father on the verandah. After breakfast, they would leave for one of the motels. I, left with the women folk, attempted to look useful, which wasn't very easy because between school and Arjun, I'd never found the time to learn to cook. In the evenings, if Suresh was not touring and did get back early enough, we sometimes went for a drive or to the cinema where rats as big as small cats ran down the aisles. Gauri, my schoolgirl sister-in-law always accompanied us because, as Suresh's mother said, she only had her brother to take her out, poor thing.

'Suresh chettan had promised me he would only marry someone who would agree to my being taken everywhere too,' Gauri informed me archly one evening as we waited for Suresh to pick us up for the six o'clock show of *Padayottam*.

'I don't mind,' I said quickly, not very sure of whether I ought to mind or not. At fourteen, Gauri was closer in age to me than Suresh was, and there seemed to be potential to make a friend. She had already shown me how to stamp my feet every three minutes in the cinema to prevent the rats from coming scampering over our feet, reducing us to hysterical titters. 'I really do like it when you come as well,' I said with more conviction.

'You realize, of course, how lucky you are,' she continued, 'to have in-laws like my parents. My older sister, Sathi chechi, really has a hard time with hers. Always interfering with everything, useless people.'

I'd met Sathi's in-laws at the wedding. They had seemed to be a timorous old couple, as much in awe of the Maraars as we were. 'But they live quite far from here, don't they? Pathanamthitta or somewhere?' I was genuinely curious.

'Yes but they visit her and us about once every six months and they want to poke their noses into everything. I never speak to them politely if I can help it.'

I wondered how she got away with it. My parents expected me to be polite to everyone, even children. She was still talking, now getting quite animated. 'Do you know, I refer to your father as "Air Commode". Only air comes out on the lavatory. It always makes everyone laugh.' She giggled loudly and looked slyly at me to gauge my reaction.

My father had worked hard to acquire the rank of Air Commodore and it hurt me deeply now to hear him referred to so rudely. I shot a look at my mother-in-law who was stringing flowers near by. She was laughing too, proud of her daughter's clever wit. I looked down at my feet and wished I could be less sensitive.

Mother-in-Law, who I'd been told to address as Amma, was showing little sign of thawing towards me, although I did notice that she certainly wasn't universally icy. She absolutely adored Gauri and was full of smiles whenever Sathi visited, which was frequently as she and her family lived just down the road. Amma was also a dedicated grandmother, full of treats for Sathi's three little girls. The Ammumma was Amma's widowed mother who lived with them and seemed to earn her keep by slaving all day to keep the kitchen gleaming, despite churning out vast quantities of food. I hoped that she got more of a holiday when she went to live with her son in Calicut once a year. Latha, the older daughter-in-law, was quite obviously not a part of the charmed inner circle, but, efficient and brisk, seemed to have gained some hard-earned respect. She and Suresh's older brother, a college professor, did not live in the family home but in distant Madras. I was sorry to see them being driven off to the station the day after the reception and would see them again only about once a year.

The reception had been a confusing affair. I'd woken up that morning with an overwhelming feeling of excitement at the thought of seeing my family again . . . after four long days! I jumped out of bed to brush my teeth and prepare for the day, bumping into Suresh who was just emerging after his shower. In my joy I gave him an impetuous hug, startling him. Suddenly unsure of his reaction, I looked at his face and thought he looked pleased. He did not, however, ask me what it was infecting me so. He didn't seem to notice at all – as I didn't then – that there were hundreds of opportunities like that one, missed carelessly and without thought for the price we would have to pay later. Tiny little chances to ask each other how we were feeling. To talk and share our thoughts and learn to become friends. That morning, however, the thought of seeing my parents again was obliterating everything else. I hugged myself in glee, sitting down again on the edge of the bed to look out of the window, wondering how like sad fat babies the dumpy jackfruits looked, clinging helplessly to matronly tree trunks. Suresh carried on humming to himself, brushing his hair and carefully choosing a shirt from the wardrobe.

'You'd better go with Amma to the bank locker to get out your jewellery and things for the reception,' he said vaguely.

I nodded, 'Shall I wear the necklace you had put on me at the wedding?'

'I don't know, you'd better check . . . there might be some traditional piece or something you'll have to wear . . .'

'Are you going to the motel today too?'

'Of course. Business is not like an Air Force job where you can take leave. Always things to worry about.' He was ready and about to leave the room. I was being a nuisance now, prolonging the conversation.

'What? What sort of things to worry about?'

'Oh you won't understand, unions, accounts, tax matters . . .'

I could understand, I thought. I knew all those words and *wanted* to understand. But Suresh was now half out of the door, swinging his briefcase impatiently. Holding the curtain open he said, more kindly, 'You'd better get ready soon, Amma and all the others would have had their baths by now. Married girls don't create a good impression if they stay in their rooms till late.'

I was more keen on creating that good impression with the

Maraars than with attempting to impress Suresh with my business acumen and hastily scrambled up to get ready for my bath. But baths before dawn, making sure I washed my *hair* each time and being first past the post in the kitchen wasn't going to be quite enough. I could tell, fairly early on, that some of the things I needed to create that good impression were completely out of my control. Later that morning, I returned with Amma from the bank locker, carrying my small sandalwood jewellery box. She was staggering under the weight of numerous large maroon boxes stuffed full, no doubt, with beautiful Maraar jewellery. It felt safer not to offer help in carrying them, as it might have been seen as an eagerness to get my hands on Maraar jewels. I let the driver do the honours instead. In the house, my little box was opened up and the women of the house gathered around to decide what pieces I should wear at the reception. I could feel that familiar feeling of discomfort creeping in as it was clearly an exercise in 'Let's see what these Highly Placed Delhi Officials give their daughters'. I had heard that Sathi had been weighed down with gold when she'd got married some years ago and was fairly sure my parents' scraped-together savings had not bought me enough in Maraar terms. I was right.

'Oh look, Sathi, have you ever seen such tiny ear-rings? They're like your jumikis, only ten times smaller.'

'Well they'll match the sari she'll be wearing, but we can't have such tiny ones. What'll people think!'

Oh no, what *were* people going to think of me? That my father loved me less because he hadn't been able to afford elephantine jumikis?

'I . . . I've always liked small pieces of jewellery . . . I feel they suit me better . . .' I stuttered, lying.

Amma was holding up a beautiful old layered gold chain. My father's gift to my mother at their wedding. 'Now, *this* is a nice one, is it new?'

Rare words of praise! I struggled briefly with a desire to lie again and, hopefully, look good. But this was something it was going to be difficult to lie about. 'No it's not new, it was the swarnamala put on my mother at her wedding.'

The chain was flung aside. 'Can't have her wearing something *old* at the reception. Sathi, go and get something out of your jewellery. Just make sure it's something people in Valapadu haven't seen before.'

The happy feeling I'd woken up with was dissipating at a rapid rate and got no better as, later in the afternoon, I had to start dressing for the reception. I was helped by Sathi and an aunt who did a 'tip-top' job, as they put it, in making me look like someone else. A plait of hair had been bought from the local Ladies' Store and was firmly attached to my shoulder-length Delhi tresses with a multitude of pins that now dug into my scalp. A thick layer of black eye-liner was painted around my lashes, quite unlike the tiny smudge of kohl I was more accustomed to. A pair of pretend lips were outlined around my own smaller ones with a deep maroon pencil and then painted in, giving them a sultry Tamil heroine pout. By the time I'd worn Sathi's jewellery and the brand-new Kanjeevaram sari that had been bought for me, I *was* somebody else!

When my parents arrived at the house, I was trotted out to show them how easy it had been to make me look like a Maraar. In a Maraar sari and make-up and jewellery. Maraar lips and Maraar eyes. Even a hip-length plait of hair to match the graceful Maraar tresses.

I stood in front of them, a counterfeit Maraar, hiding Delhi insides and a very heavy heart.

They looked happy and relieved, perhaps just faintly anxious? Only a small contingent had come, Ma, Dad, Ramama and Vijimami. Ma whispered that my grandparents, Mini's parents and other uncles and aunts had decided not to come because this was really the Maraars' do. 'It wouldn't have looked nice for too many of us to turn up.' I couldn't really see why but, by now, I was so eager to avoid doing anything that risked displeasure, I agreed that it wasn't worth the risk. I didn't have the heart to tell Ma, though. She looked so happy and proud.

At the reception, both Amma and I managed to fool all the Maraar friends and associates who'd turned up that a beautiful match had been made. And that there wasn't the hint of unhappiness or displeasure in the air. Amma would appear at my side every so often to introduce another face and name to me. She would proudly tell them my father's name and rank (careful to say Commodore and not Commode, of course) and smile fondly at me. I would take up her cue and smile sweetly and answer any questions put to me in soft Malayalam. It was a flawless performance on both sides.

From where I sat on a brocade sofa, through the fairy-lit bushes and thronging crowds, I'd occasionally spot my father or mother. They seemed to be enjoying themselves. My father in particular was being feted because an Air Force officer was something of a novelty in Kerala business circles. I could hear his brash confident laugh and even, occasion-ally, Vijimami's shrieky one. There was some comfort in knowing they were all enjoying themselves, and I felt briefly and genuinely happy.

But it didn't last. Soon the food had all been eaten, the vegetable-'pups' from Tastee Bakery and the banana halva from Eliyamma's Catering Concern, leaving my mother-in-law's normally immaculate garden looking as though a restaurant had been upended over it. There were dirty plates everywhere and scrunched-up paper napkins adorned every bush and shrub. The guests, who had eaten their fill and taken in the details of each other's saris and jewellery, were now losing interest and starting to leave. I knew it would soon be time for my family to leave as well, my little contingent from the land where they still loved me. I almost couldn't bear the thought, especially as I knew my parents would soon be flying back to far-away Delhi.

'Must you go, Ma? Can't you stay the night and go when there's light in the morning? Dad really shouldn't be driving in the dark. I'll ask Suresh, I'm sure he can arrange some rooms for you at the motel . . .'

My mother gave me a long hug. I don't think she was too worried. All brides in India cried, this wasn't unusual. All brides cried and then stayed and loved and got loved. That was the myth that had been perpetrated by families like mine. I was less than half my mother's age but I'd already learnt that this wasn't a universal truth. Some people could be impossible to love, and I was already fairly sure that, for my mother-in-law and me, this was going to be an undeniable and mutual fact. Suresh, I wasn't sure about yet. But the way things seemed to be organized here, it was clear I was going to have to spend more of my time with my mother-in-law and sisters-in-law than with Suresh anyway. That hadn't initially seemed too frightening a prospect, as the impression I'd gathered on my holidays in Kerala had been of families being warm, loving entities. Having grown up without siblings and cousins, I'd listened to my parents' stories of their own rumble-tumble childhoods with pleasure and envy. My parents had happily assumed that this new joint family would make up for that gap in my life, providing me miraculously with surrogate siblings and surrogate love. 'Just think, moley,' Ma had said, 'how nice it will be to always have company. You've always wanted sisters. Now see, *two* sisters all at once! *And* it will be easy for you to concentrate on your studies, as you won't have to run a house.' Ma had wanted this to be true and I listened, half-believing her, because by then it was too late to think otherwise. But it was already becoming clear that I was going to find out, the hard way, that none of those rules would apply to the Maraars. Just now, though, I couldn't bear to let my parents know what an awful mistake they had made.

Their hope had been genuine that I'd be drawn easily into the loving fold of this new family. And be able to simply swap one love for another ('She's young, she'll adjust, they always do'). Maybe I could have done exactly that. I certainly wanted to, quite desperately for *myself* more than for anyone else. There was no point in hankering after Arjun's memory. He was just that, a memory. My warmest, most tender memory . . . but from a life that was gone. Floating out of my grasp, smiling and winking, ready to burst if I had attempted to recapture it. It was true, Arjun's face still reappeared at all the worst moments, despite my good intentions. Whenever I succumbed to Suresh's nightly embraces, whenever a verbal shaft came zinging my way across the kitchen. Like Fanny in my tattered Jane Austen textbook, I wanted to believe I had principle and all the heroism of principle. But I knew I owed it to myself to put Arjun's memory behind me and put all my energies into this new life I had embarked upon. I needed to put down roots and attempt to survive, whatever it took. But I hadn't bargained for the fact that the soil I had been replanted in would be so hard and unyielding. Nor did I know of yearnings that arose from distant places, too distant to even know of. Where the columns were still being tallied, the dues not yet paid.

SEVEN

After a few weeks of marriage I knew without a doubt that I had not been Choice Number One on Amma's shortlist of daughters-in-law. Her personal choice had been the daughter of an old school friend, a plump, pleasant-looking girl I'd seen at the reception. This had been vetoed by Suresh and his father, mainly because neither of them was particularly fond of the old school friend. The thought of anyone vetoing Amma on anything made my mind boggle ceaselessly, but as the story had been narrated to me by Amma herself, I was left in no doubt.

I was also starting to discover that Suresh had said four things before leaving his parents to choose his wife.

1. She had to be pretty.
2. She had to be young so that she would 'adjust'.
3. She had to be able to speak English well, so that he could take her to Bombay in the hoped-for expansion of his motel business.
4. Nothing else was too important.

I was all of those, a perfect knick-knack for the mantelpiece of Suresh's life.

Unfortunately none of these qualities made me particularly useful or desirable in the rest of the general Maraar scheme of things. And so I came in for a lot of what could have been construed as good-natured teasing. Except that I had the nagging feeling it wasn't particularly good-natured.

It didn't take long for me to start hating myself for the many different things that gave the Maraars reason to slap their knees and laugh until tears ran down their cheeks. For my mother having omitted to teach me how to cook; for not being able to speak Malayalam elegantly; for forgetting constantly *not* to mind my Ps and Qs; for having been brought up in Delhi; for having had an aunt who, in the nineteen-twenties, had an affair that everyone in Kerala (except me) had heard about. There was so much to be ashamed of, Arjun's memory almost didn't count. Where I had naïvely believed that my love for him would be the guilty burden I'd bear in my new life, I found now there were much bigger things at stake.

Suresh and his father were not usually a part of this needling game that generally seemed to take place around the kitchen table. The first time Suresh was around, I hoped he would say something in my defence. Instead he got up from the table, helped himself to a glass of water from the fridge and then wandered back to rejoin his father on the verandah. Later I accosted him with it.

'You heard Gauri speak so rudely to me and didn't say anything.'

He looked surprised, 'When, when was she rude? I never heard.'

'You heard. She said she'd heard that my great-grandparents had never been married to each other. That my ancestry was questionable. You couldn't have missed it.'

Suresh threw back his head, laughing. '*That's* what you're so offended by! In those days no one married each other, everyone knows that! Gauri just likes to tease, that's all.'

'No one else ever seems to be teased. I'm getting tired of it.'

'Don't be so sensitive. Your problem is that you've been an only child, you're obviously not used to family life.'

'You're just turning Gauri's rudeness into my sensitivity.

Because you don't want to do anything about it. Even your mother just laughs every time Sathi or Gauri are nasty to me.'

Suresh gave me a sullen look that told me that I had completely strayed out of the good-wife realm. I could feel my heart thud, wondering how angry he would be with this, my first outburst. Anger might not be such a bad thing, I told myself, at least that would lead to some kind of dialogue. And then I could explain myself, calmly and with love. He got up from the bed and put on his shirt.

'Where are you going?' I asked in a panic. It was late at night, they'd think I'd chased him out of the house! As it happened Suresh had no intention of leaving his house. He got as far as the verandah and, turning on the lights, sat down calmly to read the newspaper. I contemplated going after him, but knew that from the verandah our conversation would be audible to everyone in the house. He'd picked his spot well, and it was one that would stand him in good stead for the rest of our life together. I was learning fast that Suresh was very practised at the art of escape. There would never be any unseemly rows, or loud arguments. Just escape in different forms. Work, business tours, company guests . . . there would be no dearth either of plausible excuses. And I knew that I would end up sounding silly if I described all those important things to anyone as Suresh's desire to escape the responsibilities of marriage. It was getting very clear that I was not to have an ally in the Maraar household. I would have to find my own ways of dealing with my new life.

It was two years before television would come to Kerala, freeing women-of-good-families from the tyranny of each other's company. Before soap-opera characters invaded spotless living rooms with their less-than-spotless lives, there were only neighbours' houses to look to for cheap entertainment. And, of course, new daughters-in-law who opened up a whole world of distant relations to whom no particular loyalty was owed. The Maraar women were not expected to get involved in the business and so, after Suresh and his father had left for work, the day stretched out in listless abandon. The supervision of servants in the preparation of lunch or cleaning of the floors took little time or effort and was usually left to the tired-looking old Ammumma. Although all the Maraar women had been educated, careers for women were considered infra-dig, as I'd gathered from various pointed remarks about my mother's 'need' to be a lowly schoolteacher. Jobs were quite simply for people who needed the extra money, and consequently unbecoming for the women of a good family. It was also undesirable to be trawling clothes and jewellery shops and wasting the hard-earned money of the men. That didn't really leave very much to do in a small town like Valapadu where everyone knew everyone else and exactly what they did.

Occasional visits to family friends and relatives broke the monotony. For these, we'd dress in our best georgette saris and sit in other people's living rooms, instead of our own – even though they were all eerily alike with identical divans and cross-stitched cushions standing to attention. The conversation, even when it was about people who lived on the other side of town, was often whispered. Sometimes we'd even visit *those* people the following week. I took my cue from the others and learnt to say, 'No, no, must be off, husband comes at one for lunch,' when offered tea and refreshments. But only murmur dissent when the hostess would pretend not to have heard and vanish into the kitchen anyway. If the refreshments were not home-made it was more grist to our mill. On our way back in the car one of us would comment on how awful the pakavadas tasted ('Fried in *old* oil at that Tastee Bakery, no doubt') and did you notice the dust under the sofa ('hasn't been swept in months!')?

I needed to fit in as fast as possible. Not fitting in well

enough was what gave the Maraars their licence to laugh at me. Ma had said it was easier to adjust when one was young. She was right, but in a few short months I could barely recognize the girl who looked back at me in the mirror. Who was she? Mrs Suresh, pretty-and-wearing-nice-saris-and . . . nothing else was important anyway. A Maraar daughter-in-law? Not quite, *looks* like one on the outside, complete with silk sari and big red bindi and flowers in her hair, but with funny Delhi ways that needed more ironing out. ('Still she says *daal* for parippu!' and '*Still* she doesn't know how to sit properly while wearing a sari' and still preferring a good book to sitting around a kitchen table and tearing some poor soul apart.) I still had a lot of sorting out to do and I set about the task with a commitment that impressed even me.

'Shouldn't you be going to the University to enrol for the correspondence course? Your father keeps writing about it in every letter.' Suresh looked mildly concerned.

'I'm quite happy like this, learning to cook and things . . .'

'You don't have to cook, the servants do it in this house.'

'I know, but women should know how to cook, shouldn't they?' It was amazing how my priorities had turned upside down in so short a period of time. 'I learnt how to make vegetable biriyani from Amma yesterday! I was thinking of making it for when you get back from work this evening.'

'No, don't bother. I'll probably be late tonight anyway. Have to go to Cochin to look for some new property.'

'Cochin? Oh, can I come too?'

'What'll you do there? I'll be busy running around. It won't be any fun for you.'

'I could do some window-shopping or something . . . I'll keep myself amused, you won't have to worry about me, really.'

Suresh looked doubtful, 'I don't know . . . Amma doesn't

ever go window-shopping or anything . . . It's not the done thing here in Kerala. This isn't Delhi, don't forget.'

Delhi, the stubborn tag I was having such difficulty dropping. 'Oh, never mind,' I said brightly, 'I'll go to Sathi's instead and take the children to the park in the evening.'

Suresh looked relieved, 'Yes do that, that'll be much safer and better than wandering around Cochin on your own. Buy the children ice-creams or something. Here, here's some money.' From his wallet he gave me a few rupee notes. That was the other thing I had learnt. That women from good families never needed to worry about money. Not where it came from, nor how to keep it safe nor what to do with it. There seemed to be plenty of it available, I was sure I only needed to ask. But asking would have been seen as avaricious and there was precious little I could spend money on in a place like Valapadu anyway. I took the occasional bits of money that came my way, trying not to seem too interested. Suresh didn't need to discuss money or his business with me – for that he had his father. We didn't need to discuss the household – for that there was his mother. Leisure time was shared with his sisters. As the knick-knack on his mantelpiece, I was still looking pretty but getting very dusty indeed.

*   *   *

'Please can we go to Thoduporam for a weekend? It's only about two hours from here, I believe.'

Suresh looked startled, 'What do you want to go there for?'

'Well, Appuppa hasn't been well for some time, and I feel I should see him.'

I could see Suresh wondering whether giving in to this request might set uncomfortable precedents for the future. 'Well, I've got Thomas Cherian from KTDC coming to look at the motel plans. I'd promised to take him around Cochin.'

I'd also discovered that Suresh actively encouraged

weekend business visitors as they provided him with a reasonable excuse to get away from his father's watchful eye and interminable business discussions. 'I could go alone, if you can arrange for one of the drivers to take me.'

No one seemed particularly enthused by the sudden assertion I was showing in arranging my own weekend entertainment. Was she slowly changing colours, having been here six months? This time I held out, using Appuppa's growing illness as the excuse. It was finally decided that I could go by boat as this would be the least unbecoming way for a Maraar daughter-in-law to travel alone. I was overjoyed. Thoduporam, and by *boat*. It would be like old times again!

The boat journey was balm to my saddened soul. The November monsoons had moved on as suddenly as they had come and vegetation was now bursting out of the banks. Fern fronds reached out to where I sat on the boat, waving wide-open, welcoming arms for a returning daughter. The boat inched its way carefully down the shrunken canal and dusk was already falling when I arrived at Thoduporam. The tiny oil lamp had been lit under the tulsi bush, throwing the house into darkness behind it, and the kolam was filling up with watery stars.

I knew there wouldn't be any of Appuppa's sandalwood-scented hugs at the top of the steps. He'd become a prisoner in his wicker chair on the verandah for two years now, from where he watched the occasional passage of life on the canal outside. Until this stopped as well. Looking back, I can't remember who went first, Appuppa or his canal, but they couldn't have been too far apart. Even on this trip I could see that both of them were nearly gone.

Ammumma greeted me at the door with a worried look, 'Are you okay, moley? Why are you alone? Why hasn't Suresh come? Have you heard that Appuppa's condition is much worse? Every month, I have to call Omanakuttan from the village to help me take him to the hospital at

Alleppey. But your father is so good, he always sends me the money I need for the medicines and taxis.'

Appuppa looked nearer death than I'd imagined. For my wedding, he'd been carried on to a van and then into the temple in his wicker chair, now almost a part of his body. He had seemed to enjoy the festivities, laughing widely and toothlessly at everyone who came up to talk to him. It was amazing how rapid the decline had been. He looked like a different person tonight, shrivelled and staring blankly at me. He couldn't recognize me. Or was he just wiser than Ammumma, realizing that the young woman standing in front of him with welling eyes was not the granddaughter he'd sent off with his blessings all those months ago?

'*De noku*, it's our Unni's daughter, Janu!' Ammumma was trying to make it sound like an event worthy of at least a celebratory smile. Appuppa mumbled something neither of us could hear and looked away.

'JANU, UNNI'S DAUGHTER . . .' But Appuppa was now intent on some invisible pageant playing out solely for his pleasure on the canal outside.

'There's no point, moley, he's stopped recognizing people for a couple of months now. I don't want to trouble your father, he's spent all that money on your wedding, I don't want him rushing down here to see us. Promise me you won't tell him how bad things are. I can manage things with Omanakuttan's help.'

'No, Ammumma, I won't tell him how bad things are.'

'Have you eaten? Come, let me get you some rice . . .'

Ammumma was once an enthusiastic woman who used to round up the children of the workers on her paddy fields and insist on teaching them to read and write. She did this sitting under a huge black umbrella next to her fields, wielding an ominous stick. The village children were terrified of her but some of them, like Omanakuttan, had not forgotten the favour and occasionally turned up to thank her in different ways. Now she seemed to have retreated into a kind of self-absorption, alternating between complaints about Appuppa's health and her own. There was certainly no room for any other complaints. I decided trips on my own to Thoduporam would only make her gradually suspicious and then sorrowful. There was no point. And no more of Appuppa's sandalwood-scented hugs by way of comfort.

Thoduporam, the next morning, was as peaceful as I remembered it, but dying as indubitably as her occupants and the canal at her feet. Greying moss was taking over the outside of the house, leaving cobwebs to attack the interior. Dad's old room did not look as if it had been cleaned in months although his hundreds of books still lined the walls like ghostly relics of a brilliant past. Most of them had no pages any more, just tattered hard covers holding together great handfuls of termite dust. The front room, lined with photographs and wedding portraits, was where Appuppa sat. His back was turned firmly on the smiling faces of all his children and grandchildren, his gaze being fixed on the canal and its invisible pageant. It was as though he was expecting someone very important to suddenly appear in a boat around the bend. A lot had changed in six months.

I wandered down to the kolam. The cement steps were covered in treacherously slippery moss because the water level had dropped considerably. I picked my way down to the bottom step, remembering the usefulness of this hideout on my last holiday here, perfect for letter writing to Arjun. And long conversations with Saroja, the maid. She had often followed me down here, using her pot-scrubbing as an excuse to ask me questions about city life. Open-mouthed, she listened to my tales of cinemas and city fashions and, in return, told me about the travails of her busy love-life. Occasionally, men wheeling their cycles on the path outside, would slow down and flash lascivious smiles at her breasts that wobbled precariously in colourful low-cut blouses as she scrubbed Ammumma's pots. Such interruptions she dismissed with a shouted obscenity and a smile, warning me that the world was full of such filthy men who were only after one thing. A philosophy I hadn't been inclined to believe then as the only men on whose behaviour I could have based my opinion had seemed as devoted to their women as one could expect. Dad, Ramama, Kunyachen, even both my Appuppas . . . happy marriages, loving friendships . . . I suppressed a sudden surge of envy. Why did *you* turn out to be the one exception to that rule, I asked my reflection accusingly, as it shimmered sadly in the water of the kolam. But it was silent, of course, as was the air all around; the canal just beyond, choking silently on its water hyacinths and the house behind me, unaware of its own creeping death.

Here, it felt like I was allowed to miss Arjun. The setting made it seem not quite so sacrilegious somehow. This was where I had sat down to miss him before. This kolam had been silent witness to the holiday letters I'd written to him and it felt appropriate now to allow it to see and swallow up the sudden tears that came rolling off my nose and chin. Plop, plop into the grey-green waters, once the colour of a much loved pair of eyes.

Was Appuppa's white turtle still in there, I wondered? I squatted down and waited for my eyes to get accustomed to the murky depths. Yes, there it was! Exactly where it had always been. I found a long stick of bamboo and, for the first time in all those years, probably because there was so little water left in the kolam, I finally succeeded in overturning the little creature. Expecting it to swim away, I watched as it turned and settled down again, underside identical to its upper surface. It had never been a turtle at all, Appuppa. Just a large round stone. Had you known, Appuppa? Was it just a wily ruse to trick me into spending many happy hours attempting to tickle it to life? I suppose that was one way to ensure I stayed safe within the compound without being tempted to wander off. Just another little myth to keep me safe.

The air of impending death now pervading Thoduporam depressed me, but I was still glad to have escaped the empty loveless world of my marital home. Something told me, however, as I left Thoduporam that afternoon, that I would not be back. I was learning fast that nothing was for ever – not people, not love, not even grand old houses . . . Appuppa and Ammumma would leave for Bangalore the following month to live with my aunt and have Appuppa treated at St Martha's hospital. He would die there six months later and Thoduporam would be sold at a high price because of the brand-new, bright orange road that could carry cars right into the area previously reserved solely for my games. I would find out much later that a large Dubai construction went up in her place, possibly much handsomer than her gentle predecessor. But without the greeny-grey canal that Thoduporam always had at her feet, the mirror in which she could admire herself all day . . .

I left Thoduporam without any proper goodbyes, of course, but gave Appuppa a tearful hug – while he kept his unwavering look-out over my shoulder for the VIP he was expecting would turn up at any minute now. Ammumma came all the way down to the bottom step to see me off, despite my protestations that the steps were now too high for her arthritic knees. 'Come with Suresh next time,' she said, 'not alone like this.' I kept waving to her, even as she became a tiny blurred figure finally vanishing from view as the boat went around the toddy-shop bend.

PART II

EIGHT

A year had passed, very slowly and inexorably in the Maraar household, and it was now clear to me that, however hard I tried, I wasn't to be one of them. But it still didn't stop me from trying.

'Is *that* how you hang out sari blouses in your house? *We* do it like this.' And I would rush to rearrange my wet, newly washed blouse hanging shamefully on the line next to the smartly folded Maraar ones, done just so. Even a badly hung blouse could announce to everyone who walked past the washing line that there was an intruder in their midst, one that could never ever measure up to the others. There for the fish-seller and the gardener and the next-door neighbours to look at and laugh at.

At my first Onam, Amma said with a big sigh, 'Now I suppose we'll have to explain all the rituals to little Miss Delhi. If it wasn't for families like ours how quickly all our age-old traditions would be forgotten.' As usual she accompanied this with some laughter, just to take the edge off, and to signal what a sensitive spoil-sport I was if I didn't know how to take a joke.

Sure we'd never celebrated Onam properly in Delhi, and Dad had always wanted us to celebrate Diwali and Holi and even Christmas with as much fervour. But in a rare, spirited defence of my family, I retorted, 'Well, in Delhi they don't give you a school holiday for Onam, so it was difficult to celebrate it properly.'

Amma was standing outside the back verandah, de-tangling Gauri's hair. This was a daily ritual after everyone's baths were done. The morning sun filtered softly through the jambakkya tree and the first round of washing was flapping contentedly in the light breeze. The Maraar women all had beautiful long tresses, carefully tended with herb-infused coconut oil. The daily rituals of hair-care seemed to take up an inordinate part of their day to my way of thinking. The busy, practical routines of working life in Delhi seemed a long way off and I wondered again, which of us had got it hopelessly wrong? I watched Amma's hands move carefully and lovingly through Gauri's coal-black tangles and curls and tried to remember when someone had last run their fingers through my hair, or made a meaningless gesture of affection to me. Suresh's nocturnal fumblings had been dutiful and already increasingly infrequent. Certainly, in the daytime I could not expect any demonstrations of any sort from him. That was the Kerala way, and I was used to it. But, even as a child, I'd noticed that married couples had a way of showing each other that they occupied each other's thoughts without anyone else noticing (except wily ten-year-olds, of course). I'd seen Ramama twinkle silently across at Vijimami during noisy family meals and had once walked in on one of Mini's parents' stolen clinches. My complicity had been bought with numerous sweets and for a while it was a three-way secret that I cherished carefully. Until I realized, many years later, that that was the way of loving that usually went on between Kerala couples.

There was, in truth, never anything terrible to suffer in the Maraar household, just a long and constant catalogue of very small things. Too small to complain about. Or write letters about. Now if I were being *beaten up* day in and day out, *that* would raise a few eyebrows, I thought. But tiny insults, so small and so subtle as to be almost invisible, could not do any grave damage, just rob me gradually of my knowledge of myself. *Don't be silly, you're just imagining things, Janu.*

Dear Ma and Dad,

I hope you're well. I received your letter last week and am sorry to hear you're not coming to Kerala this summer. I think you're right, with your trip so recently to Bangalore to see Appuppa before he died, it will be altogether too expensive to come here as well. I'm pretty sure you're still recovering from the extravagances of my wedding too!

I loved Dad's suggestion of Suresh and me coming to see you instead. I haven't had the chance to put the idea to him yet. He's having to tour quite a bit, Cochin and Bombay mainly, trying to buy some land to set up new motels. But I'm sure he'll like the idea as well, he's never been to Delhi. If we're coming we will try to make it around the time of the Asian Games. The weather will be just perfect then and I read somewhere that Delhi's being beautified considerably for the games. Oh how I long to see both of you and Delhi again!

Ma, I haven't forgotten about college admissions. I've been to the university and made enquiries about their correspondence courses. They start in October, and I need to show them my certificates by next month. Could you send these to me by registered post, please. You might need to go to school to collect the final mark list. If you see Sister Seraphia, do say hello to her from me!

Write soon!

Lots and lots of love,

Janu

'Delhi? When do you plan to go?'

'December would be best. I can't go at any other time because of my contact classes. It'll be the Christmas holidays then. Just for three weeks?' I was trying not to sound beseeching.

Amma was mulling over this new threat. Her initial silence gave me hope, and I could feel my heart begin to sing. Then her face cleared.

'Ah, but had you forgotten, it's your father-in-law's birthday in December. We always have special celebrations for his birthday, everyone comes for it. You can't be in Delhi when that happens! What'll people think!'

So I wasn't to get to Delhi for another year. My chances of seeing my parents and being able to tell them that I wasn't really as *terribly* happy as they'd hoped were receding. Quite what that would have achieved I'm still not sure. But, looking back, it was another one of those small, insignificant details that just did not help.

The birthday was a torment. Perhaps because Amma knew I had dared to attempt making my own plans, I seemed to be singled out for an extra dose of meanness this time.

'What are you *doing* with that vilakku? It goes *there*. Haven't they taught you *anything*?'

And, 'You're not wearing that old thing again that people in Valapadu have seen a hundred times already. Sathi, give the girl something decent to wear.'

And, 'I must have a photograph taken with all my children. Gather around all of you! No, not you, I said *my* children.'

I was nineteen and I felt completely annihilated. It felt like I had not a friend in the world. Memories of Arjun and Leena and the others had receded into a never-never land in my head, sweet to remember but quite painful and really very pointless. Leena's occasional sketchy responses to my long, sentimental letters had started to dwindle. And Arjun? Arjun had *gone*. He was in *England*. Far away, a part of my better-left-buried past. He would have forgotten me anyway. England was no doubt full of pretty girls for whom arranged marriages would be a laughable, crazy idea. They wouldn't let him down like I had done. And if he did turn around and tell me to be off, could I bear it? I'd had rather a lot of rejection lately and didn't really want to risk any more. This was my life now and I was going to have to make it work. I needed to complete my BA and get a job, that would keep me busy.

I watched Vinnu, Annu and Joji run breathlessly through the hall and flop down next to their grandmother, a sweating, laughing, heap of children. She smiled fondly down at them, and pulled Joji on to her lap. Perhaps, just perhaps, having a child would solve my problems more easily than a BA and a job. That's what I'd do, I'd have a *child*! She, as their grandchild, would be loved. Especially if she turned out to be the much-longed-for first *grandson*. And, as his mother, I'd receive a sort of instant double-promotion, so to speak. Be elevated to the position of Good Mother and Good Daughter-in-Law. And spin out the rest of my days basking in a kind of reflected glory and blissful motherhood. In the bathroom that night, with curious geckoes looking on, I pulled my Copper-T out.

As it happened, Latha, the older daughter-in-law, beat me to it. The following summer she gave birth to a gorgeous baby boy, receiving the certificate and double-promotion that I'd hoped for.

I got pregnant soon after and told Suresh about it tremulously. He looked confused and I hoped a little pleased. But all he said was, 'Amma and Sathi will know what to do. I'll ask them to take you to see Dr Gomathy.' It was decided that I could go to Delhi to have the baby, as is the usual custom. Girls go 'home' two months before they are due to give birth, to rest and have oil baths and to turn to their mothers when they are in pain. And so it was that I returned to Delhi finally, two and a half years after I had left it with my small blue vacation suitcase.

I wondered why Suresh had taken even the news of my pregnancy with the same studied indifference he had shown to all the other facts of my life. My homesickness, my complaints about his family, my loneliness at his ever-lengthening trips away. Perhaps, saddled with a teenager many years his junior, it had been easiest for him to adopt an avuncular, half-amused and half-irritated attitude to marriage. 'Companionship' was probably the last word either of us would have chosen to describe our relationship. Would fatherhood change that? Make him *want* to spend more time with me, perhaps?

But what was important for the moment was that I was to be in Delhi again, about to see my parents after an eternity. Suresh booked me on an Indian Airlines flight from Cochin, promising to arrive in time for the birth. I left the Maraar household without many regrets. The feeling was possibly mutual because Gauri said, 'Oh goody, so I can go back to getting Suresh chettan to take me to the cinema without you tagging along as well.' And Amma, as usual, laughed at her daughter's sense of humour.

As the plane circled Delhi, I looked down for Delhi's trademark Gulmohar trees that burst into fiery red and orange blooms in the summer time. Peacefully green, no flames in the forest at this time of year. It felt right. I was going to be a mother soon and perhaps, finally, all my demons could be laid to rest.

Delhi had changed in the time I'd been away. The Asian Games had bequeathed on it many sweeping fly-overs and wide new boulevards. It looked beautiful. City of my youth, city of happy, happy times. My parents were delighted to see me and Dad escorted me gently to the car, as though worried I was about to crack open any minute. I'd never seen him drive so cautiously.

'Look, over there, Janu, that's Khel Gaon where most of the events took place and the athletes had their quarters, I'll drive you around it one day next week.'

Ma turned around in the front seat next to Dad, 'I do wish

you and Suresh had been able to come for the Games. It was a glorious time in Delhi. You would have loved it.'

'Don't be silly, Mani, they had to be in Kerala for something as important as Maraar Ettan's birthday. I'm glad you stayed for that, Janu, it wouldn't have looked good at all to have skipped away for this. There'll be other Games in Delhi.'

'You haven't seen the new Hauz Khas village either, have you, moley? Well that came up as well after you left. They've converted the whole village into a shopping area while retaining the village atmosphere. There's a lovely shop selling things made by village women. No middle-men, the money goes straight to the villagers, that's the best part. I'll take you there to buy some of the gifts and things you'll need to take back.'

Ma was already talking about going back, but I had my eyes fixed on Chor Minar which was going past the car window now. Its yellow stones were glowing golden in the winter sun, and the warmth of old memories. Helloji-how-was-your-life-ji-do-you-ever-stop-to-remember-me? I was your pretend-wife once in this funny tower in the sky and we had a brood of invisible children and I loved you very much, remember? Arjun was my most precious memory, without a doubt. The thing that I came back to every time I felt unloved, which was frequently! A reminder that I was capable of loving and being loved. For me. *Not* for being anyone's daughter/wife/daughter-in-law. That reminder had stemmed my tears on bleak occasions. But I knew always that it would have to remain tucked away in that most secret part of my heart. I knew also that wherever Arjun now was, he'd have found happiness in new beginnings. I cupped my hands on my stomach as I felt my baby move reassuringly inside me.

Those three months with my parents were the best days I had been given in a long time. It was almost like going back to being their daughter again and not someone else's daughter-in-law only on temporary loan to them. Paraya Dhan, the treasure belonging to another house, that was how North Indian families ruefully described their daughters. I occupied my parents' house in a way that only a daughter can, without feeling I had to skulk about trying to look useful and unobtrusive at the same time. Here I was also free of the wearying round of visits, so much a part of feminine life in Kerala. In Delhi, it was easier to see only those people we wanted to see, not those we had to because we were related through our second cousins' sisters-in-law.

I sunned myself on the back verandah, eating oranges and reading books. Every evening I walked with my father to Hauz Khas market so that I could feast myself on the gol guppas I'd craved in Kerala. 'I don't know, all these terrible germs,' he'd mutter disapprovingly, as the gol guppa man would dunk his entire forearm into his pot of liquid. But I'd squeeze Dad's arm and he would pull out his wallet. I spent hours chatting to my mother but she always received carefully edited versions of my life in Kerala. Why I did this I'm still not sure. Probably because they seemed so happy and it was on the myth of my happiness that theirs depended. In any case, unhappiness was only a temporary state. It seemed impossible that it could last for ever, or even a very long time. My baby was going to see to that.

Riya arrived a week early, at midnight on Christmas Eve. She hadn't given her father adequate warning to arrive in Delhi on time, but she was received joyfully by her grandparents and her mother. I took my squalling bundle from the nurse, feeling more moved than imaginable. Here was the thing that would grow up to be the light of my life. She was a pink and purple walnut but I could see already that she was going to be my Transformer of Bad Things to Good. My potential best friend.

Suresh reached Delhi two days later, carrying gold jewellery meant for a baby boy sent by his parents. It had been bought before Riya was born, he said, in case he had to leave in a hurry. They'd hoped for a boy too obviously, but I was sure they would love Riya when they saw her, like I had done.

'She's so fond of her mother, it takes a crowbar to separate them,' my father warned as he took Riya off me to pass her on to her father. She wailed obligingly and Suresh laughed uncomfortably. He gave her back to me, 'I think she's hungry.' Very early on there were signs (that I chose not to notice) that Riya and I were to become a team. We would in fact become the kind of team on which my sanity would later depend. For the time being, though, she was my hope for the future.

The lazy cosiness of my first few weeks in Delhi had passed and now the precious remainder of my time was whizzing past in a profusion of bottles and nappies. Babies aren't really that much fun, I thought. Riya had seemed to spend all her time so far ejecting fluids endlessly from either end of her person. The sleeplessness was making me snappish. Ma was reassuring: 'Before you know it, she'll have grown up and left home and then you'll be longing for her to be a child again!' I looked down at my tiny baby who seemed not to have grown an inch in the month since she had been born. She was dawdling as usual at my breast, 'Oh I can't *wait* for you to grow,' I thought, 'I wonder what you'll be like . . . I hope *you* have a grand life, my darling . . .'

I'd been in Delhi long enough to delude myself into believing I belonged there again. I had met a few of my old friends but I was a stranger to them now, married and a mother. Arjun had not been back to India yet, although Leena did wonder if he would bother getting in touch again when he did. She bounced an unhappy Riya awkwardly on one thin knee and treated me to the details of her most recent paramour. I watched her leave an hour later, her cloth bag slung over one shoulder, on her way back to college. Our paths had diverged so far apart, we were nearly foreigners to each other now. I contented myself in the house, watching with delight my parents' joy in being grandparents. But, at the back of my mind was the aching knowledge that I had to return to Kerala.

'Riya's six weeks old now, Janu, shouldn't you be thinking of going back?'

'Well it's a long journey, Ma. Another couple of weeks maybe.'

I left for Kerala when Riya was two months old. It was an expensive extra month. That was an unusually long period for a girl to stay away after a pregnancy and Amma had had to concoct various excuses on my behalf. To the fish-seller and the servants and the next-door neighbours. She was not amused and I bore the instant brunt of it. Worse, now Riya was included (or, more appropriately, *excluded*) as well.

'You and your daughter should have stayed another six months. Why bother about what we have to say to our people here? We should have known back then that a girl brought up in Delhi would simply not be right for us. Just yesterday I was telling Shaila not to go to all these Delhis and Bombays in search of a girl for her Pramod. There are plenty of nice, well-brought up, unspoilt girls here.'

I was still too nervous to put up much of a fight and still found my Malayalam letting me down at moments that cried out for a sharp retort. Smarting from some unkind remark, I usually retreated hastily to the safety of my room. Shaking with indignation on my bed, I'd carefully construct a sharp and accurate rejoinder, craft it to perfection, practising it a few times, only to find that, by the time I'd emerged with my weapon of shiny new words, the moment had passed. I blamed my own cowardly responses for their increasing unkindness.

'Moley, Joji, come quickly, Ammumma's got your rice ready for you.'

Joji came tumbling in from the garden, covered in brambles and smiles. Her grandmother fussed around her, carefully picking bits of garden off the child. Joji's mother, Sathi, perched on the verandah and looked on lazily. Her fingers trailed gently through her long hair, the seemingly unending de-tangling process.

'Amma, make sure she finishes her rice today,' she said, 'yesterday I noticed she ate up all her chicken and left the rice completely untouched.' More trailing fingers. 'Janu, what are you looking at? Or have you no plans to feed your child today?'

Riya was playing at my feet, a placid bundle on her reed mat. I picked her up, tucked her on a stuck-out hip and picked up a plate with my free hand. It was funny how many things I could do so expertly now. Such as wear a sari, walk through the rain without getting the edge of my sari wet and serve up rice and curd on a plate, add the salt, mash it up into a neat white mound and feed it to a baby tucked on to a stuck-out hip. I had learnt not to expect any help with bringing up Riya. The bubble of the longed-for-and-much-loved grandchild paving my path to acceptance and double-promotion had burst without much ado as soon as I'd returned from Delhi. Amma already had three beautiful granddaughters and now a grandson in Madras who, though far away, was precious merely for being the much-longed-for grandson. Riya was girl number four, not a particularly special designation by any measure. *And* she bore my features. Most crucially though, she was the biggest chink in my armour and everyone knew that.

I took the plateful of rice and curds and carried it out into the garden. The garden had become our great dining room, partly because it was virtually impossible to feed Riya at a table without having both my hair and her face smeared with goo. The garden also gave us time away from the world indoors that revolved so firmly around little Joji, Sathi's delightful four-year-old whose lisping utterances could make even Amma's face go soft. The garden was filled with the buzzing sounds of busy insects. Riya gurgled with pleasure, bouncing on my hip at a dragon-fly doing a reconnaissance flight around our heads. I took her to the easiest place to cheat her into some lunch, the jambakkya tree, abundant at this time of year with its shiny pink fruit. Entranced, Riya looked up, reaching out with chubby fingers to catch one of these hundred pink plastic tree-ornaments dangling there purely for her pleasure, while I quickly shovelled some rice into her mouth.

The afternoon sun trickled through the leaves. Despite the shade, it was hot and I could feel my sari cling clammily to my bare waist. Kerala was always hot, it did not have the respite of seasons, except when the heavens opened on the first day of school each year. All through May, the monsoons waited patiently, whiling away the last of the summer holidays in lazy, long, hot afternoons. And, almost unerringly, on the first of June every year, just as the children are setting out with their new slippers and new books and newlywashed hair, the sky starts to rumble ominously. To the yelps and screams of happy schoolchildren, morning turns rapidly to dusk and the rain comes pelting down. As with a lot of other things in Kerala, it was a fact that was accepted cheerfully. No one thought of putting back or putting forward the opening date and, for generations, Kerala schoolchildren have survived a good soaking on the first day of term.

I'd stopped trying to remember the corresponding seasons in Delhi by now. Months ago I would think: May? Oh blazing hot now certainly . . . December? I'll bet they're enjoying the crate of winter apples Kunyachen sends from Simla every year . . . October? Delhi will be suffused with the smoke from Dussehra bonfires, making everything look prettier than it really is . . .

I'd certainly stopped calculating the time in England. I used to reckon one-minus-four-and-a-half (or one-minus-*five*-and-a-half from October to March) . . . 8.30 a.m., Arjun will be attending a class probably; 5 p.m., he must be playing cricket now; 7 p.m., night would be falling over his flat. I knew he probably never thought of me at all.

Even though Arjun was a lost dream, the thought occasionally crossed my mind that I could still leave Suresh and leave Kerala, perhaps to return to Delhi. My BA had been floundering for a while, mainly because of Riya. If I returned to Delhi, I could perhaps re-start my BA and my parents would help with Riya's care. I justified it to myself – I'd given the marriage a fair chance, no one could deny I'd tried my best, changing my whole personality to fit in with the Maraars. The fact that I hadn't succeeded, despite all that, couldn't be seen as my fault, could it? Surely my parents would see that. I'd tried it their way so now they would support me, I was sure.

I never had the chance to find out. In July that year the screaming of a telephone in the middle of the night was to bring the first of many nightmares. Dad had collapsed in his office and died of a sudden heart attack, a month before he was due to retire from service. I now only have staccato memories of that terrible night. A series of black and white photographs. Riya, awake and yelling without knowing why, Achen taking charge of the telephone, Suresh trying to be kind to me as I sobbed for my father, so far away . . . Phone calls full of disbelieving cries and confused tears were flying around. It was decided (I can't remember by whom) that Ramama would fly to Delhi and make arrangements for Dad's body to be brought on an Indian Airlines flight. To be returned to Kerala, the land he had loved so dearly, and been so sure would care well for me. Dear, kind, solid Ramama would be of more practical help to Ma than anyone else.

Suresh and I were at the airport the next day to receive them. Ma's face looked like that of a confused little girl. She suddenly seemed so terribly young. We fell into each other's arms, with all of Cochin airport looking curiously on.

'Moley, you are all I have left . . .' she whispered, sobbing, as we clung to each other, imagining vainly that we would derive comfort from each other. Who was to know of the pain that still lay ahead?

Dad was cremated the following day, giving all his relatives and well-wishers time to gather and pay their respects. So many things seemed so inexplicable, but the most meaningless thing of them all was that poor little Thoduporam Ammumma was still alive, and would outlive her beloved son by two whole years. She arrived on the flight from Bangalore and was brought straight to the crematorium. People pushed and shoved to see better as she broke free from her daughter's grasp and ran, forgetting her arthritis, to where Dad lay, throwing herself down on top of him wailing, 'Endey mon! How can you go without taking me!' And then, looking up accusingly at the shamefully silent sky, 'Guruvayurappa! Look at him! So young! Oh why could you not just take me?'

Other people's sorrow is always a fascinating thing, but this was too much even for the faceless crowd that had gathered. People who did not even know us started to wail and beat their chests, remembering probably their own worst sorrows . . . 'Ishwara!' they cried, 'What has this poor woman done to have her son snatched away like this! What great sin has made her deserve this!'

I wanted to stand up and explain to them that my Ammumma had lived a blameless life. *And* had taught dozens of children to read and write. That this was just some awful, terrible, meaningless mistake. But they would only have looked at me disbelievingly. Mistake? Meaningless? Nothing is ever meaningless, they would have said – centuries of belief validating them. There's *always* a reason for everything.

*   *   *

Later that month, I accompanied Ma to Delhi to help her pack up all her things so she could come back to make Alleppey her home. Everyone felt she and Ammumma, who had also been widowed for so many years, would give each other support and company. They also said that for Ma there would be comfort in being able to return to her childhood home. We took a week to pack into a few large tea-chests the whole of Ma's and Dad's life together. Their achievements and joys and the retirement they had planned with such care.

As the relentless Delhi heat melted the roads outside to a sticky softness, neighbours and friends arrived with chappatis and food, and to say goodbye. But even as we continued to mourn helplessly for Dad, I was conscious of (and ashamed of) one thought that kept repeating itself in my head. I was not only losing, one by one, the few people who truly loved me, but with the loss of my father my escape route had closed itself down as well. There would be no Delhi for me any more. My childhood home would now house another family with its own joys and sorrows. Without that and without the support of my parents, if I did leave Kerala with a baby and no education to speak of, how far could I go?

There was a small compensation, though, in those dark grieving months. Ma was now a mere two hours away from me. So even if I couldn't get away from the Maraars on a permanent basis I could still manage the occasional few days in Alleppey. For the moment that was good enough. I could not unload my problems on to Ma, of course. One look at her sad face was enough to quell the tiniest complaint that might bubble up from inside of me. I was not going to put her through any more pain. I would have to get on with it now and concentrate on completing my BA.

NINE

'I keep telling you there's something wrong with the child.'

I had learnt, much to her chagrin, to ignore Amma's various pronouncements. She was not going to get under my skin, especially not by taunting me about my daughter.

'Look at the way she always keeps her mouth open. By now she should have learnt to swallow her saliva. Joji was rolling over when she was three months old. This one isn't even trying!'

I remained unperturbed. It was always either Vinnu or Annu or Joji who was plumper or prettier or quicker at everything. Riya was never going to live up to Maraar expectations, in the same way that I had so spectacularly failed. I looked at Riya who was lying on her mat wearing a thin muslin dress with yellow rabbits frolicking on it. Her bib was soaked through, but she gurgled contentedly seeming amused by the conversation. Then her legs kicked out and she appeared startled, wiping the smile off her face. I laughed and swept her up in my arms.

Amma got up and left the room, muttering. Her own brother, seven years younger than she, had been born with a severe learning disability, a foot that dragged uselessly behind him and a heart so weak that he had lived for only twelve years. This, I thought to myself, had obviously made her believe she was some sort of an authority on 'children who had something wrong with them'. My carefully acquired ability to swat her remarks away with a laugh or a quick trip to Alleppey was standing me in good stead and annoyed her immensely. She could say what she liked, I knew my baby was beautiful and was going to grow into my best friend.

A month later I discovered I was wrong. Dr Sasi-the-famous-nephrologist had an old paediatrician friend of his visiting. Amma insisted we take Riya over to their house which, one still and sultry evening, we did. Theirs was an enormous, modern house nearby, kitted out with all the gadgets acquired during Dr Sasi's two-year stint as Senior Registrar in a Newcastle Hospital. This visit, as far as I was concerned, was like any other, except for the presence of Dr Vijaya-the-famous-paediatrician. I would briefly join in the conversation, smile while Amma explained to Dr Vijaya who I was and whose daughter I was. Then, using Riya as an excuse, I would escape to Sathi's geometrically laid-out garden and show Riya the love-birds in their outdoor cage and the painted gnomes cruelly displaced from their market-stall in England. Already they had started to pale visibly, the one with the fishing rod in desperate need of a new pair of trousers to replace ones that had all but peeled away in the heat of the midday sun.

By the time I had seated myself on Sathi's Argos sofa the sepulchral atmosphere and the stern expression on the face of the paediatrician as she examined Riya had started to work on my nerves. I could hear the seconds tensely tick themselves out on the kitchen clock that Sathi had liked so much she'd hung it in the drawing room. Tick . . . tick . . . tick said the teapot with the smiley face to the scone. I was still quite sure the surly expression on Dr Vijaya's face would change in a minute. She was just about to break into a smile and say we'd made a horrible mistake. Then we could all laugh and apologize for having wasted her time. But it didn't. Without saying a word the-famous-paediatrician-Dr Vijaya continued to examine Riya who had started to whimper and struggle. Keen for Riya to be putting her best foot forward, I tried to hush her by jiggling her on my knee and promising her all the goodies that she loved. But she was having none of it and soon she was blue in the face, screaming her annoyance at the doctor's fingers that were roughly examining the top of her head and the inside of her mouth. Through her wails, I could see the-famous-paediatrician-Dr Vijaya turn to Amma who was looking eagerly at her. Through a tunnel I heard her words, bald, flat and uncaring, 'This child is *deffinnitely* mentally handicapped. There is *no* doubt, see she has all the features, high arched palate, tongue-thrust,' concluding with a flourish, 'in fact I think that she will never even speak.' Amma nodded her approval and Dr Sasi-the-famous-nephrologist congratulated his friend on her expert diagnosis. Sathi, my sister-in-law, continued to pass around the palaharams and tea.

The world was spinning around me. No other being existed in that swirling universe, just a heart-broken, wailing baby fused to my body on an Argos sofa. Together we swirled through this shocking new sorrow. I could hear Riya's heart pound in fear through the thin sweaty cotton of her dress, echoing the words that were pounding inside my head: *mentally handicapped*, what a strange far-away word, take a *second* opinion, *who* docs this woman think she is, the world's *authority* on mental handicaps, there's *bound* to be a good doctor in Cochin, or in Trivandrum, it's simply not *true*, these are lies, *lies*, a Maraar *conspiracy*, that's what it is, a conspiracy to complete and then set the seal on my unhappiness . . .

I picked at the plate of uppuma that was placed in front of me, still whirling through another world. Riya was whimpering now, temporarily distracted by the uppuma bits I was putting in her mouth. The conversation floated around the sofa . . . opportunities for paediatricians in England, life in the cold wet of the north, racism in the NHS . . . Riya started to cry again, dribbling spitty uppuma on to my arm, suddenly seeming to remember the new tag she'd so abruptly acquired this evening. Deffinnitely Mentally Handicapped on a little wrist band, to carry with her through life. She brought up great big shuddering sobs with the sorrow of it all. Even the gleaming peas in the uppuma weren't proving much of an antidote on such a sad occasion. She'd given me my excuse to get out into the garden, finally.

We stumbled out, blinking in the sunshine. How odd that everything should look exactly the same as before. Birds and bees and flowers were all doing their usual things, oblivious to our world that had just turned slowly and surely over. I took Riya to the love-birds that never failed to thrill her. Her chubby fingers gripped the wire mesh and laughter bubbled up through her tears. Together we watched the tiny bundles of blue and yellow flutter weakly from one end of their cage to the other. They looked happy enough, twittering their silly glee. You poor, stupid birds, I thought to myself, you don't even know you have no freedom, so complete is your imprisonment. The Geordie gnomes were in their usual forlorn cluster around the ornamental cement pond, fishing hopelessly for the fish Sathi had attempted to breed but that had long since died. Their rosy-cheeked happiness had dimmed discernibly over the years. Who could blame them, plucked away from the cheery companionship of their hundred brothers in an English market-stall to be transported to this hot, still land where the sun beat down so mercilessly. Helpless mute witnesses to the slow murder of goldfish that had choked one by one in the heat of cement-enclosed water.

'Enda, Riya moley? Enda karayannu?' Sathi's gardener was making small talk with Riya. The kind of tête-à-tête she warmed to instantly. Perhaps that hard-fingered doctor indoors could have taken a few tips, I thought, as the old man came across to hear Riya's babble better. He bounced himself a few times on matchstick-thin legs, laughing a crackly laugh, hoping to be rewarded with her usual hundred-watt smile. But Riya was feeling serious today, screwing up her mouth in an earnest and high-pitched patter, tears still lodged among her lashes. It's no laughing matter, she seemed to be saying – just wait till you hear this – that famous paediatrician has told us that I'll never speak, imagine that! The old man cocked his head on one side and said solemnly, 'Oho? Oho?' a couple of times, as though she were making eminent sense to him. And, promising to take up her suggestions for the landscaping with Sathi kunyamma, he wandered off to nurture some other tender new shoots.

It was only after we returned home, that Dr Vijaya's words sank into that part of my brain that I had attempted to shut down over the years. The part that allowed for pain and self-pity, such useless emotions that would never help me escape my own personal gilded cage. I rushed into my room, throwing Riya and myself on to the bed and wept as though I could never stop. Thousands of unshed tears were finally given their freedom to course through my shaking body and emerge in loud unfamiliar sobs that sounded strange and noisy even to me. What new sorrows awaited me, Mullakkal-amma? Hadn't I attempted to live a flawless life! Had I done anything that deserved such unending punishment? Why me? Why me? Why me?

I must have wept for an hour, barely aware that I had set Riya off again. I could hear her screaming alongside me on the bed, sharing my sorrow from miles away. After a while she seemed to tire of her uncomforted pain. Gradually her tears stopped and she started to examine her toes, only letting out an occasional whimper. Her silence had a calming effect on me. I watched her from the other side of the pillow, with new eyes. Not the unquestioning, all-accepting eyes of a mother any more. But that of a curious and concerned stranger. Yes she did have hair that stuck out at the back of her head and two little fleshy bumps underneath each eye. Her mouth was always open, and she was flaccid rather than plump. At seven months she still hadn't started to roll over. But she was still beautiful. With tiny perfect hands and tiny perfect feet, each decorated with its own tiny half-moon nail. She had a beautiful button nose and an ability to smile and respond to my high-pitched playful calls. Simply *beautiful*. 'Deffinnitely mentally handicapped' babies were never beautiful, were they? I didn't know, I'd never seen one before. I'd seen people in Delhi, looking different and behaving oddly in markets and on buses and had quickly looked away so as not to make the embarrassment of their families worse. There was also that child of one of Suresh's cousins who lived in Changanasseri. On one visit I'd watched in painful fascination as it lay on a string bed, flies buzzing all around. A baby's mind in a ten-year-old's body, condemned to life on a string bed and a verandah. There was not one thing that connected Riya to that strange unknown world. I'd see to it that she was protected from that. I felt sudden panic rise in my throat again, did this mean she wasn't my potential best friend any more? She almost *deffinnitely* couldn't be if, as Dr Vijaya-the-famous-paediatrician had so blithely announced, she would probably never even speak. That was pretty integral to a best-friend relationship, the ability to speak, wasn't it, *wasn't it*?

It was getting too tiring to think. I lifted my tear-wracked body off the bed and picked up a towel to wash my face. Riya kicked her legs, whimpering her desire to leave the room too. I picked her up and took her into the bathroom to wash the sweaty fear off her tiny body. Clean and tearless and puffy-eyed, we emerged from the room. From the kitchen I could hear the cheerful clatter of dinner sounds.

*   *   *

Being able to cry together must create the strongest of human bonds and Riya's problems could have become the glue to fix me for ever to my husband and my in-laws. But the Maraars were not a crying sort of family. And if they did shed any tears over their newest grandchild, certainly I never saw them. Not even from Suresh, strangely. His response to my early sorrow had been complete disbelief that a child of his could have *any* sort of problem. I could understand this, disbelief having been the stick to guide me through my own first few days of swirling dark shock. But for Suresh escape lay in longer and longer periods away from the house. I envied his being able to get away from everything – and wished that I could announce an impending business tour with the jaunty swing of a briefcase.

Why the Maraars remained untouched by Riya's apparent problems was something I could never understand. Their rejection of me, though hurtful, was something I'd been able to rationalize. But Riya? She was their flesh and blood. Could it be that Amma's early experience of caring for her handicapped brother was now frightening her off the prospect of being saddled with *another* child like him? Was it *image*? Could it really be they cared more for their privileged world of swaying plaits and silk saris than for Riya?

I wasn't doing too well myself at this stage, and had taken to scrutinizing other babies wherever I went, in sidelong, envious glances. I could see that, as Riya grew, she was either doing things other babies didn't do or *not* doing the things all the rest of them seemed to be able to do so effortlessly. Even by the age of one, she had not figured out that dribble was to go *in* and not *out*. Eager for her to dispense with bibs that seemed to signal from miles away that there was something 'wrong' with her, I preferred to develop my own reflexes and a watchful readiness with a handkerchief. Still unable to speak, and displaying no desire to walk or crawl, she also developed a fine ear-splitting yell that had me scurrying to get her whatever it was she wanted. When I had begun to despair of her ever being able to walk, she finally dragged herself up and decided to give it a shot, clumping around with an inelegant, flat-footed gait – and an enormous smile at her new-found freedom. I was over-joyed but remembered that other babies her age had by now graduated into running and jumping and chattering cutely. Our endless game of Catch-Up was making it difficult to rejoice in Riya's achievements, however hard won. The only real blessing being that Riya herself, blissfully unaware of being bottom of the class, was meeting every challenge in life head-on and beaming with joy. My potential best friend not only seemed intent on letting me down at every step, but was enjoying herself hugely as she went about it.

I was exhausted, but didn't realize at first that it wasn't Riya who exhausted me as much as my desire to have her appear lovable and be accepted by the Maraars. And I can't say exactly when I freed myself of this oppressive burden. It wasn't a sudden revelatory thing for sure, but over those first few weeks and months of Riya's life the knowledge gradually seeped into me that Riya was never, ever, going to be a Maraar child. She was not going to provide me with a passport to their love and affection, she did not in fact have one herself. My struggle was over. I grabbed at the realization with a weary but dizzy, almost overwhelming sense of liberation. I was free. I neither had to struggle for their approval any more, nor put Riya through the same hopeless loop. I wasn't sure why I had so easily given up my own right to be loved, allowing it to fade into oblivion somewhere long ago. But a child like Riya, left unloved, would simply wither and perish. Couldn't they see that her kind of innocence could only understand love, not the lack of it? My own rights had not seemed worth fighting for, but

Riya needed me to be her voice and a battle on her behalf would be far more satisfying. I was soon going to become the thorn in the Maraar side.

'Aren't you ready yet, Janu? What are you doing, hurry up and give the child to the servants or we'll miss the muhurtham.'

'I'm not leaving Riya with Thanga, Amma, she doesn't have the patience for her. In fact, I think she even smacks her sometimes.'

'You think you're going to be able to bring up a child, especially a *mentally handicapped* one without a few smacks? You must be crazy.'

'Maybe I am, but I'm not going to this wedding if I have to leave Riya with that Thanga.'

'Don't be difficult, what will I tell people if we turn up without you? Especially since you didn't come to Eli-yamma's house-warming either.'

'I'll go only if I can take Riya with me. She'll be quite happy since Sathi's kids will be there too.'

'Sathi's children are different. They won't start screaming halfway through the ceremonies, they're well behaved. We never used to take my brother anywhere either, he was always quite happy at home. You'd better get used to leaving her behind. I'm not having people pointing at us and pitying us, our family has always been admired in this town.'

Even without words, Riya always managed to make it eminently clear that she liked outings more than anything else in the world. The family drivers had taken to describing her as their latest car accessory, stuck as she invariably was to one dashboard or the other. I said with as much firmness as I could muster, 'Like it or not, Riya isn't one of Sathi's love-birds that can be caged for life. Either she goes to this wedding or neither of us does.'

Amma backed off, her eyes glinting in alarm behind her glasses. She wasn't used to being thwarted and she wasn't used to the new sharpness in my voice. Increasingly, Riya and I were allowed to stay at home as this was preferable to giving people in town reason to gossip and nudge each other pityingly. Increasingly Riya and I found joy in each other's company, away from the wearying round of weddings and engagements and visits to second cousins' sisters-in-law. After everyone had left, we would unfold a rattan mat and sprinkle it liberally with toys and books. Lying there, side by side, with the sun filtering through the designs of the window grilles and the slow creak of the ceiling fan throwing cool air down, it was almost possible to imagine a sort of happiness.

Suresh, in those first few years of Riya's life, was to become more and more aloof. Caught between a father who was in essence also his boss, a sharp-tongued mother, a demanding younger sister, a young wife full of complaints and a baby who did not do all the charming things other babies did, he found that life outside the family home was starting to seem increasingly attractive. There were many urgent trips to Trivandrum and Cochin and Bombay. And he packed for those trips with increased excitement, no doubt in happy anticipation of comfortable hotel rooms, the flattery of business and drinking cronies and the joys of a new bottle of Jack Daniels. I watched him leave for his trips with diminishing sorrow and confusion. Previously I had mistaken my loneliness among the Maraars for a kind of love for him. He was the only person I had attempted to speak to about some of the pain, even my parents had been unaware of its extent. The fact that he neither could do anything about it nor seemed particularly interested in finding a solution was a fact I merely accepted. In desperate need of an ally, I had not stopped to notice that the ally I had chosen was completely occupied with his own concerns and with an overwhelming desperation for a stiff whisky.

By the time Riya was three, I had accepted that there

would be little room for her in Suresh's life. He did not dislike her, and it gladdened my heart to watch on the rare occasions that he took her into his arms or threw her into the air making her gurgle with pleasure. But even I could see that, all in all, she was to Suresh a terrible disappointment and an inconvenience. It was inconvenient that she needed to be taken to doctors and specialists. It was inconvenient that his mother was not fond of her. It was inconvenient that she wore me out completely, leaving him with an even more irritable wife than before. It was inconvenient, most of all, that he could make no sense of the future with a child like her. Most other men knew their daughters would require schooling and music lessons and marriages into good families. But what Riya would need was unknown and far too frightening to contemplate. It was easier to pretend the problem simply didn't exist.

'Oh Suresh, how can you be so old-fashioned, children like Riya are not kept locked up any more, whatever your mother might think. There must be special schools and specialist centres in Kerala.'

'At home, she'll be protected and looked after. We can even employ someone specially to care for her so that you won't have so much to do.'

'You know as well as I do that I don't mind the time she takes up. It's infinitely preferable to rushing around Kerala marking attendance at boring weddings. I do loathe those awful messy sadyas, having eaten at least a hundred over these years. Riya needs to be at school, just like any other kid. Someone told me the other day about a special school near Palamukku, behind the main post office. I think it's worth checking out.'

The school turned out to be a dismal place, with twenty children of assorted age, size and disability. Sheela Kuriakose, the woman in charge, appeared to have her heart in the right place and had trained in Special Education in

England. But she looked wearily around her tiny school when I asked her about her staff.

'We have to have been in existence for three years before the government will give us some funds. We really can't afford to pay for qualified teachers at the moment and have to rely on volunteers and people who'll work for a pittance, unfortunately. If we start charging parents fees for sending their children here, they simply won't send them. Why should they? It'll be easier for them to keep the child with a servant at home.'

I surveyed the two-room school. It was lunch time and the students had been seated around two long benches covered in oil-cloth. All of them, even the teenagers, were wearing bibs. Despite the clatter and chaos of food going everywhere but where it should, there was a strange silence about the meal. A horrible absence of words. Except for the teachers' voices encouraging or admonishing, the happy chatter of a school lunch time was missing. No long-winded explanations to avoid the ubiquitous rice and curds, no vroom-vrooms of someone pretending his spoon is a car, no efforts to do a surreptitious swap (Psst . . . I'll give you my idli if I can have your sandwich).

One child seemed to be expelling as much rice gruel as was being pushed in. I watched in fascinated horror as the teacher squashed the child's cheeks together, to insert a spoon expertly into the narrow aperture thus formed. In the second it took for the teacher to refill her spoon, out would come the gruel, sliding down the side of the child's mouth to drop into her lap. It could have been funny if there had been a sense of mischief about the whole exercise. But a cold hand wrapped itself around my heart as I saw what could only have been utter helplessness in the girl's eyes. Was she desperate for the gruel to go in and not out? Did she loathe the damn thing? Was she longing for a *sandwich* perhaps?

My heart was still thudding painfully as I left, clutching Riya's small palm in my hand. She looked up at me, babbling her incomprehensible chatter and smiling widely at the prospect of another trip in the car. I could not picture her in those desolate surroundings. She was growing rapidly into a cheeky toddler with a distinct personality. Although her vocabulary was still confined to only a few words, peppered generously with the petulant 'poda' she'd picked up from the servants, she had become a dab-hand at a certain 'Ah-ah-ah-ah' speak which, combined with much finger pointing and gesticulating, conveyed her feelings perfectly adequately. She had the flattest feet the orthopaedic doctor had ever seen, and had to wear heavy black shoes that endowed her with a noisy clumpy gait. But she was curious and confident and had a smile that could stop my heart. Ma and Ammumma, frantic in Alleppey, had asked Ramama to look for specialists in learning disabilities and I made a short trip to Bangalore in search of a diagnosis that might sound less terrible than 'mental handicap'. But it was no use and everywhere that we went, the diagnosis was apparent in all the curious stares and elbow nudges that said clearly and with barely masked pleasure, 'Aiyyo paavam, it's mental handicap, you know.'

I was sure I wanted something better for Riya than Sheela Kuriakose's special school. I'd read in a magazine recently that integration was the latest trend in the West. That children with disabilities in places like England and America were put into normal mainstream schools, which was proving beneficial to the other children as well. I had met the principal of the local primary school at a few functions. Fifty-something, she had exuded a certain kindly no-nonsense air. Perhaps she could be persuaded to take Riya into their nursery.

It was agreed that Riya could join St Thomas's nursery in the summer term, after her fourth birthday. The principal had listened and agreed that there might be certain mutual advantages for all the children at the school. Riya would have to wear the uniform and attempt to fit in as well as she could. But if there were complaints from any of the other parents or if the teachers felt unable to cope, Riya would have to leave and go elsewhere. I was overjoyed. A semblance of normality at last! I could already picture Riya making friends and learning to be independent of me.

And so, Riya set off every morning wearing her chocolate-brown uniform and carrying a brand-new school bag with a picture of Mickey Mouse on the flap. Proudly and happily I took my place with the other mothers outside the school gates at one o'clock for the noisy exodus as the school bells rang. It was one of my most cherished sights to see Riya trundling down the path, carrying her own bag and water bottle at the end of the school day. My school-going child! I did not want to think too far ahead. To the day that Riya's classmates would all learn the alphabet that would always be gobbledygook to her, or to the day that they would all gang up on her because she was different and could not speak like they could. If that was going to be a problem a year or six months from now I wasn't going to let it spoil my present happiness.

As it happened, Riya did not last at St Thomas's even one term. I first heard of The Tests outside the school gates.

'*Tests*? But they're only four!'

'I know, but the teachers have to decide if they're ready to go into first grade or not,' replied the young mother I'd befriended at the gates.

'What sort of tests? What will they have to do?'

'Oh, recitation of the alphabet, counting till ten, backwards and forwards, singing Humpty Dumpty and the National Anthem . . .'

'The National Anthem! Counting from ten *backwards*!

Riya doesn't even know what a number is, leave alone count them. Does your Vrinda know her numbers?'

'Well she doesn't understand numbers exactly, but I've been reciting them to her every evening, two or three times, so at least she can say them . . .' Noticing the look on my face she added, 'You can teach your daughter too. Just keep repeating the letters and numbers. She'll learn them.'

'No she won't, you silly woman,' I thought silently, 'she doesn't have the kind of brain your daughter has. Messages keep flying around inside her head without getting to the right destinations. Like a post office gone mad. What hope is there that she'll learn to count forwards, leave alone counting *backwards*.'

When I was summoned to the principal's office, I knew it was bad news. Her air wasn't that kindly any more and sitting next to her was Lisa-teacher, Riya's pretty little class teacher. Lisa put on her sympathetic I'm-only-here-to-help voice.

'We all want to help Riya, but she really doesn't want to help herself. I really believe we've done our best and there's no more we can do.'

Too shattered to speak, I sat glued to my chair, struggling to stay composed. Emboldened by my silence, Lisa continued, her voice now filling with scorn.

'Here just look at the work she produced at the tests.'

I looked at a few large sheets of paper with some tiny pencil squiggles in one corner.

'And look at what the other children are capable of producing.'

Sheet after sheet of paper with houses, trees, mountains, rivers and even little stick-people in glorious crayonned colours.

'I couldn't even explain to Riya what a mountain is, leave alone expect her to draw one on a sheet of paper . . .' I said pleadingly.

'I think maybe you ought to work harder with her at home before thinking of sending her to school.' Lisa's pretty face had gone steely. She was blaming me for Riya's inability to be like the other children! I turned to the principal and begged for another chance, another term. But her expression was mirroring Lisa's.

'Please don't give up on her yet, I'll work harder with her at home.' I couldn't sit Riya down for two minutes so the promise sounded hollow even to my ears, but I continued, 'I know it's a bit of an experiment for you but we'd agreed that having Riya would probably be a valuable experience for the other children as well . . .'

'We had made no agreements, no promises. Please don't misquote me. I had hoped to help you but I don't think it will be possible any more.'

'Please, there's nowhere else I can take her . . .'

It was like talking to a brick wall. Twin brick walls with less power of understanding than my Riya had in that malfunctioning little brain of hers. I got up and fled from their office in tears.

The nursery class looked on in stunned silence as I swooped in, grabbing Riya's Mickey Mouse things that lay entangled in a cheery heap alongside Tom and Jerry satchels and Barbie water bottles.

'Where is she?' I barked at a frightened classroom helper. She pointed to a tiny gaggle who had stopped flinging paint at each other to watch this new drama unfold. Riya, covered in purple paint, flashed a startlingly white smile at me. I shoved my way through the crowded classroom and grabbed her by the shoulder.

'Why do you have paint all over your new uniform, you silly girl?'

Her white-on-purple smile disappeared and she started to whimper.

'What are you crying for, you stupid, stupid girl . . . you cause me all these problems and then *you* cry!'

I couldn't trust my voice not to crack, so I shook her hard and then, as she started to wail, I lifted my hand and started to rain smacks on her shoulder and on her back.

'What are *you* crying for, hanh? What are *you* crying for?'

I was my father and I was raining blows down on the thing I loved most in the world because the thing I loved most in the world would not do what I most wanted her to do. She would not draw mountains and she would not draw people and she would not draw trees. All she would do were *squiggles*! I'd done my best . . . I'd lived my life by all the rules . . . I'd done all the things I had been asked to do . . . why couldn't she . . . why couldn't she . . . why couldn't she?

Vaguely aware that other children were joining Riya in her wails I stumbled out of St Thomas's nursery class, dragging a purple-streaked Riya after me. Pushing past alarmed-looking parents huddled obediently behind the school gates, I picked Riya up and ran as fast as I could down the crowded road, her satchel and water bottle trailing after us in the dust. I needed to get as far away from the school as possible. I needed to put as much distance as I could between us and that horribly normal world back there, where children could paint purple mountains and sing the National Anthem and count from ten backwards. There would never ever be room for us there.

* * *

Riya started at Sheela Kuriakose's special school the following month. With a mixture of gratitude and anxiety for Riya's well-being, I asked Sheela if I could do some hours of voluntary work at the school. My own BA studies left me with enough spare time for this, and the offer was gratefully received. I was asked to help Pradeep, a sixteen-year-old with cerebral palsy, to prepare for the state board exams. Sitting next to his wheelchair in the quiet room (the only other room) of the school, I could occasionally spot Riya and know that she was safe. For the moment that seemed to be the most important thing, that and the fact that we had somewhere to go.

The Maraars were not overly enthused, but by this stage there was little they could do. I had taken to snapping back at them at every bit of meanness, perceived and real.

Presumably they complained to Suresh, but by now I was confident that his cowardliness would prevent him from doing anything more drastic than escape to Bombay on another trumped-up trip. Occasionally, whenever the school closed for the holidays, I visited my mother in Alleppey.

Alleppey, stuck in a time-warp, had changed little over the years. Its cinema halls still had abysmal acoustics that made the songs and dialogues spill out into the crowded streets, mingling fact with fiction. Mullakkal temple still stood grandly on the main street, silent witness to the joys and sorrows of its townsfolk. Ma and Ammumma still lived in the old house from where my wedding entourage had set out so hopefully, so many years ago. Widows both, life had more or less come to a halt for them. Here, in this old defunct trading town, still advertising itself optimistically in tourist brochures as Venice of the East, both my grandmother and mother had taken on widowhood with an enthusiasm born of practical good sense.

'I don't see why you have to wear white saris just because Ammumma does,' I argued with Ma.

'Because that's the way, moley, why fight it? And I certainly don't miss my silk saris, I don't even like looking at them because they remind me too much of your father and the good life we had.'

'All the more reason to revel in them once in a while and

remind yourself and other people of how wonderful you used to look.'

'No, no, that's wrong. This is my lot now, and I must bear it as cheerfully and graciously as I can. The past is to be left behind, a sweet memory.'

There was no arguing with that almost annoyingly saintly acceptance of everything her Mullakkalamma dished out. My own faith had undergone a radical shift and I was secretly scornful of the blind reverence with which the day's poojas were carried out. It was, according to me, a pretty poor God who couldn't even seem to get right who was deserving of punishment and who wasn't, but I hid these feelings from Ma and Ammumma. It was not worth hurting them just to make myself feel better. Dutifully, I accompanied them in the evenings to Mullakkalamma's door, bending down in obeisance at first sight of that sandalwood-encrusted face glowing in the light of a hundred oil lamps. Standing there I whispered well-learned prayers in Riya's ear because that was what my mother had done when I was little. Then we would go to the temple office to exchange our money for vazhupadus. Two rupees to have our names read out by the priest in the inner sanctum, ten rupees for the chance to buy the sandalwood that would be used to decorate the Goddess, twenty for a payasam, sweet enough to dilute all of life's bitter pills. It was a farce worth spinning out because it brought contentment to my mother's face.

Both my mother and grandmother had guessed by now that my marriage wasn't a wonderful one. My mother had once attempted visiting me at the Maraars but had found herself ignored by them, the banana halwa she had brought given away, in her presence, to the maid. It had not taken much to deduce that she had been welcome in their house only for the time that she had been the wife of a Highly Placed Official. She did not visit them again but still her exhortations to me were to accept and to forgive. She knew things were not unbearably bad and she also knew of marriages that were worse. Poor Suma chechi was even *beaten* sometimes by that so-called IAS officer husband of hers, it had been rumoured on the family grapevine. By being at the Maraars I had the dignity and the respect enjoyed by women married into good families. Deprived of that herself by my father's death, she knew how cruel the world was capable of being and did not wish it on me. It was to many women a fate worse than death.

You saw them everywhere, women deprived of their men, sad little shadows that had lost their bodies. Widows, divorcées and those who had never had the good sense to attach themselves to a man. They occupied the fringes of life, respected only if they embraced their lot in life and gave in gracefully, spending their time in prayer and reminiscence or repentance, depending on the circumstances of their particular single-unblessedness. A widow could not give her own child away in marriage, receive a new son or daughter-in-law or even be the first to fondle a grandchild. Such joys were reserved for that happy band of sumangalis, or those-blessed-by-marriage.

My grandmother's house was already a joyless place of prayer and old memories, without menfolk whose footsteps would be anticipated every evening and for whom special food could be cooked. Once the evening lamp had been lit, this was the sort of house that closed its doors. There was also nowhere that either Ma or Ammumma could go once the temple round had been done. Only women who had the good fortune to still have lives with their men went out after dark, to the cinema and restaurants and other people's houses. These pleasures had passed for my mother and grandmother and an unspoken sadness had descended over the house that had once joyfully received hordes of children when the schools closed. Now it lurked with half-shuttered windows, only dimly shining its forty-watt presence behind two huge mango trees. Despite the occasional temptation, I truly did not wish to add any more sorrow to that house.

I had however started to plan a kind of get-away, my great and at the moment very secret escape. My duties at Sheela Kuriakose's school had been extended to the early intervention group, grandiose title for a small motley band of two-year-olds with assorted disabilities. Ajay who smiled a lot but flopped over backwards if left unsupported for even a minute, Reenie who stiffened into a bundle of unco-operative brown stick limbs at any human touch and, my favourite, tiny two-year-old Fardeem who was blind.

Surrounded by this little group, I re-found a part of myself that I thought had died the day I'd fled in tears from St Thomas's Primary School. I sat with my early intervention group on a reed mat on the floor, and didn't realize at first that they were teaching me far more valuable things than I could ever hope to teach them. We learnt first of all that life offered no miracles. Everything had to be taught, learnt and absorbed at a painfully slow pace, with patience and fortitude on the part of both the teacher and the taught. Then came the lesson that huge successes sometimes lay in very little things. Our favourite game was the 'tactile stimulants' bag, my students screeching their wordless glee when they found the scrubber or stone that matched the one in my hand. They also loved to bang pieces of Sheela's farmyard jigsaw about until the hapless animals fell, surprising everybody, into the right slots. They spoke to me in their strange secret languages, completely ignoring my loud ungrammatical Malayalam and it felt marvellous when, at one o'clock, they burst into tears as their parents arrived to take them home.

I was ashamed that I had once allowed an ignorant school-teacher to convince me that Riya was the lesser of her classmates for not being able to paint purple mountains. I knew now that Riya's efforts to communicate and make friends, *despite* the muddled messages flying around inside her head, had involved much greater effort than sticking brushes into water colours. And I watched now, with my heart in my mouth, while Fardeem reached out and explored his dark world without fear or self-pity, despite the bruises he carried on his elbows and knees like an array of medals. I wanted, more and more, to be a part of that brave world, leaving the other one to the truly blind and ignorant.

'Sheela, how did you get your qualification in Special Education?' I asked one afternoon as we cleaned up the two-room school after the last of the children had left.

'Not easily,' she replied, 'it's not available in India at all, as far as I know. It was possible only because my husband had been sent to London for his doctorate. I was allowed to take up a course myself and this was the one I chose to do. Although, sometimes I do wonder if I'd have been better off with a diploma in Business Administration instead!'

'You're not suggesting a bunch of disgruntled office workers would have been easier to deal with than our Ajay and Hamid, are you?'

We laughed at the thought of Ajay and Hamid, the school's two most difficult pupils, pitted against a team of clerks and stenos in a pitched battle involving poking pencils into hapless victims' eyes. But Sheela had put an idea into my head. Perhaps I could go abroad to do a course in Special Education. And take Riya with me. She could go to a wonderful Special School, the kind whose pictures I'd seen in American magazines, bursting with toys and special equipment. I'd do well in the course and then I'd be offered a job at the end of it. I'd work in Riya's Special School. We'd get ourselves an apartment (with lots of squashed cushions). 'Abroad' wouldn't be like India. Women could live on their own and not be thought of as scarlet women or a member of some strange, unfortunate breed. Children with learning disabilities were valued in the West. There would be no more awful staring, pitying, aren't-I-glad-you're-not-me looks.

I started corresponding with the British Council and the USIS in Delhi and soon large books listing universities and courses started arriving for me in the post. The Maraars took little notice. They'd already written me off as a bit of a basket case, too caught up with that stupid charitable school that I insisted on sending Riya to. It wasn't, fortunately, seen as a harmful pastime. Better in many ways than going shopping for saris and jewellery every day, I'd heard my father-in-law remark once to a curious uncle. By now everyone in Valapadu knew of Riya's disability and I had been at the receiving end of pity, advice and the kind of smugness that indicated I had obviously done *something* to be more deserving of punishment than they were. Occasionally someone praised my determination to make something of my 'misfortune' by teaching at Riya's school and this was quickly lapped up by Amma or Sathi, if they were within ear-shot, as the best way they knew to encourage me out of the house. 'Poor thing,' I once heard Amma whisper to a woman who had fixed openly curious eyes on me over Amma's shoulder, 'she wouldn't go anywhere, you know, no weddings or anything, couldn't bear to look at other children, until we encouraged her to go and sit at this school. Now she seems to be getting slightly better.' It was, to the Maraars' own surprise, all proving quite handy really. My stubbornness to disprove them had been turned quite easily into a kind of heroism from which they could partake generously as well (*Such* good in-laws to support the poor girl and gently encourage her out of the house). All I had wanted really was a place that would accept Riya and a vantage point for myself from which I could keep both an eye on her and my distance from the Maraars. Now both they and I were on the point of receiving mayoral plaudits from the townsfolk.

There was also the invariable pressure to try for another child, a *normal* one this time. That was essential, that all-important normality. As though, by having one that walked and talked on time, I could somehow dilute the disappointments of the other. But Riya would still exist, they seemed to forget. A walking, talking sibling would only exist alongside her, not *replace* her as they seemed to be suggesting. I was fairly sure by now that the unhappiness of my marriage would also not change if I had a normal child. If anything, Riya had taken my mind off the by-comparison-minor unhappinesses of life with the Maraars. In the end, did she pre-empt my inevitable departure or delay it? She was inextricably linked up with it, no doubt, my desire for her to escape the Maraars running more or less neck-and-neck with my own. It was rapidly becoming my one overweening thought, lodged carefully into the darkest recess of my mind, marked Top Secret. I was going to *have* to find a way to go abroad.

*   *   *

There was to be a small setback. A letter had arrived on beautifully thick smooth paper. Speaking in what I imagined was a twangy American accent, it said,

Dear Ms Maraar,
Thank you for applying to Arizona State University for the MA in Special Education. I regret to tell you that it will be a requirement for you to have a Masters from an Indian University before you can apply for this course. We will keep your application on hold until you inform us of whether you feel you will be able to do this. If you need to know anything else please write to us again.
Thanking you.
Sincerely,
Janet Whitworth
Chair of Education Department, ASU, Phoenix

I had by now completed my BA, and that afternoon I wrote to Kerala University to apply for an MA in English Language and Literature as a private candidate. In a month's time, fat brown paper parcels started to arrive for me. The syllabus was unwieldy, stretching from Chaucer to twentieth-century literature and, for the first time, I was grateful that my marriage was as empty and undemanding as it was. Now I had not a moment to spare.

In the mornings, I got Riya and myself ready and at nine we set out for the school. I spent the morning there with my little gang of three, who were no longer the early intervention group. Smaller, weaker ones had joined the school. It seemed sometimes that an angry God was intent on relentlessly churning out more and more babies with broken bodies or minds to keep the numbers up at Sheela's school.

In the afternoons, I taught Pradeep, my teenage student with cerebral palsy, re-learning my own school-level algebra and geometry. At four, Riya and I returned home. After I'd given her a bath, I settled down to read my MA books while she played with her toys against the backdrop of a chattering television. When she slept at night, sleeping her funny noisy mouth-open sleep of the innocent, I wrote my notes and drafted essays that could then be posted to the exam centre the next day. Sometimes, late into the night, when the household sounds had died away and the noisy chirrup of the crickets had taken over, I looked out of the window and my exhausted mind darted uselessly to all that might have been. The faces of my father and of Arjun and of my old friends would swim before my eyes and dissolve into meaningless tears. But such weaknesses were infrequent because I knew that the next morning one of my students would probably perform some little feat that would make me cringe at my own self-pity.

Suresh was an occasional visitor to this busy life. By

now his presence or absence had become truly irrelevant. Bombay motels could claim all his time, for all I cared. And I suspect his feelings towards my MA ran roughly on the same lines. It occupied my time and my thoughts, making me less prone to putting demands on him. Hallelujah, I could almost hear him think.

The Maraars, fortunately, held their tongues. If they were talking behind my back, I was slowly starting genuinely not to care. It was only after I had completed my first-year exams that their long-suffering attitude changed.

Gauri's wedding had been fixed. She had been seen and accepted by an up-and-coming lawyer and there were two months to prepare for what was going to be the biggest wedding Valapadu would ever see. Suddenly my MA wasn't a 'good thing, keeps her busy', but 'not good at all, keeps her too busy'. Sathi announced that I was to put my MA on hold because my help was needed with the invitation rounds and snack-making. When Gauri suggested that I also give up my work at the school, I rose to the bait: 'I can't. They need me there.'

'Don't be ridiculous! If they needed you so badly they'd be paying you a fine salary to do the job.'

'I *offered* to do voluntary work, and Riya benefits from it too, doesn't she?'

'Well, if it's voluntary work, then they can't expect you to commit yourself entirely. Tell them you have other things to do.'

Despite all my resolutions, I was still not brave enough to be contrary when looking a Maraar square in the eye. Even Gauri, four years younger than me, had always terrified me with her sharp tongue and blazing eyes. Those eyes were now fixed on me, boring two little holes through my head and daring me to argue. *Fight*, I told myself fiercely, she doesn't own you, *fight*!

But years of Ma's careful bringing up invariably took over

at moments like this. Looking at my feet, I mumbled, 'I'll see what Sheela says tomorrow.' And then, in a sudden show of confidence, 'I'm not giving up my MA, though. I'll study at night.'

Sheela was full of warmth and understanding. 'You'd probably have needed some time off for your MA this year, so perhaps it's just as well. Don't let that suffer, certainly. You have to look after yourself and do all the things *you* want to do or you'll just end up resenting Riya. And don't worry about her. She's quite used to all of us now, she'll be fine here without you. Your little group will miss you though. We'll have to train Judy to take over from you.'

I said goodbye to my ex-early intervention group and, in the way that only children can, they waved me an enthusiastic farewell and turned to their new teacher, sprightly little Judy-miss. They weren't going to miss me too much in those capable hands. I felt a pang, but I knew I could still observe their progress every time I went to the school to collect Riya.

*   *   *

The wedding was now taking over the Maraar world and I tried to be as useful as I could.

'Janu, make those nankatais your mother makes for the bridegroom's family when they arrive the day before the wedding. That'll be different. We can serve them with vegetable pups at tea time.'

'Janu and Suresh can do the Trivandrum invites in the space of two days if it's done in an organized way.'

'Janu, come and help me with these flower chains. I need to untangle the strands before they're sent to the hall.'

Half of Kerala was being invited and there was much to be done. I was painfully aware that my books had been languishing unread for nearly a month, but I could not duck into my room for even ten minutes without someone barging in to have something stitched, stirred or sorted.

A paltry MA paled into insignificance next to this all-important show. I tried not to mind because I had a wonderful secret lodged away carefully in the bottom drawer of my desk.

My first letter of acceptance had arrived. Arizona University in Phoenix had written again to make a conditional offer. I would have to produce my MA certificate before embarking on the course, but they were expecting me to begin my course of study with them in less than a year's time. There was no offer of financial assistance, certainly for the first semester. But they hoped that I would be able to find the funds I'd require in the months ahead. I had inched a step closer to my great escape!

Gauri was out, shopping for saris, when I pulled *Collins Atlas of the World* off her shelf. Page 107 ... Arizona ... tucked in there between California and New Mexico ... 35 degrees latitude. It would be hot. From something I'd read or seen on television once, images of cacti and giant lizards sprang to life in my mind. And giant desert blooms that flourish in spite of everything. Riya came rushing in at top speed, taking the corner at her usual frantic tilt. I pulled her on to the bed next to me and pointed out Phoenix to her. 'Arizona,' I whispered, 'you and I will be going there soon ... would you like that?' My secret was safe in her wordless world. She looked up at me baffled, but something about the word 'going' indicated an imminent journey, which she liked very much indeed. She beamed at me as if to say, Arizona, gosh that sounds like fun, but wriggled off the bed to run in search of more immediate adventure ... My mother and her *books*, I could hear her think in exasperation. I flipped the glossy pages of the atlas over ... far-away places, distant lives ... Remembering having rushed to look up another atlas, looking for another university, some time long ago, I stopped at page twenty ... England ... and looked at Hull, still a black dot that told me nothing. He'd be a man now, all grown up and *English*. Aspirating all his Ps and Ts quite properly, playing cricket in whites . . . He might even be married now, to an English wife with rosy cheeks sitting behind a teapot and enquiring solicitously, 'Would you like another cup, dear?'

I smiled at the thought. Hopefully, Arjun was happy, whatever he was up to. Certainly I was feeling better than I had in a very long time. I heard the gravel crunch in the garden outside as the car returned with Amma and Gauri. Returning the atlas quickly to its slot, I resolved to try not to begrudge the Maraars their joy in this wedding. Walking out of the room, I joined the servants who'd already gathered around Gauri to exclaim at the day's purchases.

I dared not tell anyone yet of my plans, not even my mother. She arrived a day before the wedding with my grandmother, both of them looking lost and out-of-place in their plain white widows' weeds amid the flashy silks and gold. I noticed, without as much shock this time, that they were again completely ignored by the Maraars who were fussing and flapping endlessly over their new in-laws, a well-known cashew merchant and his wife who dripped with jewellery. The last time that had happened, I had attempted to compensate by lavishing my own solicitous attentions on my mother, incurring further irritation from the Maraars. But I could afford not to descend into puerile games this time. Hopefully my mother would never have to darken the Maraar door again. According to my calculations, in less than ten months I could be leaving this house with Riya to begin our new life abroad. I had not thought about divorcing Suresh. No one in my family had ever had a divorce and I didn't think I especially needed to incur the shame. I did not need a divorce. I was satisfied with just getting away and being able to take Riya with me.

I watched from behind the jasmine-bedecked mandapam as Gauri married her bearded lawyer. The nadaswaram player puffed out his scrawny cheeks, his screaming notes ripping through the air. Nair weddings were noisy, confused affairs, made much worse since the advent of the video camera. The families of the bride and groom allowed themselves to be buffeted about by the cameraman while the wedding took place so that they could gather around the video player and coo in pleasure after the whole stressful business was over. On the bright side, these weddings were mercifully short compared to the four-day lavish affairs of our cousins in the northern states of India.

'Vat a vunderrrful catch for Gauri, is it not so, moley?' whispered Maheswari Aunty who was breathing asthmatically over my shoulder. 'Boy is lawyer with own practice and verrry good looking also.' She sighed and added a fervent, 'Guruvayurappa!' hoping probably to thereby invoke similar bridegroomly blessings on all her female descendants.

I turned and smiled at her. I knew she was as jealous as it was possible to get of Padmaja Maraar's good fortune. Her own daughter was pushing thirty and there was no sign of a bridegroom anywhere on her tiny horizon. She had turned up at the house the previous evening with her skinny unhappy-looking daughter in tow and had tried not to look enviously at the jewellery draped around Gauri's neck. You could almost hear her thoughts: 'What chance does my daughter have when there are those like these Maraars who can drown their daughters in gold. Guruvayurappa!'

She was a woman I normally avoided like the plague, not least because she had been the person responsible for bringing the Maraar proposal to my grandmother, with vastly exaggerated tales of their wealth. ('The car boot was fullll of jewellery, my dear, when that Sathi was sent off after her marriage!') As a childish eighteen-year-old, I had visualized different gory deaths for those of her ilk, meddling match-making types who went around recklessly planning the ruination of many a happy young person's life. Now I felt sorry for her. As she saw it, she had helped many a distraught parent find a suitable match for their children. Now that it was *her* daughter's turn, it was cruelly ironic that Kerala had been struck by a sudden famine of bridegrooms. I hoped she would find someone suitable soon for her Rejani. I also wondered what she would think of my plans and the letter that lay in my drawer? A vision of her rushing to cousin Padmaja's side, beating her chest in self-chastisement sprang to my mind.

'Aiyyo, endey Padmajey! She has gone to Arrissona? Leaving such a vunderrful family and such a nice boy like our Sureshmone? And to think that I was *single-handedly* responsible for bringing her to your door! Why does Guru-vayurappan give such wicked girls good families like yours while my poor innocent Rejani can't even find a nice *simple* family . . .'

The thaali had been tied around Gauri's blushing neck and the bridegroom's sister was now adding another fat chain to the dozens that already stretched from Gauri's throat to her waist. The crowd strained to catch a glimpse of the swarnamala, always a good indicator of how wealthy the groom's family was. It was virtually a rope of gold and the pendant was . . . could it really be . . . the crowd caught its collective breath . . . *diamonds*! Maheswari Aunty who had grabbed my shoulder to heave herself up for a better look let out a deep, wobbly sigh. I wondered whether she might faint.

In a few short, confused minutes Gauri was safely and irrevocably delivered into the hands of her lawyer. Both of them took big relieved breaths and smiled bashfully at the videoman. Balancing Riya on my hip, I joined the rest of the Maraars for the interminable photo-shoot after the ceremony. Amma was in her element, ordering everyone to either sit or stand, depending on which part of the Maraar hierarchy they occupied. How much she liked them also usually dictated how near to her they got to stand in the pictures. I took up my usual position on the fringes of the group. Amma's beloved grandson was pulled on to her lap and her bevy of beautiful granddaughters were arrayed at her feet. I hugged Riya closely to me and sneaked a quick kiss on her plump arm. Luckily, she had always been blissfully unaware of all these wearying games and now, suddenly and miraculously, I found I didn't care any more either. I smiled in a way I hadn't been able to for a long, long time into those cameras.

Leaving a deliriously happy Gauri showing off her new swarnamala (with a *diamond* pendant!) to a small band of admiring aunts, I wandered among the crowd who were carefully watching the doors behind which the wedding feast was being prepared. It was worth remembering to step out of the way when the doors did open and the crowd thronged forwards. What *was* it about Indian weddings, I thought idly to myself. Food was always plentiful and almost never ran out, but the crowd always behaved as though it had not eaten in months. I had seen even normally graceful and dignified souls push with elbows akimbo and fall upon the food as though they didn't know where their next meal would come from.

When the feast was done and the last banana leaf cleared away, Gauri was taken to change into the traditional cream and gold sari given to her by her new family. She did not need my help, clucked over as she was by Sathi and Latha. She emerged looking radiant. There were no tears as she stepped into the car that would take her to her new home. Tonight she was going to her in-laws' house in Quilon and from there, tomorrow, she was travelling to Cochin where she would be setting up her own home. She looked confident and something told me no one would dare push her around in her new life. The Maraars obviously knew how to make sensible decisions on behalf of their daughters. Gauri was twenty-two, and had completed both a BA and an MA. Her parents, influential and interfering, lived a mere two hours away and she would no doubt see a great deal of them. She had been armed with the basic necessities to earn the respect of her new family. And she knew she didn't have to bother to be polite with everybody. Everyone waved and Amma burst into loud tears as the car drove out of sight. I was beginning to think my feet would not hold me and Riya up any more as the last of the guests started to make those weary we-really-must-be-off-now noises. I went back into the rapidly emptying hall . . . would this be my last Kerala wedding, I wondered? What a relief, if it was, what a bloody relief.

Maheswari Aunty waddled past me, with Rejani trailing forlornly behind. 'Vunderrfull wedding, eh moley?' Her asthmatic wheeze had developed into a hoarse gale. 'Even better than yours.' She paused briefly to pinch my cheek, 'I still remember how pretty you looked that day, how many years ago? Just like yesterday, no?'

She wobbled off without waiting for any replies, a silk-clad mountain of brown flesh. I looked at her retreating back, the generous collection of tyres adorning either side of her waist swathed modestly today in yards of sweaty green Kanjeevaram silk. Yes, many years ago, Maheswari Aunty. And, no, not like yesterday at all. It's taken me much, much longer than I ever thought to get out. Goodbye, and try not to mind too much. It wasn't your fault at all.

TEN

I knew I couldn't postpone indefinitely the task of telling everyone of my plans. The safest place to begin this onerous task was Alleppey. We were in the living room. Outside, the afternoon sun was turning fruitless mango trees into a blaze of green. Even the window shutters and Ammumma's lace curtains could only make half-hearted attempts to shut out the heavy, damp heat. Riya was asleep indoors and the house was quiet.

'Ma, Ammumma . . . I've been thinking for a while now. Next year, when my MA's finished, I want to take Riya abroad. India doesn't really have much to offer her, does it?'

Ma looked up from her newspaper but Ammumma was still half dozing on her wicker chair, unimpressed by the new Malayalam serial on television.

'Will Suresh be able to take time off his business? I thought you said it was keeping him very busy.'

'If I waited for him, Ma, I'd be waiting for ever. I think I'm going to have to go alone.'

'Alone?' Ma's voice had dropped to a whisper, but its quavering tremulousness roused Ammumma from her slumber.

'Enda, enda? What's happening? What's happened to Mone?'

Ammumma's hearing had faded over the past few years and everything she misheard seemed to voice her deepest fears. 'It's tastier fried' would evoke a worried, 'Aiyyo, who's died?' And recently, 'I think she's a good dancer' had been converted, in Ammumma's panic-stricken mind, to the dreaded cancer she was always on the brink of contracting. Ma was her interpreter, patient and calming, on all these occasions and Ammumma jiggled her arm impatiently now.

'What's happened to my Mone? Is it my Raman you're talking about?'

Ramama and Vijimami had moved to Bangalore many years ago, and Ammumma lived in constant terror of some awful calamity befalling one of her children when she wasn't around to personally fend it off. Ma ignored her and I noticed her lower lip had started to tremble slightly.

'Alone?' she whispered again. 'Why? Can't you wait until Suresh can go with you?'

'If one of you girls doesn't tell me WHAT's happened to Mone, I shall get very upset now!'

I turned to Ammumma and raised my voice, hoping it would penetrate only as far as Ammumma's tympanic membrane and not filter through the mango trees to nosy Mrs Pillai next door.

'I'm thinking of going to AMERICA with RIYA to do a COURSE. That's the only way I can show her to some SPECIALISTS there. Isn't that a GOOD idea, Ammumma?'

Ammumma appeared to have heard this and I hoped she wasn't barking up completely the wrong tree when she settled back in her chair and said, 'I think it's a good idea, you go and do that, moley. You have all Ammumma's blessings.'

As startled as I was, Ma turned to Ammumma at this unexpected response. There was still a quaver in her voice, 'You didn't hear her properly, Amma, JANU wants to go to AMERICA with Riya and WITHOUT SURESH!'

'There's no need to shout, I'm not deaf. You don't want that Manju Pillai hearing all our business do you?' Ammumma snapped. 'Look, Mani, if Janu can take Riya abroad, does it matter if Suresh is alone for a while? Just think, if there is some cure for our little Riya mole! Janu can find out all that and come back.'

'But what will people say? And what will the *Maraars* say?'

This was greeted with one of Ammumma's finest snorts, 'The Maraars! Fine people they are to stop our Janu from doing what she can for her daughter! They will not spend five minutes to help Janu with Riya, but that Padmaja has always got one of her darling Sathi's kids attached to her sari pallu like glue. Joji this and Joji that, makes me sick!' And, just to make sure she had made her point adequately, she nearly dislodged her dentures by adding the vehement 'PAH!' she normally reserved for stray dogs that came sniffing at her gate.

Both Ma and I looked at Ammumma open-mouthed. The Maraars had never been candidly discussed between us before. It would have taken complete blindness or utter stupidity *not* to notice that they weren't the loving, supportive in-laws my family had hoped for. But the disappointment had always remained unspoken, mainly because there was little that anyone could do about it. What was the point in going on about something that could not be changed? Widowhood, indifferent in-laws, a child with a disability, for aeons we'd understood that these were things we simply inherited. Somewhere in my distant past, perhaps even a thousand years ago, I'd done something that committed me to dedicating this life to Riya's care. Had I been a thirsty traveller at her door and had she taken me in, washed my feet, fed and watered me? I would never know what ancient promise I had made to her, just as she would never know what deed had robbed her of words in this life. Or how that would be compensated for in the next. But, somewhere along the way, we had both lived many lives that linked us together now. And, in much the same way I was also a part of that strange unloving clan I'd married into. Attempting to fight all that was the equivalent of trying to fight the Gods, defeating their very purpose. So what was it now that was liberating Ammumma's tongue? Was it old age or the misguided hope that there might indeed be some miraculous American cure for the great-grandchild she loved?

I could also see that she was under the impression I would only be away temporarily. That was, in a comparative sense, fairly acceptable. There would be no shame for her to tell all her temple-cronies that I had gone to do a course and to find a 'cure' for Riya in America. Provided, of course, that I came back. To the Maraars who, as we all knew now, made her sick. I briefly toyed with the idea of correcting this misconception. Thanks, Ammumma, but there is one more thing; I don't intend leaving Suresh for a while, it might be just a bit longer than that actually, like, sort of . . . um . . . for ever?

I looked at Ma's face, on which disapproval and confusion were still looming large, and thought the better of it. She knew me well and it had probably already crossed her mind that I might never return if I did manage to get away. I decided, in my cowardice, to leave it to her to explain those complexities to Ammumma.

In the meantime, there was the small problem of funding to worry about. Arizona State University had already made it clear that they would not pay for my course. There was the vague possibility that, if I did well enough, they would consider me for a teaching assistantship in the second semester. But, in a new place, with lots of different things to get used to, I did not think my chances of rising head and shoulders above the American students was a terribly realistic one. I borrowed more books from the library and started my search for a trust that would offer me a scholarship.

A few months later, after I'd collected some more letters

of acceptance (from the Universities of London, Stirling and Newcastle-upon-Tyne, all of them, unsurprisingly, without the offer of financial aid), a letter arrived for me from the Firoze Barwala Foundation.

Dear Ms Maraar,

We are very interested in your plans to do an MA in Special Education at the University of Arizona. If you could forward us your letter of acceptance from this University, we would be keen to meet you and discuss how we may help you in your endeavour.

As you know we are a grant-making body that supports students from all over India, but our trustees reside in Delhi and we hope it will not be too inconvenient for you to travel here to meet them. The date that suits them best is 8 December. Do let us know as soon as possible if you can present yourself at the above address at about 10 a.m. on that date.

Looking forward to meeting you,

Yours sincerely,

Mrs Meher Rustomji

It was time to break the news to the Maraars. I chose the soft target first. Suresh.

'I've been hoping for a long time to take Riya abroad . . . America has been doing some wonderful things with children who have special needs . . . Suresh, are you listening?'

Suresh was preparing for one of his business tours, his fourth . . . or was it fifth one this month. He was looking critically at the shirts I was helping him to fold.

'Not this blue one, is the maroon striped one in the wash? . . . What? Yes, taking Riya abroad, it's a good idea, but you know I just don't have the time . . .'

'I'm not asking you for your time, Suresh. I'm thinking

of taking Riya myself. I've been offered admission at a few universities abroad and I might even get a scholarship . . .'

I had his attention now. His gaping suitcase and his mouth were mirroring each other as he stopped packing, a bundle of trousers hanging helplessly in his hands.

'When . . .? How did you get this . . . this admission?'

'Oh, Suresh, surely you've noticed. I've been corresponding with various people for ages. I even told you about it the other day, remember?'

I had done nothing of the sort but I knew I could rely on Suresh's habit of never listening seriously to anything I had to say. Even in the early days, whenever I attempted conversation, the most attention I ever received was an avuncular pat on my head, usually in mid-sentence, accompanied by a 'Laathi'. Chatterbox. It could have been construed as affectionate, to a certain extent it probably was. But the patronizing tone of voice signalled clearly that I was prattling on again, that I was boring and that I should stop forthwith. Which I did, finally, for the rest of our life together. Unless it was to ask for money to pay for Riya's clothes or to say that dinner was served. Even in those darkest months of Riya's disability coming to light, I had felt powerless to raise the shutters that Suresh and all the Maraars had pulled down on me. Could he really believe now that I might, at some stage, have shared my hopes and dreams with him? I could see confusion and consternation rush over his face. He *was* trying to remember what I might have said about taking Riya abroad! For a moment, I felt sorry and wondered whether I ought to revert to the truth. But, there was Delhi! I still had to broach the subject of the interview in Delhi. I ploughed on.

'And now I've been called for an interview! This foundation might even pay for everything. It's a wonderful opportunity, really!'

I thrust the letter into his hand and watched while he

slowly put the bundle of trousers down to read it. He then looked at me. Eye-contact! Now when did *that* last happen? I almost couldn't believe my ears when he then asked me a direct question.

'Do you really want to go?'

Was it just a hypothetical question? Was it just rhetorical, leading up to a lecture of some sort . . . could he be angling for an argument perhaps? When he was still looking at me a few minutes later, I realized with some shock that Suresh was actually asking me what I *wanted*. It had taken all these years to arouse genuine curiosity in him for the workings of my soul! Was it my fault, was it his? Should I have attempted to shock him thus out of his apathy many years ago? Had it been my job, as a woman, to use little wiles and guiles and to have *made* him interested in me? I took a deep breath and answered softly.

'Yes, Suresh, I really want to go.'

*   *   *

The Maraars were less easy to get around. Suresh's father, normally a man interested only in his business, called me out to the verandah the following afternoon. These post-lunch verandah sessions were all-male affairs conducted while the women cleared away the plates and dishes indoors. Meant for discussing the business and other important things. Very occasionally, Amma joined the men there, but even that happened only when there was an impending wedding or some other important function which required female participation. I had certainly never been invited to one of these, except perhaps very briefly to deliver a glass of water or announce a phone call. Struck by the seriousness of the situation, I nervously took my place in front of my father-in-law, who was reclining on his beautiful old polished planter's chair. The afternoon sun was bathing the garden in hot gold. I wished someone would turn up the speed of the ceiling fan as I could feel my blouse start to cling unpleasantly to my back. A bead of sweat had gathered at the base of my neck, and was now slowly beginning its journey down between my shoulder blades, sliding under my bra strap, gathering speed to arrive triumphantly at its final destination in the clammy folds of the sari at my waist.

I was not afraid of Achen, but had never been too sure of where exactly I stood with him. He normally exuded a kindly, if distant, air but had seemed genuinely incapable of understanding anything that didn't involve making profits and generating business. It was his role in life to provide for and protect his womenfolk and, like other men of his generation, he did that unquestioningly and he did it well. The other smaller concerns he left to his wife whom he trusted as an efficient and intelligent partner. On the face of it his house was a happy and prosperous place and it wasn't for him to concern himself with petty quarrels and jealousies if indeed they did exist. I felt awkward at the thought that I had made him stop and examine that picture more closely, looking for some obvious pieces that would help him solve this sudden puzzle. Had Suresh and I had a fight? Wasn't I comfortable in his house? Was there something else troubling me? I warmed to his concern and for one moment I could feel tears pricking the back of my eyelids. Could I chance it and pour everything out? The years of feeling alone and unloved? Amma's cruel jibes? Riya's apparent rejection? Suresh's weakness for whisky that took him on all these innumerable trumped-up-trips?

I could imagine the storm that would break if I did. Suresh would promptly organize an urgent business trip. And I would be stuck with the floods of noisy tears Amma would no doubt produce for having been so terribly misunderstood. Then she would make telephone calls to summon her beloved daughters and pour her agony out to them. Next, angry words would no doubt fly around with everyone pitching in, Gauri and Sathi and Dr Sasi-the-famous-nephrologist, perhaps even Gauri's new bearded lawyer . . . then my mother would hear of it, and I would have to face her tears and possibly even Ammumma's. We'd all agreed that afternoon in Alleppey that the Maraars made Ammumma sick, but I wasn't supposed to say that to them! That would break just about every rule in the Kerala Etiquette Handbook. It was okay, clever even, to run people down behind their backs, to whisper and gossip and shoot off beautifully concealed jibes. But it was *never* done to tell them to their faces that you simply did not like them. I was going to have to take refuge in my favourite lie.

'It's for Riya. I have to be able to take her abroad to find out if there's any treatment that can make her well.'

I wasn't sure he believed me. To me it was amply clear there was no treatment in the world that would 'cure' Riya. But I did hope that in America she would get the chance to go to a well-equipped school, get speech therapy and occupational therapy and, quite simply, a better deal.

Most of all I wanted her to escape the prejudice she had seemed surrounded by even so early in life. I did not want her to be pitied or reviled, even though, so far, I had merely felt it all on her behalf. I knew neither whether she would ever comprehend prejudice, nor even whether Abroad was a place free of this cruel quality. But it seemed worth a try. 'Treatment' was something people went abroad for on short visas, coming back as soon as they were well. I could not tell Achen the kind of treatment I wanted for Riya was going to take the rest of our lives to find. Nor that I was doing it as much for myself as for her. *And* that his home was probably the last place to which we had any intention of returning. Even if Riya had finally been 'treated'.

More questions . . . Where would the treatment take place? How long would it take? What was this course I was going to do? Where would we stay? . . . I stumbled through the inquisition, feeling foolish and aware that I was sounding more and more unsure of myself. But, in the end, Achen seemed to accept, if not quite understand it. He said I could book my ticket to Delhi when Suresh returned on Thursday. I told him I would stay with one of my mother's cousins who would no doubt meet me at the railway station as well. I would leave Riya in Alleppey with my mother, she could miss a few days of school. Suddenly, I was overcome with gratitude and, forgetting an old Maraar rule for a minute, I thanked him, but he was looking out at the garden and I knew I'd been dismissed. Had he written me off already? Had I hurt him or shamed him? Or had he just reverted to worrying about the things he usually worried about, putting aside the temporary aberration I had caused? I went indoors feeling exhausted and unhappy, despite knowing I was going to get to Delhi for the interview.

I should have felt worse the next morning when Amma woke up complaining of a terrible migraine. She sat at the kitchen table drinking endless cups of coffee and said to no one in particular that neither she nor Achen had slept a wink last night for worrying about their son and wondering what people were going to say. But I noticed that Achen was his usual self and ate a hearty breakfast before leaving for the office. He even, unusually, nodded a thanks for the coffee I'd made for him and asked where Riya was. Amma carried on being a misery all day, making numerous slanted references to girls who cared not a whit for their poor husbands who worked so hard for them. And, after a whole morning of listening to her woes, I felt the last of the guilt created by my session with Achen on the verandah lift off my shoulders. If she did have a serious problem, she ought to discuss it directly with me, I thought. But as long as she was going to be addressing her coffee mug, the cupboards and the sky outside, I was not beholden to reply. I carried on with my chores, humming a happy tune.

ELEVEN

The train journey to Delhi would take two days. It felt like the first proper holiday I'd had in years. With an excitement that was difficult to conceal, I boarded the train, tucked my suitcase away under my seat and said goodbye to Suresh. I had taken Riya earlier to Alleppey and sneaked off while she had been temporarily distracted by the ladybirds in the back garden. She'd never been without me before for any length of time, but I was sure she would blossom in the warm glow of two grandmothers' combined attention. After an interminable wait, the train gave its warning shriek and shudder, and I was off. It felt magical, and wonderful, chugging my way back to the city of my childhood, minus Suresh and minus Riya. I felt free, like a teenager again and I did not care if the feeling was as passing and illusory as the towns that floated past my window.

Palghat, Vijaywada, Itarsi, Jhansi . . . there was music in those names and there was hope in every beat of the train pistons as they carried me further and further away from Kerala. Had I really grown to hate the land that I had made my home? I had spent some of my happiest times there; even as a baby I had known of belonging somewhere amidst the peace of its backwaters. My ancestors had tilled its fertile soil for generations, my grandmother had helped to uplift a whole generation of children in her village . . . and yet, Kerala had failed to take me, one of its loyal daughters, to her bosom. Despite all the futile attempts at sari-wearing and Malayalam-speaking, I had failed so abysmally to fit in.

Was it because my parents had moved away to Delhi? Because I had not been born in my grandmother's house as tradition dictated, because I'd gone to an elitist Irish convent school and because the friends I'd grown up with were Punjabi businessmen's children who spoke a sort of 'Hinglish', leaving my Malayalam laughably accented? There was always something too *Delhi* about me and Kerala had not liked that much. Just like the childhood holiday friend who had described me sneeringly as 'too fashiony', reducing mc to bitter tears behind Ammumma's hydrangeas. The odd thing was that Delhi had never taken me completely to her bosom either, possessing as I always did that faint Kerala edge. In my name and the way my parents spoke and the idlis I carried in my school lunch-box instead of parathas and pickle or even salami sandwiches. Halfway-children, we could have founded a world-wide club of people belonging nowhere and everywhere, confused all the time by ourselves . . .

'Poori? You will eat a poori?'

One of the women I shared my Ladies' Compartment with was waving a poori at me which had been stuffed with some bright yellow potato paste. She had boarded the train at Vijaywada and had already told me she was travelling to Delhi to visit her son and daughter-in-law.

'My daughter-in-law, she is a very clever girl, MA, BEd. And now she is doing MEd.! But exams are in March and she needs help. You see, she cannot ask her own mother who lives in Palghat as she has younger children to look after, her son is doing his SSLC also this year, so I said I will go as I am free, my husband having left this world two years back.'

At this point she had seemed struck by the sudden weight of memories (good or bad, I couldn't make out) and had lapsed into silence until roused from her reverie by hunger pangs. I hadn't volunteered any information about myself, but as I bit into her poori, she tucked her foot under her sari and smiled at me as though we were old friends.

'You are also going to Delhi, yes?'

I nodded and smiled.

'Why?'

To escape a marriage that wasn't a terribly *bad* one but wasn't very good either. She was still looking at me. There was a harmless curiosity in her eyes and a certain concern for why a young woman should undertake such a long journey on her own. I was sure she was the sort who would have dropped everything, perhaps even her daughter-in-law's MEd., to help another soul in need. But I concentrated on the large three-pronged diamond she wore on her nose as I replied.

'Interview.'

'Aahh?' I could see relief flood over her face. '*Jaab* interview, anh?'

If I said yes, I'd have to create a make-believe job.

'No, scholarship interview.'

'Schaalership!' She was pleased, education meant a lot to her I could see, 'So you must also be a clever girl, anh?'

Clever? Would I have been on this train if there had been less cleverness and more honesty involved? I knew she had meant to be complimentary, and thought about telling her that I wasn't really *clever*, but had achieved quite a lot merely through a combination of boredom and determination – a BA by the former and an MA by the latter.

There was a temporary pause as a bottle of lime pickle was fished out of her woven plastic bag that seemed to be overflowing with food. I shook my head in response to this new offering. She helped herself to another poori, of which she seemed to have a tiffin carrier full, and covered it liberally with potato. On top of this she placed a piece of pickled lime and deftly folded the whole thing up into a neat little tube. Once again she looked at me, moving her head rapidly up and down and puckering her lips in an earnest attempt to press another poori on me. As I demurred, she popped the whole thing into her mouth and chewed contentedly.

'What subject schalership?' I thought we had left the subject behind two towns and a village ago, and was startled.

'Er . . . Education,' and then, remembering the daughter-in-law's MEd., added, 'Special Education.'

'Special Education? What is that?'

'The education of children with learning disabilities . . . mentally handicapped children.'

'Aahh, I know, mental handicapped. I have seen, my neighbour's boy in Vijaywada, five he must be, but he can't talk and he walks funny, like this,' she pushed her knees outwards and waggled her head from side to side, her tongue covered in poori paste lolling out, 'poor girl, his mother, she is always crying, "My poor boy, my poor boy, can't go to school, can't do anything."'

She t'ch t'ched sympathetically, but built herself another three-tiered poori, before closing her steel container with an air of finality.

I sat back on my seat and watched the now brown countryside roll past the window. Riya, darling, I hope you're okay. Ammumma and Big Ammumma will take you to lots of nice places, the temple and the beach. You might even get to see an elephant if the temple festival starts while you're still there!

'So you will teach children like that. Verrry good. Special Education.' She said this slowly, Speshal Ejjucayshun, rolling it around her tongue, committing it to memory, wanting to remember to tell her daughter-in-law about it when she got to Delhi. 'Lots of money? In Special Education, you get lots of money?'

I laughed at this innocent query and said, 'No, no money at all! Lots of heartache, yes, but definitely no money!'

I knew she hadn't fully understood this but she looked at me as though I must be quite mad for being so unworldly. It was a story that would have taken up all our two and a half days on this train to narrate and so, when she asked me her next question, I decided it was best to be economical with the truth.

'Married?'

I shook my head. She smiled at me warmly; I was a young unmarried girl, I *definitely* needed looking after and this was a role she was comfortable with.

'Special Education,' she was savouring her new word, 'verry good. You *must* be very clever to get schalership. Kerala people are all very clever, very brainy,' she was tapping the side of her forehead with her forefinger, 'my daughter-in-law says there is one hundred per cent literacy in Kerala State. All the girls are brainy and educated and go to work, no?'

Yes, I'd seen them. On buses and commuter trains, looking washed out and exhausted, rushing home from work late in the evenings. To collect their children from cheap, badly run government nurseries and cook the evening meal for the family, grinding the coconut for the kootans on their kitchen stones. I had often seen Saramma, the steno who lived behind Ammumma's house in Alleppey, wash her family's clothes in a blue bucket using water from the well, usually under the light of the moon, because the corporation water stopped at eight. After that, she would fill her blue bucket again and go back indoors to clean the floor of her house, backing gracefully on to the verandah an hour later on all fours, swaying from side to side seemingly tirelessly. In the morning, she would be up again at crack of dawn, to cook breakfast and the lunches that would be packed into little tiffin carriers. Two little ones for the children, a large one to be placed in the basket of her husband's scooter and a small steel dabba for herself, small enough to slip into the handbag she carried on the bus.

She was one of the educated young women Kerala was so proud of, a gift of Communist thought and trade union ideals. Hard working, efficient and managing without any help from either government or husband. Thomachen, her husband, seemed to adore her and took his little family out every Sunday to the cinema or to eat peanuts on the beach. But he was as much a product of Kerala's paradoxical love of literacy without liberation. A kind of education churned out without the encouragement of genuine vision. Both Thomachen and Saramma were proud of the fact that she was educated and had a government job. Did it matter if, at twenty-seven, she was as thin as a rake, the stresses of her daily grind showing up only in the tiny lines around her eyes and the huge vein that lay throbbing across her forehead? She was the statistic Kerala was so inordinately proud of: 'Same stats as in *developed* countries,' they said.

I nodded at my travelling companion, 'The last census showed a hundred per cent literacy, but I've heard that they measure that by the ability to sign one's own name. I'm not sure that's a very fair system, are you?'

We'd travelled off the subject of Me, fortunately, as the train rattled and swayed through the Andhra night. An hour later the ticket inspector came around to say that it was advisable that the Ladies' Compartment locked itself up for the night. With a flurry of last-minute trips to the toilet, pulling down of berths, puffing up of air pillows and smoothing out of blankets, we turned in. Everyone looked at me as the choice for the upper berth came up. It seemed fair as I was the only 'unmarried' woman and, therefore, presumably more agile and in possession of more energy than my married sisters. I pulled down the little metal steps to climb up to my cosy third-floor berth for the night and used the rough red Indian Railways standard issue blanket to cut out the eerie blue of the night-light above my head. The train rocked me comfortably, like a mother trying to put her baby to sleep. I was enjoying every minute of my freedom. There had even been distinct pleasure in believing my own story to my fellow-travellers, Unmarried and in Charge of my Future. It didn't feel at all as though the train was bound to its earthly tracks. It could, for the way I was feeling, be soaring through the night sky, overtaking even the stars.

*　　*　　*

New Delhi railway station was as I'd remembered it, noisy, chaotic and crowded. Temporarily disconcerted by the sound of Hindi issuing from everyone's lips, I helped my portly companion unload her luggage from the Ladies' Compartment and then picked what I hoped were the two most honest faces from the crowd of porters clamouring around us. Having made sure the right pieces of luggage were assigned to the right porter, we wended our way down Platform Nine and over the footbridge, picking our way slowly towards the main entrance, avoiding dogs, cows, beggars, touts and harassed passengers. A procession of two ladies feeling slightly overwhelmed by Delhi, followed by a porter carrying one medium-sized suitcase and another almost invisible under two suitcases, one large sling-bag, a pillow and a plastic wicker bag, now fortunately depleted of most of its stock.

Before we got to the main entrance, a pleasant faced young man rushed up to us, shouting a fervent 'Amma!' My travelling companion dropped my arm and responded with a loud, happy 'Ramesha!' followed by a delighted stream of Telegu. She kept up the flow of Telegu while Ramesha touched her feet, gave instructions to the porter and took her arm, 'Come on, Amma, Usha is waiting eagerly with your favourite poories for breakfast.' It was clear that she would prefer to deliver me personally into Raghu

174

Uncle's hands before leaving, but her son, more used to Delhi ways, agreed that I was perfectly safe where I was. Making sure three times over that I would be all right and still looking uncertain of my assurances that Raghu Uncle would definitely arrive soon, she went off with her son and was soon swallowed up by the crowd. A warm lady with a good heart, and the only person I knew in the world who thought I was an unmarried girl . . . and clever!

I paid my porter who seemed distinctly annoyed that he had received so much less than his colleague would no doubt get. His vested interest was obviously in the benefits of *not* travelling light, passengers like me were a disgrace. It was a one-sided argument as I was still feeling a little unsure of my rusty Hindi. I felt sorry but avoided eye contact in the expert way of all well-off Indians who have to deal with grinding poverty on a daily basis. I continued to scan the crowd for Raghu Uncle. Aha, there he was! I'd last seen him four years ago at his daughter's wedding in Guruvayur but could have spotted his shiny bald pate from a mile away. He was hurrying towards me through the crowd and shouted over the din, 'Sorry, moley! You haven't been waiting long, have you?'

'How nice to see you again, Uncle,' I said, giving him a hug. Raghu Uncle was one of my mother's large brood of first cousins, a warm, noisy part of the family that didn't seem to mind taking two hours out of a day to pick each other up from railway stations and perform other such favours.

'Good journey? You must be dying for a bath and some decent food after all that train rubbish.' We walked past tongas and tempos, getting finally to Raghu Uncle's battered Fiat that had been blocked in by a shiny, brand-new Ambassador car. As Raghu Uncle expostulated in not-very-good Hindi with the nonchalant driver of the offending vehicle, I took in deep breaths of that smell so peculiar to Delhi in the winter months. Smoke from bonfires and roasting peanuts, caramelized sugar used for making sesame and peanut brittle, winter apples and diesel fumes. I'd missed this city more than I'd allowed myself to admit all these years. Seven years ... no, more like six ... it felt like a lifetime since I'd been here last ... was this my city of hope? I remembered coming here to have Riya, filled with hope then of the new beginnings she would bring. Now I was here again, with renewed hopes of new beginnings for both of us.

'Come on, moley, let's go now. Bloody damned rascals all these Punjabis with their big businesses and new cars and bloody damned arrogant drivers!'

I put my bag on the back seat and climbed hurriedly into the car next to Raghu Uncle. The driver of the Ambassador, who had grudgingly moved his car, put his lips together miming a dramatic kiss in my direction as we lurched off, spluttering angrily. 'Same old crowded city and messy roads, eh Uncle?'

'Oh it's terrible, I tell you, it gets worse every year. But the worst are these Punjabis, pushy and arrogant. They just don't care about anyone else.'

I smiled at Raghu Uncle's special brand of Indian racism that we were quick to forgive ourselves for, telling each other that it was really semi-affectionate. It was certainly not vicious, but based on as many unkind stereotypical notions as its version in the western world. I couldn't tell if Raghu Uncle was using 'Punjabi' in the generic sense favoured by most South Indians of everyone-who-was-cursed-with-North-Indian-roots or whether he actually meant the people who had found themselves on the wrong side during Partition and migrated to Delhi in droves in 1947. I'd discovered from friends at school that most of these people had fled their homes and arrived in newly independent India with virtually nothing to their names.

But, within years, the immigrants' drive to succeed had seen innumerable new businesses flourish. Pushiness was bound to have contributed to that success, but it was nevertheless a quality that was anathema to the average South Indian. Cushioned from the cruelties of Partition by the good fortune of their geography, the South Indian was decidedly more mild-mannered and orthodox by comparison. The North, in turn, had its own stereotypical notion of the 'Southy.' In school I had been asked accusingly why I was not small, black and wiry-haired, with brain cells that overflowed. And whether my family had a strange predilection for eating their rice and sambar in large, messy balls that they threw into the air and caught in their mouths, sambar dripping off their elbows all the time. It was an image I had considered my sacred duty to fight bitterly through my school years, usually as the only 'Madrasi' in class facing a full battalion of 'Punjabis'. More gallingly, because I talked and dressed and behaved like everyone else did, I was often complimented on how like a North Indian I was. 'It's because she was born here, you see. See even her skin is so fair,' was one of the theories propounded by a friend's mother who had been amazed she could not squeeze me into her preconception of a 'Madrasi'.

Centuries of caste, language and religious barriers had validated our prejudices. And had been ultimately responsible for my family's hopes that I could be successfully uprooted and replanted miles away in Kerala, among my own people. The belief had been genuine that I was bound to thrive better there than in this alien place with its strange pushy ways. The problem was, I suppose, that Delhi wasn't really as alien to me as it had felt to my parents. If I belonged anywhere at all, this was the place that came closest to it. I was born here and grew up here and had fought (and won) many Southy-Northy battles in these playgrounds and classrooms. I knew how to survive Delhi and would have survived a 'Punjabi' education and lifestyle; and even *marriage*, who knows? Survival was one thing halfway-children *were* good at, hopping effortlessly back and forth between their different identities. Never quite belonging anywhere.

We were driving down Rajpath now, my favourite part of the city, where the traffic thinned out on sweeping boulevards and Rashtrapathi Bhavan rose majestically on the skyline. 'I do love this part of Delhi, Uncle, we used to come here for ice-creams which we'd eat sitting on the maidans.'

'Yes, you must have lots of memories of this city. Your dear father, we were so fond of him, Shobha and I, did he bring you here for ice-cream then?'

'Yes,' I said, looking out at the expanse of green still flanked by the odd ice-cream cart. He did, when I was little, with my mother all dressed up and looking pretty no doubt. In the days when they could only afford a scooter and I used to be tucked safe and warm and full of ice-cream in between them.

And then later, I came with Arjun too, whenever we could sneak away. From maths tuition or drama practice. We often sat near that stretch of water over there, ice-cream dripping through the bottoms of our cones if we talked faster than we ate. He was my first love, Raghu Uncle, my only love, and I could talk to him for hours on end and I loved him very, very much.

I looked at the profile of my uncle that was vaguely reminiscent of my mother. Even after so many years, it was not the kind of thing I could say without shocking or upsetting him. These were all the people who were so keen to believe that I was happily married into an excellent family. As far as they could see, I'd done better than all my cousins, if things were measured in terms of houses and jewellery and Ambassador cars. There was no point in trying to explain any of it and there was nothing, absolutely nothing, that any of them could do anyway to help.

My interview was to be the following morning at India International Centre. Shobha Aunty was very sure that Connaught Place would simply tire me out, and insisted that shopping and everything else could wait until after the interview. Feeling quite pleased merely to be breathing the polluted Delhi air again, I had no argument with that and agreed that a hot bath was in perfect order. In the bathroom, I surveyed the deadly looking tiny Racold geyser and decided it was safer to ask Shobha Aunty to remind me how to use it without killing myself. It was funny how many things one could forget when they weren't needed. After a wonderful warm bath (of the sort never required in Kerala where the temperature was only ever either hot or hotter), I went for a leisurely walk around Malviya Nagar market with Shobha Aunty, coming back with a velvet horse with gold trimmings and squinty button eyes for Riya. As we watched television in the evening, I strained to understand the announcers, wondering again at how quickly my Hindi had gone rusty. When had Delhi slipped quietly out of me, leaving me more a Kerala girl than ever before?

The day ended with a satisfyingly Delhi dinner of daal and methi-aloo but I had started to feel the butterflies begin their dance in my stomach in anticipation of the following day's interview. I could not eat very much, despite Shobha Aunty's affectionate ministrations, and asked to go early to bed. I curled up under the Rajasthani quilt on which caparisoned elephants marched and peacocks gaily strutted. There was a cosy feel of childhood warmth as I snuggled under the quilt that smelt of the neem leaves Ma used to put in with our quilts every spring. But sleep took a long time to come. The night sounds here were of cars and dogs, unlike the chirruping Kerala crickets I had grown used to.

TWELVE

I was up early, and jumped in shock at the unexpectedness of the cold mosaic floor underfoot. Goodness, I was in Delhi! Shobha Aunty's tiny guest room was beautifully decorated with little odds and ends collected on her annual trips to Kerala. A tiny carved elephant with ivory tusks nestled under a potted plant and a large brass para, probably once used in Shobha Aunty's maternal homestead for measuring rice grains, was holding copies of *Filmfare* and *The Times Of India*. I got out of bed in sudden consternation, remembering that I needed to take instructions for getting to India International Centre from Raghu Uncle before he left for work. Delhi had changed a lot since I was last here and I wasn't going to let some scooty man swindle me.

Raghu Uncle was eating hot idlis with coconut chutney when I went into the kitchen. He laughed when he saw me. 'What's this, just like a little Kerala ammumma, all wrapped up in socks and a shawl! A few years in Kerala haven't made you forget how to enjoy a little cold, have they?'

'No, no, don't listen to him, moley, you wrap up nice and warm. Don't want you catching cold before your interview.'

Shobha Aunty was full of motherly concern and curiosity. She'd questioned me quite closely the previous evening as we walked back from the market about the scholarship and the course. I knew she was fond of me, but I wondered if that would evaporate very rapidly if I told her that my plans included leaving my husband. She had just about been able to understand that I wanted to take Riya abroad, and gave me a sympathetic hug when I described the ten different diagnoses doctors had offered. But I could see she was puzzled at my apparent nonchalance at leaving Suresh behind, cheering herself up by remarking, 'I suppose he can always come and join you while you're there, so you can have a holiday together.'

Now she was urging a plateful of idlis on me. I ate a tiny breakfast, as the butterfly dance had re-started in my stomach, and escaped soon for a shower.

By eight-thirty I was ready and hopping from foot to foot in my impatience to get going. Shobha Aunty made me turn slowly around, seeming to examine every inch of me, before nodding approvingly. I'd taken her advice of looking as 'Punjabi' as possible because, as she explained it, 'You don't want them thinking, some Southy kutty's come along trying to take away the scholarship that can go to my sister's nephew's daughter.' I laughed and told her it sounded like a Parsee Trust and thought for one wild moment that she would put me into an embroidered sari with the pallav worn back to front in the Parsee style.

But she obviously approved of the ensemble I'd taken hours choosing back in Kerala – a cream salwaar kameez with the barest minimum of embroidery around the neck in yellow and purple. I knew the colours looked good on me as I wrapped the purple scarf around my neck and wore Shobha Aunty's best cashmere jumper over it. A tiny bit of make-up at her insistence and I was off.

There were about ten others in the foyer of India International Centre, all looking nervous and a little green around the gills. A couple of engineering graduates from Pilani, three medical students from Lady Harding College, an archaeologist, a lawyer specializing in human rights and two social work graduates from the Tata Institute in Bombay. An earnest looking bunch, certainly. How much were they depending on this scholarship to change their lives? Suddenly I was painfully aware that my reasons for being here were not completely altruistic, and I could feel a deep pang of shame swirl its way through my butterfly dance. I still wanted the scholarship, though.

I was the first person to be called in. The room was pleasant and sunny and my interviewers were two distinguished elderly gentlemen and Mrs Rustomji, who had written their initial letter to me. I found myself warming to them as they asked me about my long journey up to Delhi and then many questions about Riya and my experience of teaching at her school. I could see they were impressed with my having completed both a BA and an MA despite marriage and Riya. Feeling as fondly of them as I was by now, I toyed with the idea of confessing how both had been achieved with an easy combination of boredom and cussedness, and then thought the better of it.

At the end of the interview, they asked if I could either wait or return to the Centre by 5 p.m., by which time they would be ready with their decision. I rejoined the others outside, all of them eager to know how it had gone. Not wishing to give too much away to what was essentially the Opposition, I said I had something else to do and hastily left the Centre.

For a few minutes, I stood outside the Centre feeling completely lost and watching the traffic go whizzing past. Call Shobha Aunty! I suddenly remembered she was half expecting me for lunch; I had to tell her I could only get back after five now. It looked like I would have to go back into the centre and ask to use a telephone. Ducking past the small group of scholarship hopefuls who were gathered forlornly at the other end of the foyer, I found an elderly usher who pointed me in the direction of a telephone.

'Shobha Aunty, I've had my interview, but I'll only know their decision at five this evening! . . . Yes, I think it went well . . . No, I don't think I'll come back for that time, I'll be spending all my time getting there and back . . . Took me an hour this morning, isn't it a good thing I left early? . . . I think I'll go to Connaught Place and look around the shops . . . Don't worry about lunch, I'll get myself something . . . I might even try to look up some old friends if I can trace them . . . I'll give you a call from somewhere in the middle of the day, shall I? . . . Oh, I'll certainly call you when I know their decision, especially if it's good news! . . . Yes, yes, I think it went well, but you can't be too sure, can you? . . . Wish me luck!'

Look up some old friends? I'd thought about it back in Kerala, but had felt struck with sudden diffidence. What if no one remembered me, that would be awful! Now I felt tempted again . . . but did I have any telephone numbers? There were some old ones in my diary but they could have all changed . . . everyone could have left Delhi, for all I knew . . . I ran my eye down a list that was at least six years old . . . Leena, Anju, Renu . . . I'll try Leena. The last time I'd met her was when Riya was a baby, she was studying for something at JNU. More recently, I'd had a wedding card, she was marrying some Rahul Batra, but she hadn't replied to the letter I'd written congratulating her.

'Hello, is this Leena Kapoor's . . . sorry Leena Batra's telephone number? . . . I'm an old friend of hers from school . . . Janaki . . . Is that Leena's *mum*! Oh, hello, aunty, how nice to speak to you again! I hope you remember me! . . . Just for a few days . . . Yes, I know she's married, I had a card last year, but I didn't have any other contact number . . . She's what, she's had a *baby*! Goodness, I can't imagine Leena as a mum somehow! . . . Where? Oh yes, I know where that is, that's quite near where I am now, so I might go and see her today . . . I'll take her number off you . . .'

Leena screeched for about five minutes on hearing my voice, reducing me to the kind of giggles that effortlessly turned the hands of the clock inside my head to a long-ago

183

past. I quickly explained what I was doing in Delhi and demanded to see her baby.

'I have exactly two hours, and I'm coming right now! . . . Yes, I'm alone, I've left Riya and Suresh back in Kerala . . . No, I can't stay for lunch, I have some shopping to do . . . I just want to see you and your baby.'

Feeling suddenly very jaunty, I hailed an auto rickshaw and asked for Khan Market. I knew I could buy something for Leena's new-born from there . . . Leena a mum! Mad, bad old Leena with her swishing rolled-up skirt, the scourge of Sister Seraphia's life! Emerging as quickly as I could from the shops, I ran for another auto rickshaw, arms full of baby clothes and a fluffy yellow duck.

Golf Links was as redolent with the air of old money as I remembered. I looked at the large mansions that were rolling past, all of them guarded by tall gates and bored security men. Had Leena married some old money-bags then? The scooty pulled up outside a tall yellow building, this seemed to be it . . . I paid off the scootywallah and made my way to a side entrance, as Leena had instructed.

I could hear a distant bong as I pushed the door-bell and soon heard the rush of footsteps down some stairs, before the door was hurled open.

'Jans! Sweetie! Oh my *God*, look at you!'

'Oh Leena, it's so wonderful to see you again . . .'

We stood rocking each other for a few minutes and the thought occurred to me that I had probably never seen Leena struck by speechlessness before. In a few minutes, though, she had regained the old familiar garrulousness that had always left me feeling faintly breathless. Pulling me indoors, she slammed the door behind us and then stood back to get another look at me.

'How *do* you bloody manage to look *younger* every time I see you, eh? Quick, give me a few tips. Just look at what one goddamn pregnancy has done to my hips, yaar!'

She patted her hand on her derrière and I could see that it had certainly grown a few inches since our schooldays. I hugged her again, 'It comes from contentment, I believe. Is your Rahul Batra looking after you well then?'

'Don't ask, yaar, he's an absolute poppet and I'm madly in love with him, even after nearly two years of marriage and I'm sure you'll love him too.'

Recalling that this was what Leena had always said as a preamble to introducing me to the current love of her life, I wondered if I should take it with a pinch of salt. But now she was married and even I couldn't be cynical at a time like this.

'I'd love to meet him. Is he here?'

'No, yaar, he'll be back for lunch probably. There is someone else here, though, who's looking forward to seeing you again. You'll never guess who . . . Arjun Mehta! Flown in on special order from ye olde Englande. Gosh, I'd nearly forgotten about him for a minute in my excitement at seeing you! Come on upstairs, that's where my flat is.'

Arjun.

After all these years.

I'd dreamt of this moment somewhere before, some moist, yearning Kerala night . . .

'Wait, *wait*, Leena!' She was already halfway up the stairs. I ran after her and hissed, 'What do you mean, *Arjun's* here? Why didn't you tell me? I can't see him again!'

'Don't be stupid, yaar, it's no big deal. He arrived literally ten minutes before you called and, when you called, he asked if he could stay to meet you. That's it. Obviously, I said yes. What's wrong?'

'I can't . . . why didn't you *tell* me?'

'Well, I could say because I didn't want to *frighten* you off. But that's not true. I just wanted to surprise you, you silly goose. What are you so scared of anyway? He's just an old boyfriend . . . I know you live in Kerala, but there's no need to be such a prude. Now, come on!!'

It *was* a big deal, Leena. You don't understand. I loved him once and I never loved another and, girlishly foolishly stupidly, I still thought of him everyday. Everyday. For about nine goddamned years. I couldn't sit in front of him now and make *small talk*, could I? Suddenly I felt close to tears.

Leena pulled me up the stairs, still chattering nineteen to the dozen. My own mouth had seized up completely and my feet felt like lead. What was wrong? This had been my favourite dream. That I'd bump into Arjun again somewhere in the world. And this time, as adults, we would be cool and sophisticated and be able to talk calmly about the past. I'd dreamt of this so often, I should have known the routine. A fuzzy, dizzy *déjà vu*, ten times over. We were in a bright living room, a figure, tall and blurred, was getting up from a chair and walking towards me. I heard a low chuckle and a soft, 'Hello Janu . . .'

'Hello, Arjun,' I heard myself say, in a voice barely audible to my own ears.

'All right?' There was a British lilt in that familiar old voice. And something like amusement.

I nodded and sank on to a sofa. I'd wondered, often, what it would be like when it did happen. I knew it would, one day. Of that, there'd been no doubt, although the place and the circumstances had always been obscure. Once – just once – in Valapadu, from the back seat of the car, I'd spotted a head in the crowds . . . taller than most of the others in the street . . . brown curls shining in the sun . . . and had swung my head around to get a look at the face, through the rear window. And had seen blue eyes and an Anglo Saxon nose. Startled and cringing at the unfamiliarity of the features, I'd turned away then, foolishly disappointed that it hadn't been Arjun. But now here he was. I ought to be pleased now that it had happened, and not in Valapadu but here, here in my city of hope. I'd dreamt about meeting Arjun again somewhere, in some distant time, often enough to *make* it happen. So it was my own fault I was sitting here like this, trapped in Leena's sitting room and trapped in my own feelings, on a sofa next to Arjun, with my hands in his.

With my hands in his! That wasn't right! I pulled them hastily away and then looked at his face. I didn't want to hurt him, but he smiled. His smile was still white and crooked, but his eyes crinkled now when he smiled! Little creases appearing on either side of those greeny-grey eyes. Those were the same, and still had, oh God, the same effect on me. I could feel a hand squeeze something inside me, robbing me in one instant of breath, thought and speech. Through a long tunnel I could hear Leena's voice asking me if I'd like a drink . . .

'Yes, yes please . . .'

But now Arjun was speaking to me again. 'Janu, you don't mind me being here, do you? When Leena said you were coming, I had to stay and see how you were. I'll go, if you like . . .'

'No!' I could hear the urgency in my own voice and said more softly, 'No, don't go. It's great to see you again too. You don't live in India now, do you?'

'Nope, my mother returned here two years ago, but I'm still in England, I'm afraid. I arrived here last week on a month's vacation. The folks had a wedding to attend in Agra today, so I thought I'd catch up on my calls. When Leena said she'd had a baby I thought, this I've just got to see! But *this*, seeing you here like this was most unexpected . . . and the nicest surprise really.'

Leena's baby! I'd forgotten!

I turned to Leena who was coming back into the room with a fresh-lime soda.

'Leena, where's the baby!?'

'I thought you'd never ask! She's in her crib, come on in . . .'

I picked up the bag of baby clothes and the stuffed duck that had been dropped ignominiously to the floor and followed Leena into a bedroom. I could feel Arjun's presence behind me and felt another rush of disbelief and pleasure at the strange familiarity of the situation. It was getting hard to separate out the *déjà vu* and old promises from the real memories and the hundreds of times I'd lain in my lonely bed, listening to the Kerala crickets, wondering if Arjun ever remembered me . . .

Leena's baby was lying on her back, staring with unseeing eyes around her. A tiny new life, carrying so much joy and sorrow from so many other lives. Who was she, who had she been? Somewhere someone was sitting and working it all out no doubt. Momentous things couldn't just happen at random, could they? I put the gifts down and picked her up gently.

'Oh Leens, she's like you! Hello, gorgeous, are you like your mum, do you think?'

'God, I hope not. Couldn't *bear* the thought of a daughter like me! The first thing I wanted to check was that she *didn't* have a libido like mine!'

We laughed at the memory of Leena's Libido and I could feel the years roll away. Were we young again? Could we dream again? Could it be that time had simply frozen over and we were now exactly where we'd been many years ago? In another house that belonged to Leena. On a sofa, where two young lovers had failed to say goodbye properly.

Time spun itself out with a sense of unreality. Winter sunshine was pouring into Leena's living room, turning all the little objects into shiny luminous things from another world. Leena was demanding to know about my life: 'Your letters never told me anything important, yaar,' she said. I thought about all the important things . . . my having failed to find love again . . . Riya's disability . . . aware that Arjun's eyes were fixed carefully on my face. I looked into my glass where ice-cubes tinkled happily, and laughed off her question, today wasn't the sort of day to bring all that up . . . But, from across the sofa, I could feel Arjun's sympathy . . . had I imagined it? Leena wouldn't repeat her question and, through the rest of the morning, our voices floated around the room, shimmering off the walls and ceiling. Suddenly it didn't matter whether we were speaking in past or present tense. We were three old friends just finished with school and about to embark on brilliant futures. Nothing else had ever happened and nothing could take it away from us this time. I wanted to bask in this warm, dreaming, golden day for ever.

That was how I left Leena's house with Arjun two hours later. I wondered afterwards whether she had guessed, but all I said was that I had to get back to the Centre and Arjun offered to give me a lift on his way home. We walked out, Arjun and I, into one of those pale molten afternoons when nothing can seem to go wrong. As if the dappled bits of sunshine filtering through the trees were rare precious blessings from some playful Goddess above.

I got into Arjun's car and we drove without speaking very much. We'd learnt, a long time ago, to read each other's thoughts and did not now need the artifice of words. I knew we were headed in the direction of his home. I'd been there just twice but had later travelled that road so many times in my head, the landmarks were floating past like familiar old faces, the shiny purple dome of Nizammuddin mosque, the nearby crematorium where people mourned their burning loved ones, Defence Colony flyover . . .

At his house, we went straight upstairs to his room. We'd played a riotous game of cards . . . with Leena and Jai and Arjun's brother the last time I was here . . . I could hear old echoes of young laughter bounce softly off the walls. Arjun leaned on the door, and it shut with a click behind him. I walked into his arms and, as he wrapped them around me, I knew a long, long journey had come to an end. I was home again, safe and dry. A gentle breeze stirred inside me, blowing away millions of cobwebs . . . those fine cobwebbed chains that had grown over unwanted dreamed-up desires, shackling them, I'd thought, for ever. I could feel that Goddess's breath blow gently down again, lifting me into her golden air, so full of promise. I succumbed wholly and entirely to Arjun and to my own being, without the slightest feeling of fear or shame . . .

Shobha Aunty's cashmere jumper fell to the floor and, as I raised my arms for Arjun to pull my kameez off, I knew he was about to see my body for the first time. Later, many days later, I would wonder at my lack of self-consciousness in the all-revealing afternoon sunlight. But at that moment, the touch of Arjun's hands on my body and the feel of his skin on mine, seemed the most natural thing in the world. Our kisses were slow and deep like the swelling depths of the high seas. Pulling us down, on to his bed, like the treacherous currents so revered by fishermen in the monsoon months. Our bodies fused effortlessly together, sunshine on sand, the rain on the sea, so wholly one it was hard to tell where one ended and the other began. Our hands and mouths reached hungrily for each other, in grateful acknowledgement to whoever had created this brilliant afternoon, finally, from my dreams. Our lovemaking was as urgent and compelling as the relentless breakers I'd watched so often on wet Kerala beaches and, when the storm had passed, our caresses were as gentle as the waters returning to the sea.

I lay with my head on Arjun's arm for a long time afterwards, and we talked of Kerala and England and the events and years that had separated us. I could feel his fingers play with my unloosed hair and heard no trace of blame in his voice as he recounted his own heartbreak. My letter had arrived on a wet Hull morning and he had spotted the familiar blue Indian aerogramme as he raced down the stairs of Nicholson Block, taking them two at a time. As usual, he'd put it away carefully in his pocket, unopened and unread, saving it for later.

'Did you always do that?'

'I had to devise different ways of coping with those first few months in England. I missed you terribly and I missed home and letters had started taking on an eerie importance. You were to be my most prolific correspondent as well! Yes, I always put your letters in my shirt pocket, where I could feel them all through the day and all through those boring lectures. And I'd allow myself to read them only when I'd returned to my room at night, because I wasn't going to get any telephone calls then like the other lads did from their girlfriends. That day I went to see a cricket match in Birmingham with your letter in my pocket. All the way to Edgbaston and back, without realizing what horrors it held in store for me.'

'And then, when you'd read it?'

'I was shattered. Shattered with the suddenness of it more than anything else, I suppose. And I was angry. And *so* lonely, suddenly. It was a Saturday, there was hardly anyone around, just some of the international students.'

'Were you angry with me?'

'Well, with you to begin with. I had to go out and run around the football ground for some hours to try and get it out of my system. Not the kind of thing I'd normally choose to do on a wet English night, I can tell you!'

'You didn't think I did it out of choice, did you?'

'I didn't know what to think, Janu, I was so hurt and confused. I nearly jumped on a plane to come back to India! I suppose I did rationalize it later, and guess that it was probably as hard for you as it was for me. I spent a lot of that winter moping around Mum's hospital quarters. Thank goodness she was around, or I don't know if I'd have coped really.'

But it sounded like Arjun had coped, better than I had. It was amazing to think he was here, next to me (without, fortunately, an English wife and her pot of tea). It was amazing also that he too remembered with tenderness our long-ago teenage love. But, after the arrival of my blue aerogramme on that wet Hull morning, it sounded like he had dusted himself down and got on with the rest of his life. I was annoyed that I felt a pang at that.

'Did you make lots of friends at Hull University?'

'Hundreds, that was the best thing about Uni. Language was a bit of a problem at first. It was weird, there we all were, speaking English and unable to understand much of what the other was saying! Accents took a while to work out, Geordie especially. I once had to ask this bloke to *write down* what he was trying to tell me, imagine that! But, after a few beers, everything takes on an incredible clarity, I can tell you!'

I laughed, 'You hated beer back then!'

'Ah, but sustained effort yields fine results. Did I tell you, in my final year I was given the coveted title of Ayatollah Martini of Kingdom Nicholblokia for downing a pint in under eight seconds.'

I laughed again, but took a deep breath before asking him my next question. 'And girlfriends?'

'Alas, none through university, broken-hearted and shattered as you left me . . .'

I knew he was joking but it was music to my ears. 'You're not telling me you haven't had a girlfriend in all these years!'

'Girlfriends . . . let's see now . . . at last count it was . . . maybe fifty-four . . . or was it fifty-three? . . . Yes that's it, I remember now, *exactly* fifty-three. Fifty-three girlfriends to date.'

It was his turn to laugh now at the incredulous expression on my face. 'If you must know, I've had two relationships, neither terribly serious. Three, if you count the last one which fizzled out last year after just four months, so you can't count that.'

I was still looking expectantly at him. 'Oh, you want the gory details do you?' he continued with an air of mock weariness. 'I'd just finished Uni and had been recruited by a firm of Chartered Accountants in a place called Milton Keynes. Hazel, secretary at the firm, made a beeline for me, couldn't resist this fine body you see . . .'

'Was she pretty?'

'Pretty? Pretty big tits, I must say . . . ouch! . . . Well, things went chugging along nicely for a while, until she discovered that I still carried your picture around in my wallet. That didn't go down very well, I can tell you!'

'Couldn't you explain to her who I was?'

'I certainly tried! I think she believed the picture was of the girl my parents had lined up for me back in some village in India. Don't think she fancied the thought of playing second fiddle to some paan-chewing village wench from Ludhiana, smelling of cow-dung and haystacks. Nothing would convince her that the picture was really of a gorgeous urban babe who'd dumped me years ago to marry some flash businessman!'

I kicked him again at the inaccuracy of this description and he laughed as he leaned out of bed to rummage around among his clothes. Pulling something out of his wallet, he turned back to me.

'Here, take a look at this . . .'

It was the picture Leena had taken of us on the day Arjun had left for England. Cracked and faded from having lived so long in a wallet, the faces were now barely discernible.

The faces of two strangers, so terribly young and hopeful I could feel my heart ache. I flipped it over, remembering that I'd written something across the back before posting it to England. I read the words under my breath: 'Someday we'll meet beyond the sea and never again I'll go sailing alone.' Suddenly I was tearful and overwhelmed once more at the care with which he had cherished the memory. But our conversation had been light-hearted up to this point and I tried to think of some wry remark. I looked up to find Arjun looking at me, his head propped up on his arm. His face was serious now and he seemed to take a deep breath before speaking slowly.

'That could still happen, couldn't it?'

'What?'

'You don't think I'm going back without you, do you? Having just swum the high seas to find you.'

He was only half joking. He actually believed we could pull it off this time! Could we? *Could* we? Guruvayurappa, give me strength! Please, this time let me breathe the word 'Yes'! And why was I invoking the God in whose sacred presence I had been married to Suresh . . . in whose presence Riya had been fed her first mouthful of rice? Did I think *He* was going to understand!

'Arjun . . .' I could hear the tremor in my voice and I could feel waves of despair crash over me again . . . 'what about Riya, my daughter . . . my marriage, I mean I can't pretend I'm not married, can I? My mother, she'd kill her-self . . .'

The expression on his face was grim. There were no storms raging in those eyes now and the crinkles had all gone. I was sticking another little knife into him, this time more effectively, face to face, rather than in a cheap blue aerogramme.

'Arjun, what exactly are you suggesting?'

'I'm telling you not to go back to Kerala tomorrow. Stay

194

here with me, my parents will not mind. I'll get you a visa for England . . .'

'Not go back . . . at all? Arjun, you're forgetting . . . I can't abandon Riya . . .'

'Bring her, send for her, we'll take her with us.'

'But I'm still married . . .'

'So *what*! We'll live together. As long as Riya's with us, you don't really need anything else do you?'

'There must be some laws against people doing that kind of thing, Arjun . . .'

'Who cares! All I want is never to lose you again.'

'Arjun, Arjun listen to me! You've forgotten, I'm so close to getting out anyway. The course and the scholarship! I think it's best if I return to Kerala now and aim to leave for my course as planned. *And*, I could try to get to the University of *London* instead of Arizona! They've offered me admission too, remember? Then at least we'll be near each other. And you'll get the chance to see Riya as well. I can't assume you'll be able to cope with her, she can be extremely hard work, Arjun. What do you think? Please, please, it's more likely to work than anything else . . .'

He was still unhappy, I could see. He was sitting up now and running his hands through his hair in frustration and anger. His voice was filled with sorrow.

'I lost you once. And I wondered *so* often if you might have been able to resist your family's pressure to get married if only I'd been in India. With what confidence can I leave you behind again? How do I know the whole horrible sequence won't happen again? What if they don't let you leave?'

'They can't stop me now. Just another few months, Arjun. Wait for me, please. I'll be there in September, I promise.'

I pulled him down again and laid my body over his, holding him as tightly as I could to cancel out the years of pain. My hair fell in a curtain around our faces, as though making a feeble attempt at guarding us against everything, even God's wrath. I used my fingers to hold his head captive as I brought my face down to cover his face with kisses. Again and again we kissed and made love, and I wondered how I'd denied myself such sweetness before. If I had known such sweetness and bliss, would I have ever been able to give it up? Would I have ever been able to put the love of my parents, my own reputation and the honour of old illustrious families before a desire for more?

But today I'd fallen prey to the treacherous call of the high seas, to the howling, beseeching wails of a greedy Kadalamma, the Goddess of the oceans. I would never be free of that desire again. Today, nothing else mattered, not reputation, not a mother's love and not the honour of ancient illustrious families . . . I knew there would be a price to pay . . . perhaps tomorrow, when I'd have to board that return train to Kerala. Or, next month, when facing the tear-ravaged face of my mother. Perhaps it would happen on some dark wet night, when I would be surrounded by mad women weeping blood as they bashed nails into a tree with their heads. Or maybe even in another life . . . But today I wasn't to think of all that, today Kadalamma had me riding the highest crests of her ocean waves in a reckless dangerous game, while she stood aside and laughed her howling laugh, knowing I was so perilously close to drowning in her murky depths.

*   *   *

I returned with Arjun to the India International Centre at five that evening. It felt as though I had been away a whole lifetime and travelled through another universe to return and find that no one else had moved on at all. Ten Rip-van-Winkle scholarship-hopefuls were sitting around in the foyer in various states of exhaustion. The tension in the air was now palpable and I wondered if, in the course of an afternoon, the winning of a scholarship had taken on as much importance for the others as it had done for me.

Mrs Rustomji emerged wearing an enigmatic smile.

'The other trustees have asked me to inform you, *all* of you, that they have enjoyed meeting so many bright young people today. It is always a wonderful feeling, every year, to see that our country produces so much talent and so much hope for the future when we conduct these interviews . . .'

Oh no, what a time to deliver a *speech*, I thought to myself . . .

' . . . And every year it makes us sad that we cannot help *all* of you in your worthy endeavours. What I would like to say to those of you who do not make it this year is, *please* do not go away thinking you are not doing something useful and something worthwhile. Without *exception*, we have been impressed by all of you and would like to wish you all the best for the future. This year we have decided to award scholarships to three people. I will read out their names and would request the three of them to stay back, so that we can collect some more of their details . . . Anasuya Dutta . . . Bhaskar Lamba . . . and Janaki Maraar.'

I looked across the foyer to where Arjun was leaning against a table. His sudden smile was full of those delightful crinkles I was still getting used to. Our dream was in the process of materializing, we were going to be together for at least a year, everything else would fall into place. I was being congratulated and Mrs Rustomji was beckoning us to follow her. I threw another look at Arjun. It felt right that, with his return to my life, things were starting to work out again. As though everything that had gone wrong was somehow something to do with his absence. I forgot, of course, that very soon we would be saying goodbye again. Already the train that would take me away from him tomorrow was making its way to Delhi, thundering up the north Indian plains. Tomorrow he'd fade back into my dreams, almost as if he had never been there at all, leaning on that table across the foyer, with that new crinkly smile on his face and a very old love in his heart . . .

The scholarship would cover the course fees and make a generous contribution to living expenses. We would have to use our own funds to cover the rest or try applying for a top-up grant. As foreign students we could request permission to work and it was always a good idea to do that as it helped the breaking-in process. Yes, I could switch to the University of London if that suited me better, except I was to forward their offer of admission as soon as possible. We were to stay in touch and inform them if we had any problems getting student visas. We were to let them know if we had problems during the course. Were we to let them know if any of us fell in love again and happened to scale the heights of ecstasy? I supposed not. I was not concentrating any more. I needed to get out now and be with Arjun again.

'I knew you'd do it!' he said as we got back into the car.

'That's nice, because I certainly didn't have a clue!'

'Are they paying for everything?'

'Well, all the course fees and some help towards living expenses, but I'll have to scrape the rest together. I wonder how much the ticket and visa will cost?'

'About five hundred pounds, thirty thousand rupees? Look, don't worry about living expenses, I can take care of that.'

'You're a sweetie, but I'll have to show them I'm able to pay at this end before they give me a visa, I believe.'

'How much do you have in your account now?'

'Oh, about five hundred rupees. Enough to buy myself a sari if I should so fancy,' I laughed.

Arjun looked astounded, 'You don't say . . .' and then shook his head in disbelief as he realized it was the truth.

I was the daughter-in-law of a good family, I wasn't *sup-*

posed to worry about money. I was even a partner in their flourishing business, worth a lot of rupees. Exactly how much, I did not know, it was my job only to sign papers that were brought to me. Asking any questions would only have made me seem avaricious. Very undignified, my mother would have said. I was gradually beginning to see how a good upbringing was really a terribly unhelpful thing for a girl in Kerala. How much better if parents taught their daughters the arts of feminine wiles to keep their husbands interested, and taught them also to transform themselves into clever accountants whenever the situation demanded a quick look into the husband's bank accounts. I did not even know where Suresh kept his accounts leave alone how much money he had. The Maraars were right. All my coy pleases and thank-yous hadn't got me very far.

Arjun drove me to the main crossroads at Malviya Nagar. From here, I told him, it was a ten-minute walk to Shobha Aunty's.

'I have to get back to them before they send search parties out for me, Arjun.'

'Couldn't you come out again at night? Make up some excuse . . . I'd like you to meet my parents, they'll be back around ten tonight.'

'Arjun, my train's early tomorrow morning and I have to be up at crack of dawn for Raghu Uncle to take me there. They're going to think there's something definitely fishy going on if I ask to go out again that late. Please don't let's do anything to jeopardize anything now.'

Arjun nodded and I asked him suspiciously, 'You won't do anything silly like turn up at the railway station tomorrow, will you?'

He laughed, 'Now *that's* an idea. Watch you squirm under the benevolent gaze of your Uncle Raghu!'

He laughed again at the expression on my face and said,

more seriously, 'Janu, my love, I will not do *anything* to jeopardize our future now, I promise. I will not call, I will not write. I will vanish into your future and wait for you there, however long it takes. If you need to contact me, you know where I am, and you know where my parents are. Just don't doubt me, let me know what's happening if you can and, most of all, just make sure you *get* there.'

I slipped across the seat to put my arms around him one last time . . . would it be months or years before we saw each other again? Guruvayurappa, keep him safe! Whatever strange games you're playing, please don't let any harm come to this dear, sweet man. Tears were pouring down my face as I pulled away from Arjun. I knew bus drivers and peanut-sellers were looking curiously into the car, some of them making lascivious remarks about parting lovers. One of them burst into song as I stumbled out of the car and I could hear the leering lyrics of the latest film hit as I ran down the road. The words were ringing in my ears as I neared Shobha Aunty's gate.

> Heer Ranjha . . . the two lovers who'd swum out to
>   meet each other out of sight . . .
> perishing together on a stormy night . . .
> the world's anger represented by the water's might . . .

I wiped my face down with my scarf, readying myself to step back into my old role. Kerala's longest-running production, running for nine years, coming up to ten, the Martyring of Janu. Played to perfection for so long now, that part had *become* me. How on earth was I going to start unravelling that? At some point, people were going to find out I'd done all the things a lucky-girl-married-into-a-good-family never did. Scheme to leave her home and her husband, pluck a handicapped child away from her father!

('Did you *hear*, she even took up with some lover from her school days so that he would take her abroad?') Scheming, heartless, adulteress, these words were all waiting for me in the wings. Some would come from the most unexpected quarters, Raghu Uncle and Shobha Aunty too, but for now I was still their poor, sweet Janu ('Do you know how *well* she has taken the birth of her handicapped child, devotes her life to the child, poor thing').

'Moley! There you are, I was starting to get worried!' Shobha Aunty was lighting the evening vilakku in her front room. I folded my hands to the little figurine of Devi and pictures of Ganesha and Guruvayurappan, looking for traces of censure in their eyes. They looked peaceful, giving me their usual serene gaze and I took a breath of relief. Shobha Aunty put a dot of vibhuti on my forehead before asking me about the scholarship.

'I've got it, Shobha Aunty!' I tried not to look overjoyed as I gave her the details.

'So when do you think you'll leave?'

'September, probably, it'll be starting to get cold there, I suppose.'

'Cold? Arizona's hot all year round, isn't it?'

Faux pas number one! I'd forgotten that my destination had been America even as recently as this morning! Oh Shobha Aunty, what happened was this, you see, some playful Goddess picked up my world after I left your house this morning and shook it around. Like those kaleidoscopes with cheap bits of coloured plastic in them. Look at me, don't I look different to you? Everything has turned upside down in some mad delightful realignment and all because I've been to heaven and back in the arms of a wonderful man.

I could feel my colour rise as I said, in what I hoped was an airy fashion, 'I might actually go to England, you know . . . it's only a possibility, though . . .'

'But yesterday you were saying facilities for Riya would be better in America?'

Yesterday I didn't know England was going to become the centre of my life again. What time is it? Seven minus five and a half, must be afternoon in England now . . . 'This . . . this Trust seems to have a preference for British Universities . . .'

I made no eye contact, either with Shobha Aunty or with the pantheon of Gods that were watching me carefully from the wall. I was sure Shobha Aunty would now guess I was up to no good, or perhaps this would be one of those pieces that would fall into place during a distant conversation at another time. Something else to brand me with when the time came. ('What a bare-faced liar *she* turned out to be, eh? Going off, in *my best cashmere jumper*, to meet her *lover* with such an *innocent* face . . . can't trust anyone, I tell you!')

I said I needed a bath and locked the bathroom door with some relief. While the water was running, I looked at myself in the mirror, curious to see the face Arjun had seen today and still, miraculously, loved. The heat from the water was misting the mirror up, making my face look like an advertisement for a luxury soap, tiny laughter and pain lines that had etched themselves around my eyes over the years made invisible by the soapy mist . . . Arjun and I had missed the best years of each other's lives. Would it be possible to embark on a new one with whatever was left? Telling each other about the wonderful things we could have done together? I had taken my youth, neatly packaged it up, tied it together with a gilt bow and given it away to a stranger who hadn't even been particularly interested. And now I had to go back to him, on a train bound for Kerala, tomorrow. How tempting to just take Arjun's offer and run away from it all. I could send later for Riya, they'd never hang on to her, that's the last thing they'd want surely. I wouldn't be around to hear the sniping and the censure, it wouldn't hurt if I didn't know what they were saying. I had no other children, or siblings, whose honour I would be damaging for ever and whom nobody would therefore ever want to marry. In that sense I was free. There was only my mother, and grandmother, to think about . . .

I saw their faces replace mine in the mist of the mirror and felt my heart constrict at their stricken expressions. Could I live a happy life in far-away England, knowing that my mother and grandmother had locked themselves up in their house of sorrow for evermore? They had brought me up and done for me what every well-meaning parent would have done in arranging a marriage. They had carefully picked the best family they could find and thought they had not just done their duty, but done it well. Could I punish them for that with the sneering whispers and pitying looks that would follow them everywhere? I knew the cruelty Kerala was capable of, I was going to have to board that train and deal with it myself. With courage and honesty. That approach couldn't fail to work, could it?

*　　*　　*

The railway station was buzzing even at six in the morning. Despite my earlier plea, I half suspected Arjun would be among the milling crowds. But he wasn't. He had kept his promise . . . to vanish into my future, as he put it. Nine years ago, he had vanished into my past, quietly and without a fuss. Now I was asking him to vanish into the future. If it wasn't so sad, it could have been funny.

My return journey was to be in the relative luxury of Indian Railway's first class because I had not been able to get a berth in the Ladies' Compartment. As a child I'd taken air travel for granted, not realizing it was one of those things that would die with my father. One of the many perks that came with being a Highly Placed Official, along with excellent marriage proposals and obsequious attention at Maraar weddings. Suresh had offered to send me to Delhi by air, but I had felt obliged to save some Maraar money in return for their unexpected acquiescence towards my plans. Now I was grateful it was also going to give me the time to gather my thoughts. I had to be clear about what I wanted before Kerala was upon me in two days. Should I play it safe, sneak out and never return? Would it be better to confront the situation and ask Suresh for a divorce? Despite my desire to leave, divorce had never seemed necessary, but now things looked different, Arjun's occupation of my future had changed all that. Might Suresh and his family actually be quite relieved to see the last of Riya and me? They'd even be able to find a 'proper' Malayali girl for Suresh, the sort that Amma still seemed to hanker after in her various little digs at me. Suresh would still be extremely eligible for marriage, men never had much trouble finding a second spouse. It was only divorced women who seemed to get stuck with one-eyed widowers who had a brood of noisy children to bring up. While older women simply faded away. Into poorly lit houses that lay slumbering behind mango trees after sunset.

The train gave a warning tremor of its intentions and there was a sudden flurry of passengers jumping on and everyone else, friends, relatives, acquaintances, tea-boys, cool-drinks sellers and porters, jumping off. I leaned out of the train window to wave goodbye to Raghu Uncle who, determined to keep his word to my mother, was going to wait until I was well and truly out of sight. With a few heart-rending groans, the train started pulling slowly and reluctantly out of New Delhi railway station. 'Best of luck, moley!'

Thanks, Raghu Uncle, I did have the most wonderful luck while staying with you! All the people who'd jumped off, vendors and snack stalls were now moving along the platform faster and faster as we gathered speed, becoming a dizzy Delhi swirl. But in a few minutes, the Delhi scenes

and Delhi smells had gone . . . whizzing past my window
. . . followed by idling trains in a shunting yard . . . followed
by enormous hoardings for a sex-doctor curing everything
from 'pain to importance' . . . followed by children's brown
bottoms all shitting in a row . . . goodbye smelly, dirty
city of my childhood, where hope still lived, dear Delhi,
harbouring my love in there somewhere . . .

We were now doing a comfortable chug, and the train
took up its cheery beat, carrying me further and further into
the depths of India.

> Dear Delhi,
> I'm so sorry
> That I can't stay for tea,
>
> But, you see
> I must simply
> Reach Kerala by three
>
> I have to be
> At Alleppey
> In a temple by the sea
>
> Where really
> Quite angrily
> They're lining up for me.
>
> Some looking at me sadly
> Others with fury
> A thousand ghostly ancestors
> Waiting to punish me.

There was none of the bonhomie of the Ladies' Compartment on this return journey, and no friends to make. I had
other things to think about anyway. Stretched out on my
upper berth, closing my eyes tightly to keep the pictures
from fading away, I let my mind return again and again to

my stolen afternoon with Arjun. Every time I thought of Arjun's fingers moving gently over my body, I could feel the goosebumps leap up and something in my stomach constrict, almost painfully. I looked for traces of guilt infusing that cocktail of pleasure and pain, but couldn't find any. Not even when I thought quite consciously of Suresh and Riya. What was wrong with me? Had I been inured to guilt from the moment that I walked so calmly into Arjun's arms? Was it because that was what was meant to be, because of some promise so ancient I could not even remember it now? Had all feeling perhaps died in me when I had got married and come to life again only when Arjun touched me yesterday? You couldn't feel sorry for things you did in another life, the only expectation being that you paid for them in another. Even as I was hurtling back to it on the Kerala Express, my marriage to Suresh felt a whole lifetime away, even though technically it wasn't. I was both fooling myself and attempting the impossible in trying to return to a previous life. That was mixing up the divine order of things, nobody ever got away with *reversing* the karma wheel. But I wanted my one lifetime with Arjun now and thought I'd be able to get away with it if I offered to pay the price a hundred lifetimes over.

THIRTEEN

I could see that Kerala's thulam varsham had started, a month late, as the train traversed the green length of the state. This second monsoon was the gentler cousin of the first that hit Kerala's shores with such dramatic fury in June. Returning over the Western Ghats, these rains had lost their purpose in the mountains somewhere and cast themselves instead over the land in a sad weepy mist. The floor of the train was starting to get wet and muddy from the hundreds of pairs of chappals and shoes that were getting on at every stop. Grumbling passengers pulled up their suitcases to prevent them from getting soaked in the muddy puddles that were forming. Suitcases full of Delhi milk sweets and nylon saris from Karol Bagh for waiting near and dear ones.

Suresh was at Cochin railway station, with a strange new confusing respect in his eyes. I had got the scholarship, as he knew from the phone call Shobha Aunty had insisted I make. He must have known that the only thing that might hold me back now was gentle persuasion. It looked like I was in for some pampering.

'We're going straight to Alleppey now. I believe Riya's been fine, asking for you a lot, though. Your mother wanted to know if I could leave you in Alleppey for a couple of days to do your father's beli.'

I'd forgotten. It was my father's death anniversary tomorrow and I, as his only child, would have to perform the rituals that kept his soul at peace. I'd forgotten. Lying in the arms of a man my father had once hit me for loving, I had forgotten so easily about duty and responsibility.

In the car, I told Suresh about the interview and knew that he was listening. It felt odd, the knowledge that Suresh was actually listening, even though I knew it was only because he was still devising ways to prevent me from going. Even the questions he asked were designed to find the one loophole that would witness the collapse of my scheme. What about Riya's schooling? Wouldn't that have to be paid for? Special Schools were bound to be expensive. How would I cope with my studies and Riya? Wouldn't she miss everyone else? I looked wearily out of the car window, at houses with their dripping wet thatches and cyclists wobbling under large black umbrellas. Should I put a stop to the whole thing by asking for that divorce now? If I told him about Arjun, would we go careering into that tree over there?

I could see Riya bobbing about impatiently at Am-mumma's door as we arrived at the house in Alleppey. As I disembarked from the car she became a tiny cannon-ball that rushed straight into my stomach, nearly knock-ing me over. I laughed in delight and bent down to pick her up.

'Amma's puchkie darling! Where have you been?? Oh, you were with your Ammumma, were you? I did wonder where you'd gone! Oh my goodness, a new *dress*. Who bought you that?'

She pointed at Ma and chortled as I buried my face in her plump little body, feeling a sense of utter relief that I had not succumbed to the mad, momentary temptation of leaving India without her. She wriggled out of my arms now to twirl around showing off her new pink dress. A plump, pink, prancing flower in orthopaedic shoes, among Ammumma's lush, wet plants. Oh my darling, I cannot believe how near I came to leaving you. What sort of madness must have been possessing me? Never, never, *never* any happiness at your cost, that I promise. The skies above growled gently as though warning me that there were others who had heard my rash pledge.

We went indoors as fat raindrops started to splatter around us. Suresh said he would stay for lunch before leaving for Valapadu, returning for Riya and me in a couple of days. I felt sudden shock at the thought that I would have to sleep in my marital bed less than a week after having made love with Arjun. I could not be as brazen as that, however desperate I was to get to England now with Riya. The truth, please God, let the truth make everything work. I'd have to explain everything to Ma first, and then ask her if she could shelter me from Maraar fury in this house at Alleppey. The smell of rice and sambar wafting out of the kitchen was suddenly making my stomach turn and I could barely hear Riya's loud, tuneless rendition of 'Tee Tee Teevandi' . . . as she chugged around the dining room being a train with a deafening whistle.

I bathed away the grime from the train journey in smoky water warmed in the large copper vessel that was brought out only through the thulam varsha months. But I could only pick through my lunch, half-listening to the plans for my father's beli the next day.

'We'll ask Jose if we can hire his taxi because it will be too early for buses that go towards the beach. I've asked the elayathu to be there by six. He's going to arrange for all the things to be bought for the ceremony.' Ammumma was in charge, these were her areas of expertise.

The beli was to take place at a tiny temple overlooking the sea, renowned for its powers of invoking the spirits of the dead. Here we were going to offer cooked, unhusked rice and gingelly to the spirit of my father so that his soul could continue to rest in peace. If this was not done as a yearly ritual on the star date that he had died, the belief was that his soul would escape and wander around the earth, seeking destruction and revenge.

'Do you know, when they do seek revenge for all the wrongs done to them in their lives, they arrive, strangely at their old loved ones' doors. The elayathu once explained that was because, as spirits, they got confused and wreaked revenge on the wrong people. That's why the responsibility falls on the children to ensure the soul is kept at rest.'

'What poppycock, Amma,' Ma said dismissively, 'these are all man-made rituals created so that people remember, at least once a year, the ones they've lost. That's all. It's a good and healthy remembrance ceremony, even the western people have their memorial services. Your elayathu will tell you anything to make sure you give him plenty of opportunities to make some money. Spirits that seek revenge, I've never heard such rubbish really!'

Ammumma looked annoyed and outside the sky darkened and rumbled again.

I spent a sleepless night, trying to find the words I'd need to explain to Ma that what was left of her life was also about to fall apart. I was still tempted to hold my tongue until I actually left for England, but I had not bargained for having to go back to Valapadu and pretend as though nothing had changed at all. As though the gentle hands of a passionate lover had not travelled all over my body, exploring its every hollow and rise. With Suresh's new eagerness to please me, I knew he would probably try to spend more time with me . . . take me out . . . sleep with me . . . I could not bear the thought. Arjun was waiting for me, in that promised future somewhere. He had made no demands, extracted no pledges . . . I could not betray him. I'd have to tell Ma tomorrow, it couldn't wait another day. We'd have to speak to Suresh and prevent his coming back for me the next day. But tomorrow was my father's death anniversary, a day reserved for remembrance. Ma wanted to spend it remembering my father, not being told that her married daughter had slept with another man. The man her beloved dead husband had once caned his daughter for loving. I tossed and turned all night, listening to the incessant, despairing weeping of the rain outside.

The sea was stormy the following morning and the tiny temple looked like it might be swept away if a particularly strong wave came along. Angry breakers were thrashing against the rocks as though willing them to dislodge the grey stone temple precariously perched on top. Two Gods at War. Rain clouds had gathered over the horizon that rose and sank like the heaving chest of a grief-stricken Goddess. In the dim pre-dawn darkness, and as the distant clouds started to weep again over the sea, it was impossible to tell where one began and the other ended. Like two bodies making passionate love, like two lovers who could not bear to be parted . . .

The elayathu had laid everything out on the damp, dark floor of the temple, blackened oil lamps, joss sticks, a pan full of glutinous red rice, shiny black gingelly seeds, banana leaves. There were none of the cheerful accompaniments to a normal day out at the temple, tiny white jasmine buds, tulsi leaves, scarlet and yellow hibiscus and chrysanthemum flower chains, bananas, jaggery, coconuts . . . all God's favourite things. This God, to my fevered, sleepless mind, looked very angry, glowering out from the darkened inner sanctum, black stone decorated in blood-red sandalwood with stone holes where the eyes should have been.

As the ceremony started, I was asked my name and the name of the star that had governed my birth. These were to be chanted along with the invocations to my father's spirit and the spirits of all my ancestors, assuring them that this child of their loins, still present on earth, was there to protect and preserve their names and their spirits. Over and over, I could hear the elayathu intone Janaki . . . Revathy

. . . Janaki . . . Revathy . . . along with all his prayers and invocations. He was dinning it deep into my consciousness somewhere that, as the only child of my parents, I carried with me the collective responsibility towards my clan. They were all there, watching me now, rows and rows of ghostly ancestors, some looking at me sadly, others in anger and others in fury. Then they started to close in on me, surrounding me, crowding in on me, blocking off the light and choking me of air. Their voices were getting louder and louder, now they were screaming and howling. I couldn't make out the words except for their incessant Janaki . . . Revathy . . . Janaki . . . Revathy . . . as if reminding both themselves and me of who I was. And who I'd forgotten I was. Outside, the rain was beating down harder and harder. Lightning bolts were being hurled hissing into the boiling sea that had started to howl as if in pain. Fishermen who had gingerly ventured out that morning shouted hasty instructions to each other to return, their little catamarans rocking dangerously in the rising waters.

I could feel the damp rise up through the floor of the temple and enter my shivering body. Still I carried on, my fingers shaking so badly I could barely pick up the handfuls of rice to shape them into balls along with the gingelly seeds and place them as offerings to my ancestors. I tried to find the words to tell the elayathu that perhaps I had been a poor choice to appease my ancestors today as they were all, without exception, either sad or angry with me. They needed someone they could trust their honour with. Please, please, could somebody else do this? The wetness beneath me had become unbearable and I jumped up, suddenly unable to carry on . . . there, on the floor where I had been sitting, was a dark wet patch . . . was it . . . it couldn't be . . . blood? My sari was stained . . . great red blotches on white cotton . . . and now I could feel it dribbling down my legs. I could hear my grandmother scream through a long tunnel

. . . her screams mingling with Kadalamma's howls from the sea . . . With surprisingly strong hands she grabbed me by the arms and flung me out of the temple. I stumbled out in a daze . . . and then fell in a heap on to the sodden rocks outside.

We returned to Ammumma's house, a small band of shaken and frightened women, the memory of my father hanging over us like an angry cloud. What terrible things are going to befall us, Guruvayurappa, to have defiled a temple like that! Didn't you *know* your period was due? *It wasn't due, I don't know how that happened*. It's a terrible curse to defile a temple like that . . . Ishwara! . . . That elayathu will have to do all kinds of poojas to clean it up and restore its sanctity. Sometimes a temple can never regain its sanctity after it's been debased like that . . . Why did it fall on us to besmirch that sacred place . . . I get a bad feeling something awful is going to befall us . . .

That's when I told them about Arjun. That I'd met him again, and loved him again. And that I was going to ask Suresh for a divorce. Fear, confusion, anger, disbelief . . . the events of the morning were small by comparison . . . only a very small precursor of things to come. My mother took to her bed with the shock of it . . . the few times that I went in to see her, she was lying on her back, staring sightlessly at the ceiling, tears rolling silently down the sides of her face. My pleas that she eat something or have just a cup of tea were all met with this strange, silent, unseeing grief.

My grandmother, stronger in spirit, told me I was mad to even think I would get away with it. The events at the temple in the morning were proof that there were forces much stronger and far more powerful than us, mere mortals. Did I seriously think I could defy centuries of tradition and go off into the world on my own, scholarship or no scholarship? Would I have dared to do such a dastardly thing if my poor father had still been alive? And did I think this, this *Arjun* would wait for me and then make an honest woman of me? Men like him were everywhere, opportunists always on the look out for some new fun. What guarantee did I have that he would be there when I arrived in England? And Riya – would anyone bother about a child like her? Her own father and grandparents found her difficult to love. Did it ever enter into my foolish head that she and I would be out on the streets within a month of trying to take up with a new man? And then what? Another man, and another, and another. At least in Suresh, I had somebody steady and reliable. He had his faults, but then which man didn't? I should be grateful he did not beat me like paavam Suma chechi's husband did. She put up with that, didn't she? And me, I was spurning a good man! Mullakkalamma, where did such arrogance come from? And his family, whatever their flaws, were respectable and upright people, I would always have a comfortable home with them. But these other people, I didn't even know who they were! Some people I'd met years ago, when I was a teenager in Delhi! They weren't likely to offer me a home with them, were they? More likely, they would be persuading their son right now that he could do much better than marry, not just a divorcée, but a divorcée with a handicapped child! What had *they* done to deserve this, Guruvayurappa!

I listened to Ammumma's tirade with my head in my hands. It was all true. How on earth could it work? I could have just gone back to the Centre from Leena's house and never sipped from that cup of poisoned, beguiling sweetness. Arjun would have slowly slipped back into the darkest recesses of my mind and life would have gone on for me the way it had for so long, not good, not bad, but the only possible way now. Occasionally I raised my head to look at Riya who was running in silent tearful panic from room to room, distraught at her mother's raging guilt, her great-grandmother's anger and her grandmother's terrifyingly silent grief indoors . . .

Suresh arrived the next day. He did not think it odd to see my mother's puffy face, assuming probably that the memory of my father had overwhelmed her yesterday. We told him the ceremony had gone well, and I knew my mother and grandmother were nervously watching my responses to him, to judge whether I had taken Ammumma's advice seriously or not. She had packed my suitcase at night, throwing in clothes and advice in equal measure, and now she told the maid to bring it out and put it into the car. Was there no room for me in Alleppey then? What had happened to Kerala's proud old matrilineal Nair tradition? When women ruled their homesteads with spirit and verve and got rid of the men who did not live up to their standards, merely by leaving their slippers and umbrella outside the closed front door. These were the stories I had been told as a child about my heritage, but everyone always laughed as though those were traditions we were well rid of. The Nair Act did well to abolish all that rubbish, they said, it's taught our men to take responsibility towards their children seriously. Best to join the rest of the country and become *patriarchal* instead, it seems to work for everyone else.

Because the Nair Act had taken a hammer to Kerala's matrilineal system all those years ago, I had to return that day with Suresh to Valapadu, with Riya in the back seat of the car and the picture of my mother's tear-ravaged face hanging before my eyes. The road to Valapadu had never seemed to fly past faster, there seemed to be nothing I could do to stop it, to slow it down. We were already going past the turning for Thakazhy, where the world had, for many happy years, ended at the primary school. Today the national highway was flying past Thakazhy, past the ghost of sleeping, dreaming Thoduporam, to Valapadu. At about fifty miles per hour, to my in-laws' handsome large house where the floor would feel cold under my feet and upright cushions would stare balefully at me as they marched stiffly across the divan. I could not do it. It was imperative that I never got there. I had to tell Suresh what had happened. It was going to have to be by negotiation rather than plain escape. I was forgetting that my personal hostage to fortune was noisily occupying the back seat, babbling and dribbling down the front of her new pink dress.

'Suresh, can you pull in somewhere? I have to talk to you.'

Had he guessed? Or was it the unusualness of my request that made him pull in without any questions. At a tourist complex I'd passed many times on my way to Alleppey with one of the drivers. I'd often seen family cars drive in and unload their happy occupants as I whizzed past on my way to visit my mother. This was the first time I had stopped there. Suresh ordered a fresh-lime soda for me, a glass of Bournvita for Riya and a whisky for himself. Make it a stiff one, waiter, he's going to need it, ha ha.

'Do you want some lunch now or should we wait until we reach Valapadu? It's only another hour from here.'

'It can wait, there's no hurry.' In fact, after you've heard what I have to say, you might reconsider your desire for some lunch. Do you want to order yourself another whisky before the waiter goes?

Suresh was looking at me. He looked uneasy and I could see that a little yellow gunge had gathered on the edge of his eyes. I recognized one of his signs of stress. I was going to make it much worse now, convert his nagging suspicions to stark reality with one wave of my wand. I was glad I'd chosen a public place, he couldn't flip his lid and hit me here, could he? Or do a bunk with Riya, leaving me stranded halfway between Alleppey and Valapadu? Stuck between two towns like a naughty schoolgirl trapped between two strict elderly aunts. Both with an equal dislike of me, being as I was too, too *fashiony* by halves with all my tall talk of scholarships and England and *divorce*. Tourists, travelling families and let's-just-stop-for-a-drink couples were busy ordering food and drinking under colourful flapping garden umbrellas. 'Today's special is chicken fry and fish molee, saar. Fish molee is very good, saar, fresh nemeen, bought just today.' The sun was out, turning raindrops clinging to leaves into a million trembling diamond drops. I took a deep breath of clean sunshiny air, redolent with the robust aromas of wet mud and damp grass.

'Suresh, I have to ask you . . . please, I don't want to hurt you . . .' I knew I was sounding weak and pleading and not firm and assertive as I'd planned. 'Suresh . . .' It was coming out now, all in a rush, nothing could stop it now, 'Suresh-Iwantadivorce.'

He looked at me with a kind of pretend-surprise on his face. He wasn't shocked, but I could see he felt obliged to have shock, hurt, horror and sorrow march across his face now, one by one. Bring them all out, let her see how cruel she is. 'Janu, (*pleadingly*) you can't mean it . . . we're happy together, aren't we? . . . Why, why?' A tearful tremor had entered his voice.

'We're not happy together. That's the point. I'm not happy with you, I suppose I've never been. It's not your fault, I suppose, we're just different. We seem to need different things from life.'

'That can't be (*hurt*). Why have you not said anything before (*surprise*)? I realize I have not been the best husband, but it's not my fault, I have a business to run (*self pity*). In the past few years, it's kept me too busy, but now, from this year, things are going to be different (*hopeful*). I'll get much more time for you and Riya, we'll be able to go on holidays together (*eager*), like Chettan and Latha do. Maybe even go abroad (*trump card*)! Mr Kunyali was mentioning the other day the possibility of a hoteliers conference in Singapore. You'd like that, wouldn't you?'

'Suresh, there's no point, it's not you . . .'

'My parents, my mother . . . I know she has a sharp tongue, but she means no harm . . . just yesterday I heard her say to Thanga how much she missed you and Riya when you were away (she *did*?!!). She adores you really, just doesn't know how to show it. And Sathi and Gauri too, they all love you (*lies*).'

We fell silent as the drinks arrived. 'Any small items, saar?' the waiter asked and, without waiting for a reply, went into his practised patter, 'Chicken kebab . . . beef oluthu . . . vegetable cutlass . . .'

Suresh turned on the waiter in sudden fury, 'Idiot! If we wanted anything wouldn't we have asked for it?' The waiter flinched and returned hastily to the kitchen. I watched his retreating back and thought sadly, No small items, thanks, very *big* ones happen to be on our agenda actually . . . divorce . . . adultery . . . broken promises.

Riya who had been gawping at all the people drinking their drinks and tucking into their fish molees, sat up eagerly and then started to bawl at the sight of her glass of Bournvita. 'Bovi vendaaa!' she hollered in tearful annoyance at the prospect of yet another milky drink. It normally took me just a few minutes of firm conversation with Riya, in special Riya-speak, to sort her out at times like this. But, quick as a flash, Suresh had leapt to his feet and scooped her up in his arms. As taken aback as I was, Riya stopped whimpering and looked in interest at this relatively unusual event. Why had her Acha picked her up? Was she going to be taken somewhere really special now, to the land of fizzy drinks perhaps?

I watched warily from under my colourful flapping umbrella while Suresh carried Riya around the tourist complex. They stayed within view and I could see Suresh pointing out flowers and leaves to her, while she continued to look around in breathless anticipation of that giant fizzy drink. Suresh was not going to give in easily, in fact he was going to make things worse by transforming himself into a painfully attentive husband. That was the best way to escape this new trauma. He might even end up by accompanying us to England if I was allowed to go! I was going to have to tell him about Arjun. I felt faint. The colourful umbrella above my head was flapping and twirling in a crazy dizzy dance.

When Suresh and Riya returned to our table, bearing an enormous glass full of gloopy green syrup and vanilla ice-cream, topped with a cherry and wafer biscuit, I told him about Arjun. That I had known him when I was still at school, that I would have liked to have married him one day, that my parents disapproved, that he had gone abroad and that I allowed my parents to arrange my marriage for me instead. I had not kept in touch with him (I know you don't believe me, but that's the truth), but I had met him again, in Delhi. He still loved me and was willing to marry me. I believed I still loved him too, but, for the moment, I wanted to go for my course and try to put Riya into a good special school. I didn't know yet if Arjun and Riya could get on. Before anything else, however, I needed that divorce so that I could try starting again, on a clean slate. With every word I uttered I knew I was taking one more unreturnable step into the territory previously trodden only by very foolish or very bad women.

Something shifted inside Suresh's eyes. I had, in one fell swoop, removed a terrible burden from his shoulders and transferred it squarely on to my own. I was no longer the injured party, he was! I could no longer call the shots, he could. He did not have to feel guilty any more. Looking back, I wondered why I hadn't noticed that Suresh seemed so free of sexual jealousy. I had not told him in so many words about that one afternoon of passion with Arjun, but surely he would have guessed? That was what I had been banking on, that Suresh would be so consumed with anger and shame that he would throw me out of his life forthwith. That he would drive me straight to his house, order me to pack my things and then throw Riya and me out, on to the unforgiving streets of Valapadu. I thought that, as in the films, we would next see each other only in court.

Instead, Suresh started to talk quickly and quietly, in his normal voice this time. The gamut of emotions had gone, the shock, horror, sadness and anger, paraded out one by one, weren't needed any more. The matinee had finished, no heart-rending songs were spewing out of the cinema hall with its too-thin walls. As Riya eagerly slurped her way through what had now become a pale green sludge, Suresh said he would give me the divorce I needed. Why hadn't I told him about Arjun before? He would have gone himself to his parents and mine and helped me to marry him all those years ago. Now we would have to deal with it more carefully, too many people were involved and too much was at stake. I was to leave it to him. For now we would have to go back to Valapadu and pretend, as though nothing was too different. He would help me arrange for my tickets and visas. He and I could file for a divorce, he didn't know how long it would take, but we'd do it quietly so that people weren't given a chance to talk. I was not even to talk to his parents about it, they would fuss too much and the whole thing would be blown completely out of proportion. He would tell them when the time was right.

As I wiped Riya's sticky green face and fingers with a wad of tissues, I could feel a fluttering inside me. It had been a lot easier than I'd imagined in the end. The distant beat of tiny temple drums inside me weren't warning me of something, were they? It had certainly been an odd reaction from Suresh. Was he in shock? Was he really not unhappy at all to give me a divorce? Had I *flattered* myself into believing that I mattered so much to him he would be devastated? Maybe he was in love with someone else! That was probably it, all these years that I had silently borne an unhappy marriage, had Suresh been going through the same? Was this his chance for freedom as well?

We drove to Valapadu with the uneasy truce hanging between us, a third ghostly passenger in the front seat, Mr Truce, with one arm slung around each of us. As we neared Valapadu and started to climb the road that wound through rubber estates, Riya threw up in the back seat, covering herself, her water-bottle and her new velvet Delhi horse in a thick green lumpy sludge with a cherry on top. Arriving at the house in a flurry of vomit, soaking tissues and exhausted tears, no one noticed the new understanding between Suresh and me. The pact that I hoped was going to give each of us the freedom that we craved.

FOURTEEN

I knew in the few days that followed that there were whisperings going on behind my back. Between Suresh and his father, Suresh and his mother, Amma and Sathi and even the silent Dr Sasi-the-famous-nephrologist. Again I could feel the temple drums in my stomach, but I hoped the whisperings were only Suresh broaching the subject of divorce as he'd agreed. This family had never been one for open arguments and confrontations. They'd always followed their strange, non-verbal, roundabout, barbed-shaft system of communicating their feelings that had seemed so peculiar to me in the beginning. I had never attempted to learn those games and thought it best to leave it now to Suresh.

Those were surreal days with their outward semblance of normality while underneath bubbled the lava of hate, impatient to escape and destroy everything in its path. Looking back, it gets increasingly difficult to work out exactly who knew what. Had Suresh told anyone of our conversation at that café where cheerful garden umbrellas had flapped? The outward trappings of our marriage stayed intact, but so they had even long after the briefly attempted and hoped-for love had died – so soon after our marriage, so many years ago. Now, however, a farcical edge had crept in as well. Burlesque, I thought, my MA knowledge coming in handy.

After the last dinner plates had been cleared away, the table wiped and left-over rice put away in the fridge, I would fill my small steel kooja with drinking water and make for my bedroom. Riya would be sprawled all over the bed in the unconcerned manner of children. Rearranging her plump limbs and removing her thumb from her mouth, I would crawl in next to her, watch her mouth continue to work for a while and then pull the sheet up to my chin. Some time after that I would hear Suresh and his father come in from their nightly session of business and politics on the verandah and lock the front door. Then the bedroom door would open. This was often the only time that couples like us got to be alone together. What did other people do then? Did they smile, like co-conspirators in some delicious crime, silently reach out for each other and make love? Did they push their sleeping child over to one side of the bed, making up a careful barricade with pillows, and then talk into the night, holding each other in warm, sleepy arms? As the lights would be going out one by one in the small town of Valapadu, Suresh and I would lie side by side, our sleeping child between us, staring up at the ceiling, dreaming our separate dreams.

I wondered sometimes what Suresh was thinking. How had I come to miscalculate his reaction to my asking for a divorce? I'd never been confident that he cared too much for me, but I hadn't realized that he cared so little. What surprised me more was that he didn't seem too concerned at what his parents, or (even worse) his friends and cronies would say when the news broke. It was puzzling certainly and I should really have examined that picture more carefully. But I found refuge, as usual, in my foolish dreams . . . September . . . I would be thinking . . . just a few months away. Will it be cold in England? Should I pack a cardigan into my hand luggage?

I talked quite openly now about my plans to leave for England, to visitors or relatives, sticking to the same story I had spun to Shobha Aunty. The Foundation preferred

British universities, so I was thinking of going to England instead of America. The course would take a year. Yes, I was planning to take Riya with me. The Maraars never asked any questions, only looked across at each other over my head and behind my back. Suresh merely looked sad, and I felt my usual pang. It would be the end of an era for him and for me, for whatever it was worth. And, as Ammumma had said, he wasn't a bad man; despite everything he had never once *hit* me, like paavam Suma chechi's husband did.

It was on a sunny February morning that I found out what exactly Suresh's truce would entail. Dr Sasi-the-famous-nephrologist had spent two hours with Suresh and his father on the verandah, not unusually for a Sunday. Amma was making occasional appearances, with an air of self-importance. A couple of times, Dr Sasi came in to make phone calls and then went out again. Sathi, who had asked me to help her finish a patchwork quilt she was making, asked me casually for some detail about my course. I was surprised and touched, this was the first time she had shown any interest. I attempted to explain, warming to my favourite subject, until I noticed a strange, knowing smile in her eyes.

'What's up, Sathi? You're smiling . . . I haven't said anything funny, have I?'

She looked alarmed, 'No, no, I wasn't smiling, I was thinking of something else . . .'

Something inside me was starting to stretch and snap. I'd had enough of these people and their sneaky roundabout ways. I'd never been openly rude before, but maybe the time had come for some plain speaking.

'You don't, any of you, think I'm going to make it, do you? It's a bit of a joke, isn't it? Janu and her silly scholarship. Well, I've got the scholarship and I intend to go. And Riya will go with me . . .' My voice was going shrill and I stopped short of announcing that I also had no intention of returning, when Suresh and Dr Sasi came rushing in.

'Enda, enda, what's wrong?' Suresh looked distraught.

'Nothing,' Sathi replied, 'we were sitting here calmly stitching when she suddenly got agitated, shouting something about her scholarship and taking Riya with her . . .'

Suddenly Suresh was holding me by the arms and saying to Dr Sasi, 'See, this is what I mean. It's been like this for weeks now . . . all this talk about scholarships that don't exist . . . and running away with Riya . . . I can't ignore it any more, she needs help . . . she needs treatment. Sasi-chetta, help us!'

I could not believe my ears . . . Treatment? . . . Help? I started to struggle out of Suresh's grip as his plan dawned on me, he was trying to convince everyone I was mentally ill! It was preferable to have people sympathize over a wife who was mad than to bear the shame of one who wasn't mad but wanted to leave him!

They were all in the room now, Achen looking alarmed, Amma enjoying the unexpected drama on a quiet Sunday, the servants crowding curiously at the door and Mr Truce, leaning on the wall with arms crossed, laughing a toothless eerie laugh. Furious that Suresh wouldn't let go of my arms, I struggled even more, kicking out with my feet. I had to keep talking to convince them I was not mad! Tell them everything, give them the *details*. Details would make me sound sane.

'It's not madness, I'm not mad, believe me . . . if I was would I have been able to go to Delhi on my own and get through a scholarship interview? I have it all there, in my room, in the drawer, their letters about the scholarship . . .'

I could see Amma shake her head at Achen and whisper, 'No letters, I've looked. She's obviously imagined the whole thing.'

Sathi added, 'And we stupidly allowed her to go off to Delhi as well!'

But I had letters as proof! Where had my letters gone? I twisted around to see Suresh's face, 'My letters from the Trust, where are they . . . Mrs Rustomji's . . . you've taken them, haven't you?'

I was screaming now, in horror and disbelief, and I could hear Riya take up the chorus somewhere in the next room. My baby! Bring her to me, she hates that Thanga, don't leave her in her care! Dr Sasi was bringing a syringe over to me and plunging it in my arm, Maraar faces were swimming around my head, Maraar heads in a mad Maraar whirlpool . . . he couldn't get away with this, there were hundreds of people who could vouch for the fact that I was perfectly sane . . . I couldn't think any more, everything was blurring . . . peaceful, quiet darkness engulfed me.

I came to in a hospital bed. The events of the morning . . . was it this morning . . . or some time long ago . . . came drifting slowly back to me. I had to see a doctor and explain everything to him. I attempted to leap out of bed in a panic, and fell back in a daze. My head was spinning and my legs wouldn't move. I couldn't move! I was trapped on this bed! I tried to call out, but the words would not come. What had they done! My tongue would not move. I felt weary and drained. I desperately needed to get back to sleep, I was too tired to struggle . . .

. . . maybe I could deal with it tomorrow . . .

Days passed in a daze . . .

. . . Days? Daze? Which was one and which the other?

Evening haze and daylight glaze . . . everything becoming one . . . Where was I and where was the world . . . had we ever truly known each other? . . . The white of a hospital ceiling . . . turning slowly to gold . . . the black of a hospital ceiling . . . swallowing me up in sleep . . . geckoes on the walls clicking their tongues at me . . . people, people all around clicking their tongues in sympathy . . . whispering, pointing . . . my mother's face crying . . .

I have no idea, to this day, how long I lay there in my stupor. I had been taken to the mental patients wing at Trivandrum Medical College. Dr Krishnan Menon, another old crony of Dr Sasi's and, needless to say, a-world-famous-and-expert-psychiatrist, had seen me and pronounced me manic and suffering from delusions.

I had a histrionic personality, he said histrionically.

Gone insane because of that handicapped child she has, paavam, they said pityingly.

She was my sanity, I tried to say but couldn't.

The drugs they gave me were powerful, but through that hazy daze, I could remember many things. I was Janu, my daughter was Riya, my husband had betrayed me which is why I was here. He had betrayed me because I had betrayed him, one long-ago afternoon in a city called Delhi. Sometimes I could even remember the man I loved and his name came at me in soft far-away whispers from a nearly forgotten past . . . Arjun . . . I couldn't remember his face very well, the features getting lost in the hundred other faces that came to peer at me from above. But I knew he wasn't just a part of the past but was waiting for me in my future somewhere. That wasn't delusional, whatever Dr Krishnan Menon said. But knowing all this was a bit of a waste because my tongue was too weary to lift itself and speak, my hands were dead weights lying by my side. Even the greatest effort could not budge them an inch. Capable and efficient nurses were caring for me, Thresiamma and Molykutty, with rough hands and rough voices. Suresh supervised my care, with help from his mother. So devoted they are to that poor girl, they said, clicking their tongues in amazement that bad things could happen to good families too.

Finally after a lifetime, my mother, caring for Riya in far-away Alleppey, heard my silent screams and knew she could not be a helpless bystander any more. Telling (not asking!) my grandmother that she was leaving for Trivandrum and leaving Riya in her care for the day, she booked Jose's taxi and arrived at my door. I could hear the conversation in the corridor and realized with some surprise that Ma was capable of assertiveness too. I wanted to cheer her but couldn't, of course.

'Padmaja chechi, how long can she be kept here like this? I feel she will recover faster if I take her home with me. There, with Riya, she'll get better much sooner, I can assure you.'

Suresh's voice sounded annoyed, 'Look, we should be doing what the *doctors* tell us to do, not taking decisions into our own hands.'

'Suresh, I know my daughter, she will not recover here in this god-forsaken place. In Alleppey she will be happy. Riya misses her too, she needs her mother, I do not have the words to explain to the poor child where her mother is . . .'

Ma's voice was starting to wobble and crack up. Don't stop now, Ma! You're doing so well! Please!

Suresh was speaking again, now he was solicitous, 'Ma, we all know this is not easy for you, but it's not easy for me either. I have given up my *business* to be here at her bedside and care for her. Only because Dr Krishnan Menon is the *best* person in Kerala for Janu's treatment. Why, maybe best in *India* even.'

Don't listen to him, Ma! He'll start trotting them all out now one by one, hurt, sorrow, anger, shock, the whole parade. Don't get taken in! Talk to his *father* if he's there.

As if on cue, I heard Ma say, 'Maraar Etta, you are like my older brother, you tell me what to do. I can't stand by and watch this any more . . .'

Achen sounded pensive, 'Perhaps you have a point, in

Alleppey she can slowly get back to a normal routine with your help. The child's voice calling her Amma will remind her of who she is. This here is really a terrible situation. What do you say, Padmaja?'

He wasn't in it! It wasn't entirely a Maraar conspiracy as I had feared. I never found out if the others, Amma, Sathi, Dr Sasi, were in it with Suresh. It was possible that Suresh had successfully sold them the idea that family honour would be better served by a daughter-in-law who went mad ('Poor thing, who wouldn't go mad with the grief of a child like that?') than one who had run away with another man. But I didn't know that for sure and, having travelled to many different dark and distant worlds on that hospital bed, it didn't seem important any more. What was important was that my mother had arrived, alone and frightened, to be my voice.

Look at her, who does she think she is, coming here in a *taxi* on her *own* to tell our menfolk what to do! Amma's voice said those words without saying them. She was not pleased with her husband, 'I agree with Suresh that we should do what Dr Krishnan Menon and our Sasi say. Who are *we* to tell them how to do their jobs?' But by 'we', of course, she really meant only my mother. Don't give up, Ma, they'll have me in here for ever if they can manage it! My insides were melting with despair. They were all coming into the room now! Dr Krishnan Menon was doing his rounds. Thresiamma and Molykutty were doing their familiar frightened flutter before the famous doctor. And what was this! A small, plump, quivering figure was blocking the path of the busy, famous doctor!

'Doctor, I want to take my daughter home today. I feel sure she will recover better if she is at home with her child. The child needs her too . . .'

The doctor pushed her aside and stared down at me instead, with stony eyes. Eyes as stony as those of an angry

God in a dark, wet temple. His voice was angry and sent little sprays of saliva down at my face, '*What* are you saying? Look at her! Does she look like she is in any state to travel? She needs Haloperidol, not a *mother's sympathy*!'

These last two words were spat out scornfully, landing on my face like a gob of spit. What a terrible antidote to suggest for a good doctor's careful medication. *Mother's Sympathy, pah*! My mother's eyes were filling up, oh no, she wasn't going to be able to stand up to this man (Famous and World-Renowned and Very-Full-of-Himself). Suresh looked tense but pleased. Achen was anxious. Amma was saving it all up to tell Sathi and Gauri on the phone later today. ('You should have *seen* Janu's mother's face, just because she's been the wife of some High Official she thought she could come in with all that *Delhi* style and tell the doctors what to do!')

'Come on, hurry up!' The doctor was snapping his fingers at the two terrified nurses who were looking on open-mouthed. They promptly broke into their frightened-flutter flamenco again, bringing phials and Haloperidol bottles to the famous doctor. He pinched my arm roughly and plunged another needle in.

'Doctor, I insist.' The small plump invader was taking over the careful running of the mental wing now! 'Nobody can force my daughter to stay here. I will see to it that she is safe and cared for. I will give her all her medications, I will administer them myself, I give you my word. Please.'

Dr Krishnan Menon was not used to having his advice thwarted. He was furious. But in his fury lay my salvation.

'Take her out of here then! Come on, pack all her things! I'm not keeping any one here against anyone's will. Some people think they know better than specialists who have trained in their subject for *years*. Do you know, I have written *papers* on her illness. I am called to JaPAN to give lectures on the subject of delusions. But you think you know better! Take her out of here and show her to some family *quack* for all I care! Now! This minute!'

Now they were all doing the frightened-flutter flamenco, getting clothes and medicines together, all except me because I was falling asleep again. This damned sleep came on at the most inopportune moments sometimes. Half drowsing, I was aware of being helped up and into a car and driven back to Alleppey . . . first milestone Attingal, stopping at a church for Jose to put some coins into a peeling box at its door . . . an hour later, crowded Quilon smelling of fish . . . then glimpses of the sea through rocks and fishermen's boats at Haripad . . . the road to Thakazhy . . . which used to end at the primary school and from where you could only get to sleeping dreaming Thoduporam by boat . . . once, in another life, was it? When Thoduporam was not a concrete Dubai monstrosity and when Kerala was for summer holidays and not for ever. I laughed out loud at the sudden memory of a water turtle who had stoutly refused to be tickled and sent on its way for a swim. I could hear Ma start to cry silently beside me again.

*   *   *

My mother was as good as her word, administering Dr Krishnan Menon's medicines every few hours, usually with eyes brimming over with tears. I knew that as long as the medicines went on, I would continue to have a tongue made of lead and a body that would not co-operate with its thoughts. But I could not tell them that and so I watched sadly as my mother and grandmother carried me from my bed to the bathroom, to wash and bathe me. They would then wipe me down carefully and dress me in colourful saris and blouses that were now far too big for me. Not four pointies like a cow any more, Mini, but no pointies at all, see!

Riya seemed not to mind too much, only occasionally battering me wildly with small fists when I would not respond to her gifts of wild flowers and insects. I knew Suresh had visited once, I could hear his angry voice in the living room. I could not hear the words that were exchanged, but realized later that it was that evening, after Suresh had gone, that Ma stopped giving me the medicines. I could hear her discuss it with Ammumma.

'Shall we try to see how Janu responds if we stop giving her the medicines? Two months and they don't seem to have done any good at all. . . .'

'Aiyyo, moley, how can you stop the treatment without asking a doctor?'

'What's the worst that can happen, Amma? Please let's try just a week without them.'

Ammumma, whose own existence now revolved around a vast collection of pills (pink for the heart, yellow capsule for the stomach, small one for BP), agreed reluctantly, 'I've prayed to take her to Chottanikara as soon as she can travel. Only Devi there can save her!'

Chottanikara . . . temple of the goddess who took care of people's minds. I'd been there as a child once with my grand-parents. We'd carried vegetable uppuma and mango pickle in a large plastic dabba with banana-leaf plates and gallons of home-made mango squash in two water bottles, and travelled in Ramama's brand-new car. Ammumma had wanted the car's first journey to be to a sacred place. 'Chottanikara will be a grand destination,' Appuppa had said. And so it was. Ramama's new car had a built-in cassette player, which none of us had seen in a car before, and so we drove with film music blasting our ears all the way there and back. Whenever the volume dipped, Vijimami would take over in her shrieky voice, collapsing in even shriekier laughter at the expression on my face between the hands that I kept clapped firmly over my ears.

The temple was as crowded as all temples are, to a child of my size, a forest of walking, thin brown sticks protruding from mundus and saris. But what made this one different was the clearing in the middle for all those people 'who'd lost their minds', arriving at Devi's door because she was going to help to retrieve them. I watched in awe, peering from behind the safe curtain of Ammumma's sari, as the temple drums took up their beat, faster and faster, while the people-without-minds beat their heads about and swung their hair around, faster and faster.

'What are they doing, Ammumma?'

'Evil spirits have got inside their bodies, moley.'

So that was it, the evil spirits had climbed into these people's bodies and were fighting to get hold of their minds. One of the women seemed to be struggling with a particularly evil spirit as she had now sprung up, her entire torso moving in time to the drum-beat, her hair swinging around in a long black circle. From her waist to the ends of her hair she was a long black whip, beating the air, making it swish and sting as though she could never stop. Suddenly she sprang with a loud cry to a knarled old tree covered in nails and started to hit her forehead against them. The crowd took a collective fascinated breath and a collective horrified step back. I hid my face hurriedly in Ammumma's sari, because even I knew a lot of blood would probably follow such a bashing, and felt Ramama scoop me up in his arms to carry me off.

'Why did she do that, Ramama?'

'Because, poor thing, she must have done something terrible in her past life to be suffering so much agony now.'

I would go willingly to Chottanikara again because I knew I had an apology to make and because terrible deeds of past lives had to be paid for in present-day currency. My account had not been debited yet for a golden December afternoon in a far-away life. A week after the medicines had stopped, the veils in my head started to lift, my arms and legs found their muscles and my tongue found its words again. I could have my own bath, wear my own clothes and, best of all, speak my thoughts again. Ammumma arranged for Jose's taxi to take us to Chottanikara. For my mother and grandmother it was a fervent thanksgiving. For me it was a reminder that happiness was given, never taken. Careful calculations were being made all the time and, as people lined up patiently for their share, it had not been my right to steal such a large portion of radiant, sunlit, unalloyed and, at that point, undeserved joy.

We filled the boot of Jose's car with provisions, pots and pans and a hot plate. Ammumma had arranged for a room in the temple lodge, so we needed supplies for a week. Riya charged happily between the car and the house, banging a plastic mug on the bucket she wore over her head, as excited as I must have been on that journey when I was about her age. In Ramama's new car that spewed raucous music and childhood happiness.

You did not see Chottanikara until you were virtually upon it. It did not rise above the world on a sea of stormy rocks, nor did it welcome its pilgrims with the towering gates of Mullakkal. It did not, unlike Guruvayur, announce its grand presence long before you got to it with a parade of shops selling temple pictures and temple things like coconuts and sandalwood. It tucked itself instead into a small green copse as though hiding, like its tired worshippers, from the relentless stares of a cruel world. It was, to my weary mind, both balm and comfort.

We stayed at the temple for a week, rising before dawn for baths and the early prayers. We ate frugal meals of rice gruel and coconut chutney and allowed the chanting prayers of the priests to seep into our consciousness through the day. In the evenings, we would sit with those poor helpless souls who still beat their heads against the old nail-covered tree, still weeping its bitter sap of human blood. I whispered a multitude of heartfelt apologies to Chottanikara Devi, folding my hands before her mysterious figure, genuinely sorry for my sin. But I knew, better than anyone else, that if Arjun appeared before me in some tender, wondrous dream, I would merely do it all again. Was it possible to apologize for taking something that you wanted more than anything else in the world? Did it mean anything at all to weep for past misdeeds, knowing that they would be played out again and again, in a terrifying, rousing, inexorable circle, so much like the crashing waves of the sea.

Somewhere in the dark peace of Chottanikara, my mother and grandmother accepted sorrowfully that my marriage to Suresh had to come to an end. For them, there would always be shame and anguish surrounding that decision, but the episode in the mental hospital had made it clear that there was now no other road to take. Arjun's name, however, was still taboo. He was the person who had come blazing back into my life unannounced and uninvited, turning all their lives upside down. If he had not reappeared, would I have ever wanted to end things with such finality? Would I have gone to complete the course, and then come back at the end of it, even if merely for the want of anything else to do?

'Ma, I had told you, long before I went to Delhi, that I was going to go away.'

'You said *nothing* about not coming back.'

'You knew I wasn't thinking of coming back, the course was going to be my escape, Ma.'

'You would have gone, but you would also have come back.' She looked so certain and she looked so sad.

'I would have tried my best not to, believe me.'

'You never said so.'

True, I had not said so, but I was trying to protect you, Ma. Don't all children do that when there's something too painful to tell? Your pain would have been far more than mine, I know. I could not have saved you from it completely, even though I tried that at first. But I could put it off and that seemed considerate at the time. Duplicity had nothing to do with it.

The next day, walking around the temple after saying our prayers, I knew her demons were still raging. 'Was it really that bad, moley? Bad enough to *leave*?' There was more anguish in her question than anger.

I looked at the gnarled old banyan tree under which the stone snakes sat, gazing out at centuries of human endeavour and failure. I wanted to be truthful and thought for a while before I replied, 'No, Ma, it wasn't unbearable. I could have put up with it for the rest of my life, people suffer much worse things, I know.' I turned to her, really wanting her to understand, 'But it wasn't good enough, either. Both for Riya and for me . . . should it be so terrible just to want something better, Ma?'

She was silent, the concept of 'better' simply did not exist for women of her generation who took what they were given with tolerance and fortitude. I knew she was wondering how, in bringing me up so carefully, she had got it so wrong? Why had she failed to teach me acceptance? Wasn't it merely arrogance to think that we could take matters into our own hands? To take over the writing of our own stories.

Arjun's reappearance should have been seen as fortuitous, but had, in reality, infused everything with an air of deceit. What was the single most beautiful event of my life would, to most other people, seem facile and sleazy. My mother had taken my happiness and converted it so easily into her pain. How could I later stop everyone else from converting it into the sneering laughter that would rock her world for ever? For now I had to keep the silent memory of Arjun's face wrapped safe and close to my heart. I carried it with me everywhere, as I bathed, as I ate, even as I walked around the parikrama of Chottanikara temple in a meaningless act of penance. In the midst of sleepless cricket-whirring nights, it came to life miraculously and gently, not with the childish yearning of many years ago, but with the knowledge of a woman who has had her entire being loved one glowing afternoon.

Kerala was waiting with its censure. Soon it would have reason to sit back and rock on its heels in cruel laughter, slapping its friends on the back and wheezing with the fun of it all. Ammumma who had always wanted us to be well-dressed ('otherwise what will people in town think!') would have much more to bear than Mrs Pillai's whispers about Ma's cotton saris. It would soon be said, in toddy shops and street corners and smart living rooms, that her grand-daughter, married into *such* a good family, had slept with another man. ('*Simply* to be able to take her handicapped child abroad, you know!')

Suresh and his mother had been to the house at Alleppey while we were away, we were informed by Mrs Pillai on our return from Chottanikara.

'Oh, we postponed our return and couldn't inform them from there, you see, no STD booth anywhere near the temple and also the phone lines were all down all week . . .'

Ammumma was wasting her rambling explanations on her savvy neighbour. Mrs Pillai nodded knowingly and gave me a searching look. 'Okay, moley?' she enquired solici-tously, looking no doubt for signs of delusions bordering on schizophrenia.

'Yes, aunty,' I said, trying to look as sane as possible while pushing Ammumma into the house. Ma was wringing her hands in the living room: why had the Maraars come and what had they said to Mrs Pillai next door?

'Don't worry, Ma, we'll handle it when they come again. I'll have to call Suresh and ask him to come here so that we can discuss a divorce anyway.'

I could see both Ammumma and Ma flinch openly every time I said the d-word. It would be a long time before any of us could roll words like 'divorce', 'custody' and 'Arjun' out of our mouths without looking over our shoulders for Mrs Pillai or the townsfolk who were still waiting for the news to break or even all our ancestors who crowded the forty-watt half-darkness of this house. No one in the family had ever been divorced before. It just didn't happen in decent families like ours, which was why poor Suma chechi put up with her beatings about twice a month, turning up at family functions looking tired and defeated, but married.

'How long are we going to avoid telling people, Ma? I'm going to be here until I can leave for the UK. September's six months away! Isn't that just a bit too long to pretend I'm only on a casual visit?'

'I can't go around *telling* people you're back here because you want a divorce, can I?'

'Why not, they're bound to find out sooner or later?'

'How can you talk so shamelessly? Oh God, what sort of news are the Maraars going to spread about you? You will never be able to live in Kerala any more! And how will we be able to bear the shame! Why did you tell Suresh about meeting that boy in Delhi? You should never have told him that and nobody would have known.'

'Ma, if I hadn't told him he would never have even considered a divorce. I thought it was best to be honest.'

As it happened, Suresh was not considering divorce as an option at all. He turned up again, on his own this time, looking surprisingly smart and cheerful. He had obviously hatched Plan Number Two.

'Look, Janu, you had loved this boy when you were a teenager. It happens all the time, it doesn't matter. You made a mistake when you met him again in Delhi, but I can forgive you for that. You're my wife, I have to forgive you . . . And nobody will ever know what you did, I promise I will not tell anybody.'

'I'm not sure I'm ready to forgive *you*, Suresh, for that awful trick you played, getting me into that mental hospital. You were thinking of leaving me there for ever, weren't you?'

He looked hurt. 'What are you saying, Janu, I was so upset, so worried, I didn't know what to think! I really thought you were ill and needed help, the doctors all said so, didn't they? I took care of you *myself* through those days, you ask anyone, Janu.'

I looked at him in disbelief, either he was an idiot or he thought I was one. Even in his most desperate bid to save our marriage, I could not believe that he genuinely thought I was mentally ill. Nor could I now stomach his magnanimous willingness to forgive me my escapade in Delhi and have me back. And why *was* he so keen for me to go back? Was it to wreak some worse revenge? Was it the kind of desire that develops for something that can never belong to you again?

He was going to stick implacably to his plan. 'I love you, Janu, I cannot even bear to think about my life without you. I will never divorce you. Never! Stop all this now and come back to me, they are all waiting for you at home. Come, get your suitcase now.'

Ma appeared at the door. For one terrifying moment I imagined she was going to join him in his pleas. But she looked steadily at him and said firmly, 'Suresh, I think you had better accept what Janu says. We have already tried talking to her, but she has made up her mind. Explain everything to your parents, if you haven't already.'

'Ma, even you are turning against me?' He was now genuinely shocked and hurt. Having always craved a son, Ma had showered a lot of importance on Suresh. And every Indian mother hopes that her daughter's chances of happiness will improve if she treats her son-in-law like a king. Now even Ma could throw that particular caution to the winds. Suresh could not believe he was actually being asked to leave.

He returned, a week later, with his parents. Amma was carrying a box full of my favourite rava laddoos. And an expression that was a curious mixture of penitence and annoyance. She did not like having to kow-tow in such a humiliating fashion to a daughter-in-law, but family honour was obviously worth a great deal. She fell sobbing into my arms, 'Moley, Janu!' She had never used the affectionate 'moley' tag before, previously reserving it only for her own daughters. I looked in embarrassment over her shaking shoulders at Achen. He looked confused, but was obviously fairly accustomed to his wife's occasional hysterics and said nothing.

It was all very strange. The Maraars were here. Under normal circumstances, Ammumma would have been bringing out her best china and the maid would have been sent out the back way quickly to buy some hot vadas and chutney from Kerala Coffee House down the road. But today Ammumma sat red-eyed in front of them and Ma hovered around, wringing her hands. I could almost read her thoughts: Once these people were here to ask for my daughter's hand in marriage to their son; today they have come, oddly, to ask for it again. Even back then it would have been considered arrogance to turn them away. Now it's nothing short of sacrilege.

It looked like I would have to get the conversation going. I tried to keep my voice from trembling.

'I hope Suresh has told you, I've asked him for a divorce.' You might have thought I'd been saying that I'd asked Suresh for something as innocuous as a suitcase if you weren't listening closely to the words.

But Amma had heard them, 'Aiyyo, moley!' she wailed.

240

'You are our child, how can you leave, where can you go? Just yesterday I was telling Achen, you ask him, how I always knew you would be the one to look after us in our old age. How can you talk about leaving us?'

I was confused. Suddenly we were talking about *their* future, and about my broken promises to them. I was not asking just Suresh for a divorce, but his whole family for one. I knew there were unwritten contracts in every marriage. To preserve and protect not only the person one was marrying, but in a sense their whole family as well. Among us families married families. And the separation of a couple meant the consequent tearing asunder of whole groups of relationships and acquaintances. I was asking hundreds of people to go back to being unrelated again. It was amazing to think how often that complication would have seemed reason enough to keep a marriage intact.

But their eagerness to have me return was still surprising under the circumstances. Had Suresh not told them about Arjun? Surely that bit of knowledge would put them off me for ever. Briefly tempted to take the bull by its horns and tell them myself, I could feel the pleas emanate from Ma next to me (*Please* don't say anything that will make people talk more badly about you than necessary; *please*, it will kill me to have those names attached to you . . .).

'I have to go abroad, I've decided. I'm taking Riya with me and I will be trying to stay on there. I'm not coming back and it's best for both Suresh and me if we are divorced before I go. Please.'

'What have we done, what has our *son* done to deserve this?' Amma was getting incoherent. I looked at her and wondered where I should begin. Did she really not know of the wistful hope with which I, as an eighteen-year-old, had come into their lives? At eighteen all I had wanted was to make my marriage work, having quite firmly put happy memories of childhood and Arjun into a small box marked

'Do Not *Ever* Open Again'. To achieve this, I had subsumed my Delhi self to fit in, hoping to be loved. I was still young enough to have warmed to some kindly mothering, but had found myself way down on Amma's list of people deserving warmth and affection. And what had her son done to deserve this? Again, not very much. It was more a case of what he *hadn't* done, I suppose. And perhaps the punishment was too severe for the crime. But I was not attempting to make any accusations here. I had always and only said that *I* had needed to get out. Even before Arjun had come along and made it imperative for me to do so. Was that a crime? I would soon find that, in most people's eyes, it was.

Suresh came again and again to Alleppey, sometimes with his parents and sometimes on his own. His visits always followed the same routine, he was obviously hoping the dripping-tap effect would eventually wear me down.

'Janu, enough of this now, you are my little wife, you need me just as I need you. Riya needs both of us. My parents keep praying all the time for this madness to pass. We all need you.'

'You don't, any of you, need me. In fact you've never needed me, and that's one of the reasons why I was so sure it really wouldn't matter if I left, Suresh.'

'Things will be different now, I promise you. Please come back and try it, for just a month.'

'I've tried everything already, Suresh, without you even noticing. I gave our marriage my best shot, but it didn't work. Now let me go, please. We can both start new lives.'

'I don't want a new life, I want you. Janu, people are already talking because you are here. I haven't told anyone about what happened in Delhi, so you can still come back without any shame.'

It pained me that Suresh was still so keen to have me back. He seemed to have swallowed his own version of 'little wife' and sudden 'love', and at times it did seem possible that it had taken my departure for him to feel I had some worth. But I was more and more convinced that his biggest motivation was his overwhelming desire to avoid the awful stigma of divorce. I'd heard him laugh uproariously at the news of Oomen Chandy's divorce last year. 'He should have known better, letting his wife go off and act in TV films,' he'd said, 'ran off with some producer type to Bombay, she did' . . . To now have other people talk about *him* like that would be unbearable. Having me back would be a small price to pay to avoid that, and so the campaign continued. Sometimes there were tears, sometimes anger, churning emotions that rolled weeks into months. Blame and remorse got mixed up into a bland meaningless porridge that we were both forced to eat, like prisoners who hated each other but were forced to serve endless life sentences side by side.

I wrote occasional brief letters to Arjun, telling him about the events, and silently pleading for him to be waiting at the end of it all. I had asked him not to reply unless there was something important to say, painfully conscious that receiving letters bearing foreign postmarks would be tantamount to rubbing my mother's and grandmother's noses in their shame. Sometimes that old chilly hand would wrap itself around my heart as I imagined Arjun giving up on me. I would arrive in England, it would be cold and wet, and Arjun would not be there. With trembling hands, I would call the number he had given me and find a stranger at the other end. Even worse, Arjun would *be* that stranger, remote and distant, unwilling to recognize me. Having met him and loved him again, it was hard to remember a time when Arjun was not a part of the future I had planned for Riya and myself. His reappearance was only a wonderful bonus. But, like everybody else, I was also increasingly convinced by the picture of my running away merely to be with Arjun. It was becoming an effort to remind myself that there was a life that I had planned for Riya and myself, much before Arjun had arrived to occupy that place in my future somewhere.

By May, Suresh's visits had taken on a new tone. In the slow brooding heat of those summer days, his voice had changed from wheedling and pleading and taken on a threatening edge. This was unlike the quick treachery of the events that culminated in the mental hospital, but more open and risky and unafraid.

'Don't think you'll get away with this,' he said once, after another wearying argument in Ammumma's living room.

'What do you mean by that?'

'I have influential friends everywhere.' He shrugged.

I gave him a long look. His eyes shifted, but he mumbled under his breath, 'My influence can even extend to England, you know.'

My heart was beating wildly and I could hear the helpless whine of a bluebottle trying to head-butt its way out of the window next to me. I jumped up from my chair and opened the window in a panic, flapping at the stupid insect with the end of my sari pallu, and watched it whizz away, weaving through the bushes in confusion and glee.

'Get out,' I said to Suresh. He looked at me open-mouthed. Through the weary months of argument, I had maintained a forced equanimity because I hadn't thought confrontation would get me anywhere. But it hadn't worked and there was nothing I could say to this latest threat, real or implied I could not tell. Suresh had obviously grown used to my quiet placatory talk and could not believe I was standing in front of him now with blazing eyes and a finger pointing at the door. He got up very slowly, came right up to me, so close that I could see that a hair in his nose had curled right over his nostril. I did not back away even though my knees were about to give way, and just as suddenly he turned and walked out without another word.

I sank on to Ammumma's wicker chair taking a deep breath. Was it just an empty threat or could he really do anything? Did he have any addresses? I remembered the papers he had taken from my drawer in Valapadu, they had all the addresses, even Arjun's that I'd quickly scribbled on the back of my scholarship agreement that day in Delhi. Suresh had brought them all back in one of his early visits to Alleppey, when he was still trying to use charm to persuade me to return. He must have kept copies for himself. He would know where Arjun lived. If he did try to harm one of us at all, it would be Arjun and not me. He was clever enough to know that would cause me more suffering than anything else.

Ma came running in, panicking at the look on my face, 'Enda, enda, what's happened? What did he say? Tell me?'

'I think we're wasting our time trying to reason with him. We need to see a lawyer, Ma.'

'Aiyyo, moley, who? Who can we see who will not judge you? And who will give us good advice? And be discreet? Mullakkalamma, help us!'

The next morning we picked our way around the steaming municipal rubbish piles to the home of a lawyer, distantly related to us. A peon showed us into a small, newly dusted office, lined with leather-bound books. A huge portrait of a grey-haired man in lawyer's robes hung on the wall facing us. He was wearing a garland of tinsel flowers and looked important and cross. After we had been served a cup of tea each, a smaller, younger version of the man in the picture came into the room through a faded curtain starched into stiff submission at the door. Ma and I got up, folding our hands in greeting.

'Mani chechi, what brings you here? I think I last saw you at the temple festival. Just the other day I was saying to Kamala that we must come around and see you and Amma. How is she, in the best of health, I hope?'

'Amma is pulling along, heart problems, BP, you know, all the complaints of old age. You have seen my daughter before, haven't you? Janu.'

He looked at me and nodded, 'Ah, yes, of course, Janu. Married into T. K. K. Maraar's family, is it not? I know them all very well, T. K. K., A. K. K., and the young fellow, what's his name?'

'Suresh.'

'Yesyes, Suresh, fine fellow. I attended your wedding, you know, had invites from *both* sides. I know them all very well. In fact, I saw your husband just the other day at a Rotary Club Conference in Cochin. He was with G. K. Cherian.' Noticing the blank expression on my face, he added informatively, 'Congress MLA. They left together also. So, you are Suresh Maraar's wife, eh? Verygood, verygood.'

He looked pleased that we were able to boast of such fine connections and consequently extremely happy to be of help.

'So, tell me, how can I be of assistance, chechi?'

Was there a nice way to put it? Was there a simple way to say, I know you think my husband is a fine fellow and that my marriage is a wonderful alliance, but do you think I could prevail upon you to give me some advice on how to . . . um . . . *divorce* the fine fellow?

Ma opened up with the timid quavering voice I was getting used to.

'Please don't think badly of us, of my daughter particularly, but, for many different reasons we are thinking of asking them for a . . . divorce . . .' she whispered the word, making its entry as it was into the wider world for the very first time.

It certainly had the expected effect. Madhava Menon's glasses nearly fell off his nose and his voice became a shrill squeak, 'Aiyyo, why?'

'Very difficult to explain,' my mother continued, 'many different reasons . . .'

'Beating you?' he asked me, the shock rendering his speech into telegrammatic utterances.

I shook my head, no, not beating me . . . yet.

'Too much drinks, eh?'

'Partially that, although it's not really the issue . . .'

'Maybe he is having affairs then.'

The man in the picture was looking very cross now. Perhaps *he* knew it wasn't Suresh having the affair but me. A certain horrified recognition dawned on Madhava Menon's face. He dropped his voice so low, Ma and I had to lean closer to the table to hear his awed squeak.

'He is *AC–DC*, eh?' I looked at him blankly. 'You know, *otherwise* inclined, sexually speaking.' He accompanied the word 'otherwise' with a sideways waggle of his head and a knowing, we're-all-adults-we-can-talk-about-these-things expression on his face. He was still whispering, 'I hear it is on the increase in our society also, all this MTV and American ideas coming in.'

Poor Madhava Menon was struggling to make the pieces fit. Requests to draw up divorce petitions must have been rare in this spick and span little office. Petitions to evict siblings from ancestral property, yes. Filing angry cases against once-trusted business partners, often. But divorces were still rare and fell firmly into the better-to-be-avoided category in Madhava Menon's little book of life experience.

Somehow Ma managed to spill some of the details of my own life's experience out in long, rambling sentences, still full of pain and doubt. I did not think she had done too convincing a job and neither, it seemed, did Madhava Menon. He took off his glasses and rubbed them absently with a handkerchief that had yellow stains on it.

'I don't think divorce is really the best thing for a young

girl. Better-to-be-avoided.' Of *course*, I knew it wasn't the best thing, I'd acquired that bit of knowledge first-hand. It was just surprising to hear a lawyer say that. Better-to-be-avoided certainly, but sometimes not-really-possible-to-be-avoided.

'It will not be easy to get a divorce without being able to prove mental or physical cruelty. Or adultery. You are sure he is not having any affairs, eh?' He was looking at me hopefully. I shook my head. He had obviously not understood that I did not have a *clue* as to whether or not Suresh might have ever had an affair. All I did know was that he had never been there when, as a young bride, I had needed his friendship and guidance. He had also absented himself when Riya needed him and when we needed to face her problems together. I did not *know* whether he had ever had an affair, I was not his confidante, I did not even know who all his friends were. He had never helped me create a life for myself, he had never explained to me what his business was all about, he had never looked across a crowded room at me to signal that a certain partnership existed between us. As far as I could see, he preferred the company of a large Scotch on the rocks to me! Was there a name for all of that? And was it important to be able to name things? For years I had searched for a name for Riya's difficulties, as though that discovery would have solved all the problems. Now here was this man asking me to put a name to what was essentially just an empty shell. A marriage that had never been.

'Incom-pitibility!' Madhava Menon seemed to have found the name we were looking for. He pronounced 'incompatibility' all in a rush, like an income followed by something quite pitiable. We were getting warmer.

'Can that be a ground for divorce?' Ma asked.

'Yes, yes, incom-pitibility is accepted . . . but only in the case of mutual consent. Both parties have to agree to

248

separate for six months and, after that only, the divorce is granted. Very uncomplicated.'

Actually terribly complicated, I thought, Suresh's never going to co-operate, especially now that he knows I've much more to gain by the divorce than he has. And six months, I don't have six months here. My course starts in four months' time.

'Does one have to be physically present for this to happen?' I asked.

'Oh yes. Both for filing and for finalizing, both parties must be present, otherwise it is invalidated. Physically present for filing and finalizing,' he repeated, pleased with his sudden alliterative skills.

My heart sank. It would not happen before I left for England. Ma looked at me and signalled that we should leave. We got up with a scraping of chairs. Madhava Menon came around the table and put an avuncular hand on my shoulder, squeezing it conspiratorially, 'Moley, why all this divorce and all, eh? You go home and think about it. Such a serious step to take. After all, these are all small problems that can be talked over and sorted out. Maybe I can have a word with Suresh, yes?'

Oh no, please, I thought. 'Thank you for your help,' I said.

Ma was trying to press an envelope of money on Madhava Menon. But he was brushing it off, determined to press more help on us instead, 'No, no, Mani chechi, I can't take money from you. And also, I don't want our poor Janu mole to commence on this divorce line. Why don't you talk to my good wife, eh, moley? She is very understanding, she will give you excellent advice.' Before I could say anything, he was calling out, 'Edi, Kamaley!'

Kamala popped out from behind the curtains too soon to have arrived from some distant kitchen. She listened with nodding, wide-eyed sympathy while her husband rolled ten years of my life into a neat little nutshell, 'Our Janu here, you know, Mani Chechi's daughter, is having some small problems in her marriage. You know, little bit of neglect from husband, little bit of drinking,' he said this with his thumb pointing at his mouth indicating it wasn't just tea and coffee we were talking about, 'also, little bit of mother-in-law problems . . . nothing majorly difficult. I was saying that you will be able to give some humble advice.' He was presenting his wife to us like a trophy, over to you, Kamala.

Kamala gave me a smile full of syrupy scorn and contempt. I could read her thoughts: all these *Delhi* girls with their *Delhi* ideas of divorce, corrupting our Kerala ways. Unable to adjust, huh? Send them all to me for a crash course on how to be model wives. I will teach them how to worship the ground their husbands walk on, how to keep immaculate houses, how to cook Chinese Chilli Chicken and how not to have jumped-up ideas of jobs and careers. I will show them how to bring up model children who will look cute in their pavada-blouses and recite a-b-c *backwards* to look even cuter. I will show them that mothers-in-law are easily kept in their places with a few sharp words and a few whispered ones in the husband's ear. The trouble with these girls is that they think they are above it all. Arrogance, that's what I call it!

I would not, in a hundred years, have been able to explain to Kamala that arrogance had never come into it. Fear, yes. Wavering Confidence, Flagging Self-Esteem, Gnawing Self-Doubt . . . all those little demons with fancy double-barrelled names had raised their heads at some point or the other, clouding my belief in my own worth. Perhaps what I *needed* was a healthy dose of arrogance, actually! Two big spoonfuls of it, after breakfast every day, as prescribed by Dr Kamala of Alleppey, expert marriageologist.

I looked at Ma, the person who should have taught me arrogance and guile and how to cook Chinese Chilli Chicken to help save my marriage. You'd just wasted your time, Ma, trying to teach me honesty and kindness instead. Ma gave Kamala a hug and said, 'I will send Janu to you one of these days, so that you can give her good advice. Today we have to rush to the temple to see the priest about a bhajana . . .'

We made good our escape. We had no appointment with the temple priest, but I was grateful for the excuse. Ma was breathing hard as we hurried down the road, 'I just remembered when I saw that Kamala, she's very friendly with our neighbour Manju Pillai. She'll be on the phone to her just now, talking about you. Guruvayurappa, please don't drag my daughter's name through the mud!'

But my name was soon to become mud and worse. In a strange way, I managed to float above the whispering and the nudging elbows. Ma said it was because I was going to escape the worst of it by leaving for England. She was probably right, but my heart still bled for my mother and grandmother, for whom even visits to the temple were now marred by the tail end of carelessly trailing remarks: '. . . the arrogance of modern girls . . . couldn't care less about the child, and a handicapped child, mind . . . they could have had the pick of any girl, but went for this Delhi one, tch tch tch . . .'

Soon a more sinister element crept in. Whispers had started about Arjun's involvement in the picture. It was hard to tell the source of these. Ammumma was sure it was Suresh himself, who had probably given up hope of my returning and had nothing to lose now if my name was ruined. This was far worse to deal with, the whispers were becoming sibilant, with a sprinkling of razor-sharp words, aimed to sting and stab: . . . adulteress . . . shameless . . . promiscuous . . . materialistic hussy . . . sleeping around . . . ex-lovers . . . each word sent a new spear into my mother's heart.

For her, the final straw was a letter from Raghu Uncle

and Shobha Aunty in Delhi. They had been at the Malayali Association annual dinner in Delhi when someone told them about me and my capers in Delhi. That too, while wearing Shobha Aunty's *best* cashmere jumper. Had I no shame? At least I could have spared them the insult of bare-faced lies while living in their house.

'People as far away as Delhi are talking about you! Will we ever be able to walk with our heads held up again! Mullakkalamma, please end this suffering once and for all!'

I thought I knew my people well, but it still surprised me that Malayalis, literate, urbane and educated had found little else to talk about but me! Surely, the rumblings of trouble in the Gulf and the rising price of fuel were subjects more suitable for a gathering of Delhi's best Malayalis. After all they all had relatives who lived in the Gulf and they all had need of petrol. Of what possible interest could *my* little life be to them? Nevertheless, we retreated into our house that lurked shame-facedly behind the mango trees. Through the hot hazy summer days we sat under the ceiling fan, listening to the dull creak-creak of its blades trying to shift the hot damp air. Outside, schoolchildren ran riot, dislodging Ammumma's precious mangoes from the trees with missiles of sticks and stones. Usually this provoked her into a frenzy of activity and name-calling, keen as she was to save the mangoes for our annual visits. Now she sat by her window, reading her *Bhagawad Gita*, jumping only when an earthly missile landed too near the window. Letters from Ramama and Ammini Kunyamma, asking why no one had written for a while, went unanswered again. Ma ventured out occasionally to pay the bills and collect the rent, but came rushing back as soon as she could, sometimes looking pale and tearful. I whiled away the hours teaching Riya the English she would soon need. She could still only string two or three words together, and it was not easy to switch to grammar-laden English.

'Yes, "toila ponum" but also try saying, "May I go to the toilet, please?" Or even just "Toilet, please", moley.'

'Toila ponum.'

'Okay, try "I'm hungry". No, not "mamum", that's baby language, no one's ever going to understand that in England and you'll go hungry for ever. So start again, "Hungry – food!" HUNG-gry!'

'MAAA-MUM!'

Riya's temper was thriving and the enforced imprisonment wasn't helping much. Still, it was her presence that probably preserved the sanity of three women that merciless summer, each suffering her own special brand of agony. That was soon to come to an end as well. Suresh was about to unfurl his next plan on me.

The monsoons broke as usual in June, drowning delighted children running pell-mell to school. That morning the sky had darkened and rumbled ominously, giving warning of the watery onslaught to come. Vapours rose from the earth, their delicious muddy-wet aroma overwhelming the heavy scent of the last oozing mangoes on the trees. Crows and parrots gathered in the branches in a noisy, cawing, frightened camaraderie, a rag-tag army laying down its arms before the battle even began. Ma had stepped out earlier with some bills and wasn't there when Suresh's car pulled up silently outside the gate. He pushed open the door and a strong breeze carrying the threat of rain blew through the house, lifting the curtains like fearful ghosts. For one awful moment Suresh looked like the figure of death from one of my childhood comics that had given me nightmares for months.

'Hello, Suresh,' I said, scrambling up from my cushion on the floor, where I'd been playing with Riya's home-made flash cards. He did not reply. I could feel the icy hand curl over my heart again. Riya was lurking in the folds of my sari somewhere. In the early days of our Alleppey exile, she

253

used to run with glee into Suresh's arms, especially as he usually arrived carrying some stuffed toy for her. Today she attached herself firmly to my knees and peered around at Suresh from behind me. Either the gap had been too long, or she had a sense of what was coming . . .

'I've come to take Riya.' All in a monotone, no pleasure, no anger, just pure revenge.

'Take her where, Suresh?'

'To her house, where she belongs. You can go where you like. Live with whichever men you want. But you are not taking my daughter with you. To be brought up by strange men. How many, God only knows.'

'She's not going to be brought up by different men, Suresh, she'll always be brought up by me.' I was trying to keep my voice calm because I could sense he was possessed by some special demons today. Either demons or a couple of pegs of Johnny Walker, I couldn't tell.

'You?! You are going to bring up my daughter? *You*, who can't resist selling her body to strange men! Have you heard how people are talking about you? I can't have a *prostitute* bring up my daughter. Come on, where are her things?'

He pushed past me and nearly knocked Ammumma over as he entered the bedroom. Spotting a suitcase in the corner, he emptied it roughly and started hurling clothes and toys into it. Winnie the Pooh, pink nylon dress, vests and pants, a tiny pair of rain-proof slippers, orthopaedic shoes, all Riya's worldly possessions were being thrown together in a frenzied forlorn heap. I had picked her up now, holding her so tight she had started to wail.

'Suresh, Suresh, what are you doing? Riya can't live without me. She needs me! Who will look after her? Your mother has never loved her, please don't let her be brought up by the servants!' I screamed as he pulled her out of my arms. His face was twisted, he'd torn the waist-band of her dress.

Riya was screaming louder than I was, her face purple with terror and rage, every little curl in her profuse mop trembling on her head. She held her arms out to me in a wordless, worthless screaming plea. There was nothing I could do, except grab at Suresh's arm, but I was pushed aside into the door jamb. From there Ammumma and I watched helplessly, clinging to each other, as Suresh locked Riya and her suitcase into the back seat of the car. In a few seconds, he was in the driver's seat and the car was rolling away from the house. Riya's face was a small, creased piece of pain pressed against the back window, barely visible through my tears and the rain.

Ma returned from the Electricity Board Office an hour later and found Ammumma and me slumped in the living room, surrounded by colourfully scattered flash cards. They were all there, apple, boy, cat, dog . . . only their noisy protagonist was missing. Ammumma whispered only 'Suresh . . . Riya' and Ma seemed to understand what had happened. Today it was up to her to take charge. I had no strength left, it was as if someone had taken a carving knife to my chest and carved a great gaping hole there, the pain was almost physical. Ma telephoned Madhava Menon to ask him if there was any legal redress. There wasn't. The law dictated that fathers had legal custody of all minor children. This was a very good law, he said, designed to protect children and their mothers from absconding fathers who absented themselves without paying expenses. No laws to protect children from fathers who just hated their mothers. Ma then telephoned the Maraar household. The Maraars were helpless. They had tried to discourage Suresh, after all children needed their mothers, but he had been determined. They would see what they could do. No point in calling again, though.

For a few days no one knew where Suresh was, not even the Maraars. I found later that he had taken Riya to a hotel in Cochin, to immerse her in his tears of rage. He had fed her endless plates of chicken fry and potato chips and pineapple pastries, to keep her quiet and to show her that he was a loving parent too. Finally, realizing probably that she needed more than room service, he returned to Valapadu and employed a servant to care for her when he was at the office. He insisted, according to his mother, on giving Riya her bath and food himself. Amma made it clear to my mother, on the telephone, that she blamed me for the struggle Suresh was enduring. Was it right for a man to bring up a daughter on his own, she asked? She was obviously doing everything in her power to discourage Suresh from hanging on to Riya, but he was like a man possessed. I hoped desperately that it wasn't merely to take revenge on me, but also because he needed to compensate for the years of having lived on the periphery of Riya's life. There would be some consolation in that.

I got to speak to Riya just once, when Suresh was at the office and Amma dialled us in Alleppey to quell a bout of bath-time tears. I could hear Riya's yells down the telephone line and pressed the receiver painfully close to my ear as though that would somehow bring her near. She went deathly quiet on hearing my tremulous 'hello'. She didn't *know* how telephones worked, I thought in a panic, she wouldn't understand why she could hear my voice without seeing my face.

'Hello, Riya moley,' I said again, 'it's Amma.'

'Amma?' There were a few snuffles before I heard her voice, now suddenly subdued, make a tearful request, 'Amma, ba . . .' and, just in case I needed the English translation as well, 'Amma . . . come.'

Those weeks of English tuition had filtered through, amazingly. But, despite such an unambiguous request, in both English and Malayalam, I sat helplessly with the telephone receiver pressed to my ear, tears pouring down my face. My wordless baby had found the word in *two* languages to tell me she needed me. Normally that achievement would have been greeted with a loud burst of verbal applause from me. (*Good* girl! Amma's clever, clever girl! 'Ba' and 'come', that's *exactly* right, what a little smartie you're turning out to be, eh?) But I knew if I attempted to speak, my words would choke me. And so I sat there silently, feeling my heart burst into a million pieces, its shards piercing holes through my whole being. I slammed the phone down as though it would burn my fingers if I held on any longer. If that was how painful the sound of her voice was going to be, how could I bear it any more? If I could somehow teach myself to live without it, please let her be able to forget I ever existed.

FIFTEEN

I waited for the day Suresh would learn that Riya's pain was a high price to pay for mine. He would have to bring her back before I left for England. After all, I had always said I was going for her sake. But it was getting plainer that Suresh's game was precisely to see if Riya could be the final force to hold me back. Twice small Alleppey contingents travelled to Valapadu to ask for Riya to be returned. The first time Ma and Ammumma went in Jose's taxi. I paced up and down the house, hope battering down on my heart, echoing the rain on the roof-tiles above. They were back by lunch time, without Riya, and looking like the weight of the world lay on their shoulders. Riya had recognized them, Ma said, but had hung back, hiding behind the skirts of Kallu, the girl who had been employed to look after her.

'What's she like? This Kallu, did she seem nice?'

'She had a kind face, and I did see her take Riya out into the garden to give her lunch, under the jambakkya tree, like you used to. I'm sure she looks after her well.'

'When we came out of the house, Riya was playing with Jose, she obviously remembered him as well ... "Jonkle Jonkle" she was saying like she used to,' we smiled at the memory of Riya's version of 'Jose Uncle', 'but when she saw us, she jumped back into the girl's arms, almost as though she had been taught to do so.'

'Don't be silly, they'd never do that.'

But Ammumma continued muttering, always less inclined to adopt Ma's more benevolent view of the Maraars,

'I've heard that Padmaja Maraar spent Riya's first week in Valapadu taking her around systematically to all her friends and relations to show everybody that Janu had just dumped her on them.' Ammumma ended this sentence with one more of the prize snorts she still reserved for conversations about the Maraars.

Suresh had not been there on that visit. But his parents were sure that he would merely come back to Alleppey and take Riya again if Ma had brought her back in Jonkle's taxi. I knew also that it would be far more damaging for Riya to become a joyless little ping-pong game in the argument between Suresh and me. It was better to leave her where she was. Children survived things, I tried to convince myself, and were always willing to transfer affections on to whoever was handy. My suffering, I hoped, was much worse than hers.

It was nearly September and it was decided that one more trip to Valapadu would be worth a try. Ramama was in Kerala on holiday. He'd been finally told of all the events and had arrived to provide moral support for the two weeks that he could get away. This time he accompanied Ma to Valapadu. I watched brother and sister leave to catch the morning boat, and saw Ramama put a protective arm around Ma as thcy crossed the busy road. In a sudden clutch of guilt, I remembered how easy it had once been to make everyone happy, realizing now that I'd just as easily flipped that coin. How odd that love within families should sometimes prove such a heavy burden to bear.

Suresh was in Valapadu on this occasion and Ramama attempted a man-to-man conversation with him. It was useless, they told me later, Suresh was adamant. I could go back to him if I wanted Riya. If not, he would bring her up on his own.

'He can't still mean it's possible for me to go back? Is he the last person in Kerala to realize that we've split up?'

Ramama looked at me with some hope, 'Couples do split up and re-unite all the time, you know. If you do go back now, people will forget all this in time, something new will come up for them to gossip about.'

The temptation simply to be back with Riya was overwhelming. My heart was being torn in two. With Suresh, I'd get Riya ... with Arjun, I'd get happiness ... what sort of a choice was that? 'Yes, but will Suresh ever forget? And his parents? My life with them wasn't great to start with, now it'll be absolutely unbearable. I'll be having to pay the price all my life.'

To my surprise, Ma said firmly, 'No, there's no going back now for Janu, Rama. She's right, the time for that has passed. I will not get a moment's sleep if she returns to that house. God knows what Suresh could do to her in a temper.'

'But my Riya? How can I leave my Riya behind ...?' I had already cried an ocean of tears for my poor baby daughter. Could oceans overflow, Mullakkalamma! What *could* Riya be thinking in that wordless little head of hers? Please let it be easier for people who had no words to complicate their thoughts.

'I think that's what he's waiting to see. Whether you will be able to go, leaving Riya behind. It's his last gamble. If you do leave, my feeling is that he will soon send her back to us. It's too difficult for him to manage. Especially since his mother would much rather Riya was sent back too.'

And so it was decided that, on the twenty-seventh of September, I would leave for England after all. Loyal old Jose's taxi was arranged for the trip to Cochin airport. Pickles were packed ('You must make sure you eat properly'). Ma and I pulled down an old tin trunk from the loft and spent an afternoon altering my old Delhi clothes. Jeans and tee-shirts from another time, hastily put away when a carefree teenager was transformed into a graceful Maraar, complete with a false smile and a false hip-length plait of hair.

Once Ma had been a cheerful island surrounded by a sea of wedding silk on this floor. Today she seemed shrouded in grief, pulling out clothes from a once-happy time, now crumpled and yellowing. That old white blouse with tiny blue flowers, in material that was all the rage then. Busy Lizzie, called 'Biji Liji' by Raghavson Tailors of Connaught Place, and 'Bissie Lissie' by Venu Tailor at Alleppey. Did she remember that hot happy day-excursion to have it tailored, with the clarity that I did? Connaught Place had then been the elegant centre of Delhi. Deserving of its own special excursions from distant suburbs, in cars packed with children and bottles of iced water. We'd read recently that, like us, Connaught Place had changed and was now a has-been town centre, dirty and frayed at its seedy edges. The Biji Liji (or Bissie Lissie, depending on which tailor you were painstakingly explaining the design to) had acquired little yellow stains and went into the growing pile of clothes for poor widowed Alamelu Mami's teenage daughter, about to start college soon. She'd never know, as Ma never did, that I'd worn it the day Arjun had taken me for the world's most delicious layered parathas under the Defence Colony flyover . . . Here was the dress I'd worn the day he left. Not my best one, but I'd left the house in such a hurry . . . My only salwaar kameez, just coming back into fashion then, dislodging the dreadful maxi-skirt . . . worn at dad's investiture when he was given a medal by the President of the country . . . remember . . . remember . . . there *had* been happy times once, Ma?

But I couldn't prevent Ma's ordeal from spinning out as she unfolded the old clothes smelling of mothballs and memories. These were meant to have lain here at peace, coming out on some happy afternoon, full of giggles and squeals . . . (*Look* at this maxi, how *ghastly*, imagine wearing something this shape now! . . . Parrot *green* trousers, see the *size* of the flare, it couldn't have got any bigger, could it!) Wasn't that what other people did with their old clothes? Pull them out for the grandchildren to look at and laugh at one day. Did other people ever have to transform their pasts into the present, and then take the present and mothball it away as though it was a best-forgotten past? She folded my Kanjeevaram saris (much too grand for student life in London) and a pile of blouses with four-altered-to-two pointies, and put them away carefully amidst the mothballs and neem leaves. Was she hoping it wouldn't be long before I was back and wearing them again? Don't pray for that, Ma. Pray instead for a kinder future among people who cared less. In indifference there would be less interference. In the cold of an English winter, people would be inclined to close their doors and no one would care less if I loved or lost or lived even. There would be comfort in that, Ma, there really would.

*   *   *

The twenty-seventh of September came with a blaze of sunshine. It was definitely the end of the monsoon and should have felt appropriate for the day I was to begin a new life. A dreamed-of life abroad where everything was going to be perfect. Where Riya and I were going to have a little apartment filled with toys and squashed cushions. Where I would drop her off at a gleaming school with its own hydrotherapy pool, and rush off for my lectures. But, someone had taken a pair of scissors to those cherished pictures and painstakingly cut Riya's picture out of every one of them. Everyone else was there, the happy playmates she would have, the firm kindly teacher, the pretty young childminder, the hydrotherapy pool overflowing with squealing laughter. But Riya, little mop-headed Riya, who clumped around noisily in her orthopaedic shoes, wasn't there any more. My life had gone silent with the departure of those horrid black shoes I so loathed. In every life that I would ever live again, that sad silence was going to travel with me. Everywhere. How many lifetimes would it take to erase the memory of that terrible, creeping, yawning silence?

I said goodbye to my mother, touched Ammumma's feet, pushed through the crowds at the airport, queued up at various desks, checked in my luggage and finally boarded that aircraft. I was making all the physical motions I had waited so long to make, but where was the joy that was supposed to have accompanied it? I could not tell if, by leaving the country, I was closing off the last chance I had of ever seeing Riya again. Was it just me or did everybody spend half their lives leaving something or someone precious behind? Was it just me or did we all make promises we weren't able to keep, even given such wonderful opportunities? Ma said it was best not even to make a phone call to Riya, as there was no knowing what Suresh would attempt doing if he knew I was actually leaving. Just go, she said, we'll see what we can do to get her back. Even she knew by now that I was better off on the other side of the world, far from a mother's love that, in the end, provides pitifully meagre protection. And far from the little girl I had brought into this world, pledging rashly to love and protect as long as I lived.

*   *   *

I took off from Cochin airport, and said goodbye to the land of my ancestors from above. Palm trees waved their farewell fronds and the sea glinted a goodbye smile. I knew there could no longer be anger at such a sorrowfully departing daughter. The motherland knew, like every birth mother does, that however far a child travels, it takes only a few notes of a half-forgotten lullaby, or the whiff of some sea-laden air to bring back the love. Bonds that are forged even before the first breath is taken cannot be broken with the passage of a few thousand miles, especially when ancient promises wait unredeemed.

Was it the watery rhythm of the punt against the side of the boat, was it the whispering of the palm trees above or had it been the welcoming hand of an ancestor stroking my brow that had hushed the crying of a child that day? Would it now wipe the tears from the face of my far-away child? And promise her I would be welcomed back someday?

PART III

SIXTEEN

Terminal Four of Heathrow airport was bigger than Cochin airport ten times over. It smelt of coffee and perfume, the sophisticated smell of a foreign land – miles from the salt-sea, full-of-fish smell of Cochin airport. I'd only seen so many white faces together once before, seated behind the military attaches' enclosure at the Republic Day Parade in Delhi. Then I'd been fascinated by the different brand of English they spoke and the size of the chocolate bars they ate. Their Cadbury's chocolates seemed decidedly bigger, chunkier and a glossier purple than the emaciated melting bars we got to buy at Mota Kaka's shop. Their children were bigger and chunkier as well and looked like my collection of dolls, blonde, blue-eyed and beautiful. For days I had moped around wanting to be blonde and beautiful too. Now here I was, being tossed on a sea of white faces, *being* the foreigner, when I spotted my desert island. Arjun. Next to the British Airways Customer Relations Desk, as agreed.

I had called him from Madras airport, after a short struggle with myself to spare him the agonies of my life by vanishing into the blue. He would wait another few months and then give up on me and get on with his life, I told myself. As he had done before. It was no big deal, he would have said to a friend (or a wife) many years later. When I did call him after a few short minutes, I could not tell if I was doing it because I had promised him I would, or because I wanted to, so desperately, for myself. His voice sounded tinny and far away, but happy. *Very happy!* The Riya-hole in my heart filled up a tiny bit.

He saw me only when I was very near him. Dropping the paper he was reading, he grabbed me and lifted me high into the air, twirling me around. He was saying something that I could not hear because of the clamour inside my head and because Terminal Four of Heathrow airport was doing a dizzy dance around me. Smiling faces, blonde beautiful children, luggage-laden trollies, cafés selling croissants and muffins . . . all joined hands and danced around us. It felt foolish and wonderful, like the first day in love. But it wasn't really, much as I wanted to pretend it was. Arjun's happiness was undiluted, he knew nothing yet of the trials I'd faced, of the price I'd had to pay in many different ways and, worst of all, of the Riya-hole in my heart. But, in the innocence of his happiness, perhaps I could forget the worst too. For a few lovely moments. We walked out of the terminal building, pushing along my suitcase full of old clothes, two old lovers finally together. Leaving a trail of destruction in their wake.

He had a red car. 'It's a *Scirocco*, not a red car,' he said, pained at my failing to appreciate his excellent taste in cars. We drove down a crowded motorway. No white Ambassador cars here, I thought. I looked out of the window at a rolling carpet of velvet green, dotted with fat sheep. I was in England, and Arjun was sitting next to me, in a Scirocco! Had I wandered by some chance into one of my own dreams? Did I dare look around to see if a little pink nylon figure was occupying the back seat, head lolling about in innocent open-mouthed sleep. Would I wake up and find I was still in Kerala, still dreaming my foolish dreams? What time is it . . . ten-plus-four-and-a-half, half past two, Saturday afternoon. Riya should be having her post-lunch nap now. Did they know that she liked to have her up-turned bottom patted to help her get to sleep? For the moment I could not bear to tell even Arjun about the events that had separated me from my child. 'She'll probably join me by the second term,' I had mumbled in reply to Arjun's initial query at the airport. He had looked at me enquiringly at that, but had probably spotted the unspoken pain in my eyes and had not asked me anything more.

I marvelled at how expertly Arjun was handling the streaming traffic. Indicator right . . . change lanes . . . overtake . . . indicator left . . . back again. It was all uncannily orderly and not one peep of a horn! 'It's like a dance,' I said to Arjun, 'all these little cars swinging gracefully around each other, keeping time, careful not to step on anyone's toes.'

He laughed, 'Well I'm glad you like the motorway, because I have to warn you about Milton Keynes before we get there.'

'Warn me?'

'Well be prepared for about the most un-English-place you could hope to find in England.' He told me about it as we drove along. Milton Keynes had nothing to do with either John Milton or Maynard Keynes. Named after the tiny village it had swamped, it was a new town, still being built. He'd seen smart new offices and homes come up on farms and fields, it was a miracle of town-planning (and exceedingly unpopular with the rest of England), he said, pulling away from the motorway traffic under a bright blue sign. Goodbye little cars, I thought, thanks for the dance.

Milton Keynes was *definitely* not English. Not a trace of any of the wet green images my MA books had conjured up on hot sleepless Kerala nights. No winding country roads lined with hedgerows, no pretty little church, and *certainly* no fat-cheeked parson. But the long roads were lined with trees that someone had painted over in colours that I thought existed only in sari shops. Hundreds of shades of burnished orange and gold. We passed some gleaming buildings and a large lake, with two sailing boats painted on. It was all pristine and clean, rather like I'd imagined Phoenix would be. More large office buildings went past and the odd car before I turned to Arjun in alarm, 'Don't you have any *people* here in Milton Keynes?'

He laughed, 'We like to keep them out of sight. At ten we round up the population, open the doors to the shopping mall, and then stuff them all in there.'

'All this space!' I thought of Kerala, bursting at the seams. 'You couldn't travel ten seconds without having to swerve to avoid a child or a chicken or something in Kerala. It's manic by comparison with this . . . this *stillness*, I can tell you.'

'Are you missing it? Kerala? Does all this seem really strange to you?'

'I think the silence here will be good for my soul, Arjun.' Did I miss Kerala, where people drove with their thumbs glued down to their car horns? And where everyone was more interested in what was happening to you than to them. Kerala was in my blood, now mother to my child. I'd always miss Kerala, however much I hated it sometimes.

'I feel I must warn you about the houses here as well, Janu. Don't be too shocked, but you'll initially feel that it's all about to fall and collapse in a heap around your ears. They're all made of chip-board and wood, none of that solid stone and granite stuff of Indian houses. And the rooms will be a lot smaller than the high-ceiling halls you're accustomed to. When the chap next door moved in from some place in the country, he couldn't get his double bed in through the front door. I came back from work one day to find him sitting on his double bed in the garden, wondering desperately what to do with it!'

We drove up to a small house with a sloping blue roof and a tiny handkerchief patch of lawn in front. The doll's house I'd spent my childhood longing for. And, for that matter, most of my adult life too. Mine, to be arranged and re-arranged and played with to my heart's content. We *were* to be the dolls (albeit not blonde and blue-eyed) and I got out of the car, wondering if, for the first time in my life, I could finally place myself exactly where I wanted. Here there would be no one to tell me how to chop the vegetables and how to hang up my blouse. This was to become my home. My grown-up Chor Minar, where I could do it all for real. Here, I wanted to pretend all over again that Arjun and I were married, never having to be apart again. Like that time long ago, it was important to concentrate on the fact that we had somehow been given a glorious present, even if we had been deprived of a past or a future. It was best not to look too far ahead.

Later that night, I told Arjun about the events of the past few months and knew that he bled in the same places that hurt me too. I also told him about Suresh's threats and asked if he could move house, but he laughed it off with the carelessness of someone who has never experienced real hate. He looked so happy, I could not bring myself to tell him now that, if Riya had not been returned to my mother by the end of the year, I was going to have to get back to India and fight for her custody. Even if that meant losing our chance of a life together all over again.

We made love that night with the sweet searching curiosity of a first time. Suddenly, as never before, we were millionaires in time! Tonight there were no Chor Minars that had to be hastily abandoned as the bats began to flap at sunset. And no tyrannical trains thundering towards us, intent on tearing us apart again in the morning. Time and night-time were luxuries we had never had before, and the world seemed filled with new moonlit mysteries. Later, as we lay in each other's arms, warm and drifting with sleep, I looked out at the trembling stars, praying that the Goddess who was dreaming all this for me would sleep on for ever.

Twinkle . . . twinkle . . . stars of light . . . lovers laughing in the
  night.
Devi . . . Goddess . . . shining bright . . . keep us in your loving
  sight.
Thank you, Devi . . . shining bright . . . thank you for this lovely
  night . . .

It had been a still, blue evening but now, as the sky
darkened and melted into night, I could feel a cool breeze
rise from the nearby lake and drift into our tiny bedroom.
It was going to get cold later, I thought. I pulled up the sheet
that lay across the foot of the bed and covered both Arjun
and myself carefully with it.

*   *   *

We left for London the following weekend, to take possession of the room I'd been allocated at the hall of residence.
I had written to the University requesting normal student
accommodation ('It has been decided that my daughter will
not be accompanying me for the time being'). It was so easy
to say it on paper.

London was more like the England I'd expected from the
pamphlets sent to me by the University – all tall buildings
and tall buses and busy clicking heels on pavements. The
Institute building was a block of black glass, self-import-
antly hiding its vast stores of knowledge. Just a short walk
away was the hall of residence, a graceful white building in
the heart of Bloomsbury, with window boxes bursting with
red geraniums. How Ammumma had struggled, unsuccess-
fully, to grow red geraniums for years. Hers would every
year struggle up through the sandy Alleppey soil, be treated
to the most expensive fertilizers available at Lovely General
Stores on Mullakkal main road, before proceeding unfailingly to die. 'I'll get a picture of you in front of these the
next time I'm here and you can send her that,' Arjun said,
pulling my suitcase out of the car. Having collected my

keys from a loquacious Italian hall manager, we climbed two flights of stairs, arriving at cubby hole number 108.

'*Voilà!*' Arjun said, throwing the door open.

'When they say "sleeps one", they mean "a very small one", don't they? I'll have to get into this room and wrap it around me, like a skirt!' It was diminutive, but functional, my world for the year to come, and I loved it instantly. 'I'll unpack later, after you've gone. Now I want to see London.'

We set out from the hall, discovering that Euston station was just beyond a road that I thought would take for ever to cross. 'We'll use the pelican crossing further up,' Arjun said. *Pelicans* . . . to help me cross a road in central London? 'That's just what they're called, don't ask me why,' he said laughing at the expression on my face. Euston station was about as big as New Delhi station, except that no one seemed to have bothered to bring any luggage. Just brief-cases, handbags and newspapers . . . the British sure knew how to travel light – that must have been a handy skill when they'd set out to conquer the world. No porters and no arguments. Marvellous system, I thought. Escalators were swallowing people down into the tube station . . . what would our poor porters back in India have thought of these magic stairways, tottering as they did with necks about to snap, under towering piles of luggage belonging to wealthy Delhi matriarchs. After Arjun and I had done the escalator loop twice over, I felt I had mastered the art of getting on and off them without great flying leaps. 'I'm a fast learner,' I said to an amused Arjun, but changed my mind on seeing the tube map.

I had a lot to learn, and I couldn't have asked for a kinder, more dedicated tutor. With occasional fallibilities, as I was to discover later that afternoon.

'Look, that's St Paul's over there,' Arjun pointed to his right as we walked across a sun-washed bridge.

I looked at the majestic sweep of a long structure lying

on the edge of a river like an elaborate Kerala bracelet chiselled out of old gold. I'd seen that building many times before, pressing my nose on the glass of Ammumma's cabinet in her front room, gawping at all the precious possessions I had not been allowed to touch as a child. There it was, exactly the same picture as on the china plate that Ammumma had won as a schoolgirl for coming first in an egg-and-spoon race.

'That's *Westminster*, isn't it?'

'Oh, is it? You could be right, actually. Whoops, that's a bit of a gaffe, I suppose! That's what I mean, I don't come into London often enough . . .'

I smacked Arjun with my rolled-up newspaper, 'All morning I've been drinking in your pearls of wisdom, how many other golis have you given me today?'

'Oh shut up,' he grinned, shutting me up with a resounding kiss. We kissed again, more gently, leaning on the balustrade of the bridge, while traffic roared uncaringly past and boats tooted their horns gaily on the river below . . . what a strange world, I thought, no one cares that we're kissing in this public place . . . what a terrific world, I decided, where no one cares *at all*!

In Arjun's company it was easy to forget the past, so awash with pain. Had yesterday ever felt more long ago? Riya's face was in the face of every child we passed on the road. Never far from my immediate consciousness, something like Arjun's had been in the first few years of my marriage to Suresh. Now here he was with me, amazingly. But Riya had gone. Someone was making sure my joys would always be delivered to me in neat little parcels, not too big and not too small. Just to make sure I did not go keeling over Waterloo Bridge in an over-abundance of happiness.

We ate every meal out that weekend, wandering around looking for different kinds of food. Chinese, Japanese, Lebanese . . . 'It's amazing but we really should try to get back to the hall for meal times. I've *paid* for it up front, Arjun!'

'I'm never eating hall food ever again if I can help it,' he replied with feeling.

'There's nothing wrong with it,' I said, 'except that they serve you *fish* for breakfast. Bleah!'

'Spoken like a good Kerala girl.'

'As any Keralite worth his salt will tell you, fish is eaten at every meal *except* breakfast, silly.'

Hall food apart, after two cramped nights in my minuscule living quarters, we decided that it would be more sensible to spend our weekends in Milton Keynes. I took careful instructions from Arjun to get to Euston and catch a fast train the following weekend. But it was Monday morning now and time for Arjun to leave me on my own. 'Wish it didn't, but work beckons and, I suppose, the fastest way you'll learn to deal with things is by getting around on your own,' he said, not looking confident at all of my ability to get around without him.

'Don't worry, Arjun,' I took his hand as we walked to the car, 'this might have been Arizona and I might never have met you again and then who would have worried about me? I'll manage, don't worry.'

But hc still had some last-minute instructions. 'Racism,' he said, getting into the car and leaning out of the window, 'just cross the road if you feel threatened in any way. *Never* react. However angry you feel.'

I smiled at him. He hasn't changed that much, I thought, still worrying more about me than I do about myself. I reached out my hand and tousled his hair. Brown, now with flecks of grey!

'And the other kind of racism – far more pernicious – if anyone tries to get frosty with you. You know these receptionist types or salesmen in posh places, who'll pretend they can't understand what you're trying to say. Or who'll speak r-e-a-l-l-y s-l-o-w-l-y regardless of how well you speak English. Don't *ever* let them make you feel small. Just think of them sitting on the bog. That usually helps.'

I laughed, 'I can't wait to try that out. Don't *worry*, my sweet, if you aren't careful I'll start on you now . . . Drive *slowly* . . . Eat *breakfast* every day . . . *Don't* play too much cricket, it's bad for the bones . . .' I was still ranting as he drove away, much too fast, I thought.

For the first time in the world I was all alone. And the odd thing was that I'd never felt *less* alone in my life before. I ran up the steps of the hall of residence shouting a cheerful hello to the bemused manager. It was Induction Day today and I had already received instructions to join the other foreign students who had flocked to London for the year from so many far-away places.

We filed into a large room and grew silent as the Union president and a representative of the NHS started to speak. It startled me that among the first things discussed was birth control. A subject only spoken in whispers back home was suddenly out in the open in mixed company and I hoped that I looked suitably nonchalant too. We were advised to see the GPs assigned to us as soon as possible to discuss contraceptive pills if we needed them and it seemed the NHS's generosity knew no bounds when economy packs of condoms started getting passed around as well. The next offering was a small innocuous lipstick-shaped object. This, we were told reassuringly, was called a screamer and was to be used in the event of being molested by a stranger. The droll image of a stranger setting out to accost me and then waiting politely while I fished around in my bag for my screamer floated through my panic-stricken mind. The NHS woman was on her feet again. She had forgotten something important. In a kindly but firm tone she informed us that, while we were entitled to use NHS facilities, eyes and teeth did not come free. This was repeated again, v-e-r-y s-l-o-w-l-y, as Arjun had predicted. *No* eyes and *no* teeth. Spectacles and dental cavities would simply have to wait until we got back home. With this, most of the serious business seemed to have been completed. 'Now comes the fun bit,' whispered the Japanese girl sitting next to me. Information about theatreland, nightclubs, tourist attractions. 'I came here to do a course four years ago and saw every show in the West End,' she whispered again with a tinkly laugh, 'this time I'm here for *Blood Brothers* and *Miss Saigon*.'

I smiled back at her and didn't tell her that she was welcome to the multifarious attractions of theatreland. My weekends were all carefully reserved for Arjun in Milton Keynes. There, in that funny little toy-city where even lakes and trees were painted on (and people were all air-brushed out), was a little doll's house, with a blue roof and fibreboard walls, that was going to become my home. Not for ever, of course, but that was a word I'd left behind in my childhood anyway.

The course, which started in earnest the following day, was going to be tougher than expected, I could tell. Words were already floating around that meant nothing to me: . . . Stage 1 . . . statements . . . EPs . . . OTs . . . ADDs . . . I'd reached some kind of nether world populated entirely by tired-looking teachers, all speaking a language comprising a series of random acronyms. Most of the local students seemed to be schoolteachers hoping to be promoted to some coveted post called a SENCO after completing the course. The average age seemed to be world-weary forty-something and the tutors consequently only needed to occupy the outer fringes of this group. A far cry, I thought, from poor Sister Seraphia who had performed her guardian duties with such diligence. I was assigned to the care of Professor Bailey, who floated gaily into the tutors' quadrangle every morning on his cycle, bright red muffler flying behind him, his hair the colour of fresh snow. Best of all, I soon found that, at a speed faster than my success rate with acronyms, I was also learning to make friends again. Ailish, an Irish girl with a warm smile, and Susan, a schoolteacher from North London, had got chatting to me during a coffee break in the Union bar. Initially worried that everyone in England would speak like the characters out of a P. G. Wodehouse book, I talked to them carefully, hoping all errors would be drowned in the din of the music. Two coffees later, I decided they were both exceedingly interested in what I had to say and I could feel myself relax.

'You didn't seriously think we all went around saying Tally-ho and Pip-pip, did you?' Susan was surprised but, fortunately, tickled pink.

I laughed and admitted my disappointment, but I could feel the years of coldness drip slowly out of my heart. I had allowed myself to forget, in far-away Valapadu, that there were plenty of people in the world who were kind and warm too. That evening, I wandered with my two new friends down to Euston station to sample the South Indian food I'd heard was available in a café near there. It hadn't taken me long to work out that what was elegantly presented as English food in posh restaurants in India was a far cry from the stodge that was served up at the hall of residence. Tucking greedily now into sub-standard dosas and sambar, I felt sudden nostalgia for Ma's cooking. Poor Ma, how much pain I'd put her through!

Proudly I explained the intricacies of dosas to Ailish and Susan and, in a rush of affection, I offered to teach them how to make proper vegetable curry. The venue was fixed as Susan's Finchley flat the following day, Susan being the only one among us who actually owned a kitchen at the moment. Armed with the requisite masalas and a bottle of wine ('That's the English way, don't question it,' from a concerned Arjun on the telephone), I found my way up four flights of stairs to Susan's tiny flat, filled with ferns. Their conversation opened up new worlds for me, but I could see that it was the same emotions and the same fates that ruled over us all. Ailish was single, still nursing a heartbreak that had sent her flying away from Dublin in the summer. Susan had been divorced five years ago and seemed determined to keep it that way. I told them, tentatively, about my own marriage, and Riya, and the hole in my heart, and I knew I was not imagining their unjudgemental concern. It wasn't that Kerala had not been able to offer one sympathetic friend, but that I had been so unhappy there, I had forgotten the art of making them.

In some ways it was almost as if I could only understand the depth of my unhappiness in Kerala when I had been removed from it. I considered it extremely fortunate that for the moment I had nothing more challenging to deal with than the mastering of acronyms and the theories of Chomsky. I was even beginning to think I might have conquered my fear of vending machines, which initially had seemed diabolically intent on swallowing up my precious pennies without offering anything in return.

But it worried me incessantly that, in the midst of this busy new life, Riya's absence was fading into a silent background grief. I had no recent photographs of her to keep her face alive in my mind. Having left Valapadu for the mental hospital in such a dazed state, I'd had to leave all my meagre possessions behind. Later Suresh had sent two tin trunks to Alleppey – after he'd taken Riya – full of my old clothes and footwear and Ma's scraped-together seven necklaces. As though he was attempting to purge his wardrobes and his life of my existence. But among those sad remnants of an incomplete life were none of the things that I really needed and that I might have derived some comfort from. No photographs, no stray memories of a marriage and an occasional, certain sort of happiness.

Before leaving for England, I had trawled through Ma's albums and found a few old pictures that were now stuck on to the notice board in my room. Riya . . . posing with her head cocked to one side against Ammumma's hydrangeas, their heads almost as big as hers. Riya . . . as one of the Wise Men with a bristling moustache in her school nativity play, looking like a tiny fierce Sikh unhappy at having been snapped in his bath-robe. These were the memories I clung to some London nights, as the wind rattled my window panes and the laughter of revellers returning from the pub floated up the road.

By the time winter descended in a sad greyness over London, I could feel a sort of belonging, as much as it is possible to belong in large busy cities anywhere in the world. When a new batch of students arrived at the hall, I found myself explaining to a young man from Andhra Pradesh, shivering miserably in a Siberian great coat and balaclava, how best to tackle London. The tubes are *easy* to master, I heard myself say. If in doubt, just ask, the English are usually very pleased to help. I knew though, as Arjun had warned, that it wasn't a perfect world. I had once had an empty coke can kicked at me by a distinguished-looking man and realized, with some shock, that people in Barbour jackets were capable of racism too. Not all my course mates had been as kind, of course, as Ailish and Susan. Some of them never once bothering to speak to me, unwilling probably to waste their time with people from far-away worlds who would never understand the rigours of their teaching careers in inner-city schools, burdened further now by the new National Curriculum and Education Act. But I was too busy to bother with socializing while at the Institute and, in the evenings, the hall of residence was a warm place where African music filtered through the walls. I could slowly feel my wings begin to unfurl, and, on one particularly joyous day, Maggie Thatcher was toppled

– and students in the Union bar had clambered on to café tables, to stamp their Doc Martens and cheer as though this marked a new beginning for the whole world.

I called Alleppey occasionally and heard Ma's distant voice talk about a world that had almost never existed. Riya, she said, was fit and healthy, as far as she knew. She had been put back into Sheela's school because her behaviour had been deteriorating. Ma spoke sometimes to Suresh's mother, but Suresh had made no contact with her at all. He did, twice, with me. Phone calls to Arjun's house, full of angry tears that throbbed down the telephone lines. These were more difficult to deal with than pure, straightforward anger. He was still adamant he would not put Riya on a plane to England to take the place I'd reserved for her at a special school in Camden. Instead, he handed the phone over to a bewildered Riya, a tiny silent bit of bait who didn't have the words to entice me back. Her superhuman effort to produce a 'Ba' and a 'Come' hadn't worked once. Land and seas and a father's misguided love would keep us apart. I hung up on her with trembling hands, begging her to forgive her mother's impotent grief.

Suresh's feelings of betrayal throbbed across the oceans over those months, swirling up through the life Arjun and I were trying to fashion for ourselves. Anyone who has attempted to build a life using someone else's pain as a foundation will know that it doesn't really work. It hangs around, like an unhappy spirit, creeping up at the most unexpected moments, able to ruin a party with one sweep of its hand. Suresh's desperate mind was still searching restlessly for some way to de-rail my life. There was to be one more attempt . . . that would come at Christmas.

But Arjun and I had (and it still seems miraculous that we did) our weekends of happiness together. Again, because of the circumstances, it was merely a sort of happiness I suppose. But I was glad to have at least that. I counted them once ... forty-two weekends, Friday evenings to Sunday nights. Those, plus a week at Christmas and a week at Easter, would make it almost exactly ninety-eight days. That was what we would get, ninety-eight days together, to make up for those lost years. To create a sort of life, a sort of happiness. That could have been regarded as either a blessing or a curse, depending on which way you looked at it.

SEVENTEEN

People don't normally think of rows as desirable things in relationships but, when Arjun and I had our first one it felt as though life was beginning to be filled with a delicious normality. In December we had both our first squabble and our first row. And I found joy in the knowledge that our relationship would have none of the yawning silences that had churned emptily between Suresh and me.

We were in Sainsbury's on a crowded Saturday and I was wandering, fascinated as usual at the range of goodies available. Arjun, who I was not aware had been hunting for me between the milk and the fresh juices, descended on me in sudden anger.

'What the *hell* are you doing? I've been looking everywhere . . .'

I waved airily at the rainbow of colours that was the coffee aisle, 'We're out of coffee, I think . . .'

'And how long does it take to pick up a jar of coffee? Here, let me show you.' He plucked a jar off the shelf and said sarcastically, looking at his watch, 'Hmm . . . three seconds . . . honestly, do you have a *Ph.D.* in Procrastination or something?!'

I was cut to the quick because I knew he was referring indirectly to the years it had taken me to leave Kerala. 'How was I to know which brand you wanted?' I said crossly, sticking to the safety of the coffee issue, not wanting to bring the other one up. Not in the middle of Sainsbury's at any rate. 'You make it sound so simple, "Go and get some coffee", if you aren't careful you can *drown* in coffees here ... caff, decaff, Columbian, Kenyan, Blue Mountain, Powder, Beans . . .' I was gaining confidence. 'In India you say "Coffee" to the shop man and he brings you the familiar old Bru bottle. But this . . . this . . .' I waved my hand accusingly at the hundreds of bottles lined up behind me and concluded with a flourish, 'I've never seen anything as *ridiculous* as a whole aisle full of coffees before!'

I surprised myself more than Arjun with my little outburst. When had my tongue emerged from its protracted hibernation? Ma was the only person I ever spoke to with any amount of peevishness, and that was only because I knew she'd never stop loving me. Had Arjun now joined that diminishing list of one? I grinned at him now, pleased suddenly with my temerity. He put his arm around my shoulder, but didn't do himself any favours by enquiring solicitously, 'Jesus! It isn't that time of the month, is it?'

Squabble number two was, predictably, about his sport. Arjun, mercifully free of a girlfriend for the past couple of years, had grown accustomed to spending his Saturdays in gay abandon, playing cricket all through the summer and tennis in the winter. This to me was intolerable, 'Our time together is so limited, Arjun! Don't you care?'

'It's not limited – you do intend staying the rest of our lives, don't you?'

'Of course I do, but I'll have to get back when the course finishes to get my divorce and to get Riya.'

That was what led to our first real row.

'Have you ever thought of what will happen if he doesn't give you Riya?'

I had considered discussing this with Arjun at some point, but my Ph. D. in Procrastination had put paid to that. Now I had to tell him when he was in a bad mood. My own mood wasn't great either. I'd just posted a birthday card to Riya, with writing in it that she could never read and with the

284

knowledge that Suresh wouldn't even attempt to tell her that it meant I loved her too.

I said flatly and untactfully, 'If he doesn't give me Riya, then I'll stay there until he does.'

'That could take years, you know the Indian legal system.'

I said, even more untactfully, 'I don't care, she's the most important thing in my life. Nothing else matters really.'

Arjun looked at me with raw hurt springing into his normally gentle eyes, he opened his mouth as if to say something and then, changing his mind, got up and left the room. A few seconds later I heard the front door slam shut. He had left his tennis things behind and I thought crossly that he was sure to be back to get them before the match started. Nothing will make him give *that* up, I thought, still smarting. But he wasn't back and, by two o'clock in the afternoon, I was tearful and worried. Having re-examined my ill-chosen words, I knew how deeply I must have hurt him. But it was something that had to be confronted at some point. We weren't, unfortunately, the teenagers who had once loved each other – although, with me here as a student and minus Riya, it was so easy to drown in the delusion that we were. We were two adults who had met, in a completely new life, and were now having to get to know each other from scratch. *And*, I was hoping to add Riya to that. Not our child, born to two loving parents, but Riya. Mop-headed Riya who clumped around noisily and demanded everything she saw with an 'Ah-ah-ah'. And who belonged, half-belonged, to Suresh too, now so desperate to prove to himself and the world that he loved her too. How on earth would Arjun cope? I had to find him and ask him that myself.

I pulled on my coat and stepped out into the fading afternoon, asking myself forlornly what I would do if Arjun did indeed turn around and say he could not cope with Riya, or with my need to be with her. Three months without her had decided for me that I could not live even the most wonderful life if she was to be separated from me by an ocean. Arjun was going to have to hear me say that. I promised myself I would be brave and merely pack up and leave for India, depending on how he reacted. The course wasn't that important.

I found him on a wooden bench looking out at Tongwell Lake. The ducks had already written him off as a non-bread-giver and were now paddling miserably in a distant corner of the icy lake. I sat down next to him and noticed his eyes were red, his face frozen.

'Arjun, I'm sorry if I hurt you. It must have sounded so callous.' He was silent, and I continued, 'The thing is, I don't think I can live the rest of my life without Riya. She's so terribly difficult sometimes, but I don't have to worry about her when she's right under my nose. When she isn't, I worry about her endlessly. I'm just going to have to go back for her when the course is finished.'

'I haven't asked you to write her out of your life, have I?' he said finally. There was cold anger in his voice.

'No you haven't . . .' I started, but he interrupted me.

'Is that how you think it has to be? Either me or her?'

I thought about my little parcels of joy, not too big and not too small. But Arjun the optimist would never understand a future viewed with such trepidation. The thought of lining up patiently to wait for joys to be conferred would be anathema to someone like him.

'I'm not sure you'll be able to cope with her, that's all. She dribbles and hollers and barges about. She'll turn your life upside down. How on earth will you manage?'

'I don't *know* if I'll manage, but I've told you before, I'm willing to try.'

'And if it doesn't work?'

'Janu, for God's sake, haven't you learnt yet that things can't be planned and mapped out as meticulously as you seem to think! You want to know *exactly* how things will be ten years, five years, a year from now? Well, the answer is, I just don't know. All I know is that I'll do my damnedest to make it work – even with Riya – and, as for the rest, we'll just have to wait and see!'

I looked out at the lake serenely reflecting the sky. Ma had tried telling me something like that once too. That, whether I liked it or not, things were decreed and that it was arrogance to imagine I could personally go out and change them. But Arjun had said something about trying one's damnedest too. That sounded like a pretty good thing to emulate. But, in acquiring that wisdom, I had hurt this dear man whose fault it *wasn't* that Riya was not with me. A flock of geese passed overhead, cackling noisily about which warmer destination they ought to pick this year. I watched them fly with Air Force precision across the lake and over the motorway out of Milton Keynes. Please, Mrs Geese, if you happen to go past India, would you drop by Valapadu and tell my daughter that the birthday card (the one with the puppies on it) really means that I love her too.

I slid across the bench to signify an apology, but Arjun wasn't ready to thaw. He would in fact take another two days to thaw, two whole days out of our precious ninety-eight. Riya's pint-sized figure was casting a very long shadow. Happy birthday, moley, I thought sadly.

* * *

But it was just a few days later, nearly Christmas, when even that row seemed to pale into nothingness in the face of a completely new and unexpected terror. Arjun and I were in the kitchen, making a Christmas korma. In all his years in England, Arjun had fiercely resisted doing any of the traditional English things. The If-it's-Tuesday-it-Must-be-Egg-and-Chips Routine, he called it. I'd just finished cleaning the chicken when the doorbell rang.

'Bloody carollers, probably, I'm not getting it,' Arjun said, calmly chopping onions.

'I don't mind them that much, actually. I think I like Christmas, whatever you say.'

'You wait till you've had your tenth one here. It's just an endless round of turkeys guzzling turkey . . .'

The bell went again. 'That's odd, they're not normally so persistent.'

'I'll go,' I said, washing my hands. Wiping them on my jeans, I opened the door. A policeman and a man in plain clothes were standing on the snow-crusted steps, the man in plain clothes was holding out a plastic laminated card.

'I'm Neville Canning of the Immigration Department. I'm here to investigate a complaint of an illegal entrant living at this address. Are you Mrs Janaki Maraar?' He pronounced it Junaaki, and I thought, irrelevantly, that I ought to correct him, but he didn't look like the sort who particularly enjoyed having to struggle with strange foreign names.

'I am Janaki Maraar. But I'm not an illegal entrant, I have a student visa.' The thought crossed my mind that it was *Christmas*; what were these people doing outside on a night like this, trawling the town in search of illegal immigrants? Shouldn't they all be tucking into their turkeys, surrounded by children in silly hats?

'I'm afraid I'll have to ask you to accompany us to the police station to answer some questions. You'll need to bring your passport with you. I'd appreciate it if you came without causing any problems, or we'll have to arrest you.'

I could feel Arjun behind me. 'Can I accompany her?' he asked.

The two men looked him up and down, as though he had the potential for being an illegal entrant too. The right kind of colour, the right kind of smell (onions). And what were they doing cooking *curry* at Christmas, bleedin' foreigners, you could hear them think.

We turned the gas off and drove silently in our red Scirocco to the police station in the centre of town, with the police car following us. There was no advice we could try to give each other, we'd neither of us known anything like this before. Arjun was asked to wait in the lobby, full of unfamiliarly desperate-looking people. I was taken downstairs into a basement that was a warren of labyrinthine corridors and rooms. People were sitting in various hopeless states inside little barred rooms. I tried not to look, so as not to make it worse for them, forgetting for a minute I was really one of them. I followed Mr Canning's broad back into a tiny room and the door was closed behind me. I gingerly took a chair on one side of a scratched worn table, Mr Canning sat across from me, and started fussing around with a large, old-fashioned tape-recorder. The policeman had vanished. I presumed his duty had come to an end because I had trotted obediently into the police station, without kicking and screaming. I knew better than to do that because I'd read in the papers of illegal immigrants being trussed up with their mouths taped if they struggled. My experience with Suresh and his mental health doctors squad was too recent for me to even contemplate risking the same with Mr Canning and his immigration police squad.

Suresh? Could he be responsible for this? I didn't know anyone in England well enough to be reported for any misdemeanour. *Was* it a misdemeanour to have entered England as a student and then to be living with Arjun? I was still a student though. Was *adultery* a crime in this country? I knew in India it was a jailable offence. Mr Canning's tape machine had coughed to life, he'd said something and was now looking coldly and enquiringly at me. Oh no, now he would think I was deaf as well.

'Mrs Maraar, do you need an interpreter?' He did not

pronounce the r at the end of 'Maraar', but rolled the name out with an 'aah' at the end, as though it gave him great pleasure to say it.

'Oh, no thanks . . .' Wasn't he supposed to ask me if I needed to call a solicitor? Or was that in America? The many American and English films I'd seen through my teenage years had left me with a hotch-potch idea of life in these countries. I didn't *know* if I was entitled to a lawyer. I didn't dare ask, in case it put Mr Canning off me for good. Honesty would work best. Some of my experiences in India should have taught me that honesty did not always pay, but I was willing to give it another shot.

'It's true that I came here on a student visa. I am actually studying in London, at the Institute of Education. I only come to Milton Keynes for the holidays and weekends. That's because I'm hoping to get married to Mr Mehta, whose house it is. I can't marry him at the moment because my husband . . . *ex-husband* won't give me a divorce. I'm separated from him though, I haven't seen him in months. Is he responsible for this?'

It spilt out, in an ungraceful heap of words on to Mr Canning's scratched old table. Divorce, adultery, horrid nasty words, whichever country you were in. His machine whirred on obligingly as he asked me a series of questions, round and round, I knew I was repeating myself. As his gaze grew keener, I was aware of the quality of my English deteriorating. Stop stammering, remember to *aspirate* . . . my Indian accent was squeezing its way out, sending my tongue into overdrive. I remembered an old bit of advice Arjun had given me once, and mentally undressed Mr Canning's nether regions, popping him unceremoniously on to an imaginary toilet. From that undignified perch he continued to look intently at me, suddenly looking innocuous. He seemed to be making a genuine attempt to assess the truth of my words. Although everything was true, I felt I had to put my most honest expression on to convince him I was not an illegal immigrant, despite the colour of my skin, the sound of my consonants and the old jeans that had been altered so sorrowfully by my mother. My clothes, reeking of onions, surely would not help. Suddenly, surprisingly, his expression changed. He believed me! With the machine still recording, he told me it was illegal to enter the country on false pretences. Therefore, while it was not a crime to be living with Mr Mihitaaah, my primary purpose in being in this country had to be my course of study. When the course finished, therefore, I would have to leave, whatever the status of my relationship with Mr Mihitaaah at that time. If I did want to return as his wife or fiancée, I would have to make a separate application to the British High Commission in India. That application would then be judged on its own merits. He was doing me a favour in treating my case with sympathy and understanding, and he would therefore not insist that I present myself at a police station every week, which was normal procedure in cases like this. It would suffice if I called the Immigration Authorities at Luton every week, to inform them of my whereabouts. Hopefully, I also understood it was a very serious offence to take up paid employment without specific permission to do so.

As the machine was clicked off, I stood up on my still trembling legs. I was free to go. I was going to get my carefully calculated ninety-eight days after all. I needed to get to Arjun as soon as possible, to put him out of his agony. Upstairs in the lobby, I ran to him and put my arms around him, safe in the knowledge that it wasn't a crime to do so in this country. Suresh's last trick had not come to anything, he would soon give up, he *had* to. Was it his broken heart motivating him to cause all this trouble? Or was hurt pride a more dangerous beast? Whatever it was and despite the energy whipped up by his own pain, I knew he would soon be running out of angst as well. Surely he would need to get on with his own life.

I was right. Winter passed, one of the coldest London had seen for many years, everybody said. I had faithfully made my weekly calls to Mr Canning's Department and they had left me to get on with my course of study. As Easter approached, and the second round of assignments had to be handed in before the holidays, news from Kerala started to get better and better. Just as surely as the snow in the street corners started to melt outside, Suresh's resolve began to dissolve away. Arjun warned me that the March thaws were sometimes false and everything could just as quickly freeze up again with the final winter flurries. But I knew that things were definitely getting better. Ma said that Suresh had sent Riya over for a few days to Alleppey, and was *actually* talking about returning her to me! Girls needed their mothers, he seemed to have discovered. He had also told Ma he would give me the divorce when I returned from England. There were rumours that he was planning to get married again. Some excellent alliances were being proposed for him.

My cup was overflowing. The course was going well, Riya was back with Ma, it didn't matter that I had not been able to bring her with me. There was plenty of time for that when the divorce came through and Arjun and I could get married. I had enquired at Mr Canning's office, Riya would automatically get residence status in England when I married Arjun. I had found a good special school for her in Milton Keynes and had already given them all her details. A local Further Education college had offered me work on a sessional basis in their department of special needs, when I returned with permission to work. As leaves started to refill the trees on this beautiful, tiny emerald island, now readying itself for summer, it felt as though the sun was well and truly rising over my life once again.

I kept my word to Mr Canning and prepared to leave England at the end of July, the weekend after my course finished. Arjun had wanted to take me on a short holiday to Wales before I left. But Ma's last phone call had said that Suresh had definitely agreed to the divorce. It was best not to postpone things any more. Arjun agreed reluctantly but we both knew that, without being able to get married, Mr Canning and his Immigration squad would merely arrive again. This time to send me away for good. Trussed up and taped down if I made a fuss. We shopped for my return to Kerala. Toys and books for Riya, soaps and talcum powder for Ammumma, an umbrella for Ma. Nothing too expensive, Arjun said. Let's not overwhelm them before we're married. The plan was to get the divorce and apply immediately to return to England as Arjun's fiancée at the British High Commission in Madras. Arjun would stay in touch with Mr Canning in Luton and speak to his local MP to try and speed the application up. If things went wrong in India, I was to go to Arjun's family in Delhi and stay there until Arjun could join me.

Our last few days together took on the feel of a film in slow motion. Focus on the fact that you're getting back to *Riya*, I told myself the day my ticket arrived in a manila envelope marked Gandhi Travels, Leicester. It was a warm summer day that hummed harmlessly with the busy labours of insects. Outside, tiny pink rosebuds were nodding happily among the leaves. But the world went suddenly cold at my inability to quash the thought that I was going to have to leave Arjun again. I walked slowly up the stairs to look for the bag into which I'd started to pack the things I'd need for my journey, and put the blue and red ticket carefully away. Ticket, passport, purse with rupee notes . . . they were all there . . . all the essentials to remove me from the man I'd taken so long to find and who, in the past, had been so easy to lose. Everything that happened on the few days that followed took on a kind of slow motion that I couldn't seem to speed up, hard as I tried. On nights like that, we would make love as though it was the first time all over again, and possibly the last. Later we would hold each other and Arjun would talk about the future he was sure we would have, while I listened with longing and fear. Then he would fall asleep and I would gaze out of the window at the stars that still twinkled as though nothing had ever changed.

Would my future have room in it for both Arjun and Riya? Was there really a world in which people weren't constantly adding or subtracting five and a half hours to their time, merely to know what another part of themselves might be doing? Did other people have the kind of lives that did not involve a gradual count down of the weekends they had left? . . . Ninety-eight days . . . that was what we had been given. Ninety-eight days, ninety-eight heavenly nights, two squabbles and a row. Had they been a blessing or a curse? A blessing for the memories I would always have, if I were never to see Arjun again . . . and a curse, surely, because it would be precisely those memories that would ensure I'd never find peace ever again. Not even in another far-away life.

*   *   *

We clung to each other at Heathrow airport. Ten months ago we had flown into each other's arms here. I looked around the crowded terminal, it was the departure area, *everyone* seemed to be saying goodbye. The whole world was involved in some sort of macabre goodbye ritual. A mother was tearfully holding the hand of a hippy-looking son wearing a seed necklace and leather sandals. A small gaggle of unaccompanied child passengers shuffled past, tightly clutching their passports as they followed an officious woman in a BA uniform.

'Three times . . . three times we've had to say goodbye, Arjun . . . not even *knowing* if we'll ever see each other again . . .' Tears were now rolling down my face in quantities that would have brought an entire Indian airport to a curious halt. Even a group of phlegmatic businessmen, busy with their elaborately calm goodbye rituals and handshakes, were looking discreetly at us.

'It's only a matter of months, Janu, maybe even weeks. I'll try to get to Delhi on leave soon. And then, when your divorce comes through, we'll be married. Then no one will be able to prise us apart, I promise.' Even Arjun didn't sound too convinced by his own optimism.

His eyes were going red. It took a lot to make him cry, I had discovered to my cost in our rare squabbles. My teenage sweetheart, whom I'd needed to re-learn all over again. That we had been able to fall in love *again* was the real miracle.

Silences were brimming up and overflowing, for the first time Arjun and I had nothing to say to each other. Or too much to say to each other and not enough time in which to say it. Croissants and muffins were drooping sadly on coffee counters, as I clung to his arm, fearful to let go. The hippy traveller's mother was going pink in the face with her own efforts not to cry.

'This is the last and final call for passengers travelling on BA 192 to Madras, please proceed through security to Gate 16 . . . the last and final call . . .' I tore myself away from Arjun and, hauling my hand baggage along, ran blindly to the first passport check-point. Stuck in a queue, I could not resist looking back one last time. He was silhouetted against the bright fruity colours of The Body Shop. His eyes were still red but he was giving me the kind of smile that said 'chin up' and 'mustn't grumble' and all those infuriatingly British things he so exasperated me with sometimes. Why was he so resolutely cheerful all the bloody time. Even in the departure area of this ghastly place. He was the teenager who had generously proferred the last of the nimbu-pani in his flask so long ago and he was the man who had been given to me again as a gift in an afternoon dream once. What ancient promise had brought him to me, twice? And could I really expect it to pull the same stunt *again*. He looked now, through my watery vision, almost unreal suddenly. A tall, sad angel in a colourful, wet, perfumed, heavenly Garden of Eden . . . surrounded by a profusion of pineapple soaps and strawberry bubble-baths. Goodbye, Arjun . . . I promise I'll do my damnedest to be back . . .

EIGHTEEN

I looked down at the waving palm trees and glinting sea, as we circled Cochin airport. I wasn't looking for fanciful welcoming smiles any more. Had life in England removed me a tiny bit from the old superstitious ways I had been steeped in for so long? All that Malayali mumbo-jumbo, as Arjun called it irreverently. The touchdown at Cochin airport was as noisy and hair-raising as I remembered it. The runway was too short, they said. It couldn't be extended, *Willingdon Island* was too short, the others said. Everyone knew you couldn't change things that were meant to be. Like school reopening on the first day of the monsoons. It had always been like that, why change it?

Ma, Ammumma and Jose, my faithful Alleppey contingent, were at the airport to meet me. I could see Ma was brimming with happiness. Long absences from me in the past had been bearable because Dad had been alive then. And she had not needed to retire to a grieving, dimly lit house every evening after dark. It was wonderful to see them again. They were full of news. Riya had spent some time with them and had seemed not to have forgotten a thing, despite the long absence. She had looked around briefly for me, they said, in toilets and cupboards, as though I might be trying to complete a half-finished game of hide and seek. Then she had given up and, with no particular sign of trauma, had got on with her normal business of ladybird hunting and hydrangea demolishing.

'Did you try to explain to her where I was?' It was hard not to feel hurt at her apparent nonchalance.

'Oh yes, we did tell her you'd gone away for a while and would be back soon. But she turned her face away every time someone mentioned your name.' So the pain was as bad for her as it had been for me.

'Has Suresh definitely said I'm getting custody?'

'Well, not in so many words, he sort of suggested it . . . you know, Riya will be better off with her mother . . . all girls need their mothers . . . that kind of thing.'

Ammumma turned around in the front seat, 'We've heard that his marriage has already been fixed. Perhaps the new wife is not too keen on a child like Riya. It was Jose who told us about his remarriage.'

Jose waggled his head obligingly and said, 'Everyone knows it, chechi. She is the daughter of a businessman in Quilon, twenty-seven, spinster.'

The taxi and car driver network was one of Kerala's most efficient grapevines. Peopled mainly by young, intelligent and mobile men, with easy access to backyards and kitchens, it was a foolproof method of finding out what was happening in other people's homes. I wondered whether the grapevine was still trembling excitedly about me these days, or had it found fresh fodder and moved on to somebody else?

Ma had been hard at work in my absence. She had been to see Madhava Menon a few times and the divorce papers had already been drawn up. After we had reached home, I looked through the five pages with an addendum for Riya's custody. Petition for Dissolution of Marriage by Mutual Consent, it said. Two petitioners, no counter petitioners, filed under Section 13b of the Hindu Marriage Act 1955. It was humbly submitted that there was no legal impediment to allow this petition. Five pages in archaic, turgid legalese that would effectively write off ten years of what should have been a loving and life-long partnership. How much of that was my fault? Some of it? All of it? Ma had liked to say, *when you get married you only get half a man, the other half you have to make.* Had I not had the skills, and the guile, to do that? Or had I simply not cared enough?

It wasn't the arranged-marriage system for sure. I'd seen enough arranged marriages metamorphose into good marriages to know that. And I'd seen men and women in England, with all the freedom to choose their own life-partners, make almighty messes of their marriages. It had to be something deeper and bigger than any of us, something that trickled much further back than any of us could ever remember. What ghostly deal had Suresh and I cut in our ancient pasts that had brought us together so inexorably, to inflict pain and confusion on each other in this one? Arjun only laughed whenever I said this, saying it sounded like a good Hindu excuse for all the wrongs we perpetrated on our fellow human beings. Maybe, but I still couldn't see why I'd had to give away ten years of my life to Suresh if I'd really been intended for Arjun all along. Could things like that merely happen at random?

Perhaps it didn't matter any more. Suresh and I had hopefully paid out our debts and could now move on to other lives. The years together could more or less be put away like a photograph album rarely pulled off the shelf, and the pictures would gradually take on faded sepia tones. Many years later, we would struggle to remember names and faces, if we tried to at all. Many lifetimes later, we would simply not remember. If, by then, the accounts were squared, the dues all settled and no more promises had been made.

*   *   *

We were to present ourselves at the Family Court in Cochin at 4 p.m. on Thursday. Suresh was going to come there with his father, and Riya. I was nervous and apprehensive and there was a pain in my stomach at the thought of seeing

Riya again. Would she have grown? Would she shrink away from me? How long would it take for us to become mother and daughter again?

The court room was tiny and crowded. It seemed incredible that so many people had flocked to this place to end their marriages. Our names were ninth on the list pasted crookedly on the door. The morning's list was still stuck next to it, even though all those people would have long gone their divorced ways. I watched numbers one to four dissolve their marriages, only one person, a woman holding a tiny child, seemed upset. Across everyone else's faces was a common empty expression, their grief had obviously lain in the marriages themselves, not the ending of them. As number five went up, I spotted Suresh and his father come into the court room. With them was a little girl, not quite my little girl. God, how she'd grown! She looked like I probably had on the day of my reception, just slightly unrecognizable with the real person lurking underneath. A Maraar girl with Maraar lips and Maraar hair. I couldn't tell what was different. The clothes, obviously. They looked expensive. Her hair was longer, thankfully all her own and not pinned on. The expression on her face was blank, a certain mischievous spark missing. Our eyes met across the room. She looked startled, she'd recognized me! Her hand, clinging to Suresh's arm, was the only thing that moved, breaking out into an urgent tugging motion – look she's here, she's *here*, it was telling him. But when I smiled at her, she ducked her face behind her father. Like a small, confused, headless ostrich, clad in a Kidsworld tee-shirt and jeans. Suresh came to the back of the court room where I was seated. I stood up as his father joined us and greeted both of them. The judge, who looked like any petty bureaucrat in trousers and a bush shirt, was droning on, ending people's marriages in a bored monotone. His black lawyer's robes were cast aside on a nearby chair. Too hot to wear in this stuffy little room overflowing with the dead heat of killed-off promises.

In a few short minutes, it was over. The judge had asked us to present ourselves, checked that we were who we said we were. Checked that Suresh was willing to hand Riya over to me. Checked that there were no claims for alimony. Checked that we knew the six-month rule. And then nodded, a little sideways nod, to indicate he was done with us and could we please move on because he had other business to attend to and other marriages to dissolve.

Riya was still keeping her distance from me as we left the court. Ma beckoned to her a couple of times, but she retreated each time behind a convenient body, keeping a pair of dark eyes fixed keenly on me all the time. I turned to Suresh's father. He looked greyer and I felt I ought to say something to the old man who had accompanied his son here on such a sad mission. There were no words to express my regret. 'Sorry' wasn't a favourite Maraar word anyway. I hoped he wouldn't think I was behaving like a Hindi film heroine if I bent down and touched his feet. But conversation seemed inappropriate, and I remembered that he had been good to me once, if a bit surprised, when I'd suddenly developed a personality and a set of rights. He touched the top of my head lightly as a blessing. Had it been genuinely difficult for Suresh's family to love me when I'd been pretending to be their daughter, briefly occupying their house? In my naïvety I had imagined it would be easy to jump that chasm from daughter-in-law to daughter without having given them my childhood first. And now, from daughter-in-law, I was attempting to jump over another chasm to become just an unknown somebody again. Whose face would gradually blur and become forgotten, because there would be no snapshots and no postcards from a distant new life . . . this quiet, wordless farewell seemed appropriate for such a peculiar parting. Thank goodness Amma isn't here today, I thought with relief. Her presence would almost certainly have led to some good, open melodrama. Maybe even a proper Hindi film scene, complete with breast-beating and a dishum-dishum fight breaking out between the drivers.

Suresh avoided eye contact, turning away to say only that Riya's suitcase was in the boot of his car. He added, as an afterthought, that he wished to see her once a year, during her summer holidays. The mistakes made by her parents would have her join that burgeoning army of children who travelled mutely from parent to parent at weekends and holidays. For whom gifts and treats would double miraculously, bringing with them the added burden of double loyalties and double goodbyes and double pain.

As we walked towards Suresh's car to collect the suitcase, I felt a small hand slip into my own. Too scared to look down in case she took it away, I squeezed it reassuringly and could feel that old hole in my heart close up for ever with a gurgling sigh. Riya was back and I was complete again. Somewhere at the back of my mind lurked the thought that I might lose something else in return, accustomed as I'd become to receiving my joys in small neat packages, not too big and not too small. But there's nothing, I told myself firmly, *nothing* as important as redeeming my pledge to this little girl, given to me with the promise that I'd care for her as long as I lived.

She allowed Suresh and his father to hug and kiss her goodbye. She seemed to have come to her own cheerful conclusions about the mystery of suddenly having parents who lived apart. I wondered if, in an odd sort of way, I was blessed in her inability to question things. How hard it would have been to cope with the searing, stabbing questions of a talking, rationalizing child through all this. As Arjun had once pointed out, I might have never left Suresh at all if Riya had *not* had a learning disability. An unhappy marriage (or a *slightly* unhappy marriage as my mother had grudgingly conceded once) would have been a price worth paying for my own daughter to have had good marriage prospects. No one would have clasped their fingers together and sighed romantically at the news that her mother had run off with a man in some afternoon dream. There would certainly have been no decent alliances coming the way of that poor child. And so, women hung on in unhappy marriages to be able to give their daughters away respectably into hopefully not-unhappy marriages. And the daughters went on to have, if they were lucky, just *slightly* unhappy marriages but soon had daughters they would need to get married off some day. Riya's disability had been the blessing to free me from that circle of forced happiness. I wouldn't have to condemn generations after me to enter that spiralling cycle that just went on and on and on. Rewriting old stories so painfully over and over again.

We waited, with the Cochin dust swirling around our feet, for Suresh and his father to pull away in their car. Riya waved enthusiastically at them, hopping up and down in the dust flurries. I hoped Suresh understood that she did not intend demeaning his importance in her life. The year she had spent with him would have now linked them together more inextricably than ever before, but her bond with me had formed before she had even breathed life. Before she and I had become mother and daughter, and even she must now recognize she was whole again too. Besides, 'Bye-bye-see-you' seemed to be the newest phrase in her limited vocabulary, and every opportunity to brandish it proudly had to be grabbed.

After they'd driven off, I knelt down next to Riya, oblivious to the traffic and dust and gave her a hug that started from the tips of my toes. A whole body hug that held aeons of love and gratitude in it, going back to the beginning of not just this story but our very old one. When I, as a tired traveller, had stopped at her door once. When she had done something so selfless and so generous for me, I was still struggling to repay the debt.

'Bye-bye-see-you! Where did you learn to say that then? Who's Amma's clever, clever girl!' She chuckled deliciously and raised her arms, asking to be lifted up. I pulled her on to my hip, surprised at how heavy she had got. I was to carry her alone now. Technically this would be no different from my years with the Maraars, but in the eyes of many people I was now (let it be whispered) *a divorcée with a child*. A tainted woman, a woman with a past. They wouldn't, of course, be referring to the kind of past that I hoped I had just finished paying for. Some ancient far-away past from which my parents had carefully chosen a man for me. To keep some relentless old promise. From some life only half lived. There was no room in that story for blame and bitterness. And no cause for celebration, particularly.

It was my cue merely to move on. Had it left me better equipped for whatever would come next? Arjun had brought with him the kind of chances every life must be offered at least once. But our ninety-eight days and ninety-eight nights had been stolen, it was true, from the pain of so many people. That wouldn't pass unnoticed by whoever it was that kept the accounts. It certainly wasn't over yet. The story would continue to be written, carefully and painstakingly, and I would still only play a very small part. Would I ever know if I had taken the rules into my hands or merely had them descend on me from some unearthly place? I knew that minor characters weren't supposed to organize themselves into a riot and take over the writing of a story. But I wanted to believe conviction had played a part too. That the business of doing one's damnedest to *make* things work counted too. That was a wisdom passed on to me by an unlikely prophet with greeny-grey eyes, one day on the banks of a tranquil lake. And the whole business was surely something to do with learning to sing deeper songs, so that we got better and better at building those towers in the sky.

I spotted an empty auto rickshaw and raised my arm. The driver swung it towards us in a suicidal loop across the crowded road, his foot resting rakishly on the dashboard. Ma climbed on to the rexine seat that had a pink rexine lotus sewn on it, and hoisted Riya on to her lap. I put the suitcase at their feet and climbed in next to them. 'Main bus terminus,' Ma said as the driver revved up his diesel engine and we roared into the teeming traffic. Riya looked around us, cooing in pleasure at the garish pictures of various Gods that had been pasted in colourful profusion inside the auto rickshaw. They were all there, Ganesha with his elephant's head, beautiful blue Krishna, a sweetly smiling Devi, all bursting with calendar chubbiness and good cheer. Together, in their small noisy diesel chariot, they carried us into the falling dusk. Tomorrow, the next chapter would begin.

AUTHOR'S NOTE

In the months it has taken for my original manuscript to evolve into this book, I have become used to being asked how much of the story was truc. Early on, I took refuge in the non-committal reply that it was *semi*-autobiographical, which usually put an end to more questions, except from the very determined and the very curious.

The truth was something I, in my brand-new role of novelist, didn't especially wish to be bothered with. I thought it mundane, restrictive; fiction, I was discovering, was quite simply much more fun. But now, having reached the point of publication, I suddenly feel filled with gratitude to the readers who I hope will be making the journey with me – and with Janu. It is to them that I feel I owe this word of explanation.

I am not Janu, just as no character is ever quite the one it is based on. It is true that I did fall in love at seventeen. I, too, lost my teenage sweetheart to an English university and an arranged marriage. We met again, after a ten-year period of silence, in circumstances not dissimilar to those described in the book, effectively ending my marriage. I do have a Riya, with a learning disability, and as dear to me as Riya is to her mother in the book. But, these similarities notwithstanding, all through the writing of the book I found I was quite consciously setting out to blur the truth and fictionalize the story, precisely because that was what I believed a novelist's real job was. It is therefore obviously of particular importance to point out that reality ends abruptly on the road into Valapadu – a fictional name for a fictional town. The characters that populate this fabricated town have sprung entirely from my imagination. While I had, obviously, a husband and in-laws in my first marriage, I wish to state quite clearly that they bear no resemblance whatsoever to the corresponding characters in the book.

For those of you looking for a sequel, here's one of sorts. I married my Arjun eventually and Riya, happily, lives with us. The songs are deeper, certainly. Sometimes sweeter. I hope I remember always to be grateful I had another chance to build that tower in the sky.

ACKNOWLEDGEMENTS

There are many people to whom I owe many thanks:

David and Heather Godwin – without whose help this book would most certainly still be languishing in the depths of my computer.

Louise Moore – for believing in this book and being such a tremendous power-house of energy and enthusiasm.

Jane Ray – for faith that took root in a tiny radio programme and has remained constant ever since.

Ranju Dhawan – for reminding me, one crisp new morning on Hampstead Heath, that I could write too.

Simon Corns – for teaching me to *always keep things simple*!

Professor Madhukar Rao – for knowledge, laughter, sanity and an MA, a long time ago . . .

K. Rajamma – my grandmother, for prayers so fierce the Gods just had no choice.

Daya Misra – my beautiful feisty feminist mother-in-law, for showing me how to be brave.

Omana Nair – my beautiful gentle steadfast mother, for

showing me that in serenity there is a kind of braveness too.

Rohini – my lucky mascot and unlikely Muse.

And, most of all, to D – to whom this book is dedicated – because I knew no other way to say, thank you.